WHEN SECRETS BECKON

LAUREN PARKER RHODES

WILDFUL WRITINGS

NSW, Australia

This is a work of fiction. Its characters, places and incidents are a product of the author's imagination and any resemblance to actual persons, living or dead, or real events or locales, is entirely coincidental.

Paperback ISBN: 978-1-7637346-7-8

eBook ISBN: 978-1-7637346-8-5

ALSO BY LAUREN PARKER RHODES

Access Lauren's other books here, or at:
www.laurenparkerrhodes.com/books

DRIARN DUOLOGY
The Wife (short story prequel)
Amber Wolf
Blue Pointed Star

WHEN SECRETS BECKON

TRAITORS DUOLOGY
Traitors' Creed
Traitors' Promise

Author's note: Each of these books, with the exception of Traitors' Promise, were previously published by Lauren Searson-Patrick and have been republished, with permission, by Lauren Parker Rhodes. Traitors' Promise has only been published by Lauren Parker Rhodes.

CONTENT WARNINGS

Absent parent; violence; death of a loved one.

Reading age guide: 16-18+ (this will depend on maturity as the book is intended for adult audiences). Blue Pointed Star is intended for adult audiences and contains mature themes. It also contains mention of historical, off-page, pregnancy loss.

This one's for my Mum and Dad.

Because I know, without fail, they would go to the ends of the earth for me.
And because they still make me promise to look after my little brother...

OSKRINYA
KOAMAH
KOAMAH

Land of the Banished
REHDREE
The Atrium
SOLYNARA
KINGDOM
TALVORE

CHAPTER ONE

There's a roar in my ears, a heady swell of sound that I learned some time ago to force into background noise. Shifting my weight between my feet, I try not to let my opponent see the pain that shoots through my leg when I bounce to the right, to not show him just how hard his last kick landed.

He spins back to me, a flicker of disappointment running across his face – a kick that hard probably should have kept me down. But I see the exhaustion in his eyes, too.

My forehead is thick with sweat and it streams down my temples as I tuck my chin a little and hold my fists high. I've let enough hits land tonight, now I will give the audience what they loathe to see – a woman winning.

A deep inhale expands his chest and he runs at me as if it's with the last of his energy. I hold my fists at my chin until the very last moment when I drop – just like I've practiced a hundred times – slamming my weight forward off my left leg and grappling him around the waist, driving him backwards into the mat.

The air whooshes out of him as he lands with me strewn on top but he still whips his arm around the back of my head, gripping my braid where it lies against my scalp and literally holding me at arm's length. I pause – just a fraction – straining to look down at him. There's little I can do here without attacking his face and breaking one of Atticus's top rules. Instead, I break a different one and turn into his arm, sinking my teeth into the soft inside of his elbow.

Blood oozes into my mouth, but my bite has the desired effect. He grunts and his fingers loosen just enough for me to push forward onto his chest and drop my elbow into his throat. Releasing his skin and muscle from my mouth, I spit to the side, blood spraying the dirt as the noise of the crowd starts to take more of my focus. I meet my opponent's gaze, pressing my elbow hard enough for him to wheeze.

He taps out – two fingers pulsing the dirt floor – and the room flies back into sharp focus as I push myself to sit up again, still straddling the thighs of my opponent as his breaths heave in the dirt.

The red faces of the spectators around me, mostly men, scream, demanding a rematch. Insisting that I should never have been able to win that fight. I don't meet any of their gazes. I wouldn't be here if I didn't need Kabolshi more than them. Anyone who has enough coin to throw away on an illegal fight obviously doesn't move in the same circles as I do.

Or bear the same responsibility for their families.

The sound of stone on stone skitters along my jaw as I mark off the win on the wall. It was hard won tonight, and my chest and thighs ache from the effort of keeping my opponent down – my elbow just moments away from crushing his windpipe. We're not supposed to permanently injure anyone, no matter how hard it is to defend ourselves, no matter the damage we all endure in the process. Atticus doesn't choose the fights for any of us based on how easily we might win.

I glance at Ash, who's getting dressed – re-dressed – beside me, grateful we get to lose ourselves in each other when it suits us. These days, it's mostly in the aftermath of being in the ring – whether we managed to subdue our respective opponents or not. Tonight was another win – for me, at least. Another step towards freeing us from the debt I owe Atticus, and I will take all the hits I can endure to get out from underneath him.

The remaining space I am yet to fill with wins mocks me. I close my eyes briefly – if my maths is correct, and I can keep my win/loss ratio, I'll be out in two seasons. I clench my teeth a little. I can make that. I have to.

'I'll help you clean up.' Ash's voice is gravelly; he's taken his share of hits too.

'Make your mark first,' I say, handing him the small, worn, piece of rock.

Sighing, he marks the row underneath his wins – the row none of us want to fill.

'Next time,' I tell him, knowing the words are hollow. He hates this part of our life – perhaps even more than me.

Letting my gaze travel the rest of the walls in this small space, the one all of us use as a dressing room at different times, I wonder how many times those words have been uttered here. How many people before me were also running through the never-ending cycle of wins and losses, just needing another win to get closer to paying off their debts?

Ash and I will do it, though. I won't let it be any other way.

Kaya's waiting for me in the stone hall when I emerge, the torches making her chestnut hair burn bright. Her eyes immediately flick between me tugging my fitted black top back down and the open door. But she doesn't move from where she stands, one leg pressed to the stone behind her.

'I was hoping to'—she breaks off as Ash joins us. I look back at him, but his gaze is held in hers—'congratulate you,' she continues without breaking their stare. 'But I see you've already celebrated.'

She tries to wink at me, but it comes out as more of a grimace. She clearly knows full well what we were doing before we found her in the hallway.

'Home time,' Ash says, looking at both of us, the tiredness in his features leaking into his voice.

I watch Kaya watch Ash as he leads us out of the club. The walkways are all stone, with sconces at regular intervals. Once upon a time, I might have thought it was mysterious and wanted to unpack its secrets. Now that I know Atticus, I know it's best to leave those secrets alone.

The unspoken "king of the shadows" of Koamah can have his secrets.

'I thought you were going to put an end to that,' Kaya whispers as we move onto the street. It's dark out, but her keen eyes still scan for soldiers before we take each turn – like we all do. Ash walks ahead at each point, glancing at us a few paces behind as he disappears momentarily around the corners, staying close – but not suspiciously close – to the shadows the tall, stone-brick buildings create.

It's not quite banned, but two women out on their own at this hour would definitely be seen as questionable. Having Ash with us gives some measure of safety, but the hour of the night would still bring unwanted questions – no one wants the attention of the Koamah Military. Least of all us.

'We were,' I say. 'We did. It just'— I roll my eyes—'happened.'

'You're using each other as your own personal crutches, you realise?'

'At least it's mutual,' I say.

I glance at Ash, but he doesn't seem to hear us. Not that I think he'd care; we both know what we're doing.

Kaya laughs softly. 'One of you is going to find someone else and it's going to get real awkward, real quick.'

'We *all* know that person is going to be Ash,' I say, a touch of sadness creeping in. 'And I'm good with that. It *should* be Ash. He knows my conditions on what sort of person he could bring into our lives, and I expect him to stick with them. Things will only get awkward if he strays from that.'

Which he won't. I know that without doubt. Because my conditions are only to the benefit of Marley, and our daughter is someone neither of us will ever compromise.

The road we take is lit only by the windows in the businesses and homes we pass. I focus on the intersection ahead where the more major thoroughfare cuts through the lamplight. It is the responsibility of the neighbourhood to light their own streetlamps, something that is mostly rotated through the young adults before they can have paying jobs. Something Theo was responsible for, for a time – shimmying up the worn, black posts, lighting the oil-soaked wicks, and sliding back down again.

I push away the thought of how long ago that was. At the same time, I'm grateful he's now well and truly grown and willing to watch Marley when I need him to.

'And if I don't like her,' I say, dragging my attention back to Kaya, 'I'll just ask Atticus to leave her over the border – let the Oskrinya find her.' I sneak a look at her. 'Although, I guess they might execute her first.'

Kaya stops mid-step. 'Rubes! Don't even joke about that,' she says. But I hear the touch of a smile in her voice, even though it disappears before it can evolve into any true lightness. 'Oskrinya is a country I wish was much further away.' She shudders before falling silent as we keep walking a few paces behind Ash. We both know Oskrinya is nothing to joke about.

'Would anyone really be good enough for him in your view, Rubes?' she asks after a moment.

Kaya's all-knowing, fawn-coloured eyes – almost dark brown in this light – slide sideways to me as I glance at her, her full mouth set into a grim line.

I sigh.

'It will be hard, I won't lie,' I say, the possibility sitting heavy in my stomach. 'But he deserves someone really special.'

'And you?' she asks.

I laugh around the stone in my gut that's full of things I don't want to face, and step onto Traders' North that will take Ash and me home, wincing at the pain in my knee—

'Back.' Ash's voice is low and harsh as he forcefully shoves Kaya and me away from the intersection, retreating again to the darker street.

Kaya curses under her breath before we run, silently, for the stoop of what I think is someone's home and tuck ourselves into the space. Kaya stretches up on her toes and gently blows out the lamp, easing the glass casing back down. Just before it goes out, I see Ash hold up four fingers.

Four soldiers somewhere near the intersection – our way home.

My blood rushes in my ears and I push down the immediate desire to run back to the club, to seek shelter there. No soldiers in this city will question Atticus's rule, not in his own space. But getting there without being seen as we run down the quiet, wide street, even at night, would be virtually impossible – and Atticus's is not where we want the soldiers to know we've come from.

Worse than that, we don't want Atticus to see us drawing unwanted attention to his club. Which means we have to avoid taking on these soldiers directly. There is no way 'normal' women would be able to best them and Kaya is just as much a fighter as me. So, we wait in silence, the air pressing uncomfortably into my ears as I strain to listen to the intersection, trapped between two places we definitely don't want to be caught in. The long moments drag themselves along my skin until we quietly agree the soldiers have moved on to the next section of their patrol, and then we ease our way back onto the street.

It would only make things worse to be caught on someone's doorstep while they shout for soldiers.

And I want to go home. To Marley. To Theo.

I'm practiced enough, now, to be away from her for the short stretches of time that are required for me to keep our family world spinning. But as the moments over that time start to tick by, there's an increased tightening in my chest that's hard to ignore.

'Is it just me,' Kaya whispers, 'or do they seem to be doing more patrols each night? They should have been done here before we left.'

I can't find it in me to answer. Because if our military patrols are getting more frequent, that can only mean the threat that Oskrinya might launch another assault on our city is growing. And having Marley or Theo exposed to them – or any other threat – is not something I can easily swallow.

As we round the corner of the intersection once more, Ash and I fold into the shadows and I hold my breath as Kaya crosses the empty street, and jogs to her house five doors up. The houses on Traders' North Avenue are slightly bigger than those on the street that leads to the club. Each with a short staircase leading to the timber front door where some porches have pots of flowers framing their entrances.

Those stairs leave Kaya horribly exposed as she races up them and into the shadows before her door and slips inside. I don't miss the way she looks to her neighbour's dark house on her way in. Ash stares at her closed door for a moment and I wonder what it feels like not to have anyone waiting at home. If leaving Ash and me is, for Kaya, like it is for me to leave those I love at home.

'Mumma!' Marley squeals, launching herself at me before I've even taken my cloak off.

The heavy fabric tangles in my feet as I drop to my knees to gather her to me. I bury my head in her neck and breathe her in. The slight strawberry scent to her dark hair, so much like mine, warms my chest.

'Hi, baby girl. I missed you.' I pull back and smooth her wild hair from her face. 'How come you're not in bed?'

'Because you missed me,' she says, 'and so I waited up so you didn't have to miss me anymore. Theo said I could.'

She grins and Theo laughs behind her. He'd never let her come to the door on her own. Not only because of who could be on the other side, but because we all agreed that she doesn't need to know the sort of information that comes in the weekly flyer drops either. She can't quite read them properly yet, but the sketches that sometimes accompany the articles often speak for themselves. The news might be important, but the constant talk of hunting witches, banishing daughters, and the never-ending threat of an Oskrinya invasion is terrifying, if not numbing, even as an adult. I had to grow out of any innocence far too young, and if keeping those flyers away helps stop that for her, I will burn every single one I encounter.

'You try arguing with her,' Theo says, delight dancing on his face – one that's far too adult-looking for my liking. What happened to the child he used to be? He looks down at Marley. 'But Mumma's here now, so no more dilly dallying - bedtime,' he says and something in my chest squeezes in admiration of the man he is turning into.

Marley frowns. 'I like dilly dallying.'

A laugh sounds from upstairs – Papa. 'The best of us do!'

'Bedtime, my snuggle,' I say, placing a kiss on the top of her head.

I watch her stomp up the creaking timber stairs as I unravel myself from my cloak and hang it on the black steel peg, Ash doing the same behind me, smiling as he does – no doubt at being home with Marley. As I let my cloak go and watch it hang under its own weight, I make myself take a deep, slow breath and release it, consciously releasing today with it – the fight, Ash's loss, the soldiers. I'm home now, and that means facing a different set of challenges that all ladder up to the same thing – keeping my family alive, happy, and out of the spotlight of any unwanted attention.

My knuckles bark as I flex my hand, a reminder of the last lot of unwanted attention Theo got that I am still paying for. His face is serious when I turn back to him, tiny creases at the corners of his eyes. Watching them grow there, despite my trying to give him a childhood as innocent as Marley's, is like marking up my own personal failures as a mother – or mother-figure anyway.

'Well?' he asks carefully. The same question he asks every time.

'It was a win, Theo.'

I place a hand on his shoulder and feel some of the tension drain away. He closes his eyes for a moment, biting back the apology I know waits there. But he's said more sorries than I know what to do with. And I made my choice.

The only thing to do now is keep winning.

CHAPTER TWO

Papa is up first in the morning as usual, a hot mug of tea warming his hands as he sits by the hearth fire. It's a homemade brew of mine – one he taught me long ago, but now with a touch more ground rosemary to help ease his various pains. It's his knees that give him the most grief, probably from so many years tending to our garden and carting laden crates of supplies for the shop.

We sell small quantities of our specialty teas in the store that fronts the lower story of our house, but only to people we know, and never in the open. It's nothing but herbs and plants from our meagre garden and what I can get at the market. But, to the vindictive eye, how those things come together could be perceived as witchcraft – so we keep our remedies just for ourselves and those we trust.

'Morning, Rubilena,' he says without looking up, his warm-brown eyes focused on his steaming tea. 'Ash has headed to the club.'

I wince when my knee pinches where I took the kick last night as I bend to place a kiss on his gently lined forehead, his mostly white hair curling gently away from his face. Taking the firestarter potion from the bench, I top up the hearth before taking a seat next to him and watch the deep green flames surge before they settle into the normal warm hues.

'Did he take the balm for Kaya?' I ask, pulling the tie from my wrist and dragging my dark curls into a bun.

He cranes his neck towards the worn kitchen bench where I placed the small, brown paper wrapped parcel late last night. It's now gone.

'Yep. She still not sleeping?'

'It's improving,' I tell him. 'The empty house next door is a constant reminder. She was so used to getting up in the night to help the mother. I think it will take time, as well as the balm.'

Papa nods; there really is nothing more for us to say about it. The reminders of the people who are disappearing, and not always quietly, are everywhere. The memory of who used to live next door to us surfaces in a rush and I shove it away. That was so long ago – and very different to the banishment of Kaya's neighbours. But it was still someone who changed me forever. Someone there is no point thinking of anymore.

'Last night was a tough one, I see.' Papa glances sidelong at me, running his fingers over the threadbare, checked pattern of his favourite armchair, resigned disapproval all over him. He always looks this way the morning after. When the buzz of the fight has left my system and only sore spots remain in its wake. 'We need to talk about selling the store.'

My chest tightens a little, like it always does when we have this conversation. If only it were that easy. But my grandfather has made more than enough sacrifices for us, and I decided a long time ago they'd be enough. It's not fast, and it's not pretty, but I am working my way through Theo's debt. Then we will be able to focus on the store, and only the store. And perhaps making enough Kabolshi so Papa doesn't have to work anymore.

But having him give up his home and the business he has spent his life building is not something I will ask of him.

And it wouldn't be enough to end our Atticus problem, anyway. We'd probably have to turn to him to find new accommodation – to get a loan for something – which completely defeats the point of selling our home and business.

'We have talked about it, Papa,' I say, rummaging in the weave basket by my chair for a salve.

My right knee is swollen slightly and I struggle to pull the leg of my pants high enough to see the skin. The salve burns a little as I work it in, the stench stinging my eyes. But this is a concoction I didn't hold back on when I put everything together, and I know it will do what I need.

'This is our home,' I continue gently, 'there is no way we can sell the shop. Unless you've miraculously discovered somewhere else for us to live? And earn?'

He doesn't answer. He knows as well as I do that Atticus was the only way for us to clear the debt. Theo's debt. Ash has his own – part of the reason he stayed living here after we separated, Marley the other. But Theo's is just for being a reckless kid in a world too prepared to take advantage of him.

We're lucky, really, that this is the worst of it. That we didn't lose Theo entirely, and we were able to bring him home and work through this new life of ours. Not everyone who tries to go into competition with Atticus walks away.

But the guilt Papa carries because of my fights is evident in the set of his shoulders, the tightness in his jaw. He'd wanted to join Atticus's club instead of me, of course, but the steadiness of the store couldn't be jeopardised as well, and no one else can run it like him. It's in his very bones.

So, I beat him to Atticus and bargained to pay the debt instead of Theo. The more I win, however, the more difficult the fights Atticus selects for me get. But he at least gave me a choice on how I used my body to repay him – and I chose the option that allows me to hit back without punishment.

'Morning.' Theo's deep voice finds us in the steadily warming space around the fire. He takes a slow inhale and makes a noise. 'That stuff's revolting,' he says, nodding his head at me.

'Tell me about it. Works though.'

I look up at him, another apology flickering behind his hazel eyes and broadening jaw. I stare him down until it disappears. I accepted where we are a long time ago, and I wouldn't have made a different decision. Theo has always been mine to protect. After one of our mother's brief visits left a screaming baby in Papa's kitchen, my first coherent thought was '*mine*'.

'Okay, tea first, and then I'm off,' Theo says as Papa hands him a mug of my brew.

'Where to?' I try to stop my eyes from narrowing.

'The shop, Rubes,' he says levelly. 'It's my day at the shop.'

'Right, sorry. Got my days mixed up,' I say, returning my attention to the salve so he doesn't see the relief on my face. I didn't really get the days mixed up – sometimes, I just need him to say out loud that he's not doing anything stupid. I might be fine with where we are now, but I do not need any more complications to manage.

He makes a noncommittal sound and takes a long gulp from his mug.

'Shit, that's hot,' he says, spitting some of it back out.

'Be on watch for the patrols,' Papa says, ignoring Theo's expletives.

The hands that grip his mug are still strong, shoulders still proud, far more capable than 'papa' indicates. He's not as old as that title suggests, but it's his. And those blue eyes of his don't miss a trick. 'There's been more of them around of late. I have a bad feeling about it.'

I don't tell them Kaya said the same thing last night. It would only invite more discussion of selling things we can't afford to sell to get me out of the club and off the streets at night.

I run my tongue over my teeth. I'm sure that bite will come back to haunt me – I just don't know by how much yet.

I help Theo in the shop for the day, leaving Papa to his tasks of making and ordering and just generally doing the background work of the store. Or, as much as he can get done while he entertains Marley. He loves it, though, and her laughter is good for him. Plus, it's easier on his body than being on his feet all day.

'Sweet almond oil,' I call to Theo as I wander the store, making notes of everything we need to restock – both for sale and for our secondary uses. 'And more chicken feed.'

Frankincense, I add to myself.

Papa's shop has been part of our family since before I can remember. He used to tell us stories of what it was like when our mother grew up here and danced amongst the worn wooden shelves that circle the space; but neither Theo or I remember it as anything other than the three of us. Until Marley, of course, and she brought a light we didn't know was missing. I smile at the thought of her down here, chattering to the customers. I'm convinced some of them come just to see her and Theo.

'We've got a long few nights ahead to get ready for taxes, Rubes,' Theo says as the latest customer walks out the glass door, brown paper bag under her arm.

I groan.

'We're about three months behind.'

'Meaning we will have to backtrack and work out what we can declare and what we can't?' I ask, grimacing.

My aversion to tax time isn't only because of the vast amounts of money we have to pay to the King and Queen of Koamah. It's the time it takes to painstakingly make sure everything adds up. That every book and pencil and handmade toy and piece of fresh produce is accounted for. What we bought and what we sold.

And that it never, ever, alludes to some of the ... additional ... things I make and sell. As owners of the local shop, and the sole trader in our immediate neighbourhood with access to suppliers from all over the Kingdom, it's our duty to help provide them with what they need. Even if that sometimes takes a bit of extra attention from me. Attention, nothing else.

It also places targets on our backs for the Koamah Military. Because anything ... *extra* ... King Boaz wants stamped out. Permanently.

The little brass bell above the white door chimes as our next customer enters. I pop on a smile and turn. My lips remain frozen in what now probably looks like a sneer as a soldier lets the windowed door shut behind him.

The chime of the bell is the only sound as the door closes.

'Good day to you,' I say, forcing my smile to stay and hoping I don't have too many teeth showing. 'Is there anything we can help you with?'

He's about twenty, roughly Theo's age, and confident in his off-white uniform. So he should be, really. They train hard to get into the royal army and, from what I understand, the regime is pretty brutal once they're in, too. But then it goes to their heads and it's always, *always*, the little people they take it out on. Those they deem 'little' anyway. But this one's young, and the swaggering arrogance hasn't quite claimed him yet.

He surveys the shop and my skin prickles the more his gaze lingers. Quickly, I think on what he can see: the white-painted stone walls, the dark timber shelves that line them; a clean, slate floor (I know, because Theo swept it this morning); hessian bags of grain in two of the corners; our long, dark counter with paper and boxes stacked carefully, ready for packing customer purchases.

And I mentally do a check of what he can't see: the hidden door in the back of the storeroom (I know, I closed it); the small, brown glass jars awaiting the balms and salves that are behind that door; and the list of people and their needs – that one I keep in my head, just in case.

Casually, he wanders across the space between us, before cutting away and closely examining the shelves, peering into each basket and canister. I exchange a look with Theo, but we remain quiet. The fastest way to be banished from the City of Koamah, ending up somewhere far worse – like Oskrinya – is to offend the Crown, or a soldier acting on their behalf.

Or be called a witch.

Which is exactly what everything behind that little door will scream.

The soft sunlight catches in the man's blonde hair and lights the side of his face. It seems kind, but his behaviour scatters my nerves. Perhaps it's just because we have a soldier in the shop.

'Anything of interest, sir?' Theo asks.

The man's eyes flick up and down Theo like property, running over his too-long, caramel hair, the cut of his shoulders. I clench my fists behind my back.

'Just seeing what sort of goods you sell here, is all,' he says, glancing around the shop again. 'Never know when something might come in handy.'

Showing off his new authority is more likely.

A slow grin spreads across his face when he looks back to Theo, the sparkle in his brown eyes clear from here. He nods shallowly to me before walking out, the bell chiming again. Through the glass shopfront, I watch him walk away; there are five other soldiers on the street, all in formal patrol formation – two in the front, three in the back – as the one from the shop fills in the gap in the first row.

The rest of the day is quieter than normal, and I can't shake the oily feeling the soldier left in his absence. There is still enough business to keep us occupied, and we reach our daily income threshold to keep us ticking over.

Just.

It's a reminder how quickly the soldiers can change our fate – just their presence seems to have turned people away.

Most of the customers that do come through the large doors gravitate to Theo. He's fun and charming, and I'm the broody big sister that beats people unconscious for a living. Not all of them know that, of course, but there are definitely some that come to the club to watch – a fact we *never* talk of. I know I'm an awkward person to be around, so I forgive them for their uncertainty. Still, I make sure to look after as many as I can, so the chattier ones can give Theo as much news as possible. In this city, knowledge is power. Even if it's only how to avoid notice by the royal army.

'Something is definitely coming,' Theo says at dinner as we all sit around the small, round table between the kitchen and the fire.

Papa has made us his favourite stew, and I managed to get a loaf of bread from Molly in exchange for a birth control tonic. I've tried making my own bread several times, and it gets us by, but it's nowhere near as delicious as Molly's – I can't get the texture quite right. Birth control, though, that I've nailed.

I swallow a laugh as I remember Theo trying to make it on his own once to give to a girl he went to school with. Once my rage simmered at him almost drawing the worst kind of attention – from both her father, the head teacher, and the soldiers – I couldn't help but laugh at the glue-like substance he'd made. Unlike the silky, iridescent one I do. It was clear from that day he just doesn't have the touch.

'What's coming?' Marley says with her mouth full, spoon held aloft.

I look at Theo.

'I'm not sure yet, snuggle,' I say. 'There were just some extra soldiers around today, we're not quite sure why.'

'Maybe they just wanted to visit?' she asks. 'Papa's shop is the best, after all.'

Papa laughs and I smile, scraping a small amount of butter on my bread and hoping the sound covers the tightness in my voice.

'Maybe,' I say. *I hope.* But I know that's folly. That soldier had an agenda that had nothing to do with our goods – neither actual goods, or Theo.

'Maybe they just needed something important,' Ash says. 'Everyone has to buy things sometimes, don't they?'

But the way his smile reflects the one I gave the soldier is enough to tell me it's for Marley's benefit only.

And the soldier didn't buy anything.

CHAPTER THREE

I'm not due at Atticus's until later in the day, so I take the opportunity to spend the morning with Marley. She happily trails right behind me, one hand in my cloak so I know she's still there, as we peruse the market in the square. We gather the different herbs and base oils I need while we wait for Ash to join us. We buy food, too – I always purchase my own stock with meat and vegetables. The more they look like ordinary cooking goods, the better.

'Mumma, look,' she says, dragging me to a stall with a white tablecloth and matching bunting hanging from the simple timber frame that sits above. 'Can we buy some of these for Kaya?'

'The peonies are especially beautiful this season,' the stall holder says with a smile at Marley.

My heart sinks a little. What I would give to have spare Kabolshi to buy her flowers – either Kaya or Marley.

'Please, Mumma,' Marley says quietly, catching the look on my face. 'They're only a quart-Kabolshi, we can use the roots for—'

17

'Not today,' I say, sharper than I should, grasping for her hand.

The stall holder, a moustached man, catches my eye but says nothing.

Marley falls silent, the hint of a scowl on her face, her green eyes so much lighter than my pale-brown ones but holding the same fire, and I wish it didn't have to be this unfair.

'Here,' the man says, holding out a flower to her. 'You take it. It's too lovely a day to not appreciate the little things.'

Marley looks at me for permission before I nod reluctantly and watch her take the cut stem.

'And for you,' he says, reaching across the table and taking my hand. 'Do some good with these.'

I stare at him as a small pile of peony seeds fall into my palm, a whisper of knowing crossing his features. But a knowing of what? That they're Kaya's favourite flower? Or that they make a good cough syrup?

I try to shake off the need to know – I certainly can't ask him outright – and the seeds will come in handy. Sliding them into a pocket on the thigh of my pants, hoping I can retrieve them all later, I encourage Marley to be distracted by the next thing. And send up a wish for the stallholder to do the same. To forget our faces.

Anything I can't get here, or grow myself, I get at a different market. One I don't take Marley to. Not after I'd taken her as a baby and a rumpled old woman told me to watch her. Watch her gift unfold, but to never let anyone know. The second bit she didn't need to tell me; the first was like being dumped in ice-cold water. Not that I didn't have my suspicions – I inherited a knack for making things from Papa, so there was every chance Marley could be similar.

I just hadn't expected anyone to know that just by looking at her. And I curse myself for making the same mistake twice.

But it's a fine balance between not hiding a daughter, and letting the world see too much of her. Or me.

The market is busy as ever, the normal haggling over prices and people filling their baskets with colourful pops of produce. The colours are beautiful, all deep reds, yellows and greens, but it's the smell that's my favourite – the one that lies under the sweat of people and the stink of the city. The smell of baked bread and fresh herbs and the dirt that still cakes some of the imported vegetables.

I feel the shift in the crowd before I hear the hooves of horses thundering down Traders' Avenue and into the market. Their hooves skid on the stones in their haste, the sound echoing off the buildings that surround the square.

Soldiers.

The people around us contract as one, and I grip Marley's hand hard enough for a whimper to escape her throat. I crush her to my front, partially covering her in the side of my cloak. It's not quite cold enough for it, and the sky is clear, but it's helpful for hiding things I don't want found.

I step closer to the person in front of us, shuffling Marley with me and obscuring her further from view.

The stall holder to my right, from whom I'd just purchased a bottle of sweet almond oil, catches my eye over her table, the corners of her mouth dipping downwards slightly.

The crowd murmurs, no one brave enough to talk audibly.

A child sniffs, and my heart leaps into my throat.

Marley doesn't make a sound. She just squeezes my hand in return.

Fabric jostles behind me, and a body presses against my back. I stiffen before I realise I know the scent of his soap – a tobacco one I made.

Ash.

I exhale.

There's no telling why they have come today, but it's not hard to guess. I comfort myself with the knowledge that there is no way we can be the *three of she*. No way they can think we will bring about their stupid prophecy.

The people of our neighbourhood recognise Ash, know he only has one daughter. By extension, they know I only have one daughter. And some will know me from the shop and will have seen only one daughter, including the soldiers.

Not that any part of me believes 'three of she' would have the power to raise the dark gods and let their blood lust run free.

The crowd shifts and splits, soldiers tearing it down the middle.

'Where is Driontia of Traders' North?' the soldiers shout as they move through the people.

Ash grips my elbow.

'Driontia of Traders' North!'

As the crowd presses back further, the gap between the two sides widening. A final pair of horses makes their way into the market, something I only know by sound until I see their crowns appear over the heads of the people in front of me.

'Be still, your King and Queen arrive!' A young, male voice sounds across the market. I watch the King and Queen ride into the space, my stomach contracting as my suspicions are confirmed.

'A third daughter,' the King says, his words carrying in the thick atmosphere, 'has been born to Driontia.'

A gasp circles around the market. *Three of she.*

The Queen surveys the crowd, silently watching every individual. Searching. Her stare moves towards us, and I duck a little further into my cloak, her gaze sliding over the top of me.

'Here!' someone screams from across the square, the sound echoing around us. Marley lets out a tiny whimper as I grip her harder. 'They're here!'

My heart sinks to meet the bile rising from my stomach. A woman shouts and a little girl screams and my heart all but shatters. Ash tugs my arm from behind and we surreptitiously move backwards, against every instinct in me screaming to fight for her – this faceless, screaming child. Marley shakes slightly in my grip as I drag her with me slowly.

The girl continues to scream and fight. I can't see either of them, but I can imagine the little girl desperately thrashing to be returned to her family, tears streaking her face as she's ripped away.

If it didn't mean I'd have to release my hold, even for a moment, on Marley, I would cover her ears so her dreams aren't also haunted. Not like mine are with Oskrinya soldiers – and the blood they spilled on these streets not so long ago.

A man and woman sob somewhere near the King and Queen and the royals look down on them from their handsome horses, just visible between the press of bodies, the royal steeds' chests decked in gold and jewels.

The King shifts in his saddle as he surveys the now quiet crowd that's thick with a bitter hush.

'Look around you, people of Koamah,' he says, voice raised so it fills the square over our heads. 'Look at your loved ones, your friends, your *children*. Not one of us would be able to bear the wrath of the dark gods who have so long been locked away. Not *one* of us would survive their hunger. You are sad, heartbroken even, for Driontia and her daughters. But you know the risks. You know the "three of she" cannot exist. Look at your loved ones and tell me they are not worth the sacrifice of a few. A few who *knew* the consequences and hid their three daughters anyway, happy to damn us all.'

The crowd mutters, the swell of their agreement pressing against my chest. If the people of Koamah were in any way hesitant to report their neighbours before, King Boaz has all but eradicated that doubt. Bile starts to burn in my throat. If it's so important to the prophecy to not have three daughters, why is making my birth control an executable offense?

'The dark gods will not rise under my reign!' the King shouts above the din.

The people swim around me as I blindly walk backwards, guided by Ash, out of the crowd. Away from the little girl whose fate has been sealed simply by being born. As we reach the edges of the mass of people, a strange scraping noise comes from across the square. Turning, I find a large, wide piece of canvas being hauled up one of the buildings. Ropes on either side are secured somewhere I can't see, but I imagine soldiers tying it off.

WARNING: When three of she become one, the dark will rise with the sun.

All that's dear will be reclaimed, all that's loved will be lost to flame.

A darkness none will defy, and all but blood will die.

ALL HAIL THE KING AND QUEEN: The City of Koamah will defend us.

The black painted words send a cold shiver down my spine. The little girl they dragged away – her life over before it really began – didn't sound any older than Marley.

What possible danger could she have posed?

'Your feet are flat. Heavy,' Atticus barks.

I lift my heels, bouncing on my toes in the sparse, rectangular training room.

'Honestly, Rubilena,' he says, 'you look like all the world's problems are literally sitting on your shoulders.'

I stifle a groan and bounce a little harder. Lighter.

The echo of the girl's cries rings in my ears.

Unless Atticus has something special planned, I fight about every third day. In theory, the day after is to give my body a moment to recover. But most of my injuries are such that healing will never be done in such a short amount of time – unless I help them along. Which I can never do completely. Not when my colleagues are limping, or nursing busted faces (even though we're supposed to try and avoid the face), or wearing a brace of some sort, even with the helpful tonics and balms I secretly provide Atticus. So, I fight through them instead. The second day is to train. Given the hurts are always present, it's mostly about getting myself back into the right mindset.

Finding that mindset after the square this morning feels so much harder. But losing my fights won't help support Marley and Theo, and so I try to push the memory of the little girl's scream to the back of my mind.

Focus, Rubilena.

'Now,' Atticus commands, and I attack the bag he's strung up in the timber beams for me.

The complicated pattern of punches, knees and kicks coming like second nature. I try to let the sound of my fists on the bag drown out the screaming I heard.

She seemed so young.

I spin on my heel on the dirt floor and slam my foot into the bag. The ropes groan where they hold it aloft. The soft grunts and smacks of others doing their own training around the floor is a steady backdrop.

'Again,' Atticus says.

I spin on him.

'Why didn't you help them?' I ask, the barely contained anger in my chest coming out as desperation in my voice.

Atticus sighs, his jaw tightening before he draws another inhale. His gaze when it finds mine is like hard chips of ice, his auburn hair tied back off his face.

'Again,' he says.

I pummel the bag, refusing to drop my gaze from Atticus's.

Again.

Sweat drips down my spine.

Again.

My vision starts to blur with exertion.

Again.

She was just a child.

I slam my left fist into the bag, the side seam busting just enough for sand to start leaking out.

'For fuck's sake, Atticus! You own half the fucking city!'

He stares at me as my breath heaves in and out.

'And I own you, Rubilena. You'd do well to remember that before you raise your voice at me again.'

I have to close my eyes against his cold face, against the truth in his words. Around me, the others have fallen quiet and my stomach falls in a familiar fashion. No matter how used to it I am, the reminder that my life is not my own never sits well.

'Return to your training.'

Atticus's barked instruction is directed at the rest of the room, and it slowly returns to its usual rhythm. All of us are here training to brutalise each other in the ring.

'They didn't come to me,' he says evenly. When I open my eyes, he's dragging a palm over his mouth and chin. 'I didn't know. I can only help when I know.'

'Fuck,' I say, leaning my head lightly against the depleting bag.

The young girl screamed as she fought the soldiers. A terrified animal in a world she doesn't understand. For all I know it was the first time she'd seen the light of day. And now she will join the rest of the 'banished'.

A third sister. A danger to the Crown. To the entire world.

If the prophecy is true, that is.

There is nothing in me that believes the fate of the world is at risk because someone happens to have three daughters. I have a daughter, and I know the soul-wrenching love that brings. Love that strong could never be evil, even if it is three times more.

Knowing what the King and Queen tell us about these girls and women being banished – that they're saving the citizens of Koamah from the prophecy by putting as much distance between the 'three of she' as possible – is a lie, churns in my gut. It's their worst kept secret that none of those taken survive. It's only Queen Astra's unease about spilling possible prophecy blood on the lands of the Kingdom that delays their executions. But, once they're considered far enough beyond the borders, I can't imagine anything could save them.

I'd itched to intervene. My inaction is a stain I'll never be able to rid. But I chose Marley, just as the King wants all his citizens to do – choose your own first – and I will choose her every time. Drawing attention to myself in those moments will draw it again when the soldiers need someone else to make an example of. And I will never give them that. I just wish I didn't have to choose between my daughter and someone else's.

'She's being sent to the banished lands, Atticus,' I say heavily. 'She's not even a citizen of the Koamah Kingdom anymore. And, to get there, she will have to cross through Rehdree – how do we know the military will see her safely through that lawless expanse? And to what end? Just to have her throat slit when they arrive at their destination anyway?'

Although, I don't say out loud, if it's laws that got her sent there, can lawlessness be that much worse that the death that awaits her?

I shudder.

At least she won't go through Oskrinya. There's not a chance the Koamah Military would set foot across that border – no one is dumb enough to incite the wrath of their leader, Roan. They might be a country much smaller than the might of the Kingdom, but they are brutal with no regard for the lives of others and I can only hang on to the hope that the Koamah Military will at least make the girls' deaths quick. Parts of our city still wear the scars from the last battle Roan's Oskrinya brought here. My dreams certainly do – the colour of their uniforms, stained with the blood of my neighbours, is something I will never forget. Something that I can see haunts Papa, too, something he hoped he'd never have to protect me from, but he did.

'There's nothing you could have done,' Atticus says, placing his hands in his pockets. A sign I know from experience means he's trying to mask his own anger or the calculations that are running through his mind. It's a look he has when his fights don't go to plan. Or he's about to make yet another business decision.

'You have a plan,' I say. 'You're going to save her.'

'Maybe,' he says. 'But you should worry more about how you're going to pay me the eleven Kabolshi fine for that bite.'

Fuck. Eleven? I mentally add another fight to the empty space on the wall. Another one I will have to win.

He nods at the bag. 'Again.'

CHAPTER FOUR

I head home later than I'd hoped, the dusty pink and blue of the evening sky are just starting to break through, but I'm buoyed by the fact it's not yet full-night. I draw a few glances from the passersby – for being a woman on my own, most likely – but I'm not frightened of them. I know more than enough ways to protect myself if needed. And my choice of the fitted pants and shirt under my cloak probably speak volumes about what I can do, compared to the flouncy dresses so many other women wear.

No, I'm not afraid of them in the immediate sense; it's the additional soldiers of the royal military on the streets that send a chill down my spine, their off-white uniforms stark against the stone pathways and buildings. I watch them snake away in their rows of three, down the dirt lanes that branch off the larger stone roads.

In its own right, the military has never been something to fear before. It was once something to be revered, a career I was immensely proud ... someone I used to know ... had chosen; I'd even once hoped Theo might do the same. Theo followed him around like a love-struck puppy most days, and I was nothing but grateful. Papa was amazing at helping raise us, but between the shop and keeping us fed and housed, he was busy. So I did most of the raising of Theo. And for him to have such a good role model and friend – outside of Papa and me – was more than I could have wished for at that time.

Then I fell in love with him, and everything changed. Now, I can barely bring myself to think about the man that's now a stranger.

And the royal military changed too, becoming more and more brutal in their own right following the Oskrinyan attack. Now, they are not only the protectors of the City of Koamah, the seat of power for the Koamah Kingdom with its combined might of three countries, but the ones we fear as well. Every day, more people are rumoured to have been banished to the unnamed lands. Every day, another witch or third daughter. Like Kaya's neighbours.

Like the girl at the market.

Ash's booming laughter from the upstairs windows greets me and I jerk my thoughts back to the here and now as I make my way inside the rear of the house, sparing a quick glance at the gap in the fence I used to use so frequently. It's now almost entirely covered by a thorny bush, the only part of our small yard that hasn't been taken over by our sprawling gardens, and I shake my head at how appropriate that now seems.

Hanging my cloak on the black peg at the foot of the staircase, I try to sneak upstairs. The dark steps groan underneath me as I go, but they are making such a ruckus I'm confident they won't hear me. There are multiple voices, each of which I recognise, and I love catching them un-awares. Love finding the sheer joy on all their faces, but mostly Marley's. I love that I have been able to give her this. A family. A family that I have pulled together, have held together, despite the absence of the one person I thought would always be here. Unlike my own mother, who just drops children and runs.

As I move into the warm wash of the hearth fire and the small lanterns that dot the space and the walls, Ash does an impersonation of something I can't quite figure out. Something that has Theo snorting into his hands, and Papa suggesting it's last call for snacks before Marley's bedtime.

'Daddy cheated!' she yells indignantly.

Ash just laughs, his blonde hair falling in his face. He scoops her into the air, tickling her mercilessly until she can barely breathe.

'Look!' he says. 'Mummy made it home before sleepy time.'

'Mumma.' Marley sulks as she stretches her arms towards me, a silent demand to take her from Ash. Happy to see me but still upset about her game.

'Hi, snuggle-girl,' I say. 'Is Daddy putting you to bed?'

'Only if he reads me two stories.' Her brow furrows as she looks at him, two fingers held aloft.

'Deal,' he says, taking her from me once more and heading towards the bedroom she and I share.

I flop on the couch next to Kaya, who smiles warmly at me. Her smiles always meet her eyes when she's here, something I notice the absence of anywhere else.

'Ready for tomorrow?' she asks.

'As I'll ever be. He's paired me with Marco.'

Kaya's head whips to mine, her messy chestnut bun bobbing with the movement.

'You're joking.'

'I wish. We're first up.'

'You have to tell Ash,' she says.

'And have him do what, exactly?'

A knock sounds from downstairs before she can give her non-answer. I look at Papa, his face full of suspicion even as his eyes light with a flicker of hope. Hope that it's her. But it hasn't been her since Theo was a child.

The knock sounds again. 'By order of the King and Queen, you are to open this door!'

'Shit,' Papa curses. 'Coming!' he shouts more loudly and all but bounds down the stairs, the short spell of hope broken.

Theo, Kaya, and I are still as we wait, unwilling to draw attention to ourselves. They will know the house is occupied, given the light spilling from our windows, but there is no need to give them reason to invite themselves in. I glance over the back of the lounge, but there's no sign of Ash. He likely heard the call from downstairs and is making sure Marley stays quiet. Relief washes through me, knowing he'll protect her at all costs.

'No, sir,' I hear Papa say, but I can't quite make out the response.

'Sorry sir, I haven't seen anything like that before,' Papa says.

Another minute or two passes until the door closes and Papa comes back upstairs. But not before I hear him re-bolt the door.

'You can come out, Ash,' Papa says quietly. 'They're gone.'

Ash nods at me when he rejoins us – she's asleep. All eyes turn to Papa as we wait, but he just shrugs his shoulders towards his soft white hair.

'Something has gone missing from the Palace,' he says, dark eyebrows lifting.

We each meet him with silence, uncomprehending. Theo frowns and shifts forward from where he sits on the floor.

'And they thought it was here?' he asks.

I blink at Theo, a tiny slice of panic lurching in my gut.

'Not here precisely,' Papa says. 'But possibly in this neighbourhood.'

'That's not good news for us,' Kaya says, her lips pursing in thought.

'And what has gone missing exactly?' Ash asks.

Papa rubs a hand over his stubble. 'Well, that's the interesting bit. They wouldn't really say. I got the sense they have no idea what they're looking for. Just asked if I've seen a trinket of the Queen's.'

Ash blows out a loud breath. 'That's even worse news for us. They'll be jumping at shadows to deliver something – anything.' He looks at Kaya. 'I'd like you to stay here with us tonight. I'll bunk in with Theo and set you up in my room.'

Kaya looks up at Ash quickly, but he won't get any argument from the rest of us. There's no way any one of us would let her stay home on her own, not with more soldiers hunting around. It's always been a point of concern but, after her mother passed away, Kaya simply refused to give up her family home. Regardless of how dangerous it could be.

Eventually, she looks at me and I smile gently, a flash of recognition in her face. I think she knows I couldn't manage another jagged departure from my life.

As we ready for bed, Ash and Papa making doubly sure that the doors and shutters are locked up tight. Theo catches and holds my gaze.

'I don't have it, Rubes,' he says quietly. Wearily.

I swallow and pull him into a tight squeeze. How long will it be until I go back to never doubting him?

The crowd cheers and mocks, their voices a buzzing that envelopes me. I blink and focus on the mountain of a man in front of me. He gestures to the crowd, a sickening grin on his face, and they scream louder. Marco lifts his arms in the air and shakes them like he's already won.

It's all part of his act.

Outside the ring, he would be at the front of the line to protect me. Second only to Ash. Or Papa. But in here, where our livelihoods depend on giving the audience what they want, he will show me no mercy. And this audience is sick of seeing me win. They've been lapping up the progression of fights Atticus has been putting me through. Each fight harder and harder for me to win; more often than not, more of my blood coats the ring each time, too.

Marco is huge, built like the building that corners our shop.

And about as fast.

Atticus gives the signal, a flourish of fanfare I no longer take the time to watch. Instead, I focus on Marco. How his back foot is a little flatter than the front, his left fist held a little lower than his right. But that's his secret, his left is his dominant. The one he slams with when his opponent is distracted by the right. Or the knee he favours driving into the soft part of someone's stomach.

I let the sound die away around me, ignoring the spit that flies into the ring at my feet, wetting the dirt. These people can't stand to see a woman win. Not consistently. Even if I am the same person some of them, or their loved ones, have turned to in times of need. In here, none of that matters.

Some of them I'd be quite happy to run into on a dark street, where the shadows are my friends.

Marco waits for me, and I know I have to move. Atticus will make the stakes harder for us all if we fail to move. Some showmanship is okay, providing we pulp each other in the process. There are no pulled punches in this ring – boring the audience is not acceptable. Marco nods slowly at me as I approach, his face serious. Ready.

I duck in and land a solid punch to his ripped gut before I dance out of the way.

A soft grunt is the only acknowledgement I get.

I run at him again, feinting with my left, and land an uppercut with my right, his teeth snapping as I drive under his jaw. The impact smarts in my wrist, snaking down to my elbow.

He takes a single step back before recovering, landing his own uppercut to my middle. I follow my body's need to bend at the waist, and use the momentum in my crouched legs to deliver a flurry into his gut in return.

My left cheek cracks as he slams an elbow into the portion of my face I haven't covered well enough. I spin away, pain radiating through my head and into my cheekbone. I smash a foot into Marco's hip and he folds. I don't even let him breathe before I strike his knee on the same leg and he goes down.

I move to deliver the final blow – the knockout. But Marco lurches forward at the last moment and pulls my legs out from underneath me. And then his arm is crushing my windpipe – the same move I did in my last fight – and I know that's it.

The blackness claims me, almost as suffocating as the disappointment.

I stare at the markings on the stone wall where I can't make another, instead making my mark in the row below. It's not the first time I've lost, although it hurts all the same. Maybe worse than the first few times, when I expected nothing but to be beaten. Then I got better.

A heavy hand lands on my shoulder.

'You did well, Rubes. I'm sorry.' Marco's voice is so gentle in comparison to his appearance. The scars and tattoos that decorate his night-coloured skin do nothing to soften first impressions. Neither does his absence of hair, his head shining in the firelight.

I try to smile as I look at him, despite the pain in my face. I don't think he broke my cheekbone – I've felt that before and it's not as bad this time. But bad enough that Marley's eyes will fill with tears when she sees the bruising on my face. There is only so much I can hide.

'You need wins, too,' I say. 'I'm happy for you.'

'You're a good one, you know, Rubes,' he says quietly. His eyes widen and he sighs. 'I still can't believe you ended up here.'

I place a hand on his chest. 'It happens to the best of us. Mark your win.'

He captures my hand in his, the warmth in his calloused palm seeping into my skin. Words stumble from his mouth, a gentle, captivating sound I don't understand. But his face is sad and peaceful when he talks.

I frown at him slightly, just enough to ask my question without breaking the spell.

'Just something my grandmother used to say – *leap and you shall fly*,' he smiles, but it fades quickly. 'Most people of my home country, Solynara, don't remember the old sayings, but she never lost them.'

He releases one of my hands and chucks me lightly under the chin before scratching his win on his place on the wall. So much shorter than mine.

'Come,' he says, 'I'll walk you home. Ash will come with Kaya when she's finished.'

The door to our dressing room creaks slightly and Atticus joins us. Looking both entirely out of place in his finery, and yet every bit the king of his domain. He nods at Marco, whose eyes slide to me.

'I'll be just outside,' he says, closing the door behind him.

'How you feeling?' Atticus asks, genuine concern in his question.

'Like I've been pulverised by Marco.'

He smiles gently. 'Looks about right, too. Do you have anything you can use?'

He looks pointedly at my face and I nod back. He knows I do.

'You should all keep a low profile for a while,' he says.

The room starts to blur and my mind immediately goes to Theo. I stare at Atticus's face to keep my focus. The way his nose is slightly too large when I look at it in isolation.

'Why?'

'Nothing official,' he says. 'But there are rumours swirling that it's Roan's forces – Oskrinya soldiers – that have stolen from the Queen. Anyone seen to be even remotely different, or possibly working with Oskrinya, is going to have an even bigger target on their back.'

I think of everything I have behind that door in the shop. The way Marley knew about the peonies and what we could do—

But it's the memory of the olive-green uniforms cutting down everyone I could see that runs most sharply through my mind. As clearly harmless as my – and Marley's – abilities are, that won't stop Koamah authorities drawing connections that don't exist.

'Shit.' I curse on an exhale.

'With more of our own soldiers looking for the Queen's stolen valuables, and Oskrinya seemingly ready to make another brutal move on us, I just think it's sensible.' He pinches the bridge of his nose. 'That includes no more secret home remedies for a while too, Rubes.'

The regret on his face is genuine. He's a businessman, and fighting is part of his currency, but it doesn't mean he's not caring in his own way. Keeping a fully stocked medicinal cupboard is one of the ways he shows it.

'Do you know anything about the thing they're looking for?' I ask. Anything Atticus could use as leverage for some future arrangement must be very high on his list of wants. Atticus might hold my strings, but he doesn't lie – another sign he cares.

'Nothing I can verify,' he says, 'but it's said to be incredibly powerful. Powerful enough for Roan to do anything to have it.'

Roan? Fucking Oskrinya, why can't they just leave us alone?

I swallow. 'Why?'

'Because anyone who has it can access all the knowledge – and the secrets – of the Kingdom and everything that impacts it. It would give them the powers to erase the borders that separate us, essentially creating an empire.'

I have no idea how to respond to that. It sounds about as feasible as the prophecy.

'Marco's waiting,' he says, his icy blue gaze not leaving my face.

I turn back when I reach the door, the metal handle cool on my palm.

'Thank you for the heads-up. We'll keep a low profile.'

He glances at the wall of wins and losses as he starts to leave. 'If you hear anything – from your customers – let me know.'

CHAPTER FIVE

The increased presence of soldiers on our streets doesn't slow the stream of customers to the store like I thought it might. Or maybe the people of Koamah are quickly adjusting. But it does mean we have to be more careful when exchanging goods that might draw additional attention. We also don't let Marley come down, and I never run it on my own. Which makes me feel like a kept child, along with her, when in reality I'm the one who does most of the protecting of this family. Not something I thought I'd do on my own, not when I'd found my counter so early. Someone who was supposed to be not only my best friend, but my partner. The father of my future—

I cut the thought off. It's ridiculous how often they swirl in my mind, given how much time has passed. And they invade at the strangest times, why is that? I can be drifting off to sleep, and I'll remember the feel of his arms; or delivering a bundle of sage, and the smell brings images of his hands when he'd help me tie them. Or I'll see the laneway I saw him in last, and I travel the road of heartbreak once more. Still living in the house we shared so many memories in doesn't help, but nor do I ever envisage living anywhere else.

So I made myself adjust to the reminders. Apparently, it's an ongoing journey.

'Evening, Molly.' I smile as our local home baker appears through the door of the shop.

Her face crinkles in response. 'So good to see you, my dear.' She pats my hand as she draws near.

'What do you need?' I ask, glancing out the front windows. I can't see anyone, but I lower my voice anyway. 'How are you getting on?'

Her hand trembles a little where it still rests on mine on the dark timber counter. The sun is about to go down and she will need to hurry home. So, I take the slight shake of her head as the most comprehensive answer I will get and set about packing her things. I wrap some hard cheese in brown paper, as well as a few potatoes and a small cup of nuts. In the bottom of the cup I place a small vial of oils I've mixed for her husband's cough – a great hacking sound that shakes his body and mostly keeps him at home.

I fold the top of the paper bag before handing it to Molly, accepting the warm loaf of bread and handful of Kabolshi in exchange. It's never quite what we need, but she does her best and I don't correct her. I can't know about the pain her husband is in and do nothing. I just hope he might stay well enough for my peonies to grow, and then I can create him something different to try – maybe something better.

Molly leans forward a fraction, glancing behind her before she looks intently back to me.

'There are whispers that Roan is preparing Oskrinya for another infiltration of Koamah,' she says quietly. I glance at Theo, who's talking to another customer – a regular. 'Can you give me three times my order next time? I can pay it off?' she asks uncertainly.

I try to school my expression as a small sliver of disappointment runs through me. We need Kabolshi as much as anyone, and not being paid …

'Of course, Molly. I'll do what I can.'

'I'd suggest getting some things ready for your family, too.' She glances over her shoulder to the door then back at me. 'There's a shift in the air, Rubilena, I can feel it.'

I squeeze her arm in farewell, the long silence between us heavy with all the things we shouldn't say out loud, and listen for the bell as she leaves.

'I'll just grab your book, and I'll be right back,' Theo says to his customer before ducking out towards the storage room, and I nod at the man I recognise but don't know. His eyes are kind as he returns the gesture, reminding me of the neighbours we used to have. The man that could have been like a father figure had he not been so mysterious. I haven't seen them in almost as long as I haven't seen him. They just vanished into thin air.

Like many do when Oskrinya is involved. Our alliances with Solynara and Talvore should mean we are bolstered against the threat of Oskrinya, but we are the only country to share a border with them. And when they attack, they strike hard.

When Theo reappears and the man leaves, satisfied with his purchases, I drag out the pile of papers that mark our sales for the past few months. They land on the counter with a thud. Theo turns his head to me and flips the closed sign on the door. He doesn't lock it though, and our most loyal customers know there is always a short amount of time they can get some last minute purchases before we slide the lock into place.

'Fun, fun,' he says, walking over and eyeing the stack of cream paper.

'Molly thinks we're going to have another attack,' I say quietly. Theo glances up at me, looking a little dubious, until I add, 'So does Atticus.'

His face falls before settling into a wall of resignation. A look he is too young to make.

'Roan, I assume?' he asks. 'He didn't kill enough of us last time?'

The bell on the door chimes and Theo jerks upright. A move he doesn't make for anyone.

With one exception. He was much, much younger the last time, but the action is the same.

I watch Theo's back for a moment, gathering my calm, before I draw myself to full height and take a deep breath. Shelving all the things I would like to say.

'What can we help you with?' I ask the woman before us, stepping out and placing myself between her and Theo.

Mine.

The woman's pale skin has aged a little since I saw her last, faint lines crawling from the corner of her eyes towards her hairline, but she still looks young. Vibrant.

Someone unaffected by the challenges of parenting.

'I came to see him,' she says, her soft pink lips edging up into a smile. But there's something sad about it I refuse to examine.

'No—'

'It's fine, Rubes,' Theo says from over my shoulder.

In past visits, he hid behind me, unwilling to see her; to understand who she is and her reasons. I was his mother in every other way, not this stranger.

I *am* his mother in every relevant way.

'What do you want?' he asks, stepping up beside me.

She smiles a little wider and tucks a strand of her golden hair behind her ear, so much lighter than mine; Theo's falls somewhere in between. I would have said she was beautiful if I didn't know she has no soul behind those eyes.

'I need to give you a gift. It was your birthday not long ago, no?'

I scoff. 'You have no idea when his birthday is.'

Theo glances pleadingly at me before looking back to her. She looks over her shoulder, through the glass shopfront. Her gaze lingers on the darkening street and the cloaked people passing by before coming forward. I tense slightly. She rarely brings joy.

But she simply places her hand in a pocket of her navy cloak and draws out a small fabric bundle. She hurries the last few steps to Theo and presses the bundle into his hands. Her eyes water as she looks him over, seeming to absorb how much he's grown. I shift my feet, narrowing my gaze at the admiration on her face. He's handsome and kind, even if he has been a little reckless in the past. And she soaks him in like she's entitled to bask in his goodness.

I clear my throat. Not once have I had that look from her, but it's not jealousy I feel – just a white hot rage that she feels she can look at either of us that way.

'Keep it well,' she says, locking eyes with him before they flick to me. The weight of her gaze is heavy, and sharp with things that have never been said. For one brief moment, the question 'why' is full on my tongue. Why did you leave us? Why did you leave *me*? Why did you never help me? Why was I ... so hard to love and look after?

But I clamp my lips together. I don't need those answers from her. Whatever she could possibly say wouldn't mean anything, anyway, and I know in my core that my love and care for Theo – and Papa and Marley – far outweighs anything she could provide.

'Rubilena,' she says, taking a step towards me – no gift in the open hand she reaches out. No indication she's given me any thought before tonight. Only Theo gets that.

I step back. 'No. You can go.'

She watches me for a moment and I make myself stare back until she looks away.

'You're grown now, Theo, and the world is changing,' she says before glancing sideways at me. 'Keep her well.'

She doesn't look at me again before she hurries back out, the chiming of that damn bell reverberating down my spine.

'Don't open it Theo, she's not worth it.'

His hazel eyes are full of torn desperation as he looks at me. The man who knows his birth mother doesn't deserve him, knows who it was that did the hard yards in raising him, grappling with the child who wants to love his mother anyway. And yet I know the devastation that's on the other side of this hope. The despondency that occupies him for days, weeks, after her visits when another doesn't come.

Theo stares at the package.

The door flies open, so hard it catches the bell off guard, and it doesn't have time to chime. Early evening wind flurries around the store, the stack of papers on the counter scattering furiously into the air.

Pale sheets of paper suspend around me as a Koaman soldier steps in and the world grinds to a halt.

It's a ghost.

My ghost.

He slams the door behind him and the papers finish their journey to the floor.

'Theo,' he says.

I suck in a breath at the sound of his voice, the shock of it forcing tears to well. Unwelcome tears I blink away as quickly as they come.

'Hey,' Theo says distractedly, starting to collect the papers. He looks belatedly at me and then surprise registers on his face. 'Oh.'

It takes me a moment to comprehend it's me Theo's shown surprise at, and not the person who's just tornadoed into my shop.

'Ruby,' the other man says quietly.

Deep chocolate eyes find me, and the world disappears under their intensity. Like I'm the only one in the world.

Ruby.

Not Rubes, or Rubilena. Ruby. Like I am something precious.

I blink.

He takes three steps towards me, and I take four back, until the door to the storeroom presses against me. The handle digging into my skin.

Emotion I don't want to name ripples over his skin, and yet, still, he stares at me.

Theo clears his throat and, almost reluctantly, the ghost drags his eyes from mine and looks back to Theo as he places a misshapen pile of paper back on the countertop.

'Are you okay?' he asks Theo, the timbre of his voice washing over me. 'I saw her leave—'

Theo frowns. 'What—'

He sighs gently. 'We're going door to door on behalf of the Queen and I saw—'

'Ouch, shit,' Theo exclaims.

My eyes fly to him, the knee-jerk reaction to protect him more than enough to take my eyes from the soldier in front of me. The worn, white fabric Theo was given by our mother now has a small red stain as it flutters to the floor.

A metallic object remains in the palm of his hand.

'Fuck,' the soldier says, surprise and ... fear? ... in his voice as he glances back out onto the street. 'We have to go.'

'What are you doing here?' I ask, my voice finally coming. 'We're not going anywhere with you.'

His umber eyes drink me in, the history there almost buckling my knees.

'I was coming to warn you of the search,' he whispers. 'I didn't think
...'

He nods at Theo, who stands with his outstretched hand and wide eyes
as he looks at each of us. The two people he knows can, and will, get him
out of anything. At least, *I* will get him out of anything.

'You need to explain. Now,' I say.

He strides to Theo and grips his wrists.

'Do you know what that is?' he asks, tugging at Theo.

I don't bother to look at what he holds. Whatever she brings us is never
good; I don't need a trinket to know that.

Theo was barely more than a child when we saw this particular ghost
last – the second person in our lives to cut and run. And yet he's completely relaxed, if a little puzzled with the gift he's cut himself on. Pon-
dering the visit from our mother, seemingly not at all fazed by the soldier
in our midst.

'No,' I say. 'And I don't particularly care. If you came here for Theo,' I
frown, 'he's busy.'

Why would he be here for Theo?

Dark lashes dust his cheeks as he closes his eyes momentarily. He
glances at Theo and they share a look.

'I do sometimes come here for Theo,' he says eventually as Theo looks
away a little guiltily.

I cock my head. *Sometimes* come here?

'But it's this'—he indicates Theo's hand again—'the medallion the
Queen has been looking for that brings me here tonight. We're going door
to door – searching this time, not asking.' He swallows. 'It seems I've
found it. In the worst possible place. And I'm about to commit treason.'

The silence in the shop seems to pound in my ears.

'I thought Roan was supposed to have stolen it?' I ask, my voice barely
above a whisper.

Suddenly, the thought of Roan having it is so much more palatable
than what is unfolding in front of me right now.

His eyes flash. 'I can assure you, that's not true.' He looks at Theo
again. 'What did you feel?'

Theo swallows. 'It ... spiked me.'

Gently, he lifts the medallion with the thumb of his other hand. A small splodge of blood is smeared on his palm and I absently note its iridescent qualities.

Treason, he'd said.

The bell rings again, and I close my eyes against the sound. The harbinger of disaster. Another soldier joins us, the gold bars on his chest less than the ghost's – he's been promoted several times since I last saw him, then. Which makes sense. I knew he was made for this work, at least when it was respected and not feared. I let out an exhale.

'Good evening, how—' I begin, keeping my eyes averted from Theo, unable to see where he's currently hiding the most wanted object in the Kingdom. I try to keep my voice even, though my fingers begin to shake.

My ghost turns to the newcomer. 'I've got this one,' he says.

'Of course, sir, would you like me to—'

'No. Thank you. You may carry on down the street. I will finish here and join you.'

'Yes sir,' the second soldier says. The bell rings again.

We stand like that for a moment, each of us looking out the shopfront, frozen in place. None of us wanting to be the first to break, to propel us down this foreign new road.

Treason.

CHAPTER SIX

My knees tremble a little as I pace the living room. Papa tracks my steps.

On what might be my fifteenth lap of the room, Papa pulls me into him – squeezing hard, as if he can squash out the tension I'm trying so hard to hold in.

'Come, now, snuggle,' he breathes into my hair.

I clutch at him as a wave of emotion threatens to drag me under.

'You're not in this on your own,' he says. 'I've got you.'

He holds me a moment longer before letting me return to my pacing. Pacing that's lost a fraction of its ferocity.

'So, Roan's armies didn't steal it,' he says to our small group.

I don't know if it's a question or a statement. Most of Koamah lives in fear of Roan and his armies. He's coveted our home for so long; it made perfect sense that he would steal something precious to the Queen. Something that would give him untold power and knowledge of the Kingdom and, according to Atticus anyway, leave us ripe for a takeover. He wants our land, easy access to borders with our two sister countries, Solynara and Talvore, that make up the rest of the Koamah Kingdom, and will stop at nothing to get it. He's the reason we need to have such a ruthless military ourselves. Why my ghost was so intent on joining the service – to protect our home against the olive-green clad Oskrinya forces.

I still remember how the hems of their uniforms turned dark with the blood of Koamah.

'Apparently not,' I mumble, trying to make sense of what's happened – and what we do now.

The decisions Theo made that forced me to Atticus now seem so childish – he was never going to get his underground club off the ground. Now, he is the most wanted person in the Kingdom, the person that single handedly controls the fate of Koamah and our continent – if he wanted to.

And who will, again, be the centre of Atticus's attention once the underground king learns what Theo holds.

Stop being dramatic, I tell myself. But why else would it be so important?

'He's coming here?' Ash asks, breaking into my thoughts.

I nod. 'He said he'd explain.' I look at Ash, sure the intensity in my gaze must burn. 'But Marley stays in bed, and I need you out here. If anything looks suspect ... he doesn't leave.'

I swallow back the acidic taste that rises with that statement. Along with the question of whether or not I could really kill him. Because, regardless of what else I feel, I will never let harm come to Marley.

Ash doesn't respond, he doesn't have to.

'And if he doesn't come on his own?' he asks quietly.

Theo scoffs. 'He's not going to betray us.'

'You've got to be kidding me.' Heat stings my face as I spin to Theo. 'You have no idea—'

'Yes, I do, Rubes,' he says, standing as his voice rises. 'I have *every* idea. He *won't* come here with anyone else.'

'Since when are you so familiar with him, anyway? He said he sometimes *came* for you?' I shift my weight under Papa's stare.

'We ... kept in touch. After,' he says.

Theo at least has the grace to look guilty, but it fires something in my blood. It's a courtesy I was never extended. The last memory I have is of him in that laneway, and then he just ... disappeared. Not even a fucking letter to tell me what happened. To explain. Now, I'm ashamed how many years I kept waiting for that knowledge to come.

'How often?' I ask quietly.

Theo looks at the floor. 'About once a week.'

My stomach feels like it's just opened up at the bottom, and all my organs are going for a dive.

'Right. Okay.' My throat thickens against the poisonous ball that sits in my chest.

'He's my friend, Rubes, I—'

'He is *not* your friend, Theo. He is nothing.'

'Um,' Kaya speaks from the top of the stairs behind me. I didn't even hear the stairs creak as she came up. 'I found him outside,' she says. 'He said he was expected?'

I spin on my heel to find those dark brown eyes on me once more. I wish I could say they looked hurt at what I said, but they convey nothing. Which is precisely what I meant to him, too.

'Ted,' he says, looking past me to my grandfather. He walks over to shake his hand. 'It's good to see you again.'

Papa looks from me to Theo and back to the now plain-clothed soldier before him, taking his hand. 'You too,' he says, pulling him in for a hard embrace.

'You can talk now,' I say, conscious of the bite in my voice.

Kaya eyes me suspiciously before studying the soldier, her eyes running over his muscular legs and broad chest. As if she's trying to work out who he is.

'Have a seat,' Papa says. 'Tea?'

'Please.'

His dark hair is looser than it was earlier. Strands run free around his face, framing the tension in his jaw that's obvious even beneath his beard.

I force myself to take a breath. He came. On his own. He's committing treason for my family. For Theo. I bite the inside of my cheek.

'Fox!' Marley shouts as she flies into the living room.

My exhale catches in my throat and I choke. I don't move fast enough to stop her from throwing herself around his legs as my mind tries to catch up with the scene in front of me. His face splits into a sad smile.

'Hi, pumpkin,' he says.

I'm sure the sound of my cracking heart reverberates around the room.

That was a dream Rubilena, nothing more than a dream. Ash gave me my Marley. And I will be forever thankful for what we share. This ... soldier ... didn't stay long enough for any of those dreams to ever come to fruition.

Ash's wide eyes find mine as I seek him out. Clearly he didn't know about this either. We both look to Theo at the same time. The unbroken – until now – rule was that no one was introduced to Marley without one of us giving the okay. In our world, with the risks we take in the store and the illegal fighting ring, we can't be too careful. Not to mention that anyone can claim witchcraft or the fucking prophecy whenever they please. No, protecting our daughter from the everyday pitfalls of this life – this city – means being careful.

Theo shrugs, the picture of adolescent insolence. 'It's not like he's a stranger.'

'Maybe not to you,' I say, biting back how much I want to lash out at him for lying to me, for betraying me by allowing Fox to see Marley without my knowledge. Even if I wasn't worried about introducing her to strangers, this man is not one I want in her life.

'Did you see Mumma's bruise?' Marley whispers to Fox, like he's an old friend, as he squats down to listen to her.

I look back to Fox, trying not to be absorbed in those assessing dark eyes, and willing words to form in my mouth.

'You said no one was allowed to hurt her,' she says.

Fox's eyes flick to Ash, and back to Marley. 'No one is allowed. And I'm very sorry that happened.'

He gently disentangles himself from Marley and she moves to Ash to be picked up, her sleep-heavy head resting on his shoulder. We wait in an incredibly uncomfortable silence as he returns her to my room, his soft, comforting murmurs about no one hurting me going with him.

'Talk, please,' I say flatly to Fox when Ash returns, taking the seat next to Kaya.

Fox takes the seat Papa indicates, shifting forward so he's perched on the edge, knees bent. The fabric of his dark pants crinkles where it's cinched at the back of his legs.

Papa's patient face is watchful, absorbing every interaction. Kaya's forehead creases as she watches me, piecing it together. I'd told her about him once, when I'd had too many tongue-loosening drinks, and she'd demanded to know why I thought there was something missing with Ash. Demanded to know why—

I clear my throat in an attempt to focus my mind, but I'm too jittery to sit. So I stand, slightly on the outside of the group. We all look at Fox.

He steeples his fingers, elbows on his thighs, and I look at the point they make instead of his face. His inhale is audible.

'I need you to know,' he says, 'I will be executed simply for being in the presence of that medallion and not killing for it. Explaining what it is to you will earn me a fate worse than death.'

Papa reaches over and taps his knee.

'Not one of us will breathe a word, son,' he glances at me. 'You are safe with us, always have been.'

I clench my teeth against the surety in his voice, the gentleness when he said 'son', and the slice of pain it creates between my ribs.

Fox glances hesitantly at Ash, who nods shallowly. Not once did I consider they might have to be in the same room. The walls are tight on my skin. Theo refused to talk about our mother and the medallion until Fox was here – another small but significant betrayal that stings more than I want it to.

'The Queen's medallion was taken some weeks ago. We have been hunting for it since. Quietly at first,' he says, 'but now the efforts are being stepped up.'

'Why?' Ash asks.

'It ... holds the power of secrets and knowledge. If that knowledge can be harnessed, there is no telling what the bearer could achieve, could overcome. Decisions, punishments, laws. We don't know how far it goes. But King Boaz is worried enough about it for it to cause great unrest in the Kingdom. And unrest generally means the worst rises to the top – at least for a time.'

'So, Roan doesn't have it, but he's still going to want it,' Papa says.

'Everyone is going to want it,' Fox says. 'Whoever holds the medallion has the most power on the continent – practically the key to rule us all.'

'I don't understand – how can a medallion hold all of that?' Kaya asks.

'It … look, my source isn't one that would be trusted in Koamah – but it holds secrets. A lot of secrets, including state secrets. That knowledge in the wrong hands could very easily overthrow the King and Queen and bring down most, if not all, of the most politically influential families in the land. Leaving us all ripe for takeover by a new line.'

I narrow my gaze at him. If he's not supposed to know, *how*, then, does he know?

'What does it have to do with me?' Theo asks.

Fox shakes his head. 'I have no idea why you ended up with it – what your mother's motivation would be. I know you didn't take it, Theo.'

'Take it?' I ask. 'You must be joking. Of course he didn't take it.' My tone has less bite than it might have, because I didn't fail to notice the tone in Fox's voice as he mentioned our mother.

'But how you got it is not my primary concern,' Fox continues, looking directly at my brother, not me. 'The issue is getting you out of Koamah. Now it's marked you, once it gets used to you it will start to send a signal to show where the new power resides. A signal – kind of like a pulse of energy that will compel anyone attracted to having authority to you – that will show the Kingdom, and beyond, that Koamah is up for grabs.'

'Hold on,' Ash says. 'You're saying that now Theo has touched it, it's going to start sending out a … beacon of some kind to tell people where he is?'

'Yes,' Fox says. 'And I want to get him to a … healer before then.'

I exhale in relief and almost smile. A healer I can do, the markets are full of them. 'We can manage that, we know healers.'

He shakes his head slowly. 'We won't find what we need in Koamah.'

I grip the back of Papa's armchair, the cushion so old I easily feel the frame against my palms, and he reaches back to pat my hand. A sickness starts to whirl in the bottom of my gut, not unlike before I get into Atticus's ring.

'Where do you suggest we go?' I ask.

'I can take you to someone who can remove the mark before the signal gets too strong and anyone who covets the Kingdom – for any reason – comes for Theo, to claim it before he can.'

I laugh hollowly. 'This is ridiculous, Theo isn't going to be King.'

Theo laughs, a little maniacally. 'No. Not King. Please.'

'We'll just get rid of it,' I say. 'Leave it for your soldiers to find – have someone leave an anonymous tip.' I look at Theo in what I hope is a reassuring manner. The slightly frantic flicking of his gaze between Fox and me is evidence enough of his own loose grip on what is happening here, and I hope that same feeling in me isn't completely reflected in my face. 'We'll get rid of it,' I repeat more firmly.

'It won't be "left". I'm sorry, Ruby,' he says. 'Now it's marked Theo, you will never get rid of the claim without the medallion itself.'

'What if I took it instead?' Kaya asks.

I stare at her. Ash's eyes go wide.

'You could try, I suppose ...' Fox surveys the group around him, my family. 'But there's no guarantee it would claim you instead of Theo. And, even if it did, I'd imagine you'd be in much the same position.'

'So, we get someone else to take it,' I say. 'To try and shift the claim ...'

The implications of my words are painful as they land. I couldn't just select someone else to be at the mercy of the royal military and anyone else hungry for power. I'd be selecting them to be a target for Roan and Oskrinya, as well. Although, Atticus, maybe ... but I just don't know what he would do with *that* much power.

'What if we give it back to the Queen?' I say, changing tack.

'And how will you explain having it?' Papa asks, looking abruptly at me.

His voice is quiet, but I know what he asks. How will I keep from implicating his daughter? Do I want to? I don't care what I implicate her in, not after everything she's left the three of us to face on our own, especially not now that she's put us in an impossible position.

'Papa,' I say, clenching my right fist so my nails dig into my palm – channeling the overwhelming tightness in my chest to that sensation and not my tone at Papa. 'There is no way she didn't know what she was doing tonight – what she was giving Theo.' I make myself take a pause, to let the air expand in my lungs. 'She *purposefully* gave him the Kingdom's – the world's – most wanted item. Why would anyone, any *mother* in her right mind do that to her *child*?'

The words are bitter in my mouth even as I say them. He's not her fucking child, he's mine. But, beyond all reason, my grandfather still loves her.

'Exactly, Rubilena,' he says. 'She gave it to Theo. Do you really not consider that she might have had a reason? And a good one?'

There's something there, behind his eyes, that he's not telling me. But no matter how many times we've argued about her in the past, about the choices she's made, or even when he acknowledges what her leaving did to my life, not once has he ever backed down from the fact she had her reasons.

He just won't share what they were.

I sigh. I know he loves her as fiercely as I love Theo and Marley, and I will not be the one to break his heart by turning her in.

'I'll take—' I start.

'Nobody's taking it,' Theo says. 'It was given to me, it's my responsibility to bear. I won't risk anyone else's safety.'

I'm equal parts proud and incensed. He is growing into such an incredible man. But one that wouldn't be in this position if it weren't for our useless – and now it seems murderous – mother. If I clench my fist any harder, I'll start shaking.

Theo looks at me. 'I want it gone, not just from me. I don't want it to trap anyone else.'

Fox's face is so open when I glance at him, and yet I can't put the fate of my brother in the hands of someone I don't trust.

I won't.

'I have an idea.' I hold Fox's gaze despite desperately wanting to look away. But unable to. 'I know someone who can help us, someone with more contacts than you can possibly imagine. Thank you for explaining. You've done enough, I wouldn't want you to risk any more for us.'

Confusion clouds his features. He looks at Theo, the care there clear for all to see. He always did love him like a brother.

'Ru—'

'I'll walk you out,' I say.

He watches me for a moment before drawing himself to standing.

'You need to get the mark removed,' he says. 'But also work out what to do with the medallion afterwards. Removing the mark won't change that the control of Koamah and its allies is essentially now up in the air.' He runs a hand through his dark hair. 'A ball has been thrown, and you need to work out where it lands.'

The silence is awkward as I release the back of Papa's chair and wait for Fox to move. He looks at the group once more, opening his mouth as his gaze lands on my grandfather. But he shuts it and walks away. I follow him down the stairs and to the back door. His frame is bigger than the last time he was here, but the house seems to remember him.

He pauses at the bottom, almost pointedly not opening the door. The small space is so filled with him I can barely breathe. At the foot of the stairs, I feel the weight of the day above me, of a room full of people who need me to work this out. Work out how to be a mother to two people who need me so differently. Work out how to keep our family together without bringing the entire Kingdom, and others, searching for Theo. Searching for him ... to kill him.

We didn't talk about it upstairs, a silent understanding of how likely it is that Marley is trying to listen through her door. Having her hear that Theo is now top of the list for execution is not what I want her to know. I reach a hand out to the wall, letting the cool surface bring me back to the moment.

Fox's gaze burns as I find it on my face. There's the hint of a scar at the top of his short, dark beard that I don't remember. I would've remembered it.

'It was our *mother*,' I whisper. 'She did this to him. I—' I cut myself off, realising I said as much upstairs.

I don't need to say it out loud to Fox, anyway. He's heard it all before.

I try to squash the part of me that needs him to know Theo and I didn't get into this mess on our own. That we're not struggling without him.

'Ruby, I know,' he says softly. 'I'm—'

'It's fine,' I say, clearing my throat and drawing my shoulders back again. 'I'll work it out.' I look up at him. 'Thank you, truly, for today. I would never want to put you at risk. I can't tell you how much I appreciate you giving me the opportunity to keep him safe.' My words sound thin, even to me.

He reaches out as if he's going to touch me, and I freeze. His hand drops away.

'I want to keep him safe too, Ruby.'

'I know,' I say sharply. 'And if you don't see his head on a spike somewhere, you'll know I succeeded.'

He flinches.

'Goodnight, Fox.'

The air is cold as I usher him out.

CHAPTER SEVEN

The walk back up the stairs feels long, each step harder than the last. I brush my face with my hands to make sure there's no sign of tears before I get to the top, where Theo waits for me. Probably unsure why I turned down Fox, but, hopefully, trusting that I have another idea.

It will cost me, my plan, but so would going with Fox – just in a different way. Who knows where that road would lead. At least my option allows me to do what I know – and stay with Marley.

'Let's hear it, then,' Papa says as I appear in the living room, but the look on his face says he knows exactly what I'm going to say. What my solution is.

I sigh as I think about how long that stretch of my wall is about to get. The one I'm supposed to fill with wins. 'I'm going to Atticus.'

'That's your plan?' Kaya asks, disbelief dripping from her tongue.

'He helps people, Kaya.'

I wish, again, that family from the market had gone to him.

'If you *pay* him, Rubes. How exactly are you going to do that? People like us don't *pay* him for anything – he makes *us* the payment.'

Theo lets out a slow moan just as his hand starts to shimmer. I blink, and it's gone. He shakes his hand.

'That was weird,' he says. 'I can feel it though, the claiming. It makes sense, what Fox said about that now.'

I stare at him for a moment.

'We need to go now,' I say. 'The healers Fox talked about – Atticus will know who they are. He'll get us one and he'll help hide us until we can get the mark removed.'

'I'm coming,' Ash says. 'Atticus will want that medallion for himself, and we can't hand it over just yet – not to anyone. Not until we know what the options are and what they mean for us and the rest of Koamah. Getting Theo's mark removed – whatever the fuck that means – is task number one.'

Kaya and Papa stay with Marley as we make our way to Atticus's. I'd crept into my room where Marley slept before I left – I never leave without saying goodbye. Her little arms snaked around my neck as she burrowed in, aware of me even in her sleep. I allowed myself a handful of moments to pause there with her, her hair tickling my nose, breath heavy on my neck, before I had to drag myself away. Marley needs me, always; but, in this moment, Theo needs me more. And Marley, even if she doesn't know it, needs me to save him too. I won't give her a world without him in it.

The street is dark but, perhaps unsurprisingly now, there are soldiers still out, their not-quite-white uniforms almost glowing, and we keep as much distance as possible. The houses here are packed together, much like our road, the stones leaning into each other for support. Warm light spills out of the windows, and I catch glimpses of calmer lives as we scurry past.

Ash leads us to the end of the paved road and motions for us to stop as we approach the corner. He peers around the wall of a house with a blue door before whipping back around and pressing a finger to his lips, his face darkened by the hood he wears. He lifts a hand. Five. Five soldiers around this corner – more than we can take. No questions about why we are out at this time are good ones, and they will search us if we so much as sneeze.

I've left all my balms and remedies hidden in the house so I'm not found with them. But being accused of being a witch is the least of my worries tonight – I will die before I let them find Theo with that medallion and drag him before the King and Queen. They showed no mercy to that young girl in the square, there is no reason they would do so now. Not to someone who, on the surface, appears to have stolen something so precious and powerful.

We wait, huddled together in the shadows against the side of the stone house, until their voices dim and Ash gives the all clear.

Halfway down the next street is the side door to Atticus's. It's black and dirty, like almost every other door on this road.

I glance behind us as we step out.

'You!' A voice rings out from the shadows.

Theo freezes. I look to Ash, my heart in the back of my throat.

'Move,' he says, dragging Theo with him.

I run after them, the only option is getting to Atticus's. I don't think about what he will do to us for bringing soldiers to his door.

'Stop!' the voice shouts again, closer this time.

Footfalls close in on us. Only one set, I think.

The door creaks slightly as Ash drags Theo through in front of me.

A hand whips around my neck and I crash down backwards – back into the street and away from the door I was moments from passing through – fingers pressing into my throat. I drive an elbow into the body that's now pressed underneath me, and slam my head back. A crunch rumbles along my skull as I break their nose. Hot blood pumps into my hair and warms my scalp.

He groans as Ash appears above me, pulling me to my feet. My breaths are ragged as I draw them in through my bruised throat.

We take a foot each, and drag the soldier into Atticus's. The blood from his nose drips down his face. He struggles to sit up, but his daze and our quick momentum keep him down.

I slam the door behind us, leaning against it until I hear the click of the lock.

Theo stares at me, and I ignore the flow of emotion behind his eyes. He's never been here, despite his actions making this place so familiar to me, but he knows what it is. And he's never seen me fight anyone before.

A towering shadow falls over us, and I think Theo squeaks. But his face is calm when I glance over. Perhaps I'm remembering the sound he used to make when he was scared of what lived under his bed. The firelight torches flicker around us.

Marco's pulling security tonight and his staggering form lumbers across the small entrance from the second door. He lowers his brows at me as I remove my hood.

'Rubes? I didn't think you were on tonight,' he says.

His gaze falls on the moaning man Ash is still pinning down.

'Marco,' I say, 'I—'

He gives the soldier a long look before nodding once and turning back to me. 'I'll take care of it. Head in.'

I spare the soldier one last look, trying not to imagine the proud family he is supposed to go home to. Marco's thick forearm is tense when I grip it in thanks. His soulful black gaze holds mine as he places his hand over my own, squeezing my fingers, but he says nothing.

I lead Ash and Theo down the darkened hall, towards the fighters' changing room, but I don't care who else is here.

Atticus is the only one I need.

The creak of the internal door to the entrance sounds behind us as it closes. A series of muffled grunts and the thumping of feet kicking at the door follows us.

Then silence.

I shudder at the position I've forced on our gentle giant, the movement cracking something inside.

Atticus's office is at the back of the club where he is assured privacy. I only visit his office on paydays, when I take my small allotment of cash and co-sign the reduction in the debt I am working off. Our first negotiation was also done here, when I begged him to take me, and he gave me my choice – how to use my body.

It was the only thing I had to bargain with.

The brass door is open, shimmering in the torch light that lines the hallway, the sconces bolted into the stone. Atticus sits back in his large, carved timber chair. The plush, black velvet cushions that make up the seat and the back absorb the light. His huge stone desk, also black, sits between him and the door. Ice chip eyes find mine as I pause in the entry, as if he was expecting us.

'Rubilena,' he says.

'Can we come in?' I ask, the weight of my next series of questions making my voice waver.

He just stares back, gaze running over the three us, and I'm keenly aware of being in the very place I worked so hard to keep Theo away from. Now, Theo's right under the nose of the person I didn't want to have any influence in his life – and that now potentially holds the key to saving it.

Eventually, when I'm starting to seriously consider that he might say no, he gestures to the small array of couches and chairs in the corner, to the right of the door. Theo follows me in, slightly wide-eyed as he takes in the office and Atticus for the first time. Ash leans against the door frame, not quite in and not quite out.

Or positioned to stop Atticus leaving without helping us.

Slowly, Atticus draws himself up out of his chair and wanders over to join us, the bottom of his tailored jacket falling towards the back of his knees. Theo shifts in his seat. The small lump in his pocket – where the medallion resides – already feels like a beacon to me. One I don't know how to explain to Atticus without him wanting it. I don't miss the faint blush on Theo's cheeks. Of course he finds Atticus attractive, he's always had bad timing. And questionable taste.

Even if Atticus isn't wholly bad.

'It's been a while since we had a conversation like this, Rubilena,' Atticus says. He looks at Theo, a smile playing on his lips. 'Can I ask what you did this time?'

He doesn't mention the blood that's drying in my hair, or the marks I'm sure are on my face and neck. But then, he's used to seeing me busted up.

Theo tilts his head, no apology on his face. 'I think you'll find I'm the victim in this one,' he says smoothly.

Victim.

We both are. Victims of our mother's … what? I can barely conjure up a guess as to why she had that medallion, why she gave it to Theo. Does she believe it also holds some secret about the prophecy she once held so dear? If so, why didn't she just let the medallion claim her instead?

I take a deep, steadying breath.

'I've been marked by the medallion,' Theo says.

My heart sinks as Atticus's eyes go wide. The tiny part of me that was hoping he would tell us we're wrong, that it's not dangerous, gutters out and dies.

'*The* medallion?' he asks. 'The one that holds the secrets of the Kingdom?'

I look back at Ash, who shakes his head softly.

'Apparently,' Theo says.

Atticus sits opposite him, so close their knees touch. Theo narrows his gaze at him but doesn't look away.

'Does it feel like knowledge is flooding your veins?'

Theo's eyes slide to mine and back to Atticus.

'It's like a rush that comes and goes,' he says.

'A rush,' Atticus says, and grins, 'that makes you the most powerful man in the Kingdom.' He looks at me, realisation setting in. His eyes sadden a fraction. 'And the most wanted … I see the challenge.'

'We need to remove the mark, Atticus,' I say. 'We don't want the secrets – or the medallion.'

'Do you know what you could do with them?'

'Probably destroy a lot of people,' Theo says quietly. It's clear there is no chance he will be convinced to do that and the warmth of pride unfurls in my chest.

'And lose Theo in the process,' I say. 'We've been told there are healers beyond the Kingdom that can remove the mark. I need you to get one for us.'

Atticus chuckles and my skin prickles.

'Fuck, Atticus, this is serious.'

'It's exceedingly serious,' he says, still watching Theo. 'But you will never get one of those healers to come to Koamah.'

'Why?' I ask.

Atticus looks at me, a wave of auburn hair resting against his face.

'You've heard of the Varelai?' he asks. 'They're the witches you're going to need to get rid of that mark.'

Witches. A cold, icy feeling forms a hollow in my gut. I could be executed for simply mixing a balm for my knee – full-blown witches would be hunted mercilessly. I wouldn't come to the city for a stranger if I was Varelai, either.

I drop my head into my hands, pressing my fingertips into my scalp as if I can physically force myself to think of another solution. Varelai won't come to us, and I sent away the one person who could lead us there. Pressure builds in my throat and behind my eyes ...

'Don't despair yet, Rubilena,' Atticus says, his voice full of opportunity. 'I can get you out, you know that.'

I sniff, blinking at the grey ceiling for the tears to flow back home. He gets people to safety. I've never known where, but—

'But can you get me to the Varelai?' Theo says.

'I know someone who can.'

I snap my head back down. Atticus's face is gentle in this light, and he's never lied to me. Mostly, I only hear brutal truths from him.

'There is the question of your fights though,' he says. 'How do you intend to pay what you already owe? This endeavour won't be cheap.' He looks back to Theo. 'Although, you do appear to have something incredibly valuable in your possession. I'm sure we could—'

'I—' I start, but he holds up a hand to halt me.

'Before you talk – your debt to me is already substantial, this endeavour will certainly add to it. But that medallion,' he nods at Theo, 'could erase it all.'

Silence pervades the room.

I could hand over the medallion, the Kingdom, to Atticus right now and save Theo from this whole mess without stepping outside this office. He's not a bad man. But is he the person I want ruling the world Marley is growing up in, deciding her future?

He already rules so much of my life, could I—

But it doesn't matter. Even if we did hand it over, Fox said the medallion won't leave Theo until the mark is also removed.

'I'll take the debt,' Ash says from the door.

Atticus watches me, waiting as my heart thumps in my chest.

I turn to Ash, his shoulders blocking the light from the hallway. His gaze on mine is sad but firm. He knows I have to go – and he knows it's going to destroy me to leave Marley. I can't voice my conflicted thoughts. I look at Theo; he is just as crestfallen.

More debt to Atticus is something I never wanted any of us to have. Ash and I have literally been fighting our way out as hard as we can. And now …

I swallow, glancing at Ash again. 'Okay,' I whisper, assuming Atticus understands what I'm saying, despite not looking at him.

'You will need to leave now,' Atticus says, breaking my stare with Ash – our connected pain.

'No,' I say. 'Marley—'

'Will need you to come back to her,' Atticus says. 'The soldier Marco disposed of will be missed, and questions will be asked.'

'How do you already know about that?' I say.

'Does it matter?' He turns in his seat to face me instead of Theo, their knees finally losing contact. 'If Theo is already feeling the rush, it's not long until that rush – the pulse – is felt by others. Make no mistake, Rubilena,' he says, 'they will come. They only want the medallion – and they do not need any of you alive.'

'Okay,' I say, the tears pressing behind my eyes start to break free. I press my palms against my face. 'Okay, Theo first,' I say, looking at Atticus. 'Then we'll work out what to do with the medallion. We'll talk. After.'

Atticus leans forward and squeezes my knee. 'I look forward to it. I'll organise you some things to take. The sooner you go, the sooner you get back to her.'

'Thank you,' I whisper.

'Don't thank me yet,' he says. 'You come back without that medallion, and you will die before you pay your debts to me.'

He stands and moves to ring a bell on his desk. A scantily clad woman appears a moment later, sashaying her hips as she wanders past us. They have a whispered conversation in which Atticus appears to list things as she nods and disappears once more.

'You'll leave from here. I'll have someone meet you and lead you out.' He glances at the wall beside his desk, before heading for the door. 'They'll be here soon,' he says, leaving us alone.

The woman reappears with three packs, and talks me through the contents. My mind scrambles to hold the details, but all I can think of is Marley. Of her face when she wakes in the morning, and I'm not there. Her wild blonde hair that will need brushing twice a day to keep on top of the knots. The feel of her warm little body where it seeks me out in the night.

'She'll be fine, Rubes,' Ash says, finally coming into the office.

'I've never left her, Ash, not once.'

The tears prickle once more.

'I'll be here with her. And Kaya, and Ted.'

'I know, it's just—' I wipe the tears angrily.

'We're not you,' he says quietly, without judgement.

I don't need to say that he's right, he knows.

'I'll miss her.' My voice cracks. 'I don't even know how long we'll be. I—'

Ash pulls me to him, and I hold tight.

'I'll keep her safe, Rubes,' he says. 'And I'm sure Kaya will help with the shop as well as Marley.'

I nod against him, my soft tears leaking into the dark grey fabric of his top. 'I know,' I whisper.

A soft scraping noise fills the room and I turn my head on Ash's chest, resting my cheek against him as I look for the source.

A door-sized hole in the wall opens and a man steps out. My heart skips at his familiar shape.

A soldier of the Koamah Royal Military.

CHAPTER EIGHT

Fox's stare drags on my senses.

Part of me screams I should have known he'd given up too easily on helping Theo and that, of course, he would still be here. But then, that's the last memory of him I have – him giving it all up.

A warm flush rises on my skin as I slowly remove myself from Ash's chest and wipe my tears. Vulnerability is not something I ever intended to show this man again. My breaths are deep and forced, but I hold my head high. He will not make me feel ashamed. And I will never tell him how many of my past tears have been for him.

Ash keeps a hand on my lower back as I stand beside him, his presence as steady as ever. I glance at Theo, the tension in his shoulders draining away at the sight of Fox – transferring directly to me.

'We didn't betray you,' I say tightly. 'No one else knows of your … visit.'

I don't know why I say it. Just talking to him of betrayal stings, and yet I still don't want him to doubt me. I'm the steadfast one. Even in my anger, even though I don't want new memories with him, even though I resent him being in my life again.

'I know,' he says evenly. 'I suspect I wouldn't be standing here if you had.' Eventually, he looks at Theo and time starts to move again. 'Ready?'

I close my eyes briefly, my understanding coming more slowly than I'd like, before looking up again at Ash's oceanic ones. 'He's Atticus's contact,' I say, the words far more straightforward than this situation feels.

'Certainly seems that way,' he says. He turns me to him, hands on my shoulders, framing where Theo's fear, and mine, fight for space in my chest. 'You know I would go instead'—his fingers squeeze harder—'but I can't have you doing my fights, Rubes. The audience would demand Atticus push you too far – they've seen you win enough. And you'd have to face Marco more often.'

I frown, desperate to be in both places, but the truth in Ash's worries is hard to ignore. Atticus isn't just going to let me take a break – there are scheduled fights that need doing and he has a business to run. I trace the tips of my fingers firmly over my eyebrow. Ash staying to do my fights also potentially gives him an advantage on my opponents and possibly more wins. I can't think now about how quickly Atticus might change that because, for now, it's the only thing that's got any chance of softening my guilt about putting him in this situation. I can't let Theo go on his own, I won't.

'I know you're strong, Rubes, and you're a menace in that ring.' Ash grins, but it's sad around the edges. 'But there is only so much our bodies can take of this, and you've been at it longer than me.'

Theo tugs my arm, pulling me round to look at him. His dark, caramel hair sticks in all directions where he's been tugging at it. 'No more fights, Rubes. Please.'

I know his request is genuine – he hates the fights I do for him, and adding more will only compound his worries. But there's another request under the surface, one I know he would never voice in this room, with this audience. Perhaps when he was younger ...

'I'd never let you go without me, Theo. Never,' I whisper so only he can hear.

He exhales, the other words he wanted to say left unsaid. He knows I know. And that unspoken knowledge between us warms me a little on the inside. His hand slides down my arm, gripping my hand momentarily before he turns back to Fox, who just watches silently from the secret door.

If only I knew what was behind this one.

Fox's face holds his last question – *ready?* – but he doesn't ask it again.

'Okay,' I say to Ash and Theo. 'Time to go.'

Theo grabs our packs, and I turn to Ash.

'Don't make her sleep on her own. There's some of the stewed apple left in the cool box, she loves that.' I glance back at Fox once before lowering my voice as I talk to Ash again. 'I left my bag in the space behind my cupboard. If she gets sick—'

Ash takes the hands I'm gesturing with and presses them in his own.

'She's going to be fine, Rubes.'

I open my mouth, but he cuts me off.

'I'll remember the apple, she'll sleep with me, and I know what to do with the bag. We're good. You focus on Theo and getting home.'

He pulls me in for a hug.

'Go easy on him, he seems like a nice guy,' he whispers against my ear. 'Particularly if you like the dark and broody type.'

I pull back, but he ducks away before I can elbow him in the ribs.

I look at Theo and then Fox. I don't think Fox's gaze has left my face.

'Ready,' I say, hoping that is, in fact, true and I can save Theo and our family for a second time.

The passage Fox came through is darker and far colder than Atticus's office. But the stone walkway is clean, and I wonder if this is the way Atticus smuggles goods – and people – in and out. Fox carries a torch in front of him, the empty sconces on the walls giving no light, and leads Theo and me along in silence. I focus on the steps I take in the fight between light and shadow as the fire dances.

About twenty paces in, he stops by a heavy looking wooden door and pauses until I make up the last two steps to him and Theo. Silently, Fox opens the door into a large room, much like the fighter's change room in the main part of Atticus's club. Timber benches line the stone walls, wicker baskets underneath. In the other room, those baskets are for our belongings – mostly the clothes we wear to and from the club – and where we find our fight clothes after they've been washed and mended. These baskets are also full of what looks like clothes, but I have no idea who uses them. Fox lights three torches in a far corner and selects a basket from the floor.

'Find your best sizes in here,' he says. 'If your clothes will fit in the packs Adela gave you, you can bring them with you.'

I press my teeth together at the sound of the half-naked woman's name on his lips. Theo doesn't bat an eyelid.

The basket drops quietly onto the bench. 'There are shirts and pants in here.' He picks up another and drops it next to the first. 'And jackets in here. You'll need it all. Boots are by the door. I'll wait outside and we'll do weapons next. I just ask you be as quick as you can – we're behind already. And blow out the torches as you leave.'

He turns, closing the door without looking back.

Theo and I stare at each other a moment.

'Right then,' I say, making for the first basket. 'Oh.'

'Shit,' Theo says, picking up one of the uniforms. 'We'll be executed if they find us in these.'

I don't tell him I think we might be executed for having the medallion anyway. But he's right – impersonating the Koamah Military is a hanging offence.

Just for a moment, I look back to the closed door. Back to where the hallway lies that could lead us back to Atticus's. But already I feel like we've come too far to go back. And I know there are no options where we've come from, only where we're going.

My stomach is heavy when, a handful of moments later, we're both dressed in uniforms that almost match Fox's – Theo's hauntingly so. We're just a few rank bars lighter. How many times had I imagined the two of them in the uniforms of the royal military? Working together, protecting each other. Little did I know they'd do it anyway. But now, when Theo is actually wearing the uniform, it's a way that could get him killed instead of celebrated.

I watch the way the shirt stretches and pulls across Theo's shoulders as he turns to follow Fox and face what comes next. There's so little left of the boy I raised now.

One day I will watch a grown-up Marley turn away, too.

The weapons room is larger than the changing room. Racks and racks of sorted and categorised weapons hang on the walls. Walls of black, steel, and timber. All I can understand of their differences is their size.

Fox throws heavy black belts at us in turn before removing two smaller blades from the most depleted rack. I fumble with the belt, the weight of it slipping down my hip before I can latch it.

My breath catches as Fox stands before me, blades no longer in his hands.

'May I?' he asks.

I stare at him, paralysed by his proximity. My gaze follows the scar into his beard—

'Ruby,' he says quietly. 'I can help.'

I blink.

Theo slips a blade into a holder on his belt. How did he know how to do that?

'That'd be great, thanks,' I say flatly and look away as his fingers brush against my side.

He pulls the belt tight, and my body jerks in response. I still as he reaches to the bench for the remaining mid-sized blade and gently places it in the holder at my right side.

He moves to another part of the room, another deadly wall, and is back in front of me before I can properly draw breath. I stare at his chest, the button at the centre of my vision straining a fraction, before dropping my eyes. That's not a good idea either.

'I gather you're good up close,' he says.

My gaze flies to his face, the spark in his eyes bringing flashes of memory. Theo makes an embarrassed, half cough, but Fox doesn't look away.

'I hope you don't need these,' he says, as he slides two more knives into other sections of the belt. Dropping to a crouch before me, he lifts my pant leg and I gasp.

Theo stifles a laugh, and I glare at him.

Fox finishes strapping something, another knife I assume, to my calf and stands.

'I hope you don't need them,' he repeats. 'Ever.'

We're silent for the rest of the walk along the stone hallway, the slight crackle of Fox's torch and our footsteps the only sounds. The walk feels far longer than what would've kept us in Atticus's club. But the further we go, the surer I am he had this tunnel built specially for his use. It wasn't connected to his club by happy accident. I'd only vaguely wondered before how he managed to get people in and out – his office never once entered my mind. There must be another walkway from there too; I've never seen any strangers wandering lost around his club. Not secret ones, anyway.

The path steeps upwards slightly, a worn red door appearing out of the darkness. Fox pauses again to wait until we're gathered around him.

'It's open out here,' he says, gesturing to the door. 'You're newly inducted soldiers on your third patrol. It's unlikely we'll be questioned, but that's the story. Carry your packs in your hands, not on your backs. We need to look like we're transporting something, not venturing out on our own.'

He hands me a hat, and I frown.

'To cover the blood,' he says. Right – the itchy, drying patch in my hair.

He reaches for the handle.

'Wait,' Theo says. 'Where are we headed? We also need to look like we know where we're going.'

'Out the front door: Traders' Avenue.'

CHAPTER NINE

I squeeze my hands into fists, focusing on the nails in my palms to steady my breathing as Fox places an ear to the door. He waits several moments before blowing out his torch and dropping it to the floor, slipping us into the night.

The sound of the mostly sleeping city is static in my ears. I wonder if Marley woke up when Ash joined her in bed, or if she snuggled down in her sleep and will be surprised to find him in the morning. She'll probably squeal with delight. There won't be much sleep coming for Ash over the next few days.

Fox strides ahead and Theo and I fall in behind him, side by side. This end of Traders' Avenue, where it cuts through the end of the city closest to the border, is full of permanent market stalls where licensed shop owners can purchase wholesale goods. A place my family frequents. A handful of people slowly unpack timber crates and restock their shelves. Business ended hours ago, but the vendors still need to prepare for tomorrow's trade and deliveries.

'Oh, shit.' Theo freezes and I stop with him, looking around frantically.

Two soldiers lean wearily against a closed shop a block away, towards the heart of the city. They don't appear to look in our direction, but it's too dark to really know.

'What if—'

Theo takes a step backwards, back towards the club. Instinctively, I latch onto him – gripping his bicep and forcing him to turn to me. Dread sickens my stomach.

'Theo,' I start, but his eyes are already wide, not listening.

'Rubes,' he says, his voice sharp, 'we can't be out here. This – this *thing* – shouldn't be out here. People will go to war over the knowledge in this medallion. And that's before they even know what there is to know.' He links his hands behind his head, effectively shrugging me off, and then drops them as if the whirling in his mind is too much to be contained by them anyway.

I chance a glance at the soldiers, desperately hoping they haven't noticed us in the shadows, can't see Theo starting to unravel like I can.

'It needs to be destroyed. Think about it, Rubes,' he continues quickly. 'It could say anything – what if it says the prophecy will be fulfilled by a woman with crazy blonde hair and green eyes?'

A vision of a grown Marley flashes before me and my vision swims for a moment.

'Every woman with that colouring will be persecuted,' he continues. 'More women will die than they do even now.' He takes a step towards me. 'Worse, Rubes – what if it says the prophecy is wrong? How do you think the people will react if all their daughters, sisters, wives, have been exiled or executed for nothing? What if there is no prophecy at all, and it's a control mechanism?'

I gape at him. I have no answers for the questions he's posed. But I know he's right – people are savage under the right conditions.

'We'll be careful,' I say quietly, looking at Fox.

'I'll get a moment, Theo,' he whispers, 'but by the time I finish talking to those men, we need to move – without drawing more attention.'

His tone is firm but his face is filled with warmth when he locks eyes with Theo for a moment before he moves off to talk to the soldiers up ahead, their heads bowed together.

'Careful,' Theo says, his breathing getting heavier. 'What if careful isn't enough? What if they find me? What if I can't go home? What if – I know I'm supposed to learn something but—'

The slight crunch of footsteps approaching behind me makes my blood run cold. Theo freezes, the panic in his features making me ill.

'You okay here?' a stranger asks.

I turn on the spot, slowly, standing between Theo and the soldier. Willing any trace of uncertainty to leave my face, I press my shoulders back and stand tall.

'Yes,' I croak. 'We're fine.'

The soldier looks us over, honing in on Theo over my head, clearly unconvinced.

'Look,' he says quietly, glancing back to Fox and the other one. Fox stands close to him, close enough to silence him quickly if needed, I imagine. 'This whole search for the Queen's stolen goods business has got us all a bit ... antsy. Busting into people's homes isn't what we signed up for, I get it. But we have a job to do, soldier, and you're going to pull yourself together and finish your patrol. Understand?'

The silence around us presses in.

Theo clears his throat. 'Yes, sir,' he says, with only the tiniest wobble.

'Good man.'

We stand there, together, as we watch the soldier walk away. Ten paces. Thirty. Until he's far enough away I think we might have a shot at running if we need to.

'Theo,' I say without looking at him, 'we can do this. We're getting your mark removed. We're going to be fine.'

'And then what? The secrets of the Kingdom are at the mercy of someone else? We have no idea the horrors this thing holds – the changes it could bring about. How do we keep Marley safe from what we don't know? *Who* we don't know?'

'Right now, Marley is safe. It is you who needs to be safe, and we will make that happen one step at a time. In this moment, that means acting like the Koamah Military and getting out of the city. In the next, we remove your mark. We will work out what happens to the medallion after that.'

We're both silent as we wait for Fox, the thumping of my pulse loud in my ears.

'No one else can get their hands on this medallion,' Theo says, when Fox has rejoined us and my heart rate has slowed a little more with each step away the two soldiers take.

Fox's mouth drops a fraction before his words form. 'The Varelai ... they won't be able to remove its marking without the thing itself, Theo.'

He nods. 'If it doesn't turn out well ... you have to leave me, hide the medallion where it will never be found. Destroy it if you can. I can feel the violence of the history in this thing – people are going to kill for it without even knowing if it truly holds any worth.'

I step back a fraction, understanding what he's saying underneath those words.

'Theo,' I say again.

'We really need to go,' Fox says over me.

I pin him with a glare. 'Things are moving pretty quickly for us, Fox. Forgive me if stealing out of the city in the middle of the night with a stolen fucking medallion isn't something we're used to doing. Some of us don't just disappear.'

He pulls in a slow breath, watching the soldiers who still loiter.

'None of us mean to,' he says, before looking back to Theo. 'We'll work out what to do with it as we walk. Right now, we need to *move*.'

Theo blinks in the soft light of the few shops that leave lanterns on in their windows. Even in the dark, his apprehension is clear. As is his determination to do the right thing.

But he takes another step.

We don't pass any other soldiers on our way out of the city. Traders' Avenue is framed by a large, timber arch that announces the arrival to the city of Koamah, not too far from the Kingdom's border. It looms over us as we pass under and leave the city behind, the Avenue stretching out long before us and disappearing into the darkness. My heart grips in my chest as I walk further and further from Marley, even as it lightens as we walk closer to relieving Theo of the mark. With the mark gone, the target on Theo's back will at least be lessened. We can figure out what happens next later.

The three of us walk, voicing nothing more of our thoughts, for what feels like the rest of the night. Outside the city, the density of houses and businesses drops away quite suddenly, almost like there is an invisible wall on the city border no one wants to cross. The wide, dirt road is eerily quiet.

My eyelids are heavy, my feet aching in the new-to-me boots, when Fox finally directs us off the road, leading us into the scrub that lines the Avenue. With only the moonlight to see by, we make slow progress, the tiredness dragging on each of us.

My eyes burn with tears as a branch whips my face, leaving a hot sting in its wake.

'Just here,' Fox says, and I want to let the tears fall with relief.

Theo's stomach grumbles in response.

Fox stops just ahead, the bars on his uniform gleaming in the silver night.

'Duck as you go through,' he murmurs.

Theo moves ahead of me, grunting as he bends over and disappears. Fox gently places a hand on the back of my head as I move past him, pressing me under whatever I'm supposed to duck, the warmth of the soft weight forcing my eyes closed momentarily.

The moon disappears, and a faint panic stirs in the back of my mind at the total darkness.

'Theo?' I whisper.

'Here,' he whispers back.

'Give me a minute,' Fox says. The sound of branches scraping against each other sends a shiver down my spine.

Fox scrambles around for a moment before a spark of fire starts on the floor. The flames light our faces in black and orange, accentuating the tiny hollows beneath Theo's cheekbones.

As the flames grow, the cylindrical base of the room takes shape. Appearing to have been made primarily from sticks and leaves, a flattish, misshapen roof starts just above Fox's head.

'Won't the smoke ...' I trail off as it doesn't appear to fill the space.

'There are openings in each corner,' Fox says quietly. 'And it won't draw attention at this time of night. We'll have to make sure it's out early, though.'

He rummages in his pack and passes Theo and me a chunk of bread each before tearing into his own.

'Now what?' I ask.

'Rest now,' he says, 'we have more ground to cover tomorrow. When we're out of Koamah territory, I'll be able to get us some horses.' Fox looks at me, his eyes black in the dark. 'We have a way to go before we reach the Varelai, Ruby.'

I nod shallowly before seeking out Theo's face across the small flames. He looks away. I want to be soft, understanding. But his relationship with Fox sits heavily – that he kept it from me for so long, despite how far I go, on a daily basis, to keep his world spinning.

It's a secret between us that's burst, and now it bubbles and burns.

Theo eats in silence before lying on his side, shuffling until he has his back to the fire, and gently starts to snore. I shake my head at his impossible ability to sleep anywhere. He's been like that since I carted him to school in a basket every day. But perhaps the emotional exhaustion of recent events is taking its own toll.

His reluctance to face me doesn't make me any more patient to understand why he didn't tell me – and why he kept in contact with Fox at all. How he knew *how* to contact him. But we didn't come this far together without me learning, sometimes in difficult ways, when to pick my battles with him. I still don't always get it right.

'I'm sorry you've had to leave Marley. That must be hard,' Fox says quietly, watching the fire.

I close my eyes. He saw my tears – my sickening worry at leaving her – no point hiding it now.

'It's like being asked to choose between my heart and my lungs.' I look at Fox, trying not to notice how the firelight caresses the skin on his neck. 'You can do this right? You *can* help him?'

'Yes.'

My nose burns with unshed tears and I take a moment to make sure they stay that way. But the relief that races through me at the complete certainty in his answer is hard not to get washed away in. Neither is the realisation that I believe him.

'Thank you for still caring enough about him to do so. I admit, it's been … a surprise.'

My voice is quiet as I look back to the small fire. Theo might be asleep, but I don't want to risk waking him – he needs to rest after all that's unfolded today.

'Does he make you happy?'

'Who?' I ask.

'Marley's father – Ash.'

My throat thickens. Perhaps Theo hasn't told him everything. Like the fact Ash and I aren't actually together. But my softening to him only applies to his willingness to help Theo – the one he didn't leave behind. He doesn't need, or deserve, any more details about my life.

'He's a wonderful father,' I say truthfully.

He nods twice, his head bobbing slowly in the crackling light.

CHAPTER TEN

The rest of the night passes too quickly for me to get any sleep – not that I could get comfortable on the ground, anyway – and too slowly for the thoughts in my head to calm. Theo snores softly. Fox makes almost no sound at all. And I spend the hours listening to every sound as the night seems to breathe around us, watching the fire slowly die out.

Eventually, long after I've sat up to ease the pain in my hips, birds begin to chirp. Their marking of the new day is gentle at first, before the sun starts to shine through the branches of our shelter, and then the whole world is full of song. Fox stirs next to me and scoops a handful of dirt onto what little remains of the fire, dusting his hands on his pants. The cream coloured uniform readily catches the brown dirt – or more of it.

I watch him as he collects the small number of things he put out during the night. But I don't look away fast enough when his eyes find mine in the growing light; he holds my gaze. We watch each other for countless moments, the things to say too much ... and not enough.

I've imagined this moment – the quiet one in which he'd explain. Or I would rage. Or ignore him. Or ... somehow convey the impossible, painful ramifications of what he did. For never coming back. For leaving a hole in my heart in the exact shape of him.

But that hole has scabbed over, scarred, and even he doesn't fit in it anymore.

'Tell me you have more food,' Theo says groggily, and I look away from the face that's both familiar and new.

'How are you feeling?' I ask, clearing my throat.

'Pretty good, given I just slept on dirt for ... maybe the third time in my life.' He smiles coyly at me. I only know of one other. He grimaces when I shift my pack, coming properly into his line of sight. 'You need a wash, Rubes. And something to cover your throat.'

My fingers trail my exposed skin on reflex. It feels intact, but tender. I can still feel exactly where the soldiers fingers were when I swallow, and I know from experience how colourful bruises here can be.

'I'll get you to some water,' Fox says, his features flickering with something like pain as he drags his gaze along my exposed throat. 'But we should go now, before the sun has fully risen.'

Theo stays behind with the job of making sandwiches for the day with whatever he can find in Fox's pack. Fox wriggles aside what I can now see is a branch door, just enough for me to squeeze out, and he follows behind, closing the makeshift door once more.

I follow in silence through the scrubby bushland that surrounds us. There's no clear path between the grey and green foliage, but Fox moves without doubt – despite it still being relatively dark in the undergrowth, where the dawning day hasn't reached yet. My heart stutters a beat when I realise I'm blindly following Fox with no hesitation.

I didn't think I trusted him, not anymore.

A faint burble breaks through the layered sounds of the pre-dawn, and I try to breathe the calm in. If I could put aside my new reality, the weight of this responsibility, this would almost be peaceful.

Fox stops by the stream, and rubs the back of his head.

'This is the best I can do for now – you can ...' He motions to the stream, actively avoiding my gaze. 'I won't go far, just in case,' he says, and I stare at him as his eyes widen a fraction when he turns back to me. 'I don't mean – you'll have privacy.'

I squash the jittering in the bottom of my stomach and walk past Fox, stripping the military uniform as I go and dumping it on the narrow, sandy shore. Leaving my undergarments on, I stride into the water. My grip on nonchalance slips as the freezing water bites my skin, violently stealing my breath.

'Fuck,' I breathe to my myself. I count to three, psyching myself up and trying to get a handle on my breathing that's suddenly short and sharp.

I submerge as quickly as possible, forcing myself to stay under as I scrub my hair and scalp with my nails.

When I'm comfortable as much blood has gone as I can manage, I scramble back out, dripping on the rough bank. My hands start to shake, and the soft breeze pulls bumps from my skin as I grapple with the cold.

I dry myself on the cleanest parts of the uniform I'd discarded – the inside of the fabric – and do an awkward wiggle into the dry undergarments from my pack without exposing any more skin than absolutely necessary.

'Done,' I say when I've dressed myself in plain clothes and attempted to wring out my hair. It seems stupid to cringe at what my curls must look like right now, but I do it internally anyway.

Fox turns from his spot where the trees are thicker and brands me with his stare.

'Ah,' he says, 'you've still got—'

I touch my wet, knotty hair. It will be a nightmare in a few hours.

'No,' he says. He takes the few steps that separate us and scoops up the uniform shirt, soaking it in the stream. He wrings out the excess water before standing in front of me. 'You just have ...'

His eyes darken as they look down my throat, a crease appearing between his brows. I hold my breath, both wanting to stay and drag myself away.

'This would have hurt,' he says softly.

My neck stings a fraction where he wipes, the fabric finding scratches I didn't know were there. His eyes fly to mine when I suck in a quick inhale, concern sparking in them.

'It's fine,' I say. 'Trust me, I've had worse.'

His eyes close briefly, and I take the shirt from him, our hands coming together – just for a moment. I step back and wipe at my throat myself.

'I know what I did was—' he begins.

'Better?' I ask, angling my neck for him to check. The excessive knotting in my stomach isn't the only thing telling me this conversation isn't one I can have, and I will no emotion to show on my face.

His eyes search mine.

'For now,' he says.

Traders' Avenue – the primary supply route for the whole continent – is full of people, carts, and all manner of animals when we find it again. The stone beneath our feet is even and packed closely together, creating a cacophony of sound. Wheels and hooves and voices clamber for their moment to be heard.

Dirt channels run alongside the road, worn in the grass from decades of traffic. The scrubby bushland we'd stayed in last night doesn't quite extend to the road – the immediate surrounds are green and spacious aside from the dirt borders.

No one pays us much attention and we certainly don't look out of place amongst the various groups as we spend the day walking. If someone looked more closely, they might realise we don't have much with us to trade. But that could be explained away with the lie we have sold all our goods in Koamah and are returning home, wherever that might be. I make a note to talk to Fox and Theo about what our story is when we're out of earshot of the other traders.

Theo and Fox have also ditched their uniforms and we all wear variations of dark pants and short sleeved shirts. I'm the only one of us who wears a jacket, with the collar popped around my ears and a scrap of cream fabric Fox tore off the uniform shirt wrapped around my neck.

It's just warm enough now, as the sun continues to travel towards her highest point in the sky, for the neck covering to be a touch uncomfortable, the fabric scratching at my already sensitive skin. I grip the straps of my pack to stop from fiddling with it.

Traders' Avenue ultimately meanders through a number of countries on the continent. Both Oskrinya and the land of the banished are ahead of us somewhere, but neither Theo or I have traveled outside of Koamah before.

I glance around quickly, again, for any Oskrinya soldiers. Roan's last attack on Koamah left more dead than we were ever formally told, Molly's daughter among them. An entire family from our neighbourhood vanished – the mother simply never returning to our shop for her son's medicine. The flyer drop that came after suggested we'd won. And I suppose we had, given King Boaz still rules. But I think the definition of 'won' might be different for those whose families were destroyed.

The Oskrinya soldiers' olive-green uniforms have been burnt on my brain, along with the glint of the machetes so many of them choose to use. And it's those I constantly search for here, even though I believe we are still in the Kingdom – I don't know exactly where the border is. But there are none here. Still, I feel so far from home. I almost expect to see Roan himself cutting us down.

'Did you know this road wasn't originally built for trade?' Theo asks, rubbing his temple as he frowns.

I tug at the collar on the black jacket. 'What?'

'This road. The taxes people paid for it broke a lot of families, but it was never truly intended for a trade route. The then-ruler wanted easier access to his different lovers.'

I blink at him, wondering where that particular piece of information had come from.

He shrugs a shoulder as Fox clears his throat. 'Just something I thought was interesting.'

But, as we continue walking, I can't help but mull over his comment – is it something he has always known? It doesn't feel like something that would be common knowledge in the Kingdom. I lengthen my strides a little. The faster we can get rid of that medallion, the better.

By the time Fox points to a small collection of buildings in the distance, after the best part of a day walking, the blisters on my heels are screaming. A Traders' Station.

'I've heard about those,' Theo says. 'Are they as full of debauchery as they claim?'

I'm too tired to mock admonish him. My legs are heavy, and my shoulders and back ache from the weight of the pack. I can't even completely roll my eyes.

Fox laughs.

'Anywhere has debauchery if you look for it, my friend.' He jabs Theo in the ribs. 'But you're too young for whatever we might find here.' He laughs again, and my stomach tightens in response at the easy sound.

'Ha!' Theo shouts, briefly drawing the attention of a woman leading a donkey past us. They continue on in the direction we've come from, bulging packs hanging from the donkey's sides, towards Koamah. 'You know full well that's not true. If I recall correctly, it was you that—'

'That what?' I ask sharply.

Theo sighs and shakes his head. 'Nothing, Rubes, don't worry about it.' A private grin appears on his face as he looks ahead again.

'You two have more than "kept in touch", haven't you?' I ask, trying not to click my teeth together in annoyance – and to ignore the hollowing sensation in my chest.

I don't look at either of them, but focus on the cart we trail behind. I adjust my pack. Wicker baskets covered in thick hessian blankets bounce gently. A lone piece of pale-green something blows around the base, waiting for the wind to pick it up and release it from the cart. Looks like part of a corn husk.

'I already told you we're friends,' Theo says. 'Not my problem if you didn't listen.'

I glare at him. 'I listened,' I said. 'I just didn't want to believe you'd establish a friendship after—'

'Get over yourself, Rubes. We were friends before then, and you know it.' He wipes at the sheen on his forehead with his arm.

'And you didn't think to tell me?' My chest heaves a little heavier.

'And go through this with you every time I saw him? No thanks.'

I glance at Fox, who's studiously assessing the baskets in the cart in front, hands gripping the pack straps at his chest as he leans into the weight.

'Thanks for having my back, Theo,' I say through gritted teeth.

'Fuck, Rubes, what do you want me to say? Sorry he wanted to be my friend and not yours?' I flinch. 'He messed up. I know that, he knows that. But that's life, Rubes. You need to forgive him and move on.'

'I would suggest Marley is plenty evidence I've done just that.'

Theo scoffs.

My cheeks burn.

The three of us walk in silence until the buildings are so close I can almost feel the relief of removing my boots. A huddle of timber and stone frames a small, grass-covered square. There are four, maybe five buildings, each with a painted sign at the front that denotes their business. Tables flow over the green patch, their ownership clear from the empty glasses strewn across their tops. The tired, vacant stares of the people who have settled in for the night, their spaces claimed.

Fox leads us to the room he's secured in one of the two inns that operate here. It's up the end of the second storey, down a narrow hallway, and tucked away from view of the main floor. Theo strides in ahead and claims the sole bedroom for himself, door slamming behind him.

I sigh as I turn to Fox. 'About before ...' My cheeks heat again, annoyed at myself for having the conversation in front of him. 'We don't normally argue. Certainly not about—'

Fox removes his pack and sinks himself down on a worn but sturdy-looking chair. 'Putting aside the fact I've witnessed, first-hand, some pretty spectacular dust-ups between the two of you – I do owe you an apology. But you certainly don't owe me anything.'

I swallow, too afraid to move.

He reaches back and unties his hair, dark waves falling to his shoulders as he loosens it with his fingers. His eyes are sad when they find mine. Blood pounds in my ears.

'I messed up, Ruby. Terribly.' One hand rubs at his eyes.

I wait. Is this it? The explanation, the apology, that will make everything better?

'I never wanted to hurt you,' he says. 'And should never, *never,* have disappeared after. I just'—he inhales, and I follow the movement in his chest before looking back at his face—'I didn't know how to face you. How to explain.'

He grapples for words, and all I can do is watch him. Nothing more comes and, eventually, I gingerly make my way to the small couch in the open area near where he sits. The sudden movement, after standing still for a few moments, makes my blisters scream against the leather that encases them and I wince. What could he say, really, that would take away the hurt? What would it change? Certainly not our current situation.

I ease my boots off and peel the socks away where they've started to stick, aware of Fox's every movement as he stands and turns on the tap in the kitchenette, fussing with the cupboards. If I was at home, I'd make myself something to soothe my heels with, perhaps with aloe and green tea. But it's better my supplies are available to Marley, just in case she needs them.

Fox pads over the timber floor, having removed his own boots, and passes me a warm, wet cloth. I take it gratefully and gently wipe my heels. Suppressing the hiss that tries to escape as I make contact with my torn blisters.

'What should we do about Theo?' he asks.

I narrow my eyes at the door Theo disappeared behind. 'He'll come out for food.'

Fox holds a small, brown glass jar to me.

I glance up at him.

'It might not be as good as yours, but it should help,' he says.

Wordlessly, I reach out to take it. I'd take just about anything at this point. I wonder if this means he hasn't told anyone about the things I can make. The things I can do with ingredients that other people can't. He holds my hand, gripping my fingers until I look at him.

'I'm sorry, Ruby,' he whispers. 'I would do anything to take it back. But … I'm pleased you moved on.'

A soft knock sounds on the door, an unusual rhythm.

Fox stiffens.

'Soldiers incoming,' he whispers.

CHAPTER ELEVEN

He bounds on quiet, bare feet to the door that conceals Theo, cracking it open when he gets there. 'Hide. Now.' His voice remains a hoarse whisper.

I shove the balm Fox gave me into my pack. He scrambles around, placing our boots side-by-side near the door and unpacking some of his clothes, dumping them on the chair.

'You need to change,' he says. 'Don't look like we've just arrived. Adela will have packed you something ... casual. Or sleeping clothes.'

I rummage through the pack, going mostly by feel, and yank out a pair of soft black pants and a bright red shirt. Not needing a second instruction, I strip, refusing to look in Fox's direction. The pants are delightfully soft, but the top is far too tight and short. A strip of my stomach catches the cooling air.

Heavy footsteps sound in the hall, only moments before it rattles on its hinges.

Fox glances at the bedroom where Theo hides.

'Go,' he mouths at me, pointing to the room.

I cross the room, stopping abruptly halfway – my neck. Racing back to my pack, I desperately rummage for something – anything – my fingers landing on something silky. Charging back to the bedroom, I close the door behind me just as I hear Fox open the main one.

'Evening,' he says. His voice is muffled by the timber door now separating us.

'It's me,' I whisper into the room.

I can't see Theo, but there's only a slim cupboard that leans precariously away from the wall, or under the bed, so he's not far.

'What's—'

'Shh,' I say as quietly as I can. I unfold the silky item, a slinky top, and wrap it around my neck. Hopefully no one else will ever have to see it.

'—routine search,' a stranger's voice says from the other room. 'You'll invite us in, I assume?'

'Of course,' Fox says smoothly. 'Please do.' Shuffling sounds from the room next door. 'Adela,' he calls. 'We've got company.'

I stare at the door, heart racing. Shit.

'Del,' he calls again.

Having no idea if I'm doing the right thing, I run my hands along the make-shift scarf, doing the best I can to tuck in the thin straps and hope it's wide enough to cover any marks. I open the door and smile.

'Hello,' I say as I take in the soldier and move towards Fox, taking the soldier's attention away from the bedroom door.

Off-white uniform.

Koaman.

I breathe a sigh of relief, but it's shallow – they still look for Theo, even if they don't know him specifically.

His pale eyes take me in, at the same time Fox's land on my hips where the gentle fabric lies below the strip of exposed skin.

'What brings you to this station?' the soldier asks as he moves around the room, eyes roving over every surface. His left shoulder hangs slightly lower than the right – possibly a weakness I could use, if it comes to it.

Fox steps to me, linking his hand in mine. He grins, and confused butterflies flap behind my ribs.

'We just needed some alone time,' he says.

'And you chose here?' the soldier asks, not looking at us.

'I'm done,' a second soldier says as he comes in the open door. 'How long—'

He cuts himself off as he sees Fox and snaps to attention. 'Apologies, sir. I didn't realise,' he says.

The first soldier straightens himself a moment later and looks between Fox and the second soldier.

'It's fine, soldier.' He squeezes my hand. 'I'm trying not to work, anyway.' He winks at me.

Both soldiers laugh, apparently taking Fox's lead of less formality.

'I tried to suggest this was an unusual choice,' the first one says, gesturing to the room around us. His blonde hair is cut close to his head – far shorter than Fox's.

The hand I hold is warm, and so familiar. I bite back the memories it brings, the way my hand fits so seamlessly into his, even after all this time.

'Noted,' Fox says. 'It's not our final destination, but I was ... let's say ... impatient.'

'That explains her hair,' the first soldier says, still looking like he's trying to piece together who Fox is. He laughs again. 'I'm sorry we disturbed you, sir. I hope you enjoy your stay.' He smirks as he follows the second soldier back out of the room.

The door shuts gently behind them.

The weight of Fox's hand is heavier in mine, his callused skin burning.

He doesn't let go.

Neither do I.

'It was the best I could think of,' he says quietly. 'Sorry I didn't warn you.'

'It's fine, Fox, it's fine. I've—'

'Moved on?'

The bedroom door squeaks. 'Can I come out?' Theo asks.

I step away from Fox, dropping his scorching hand.

'Bit late if we were going to say no,' I say.

Theo sags onto the small, dark couch. It's so worn I'm not actually sure what colour it was before, maybe dark brown? He takes the medallion out of his pocket and spins it in his palm. It's almost a subconscious movement but, where he seems totally at ease, I can't drag my eyes off it.

Fox paces.

'It's not totally unusual for us to come this way,' he says. By 'us', I assume he means soldiers of Koamah. 'But there weren't any scheduled inspections for this week.' He runs a hand through his hair, pulling it off his face. 'And now they know I'm here – somewhere I am not meant to be.'

'Shit, Fox,' Theo says, the spinning medallion coming to a stop as his fingers curl around it.

'I'm not worried for me,' Fox says, pausing across the room. 'Nor should you be. I worry about the questions that will be asked.'

Theo eyes us.

'I have a theory,' he says.

Food is delivered to the room and I gratefully accept the tray from Fox, who answered the door – a knife held behind his back. Steam rises from the three large bowls, a number I'm relieved the Koamah soldiers didn't see.

'This is so good,' Theo says around a mouthful of stew. 'Don't tell Papa, but this rivals his for sure.' He mops his chin with the palm of his hand, wiping it on his pants.

'I don't know,' Fox says, 'I miss Ted's cooking. We certainly don't eat like that in the army.'

An unwanted memory bursts forth. Of the four us – Papa, Theo, Fox, and me – cooking and laughing. Eating and telling stories around our own worn, timber dining table. The way Fox's hands suddenly seemed so much larger than the cutlery, his voice so much deeper, and his opinions as deeply thought as ever. At that time in my life, I'd never not known him. Seeing him again is like being sucked under the tide of time.

Fox glances at me, memories in his eyes too. Dancing shadows.

I focus on the delightful burn on my tongue to keep me present, on all the challenges I don't want to face, and yet am anxious to, so I can go home to Marley.

'Let's hear it, then,' I say to Theo. 'Your theory.'

Theo swallows and scrapes the bottom of his bowl with a chunk of bread. I can't help but look at it and wait for him to shove it in while talking. Thankfully, it doesn't yet make the journey to his mouth.

'Remember what I said about the road and the then-king?'

I make a sound of agreement as I chew my own bread. Definitely not as good as Molly's.

'I'm pretty sure I didn't know that before,' he says, 'but now I feel like I've known it my whole life. Like, how did I ever miss it?'

Fox watches us.

'And this is a theory because ...' I prompt.

'I think it's the claiming of the medallion,' he says. 'It's giving me the secrets. For example, I know the soldier that was here first today knew exactly who Fox was, but he wanted an excuse to play at ignorance – a chance to ruffle the feathers of a more senior officer.'

Fox blows out a breath.

My first thought is to reject what Theo's saying; it's outrageous that he could know these things. But the fact he is holding the Queen's medallion, that it shimmered in his palm like it was home, is equally unbelievable. I've spent a lifetime promising I would believe whatever he told me, trying to impart the importance of the truth to him. He hasn't been perfect at it, and neither have I, but now is not the time to let the doubt start creeping in. At least, not beyond the weaknesses in my armour his relationship with Fox has created.

'We knew the medallion would start to attract people,' Fox says. 'If the telling – giving – of its secrets to you equals it making its "claim", it might also explain the timing of the soldiers' visit just now. An inspection they weren't scheduled to make.'

I look at Fox as he places his deep, empty bowl on the low table in front of us. He sits next to Theo, each of them sitting forward with their elbows now on their knees. Fox is bigger, broader, but Theo could certainly rival him in a few years when he finishes growing into himself.

But his words remind me of a concept Papa taught me long ago. One that Atticus taught me in a different way. The concept of each action having an equal reaction. Like when I'm mixing our teas and the rosemary I add responds to the brew. Or how my cheekbone felt like it exploded when Marco hit me. Two things that are intrinsically linked.

'How does it feel when you are ... given a secret?' I ask.

'Like a rush, like someone has dropped ice down my shirt ... I'm not explaining it well.' He frowns, but I get what he's saying. And the ice might start with Theo – the medallion – but the water still needs to go somewhere.

In this case, it seems to be going into some sort of invisible beacon.

'Do you feel anything?' I ask Fox, wondering if him also being a soldier has any impact on how the beacon is received.

'I don't know ...' he says carefully. 'At about both those times – when you say you learned the secrets – I did feel particularly compelled to be here, but ...'

Theo laughs out loud. 'You're an idiot. You always feel *compelled* to be with us. We're—'

'If that's true,' I cut in, unable to hear whatever else was about to come out of Theo's mouth, 'that means we have about half a day between the medallion giving you a secret and being found. If the soldiers just now came because of the secret of the road, then you now knowing the secret of that soldier recognising Fox means we're looking at more visitors during the night.'

Theo drops the piece of wet bread back into his bowl. 'So, the hunt has started,' he says without looking up.

The stew sits heavily in my gut, and I can't shake the question that, if the 'hunt', as Theo calls it, has started because of these small, seemingly unimportant secrets, what happens when it starts to share bigger ones? Like details of who will fulfil the prophecy, or if it's even true?

Theo and I take the bedroom – leaving Fox the tiny couch – for as much rest as we can gather in the hours we have. Not that we really know what number that is. I sleep fitfully as the thoughts tumble around like stones with jagged edges. Theo starts to gently snore. I press the back of my head harder into my pillow at what is now proving to be an annoying ability to sleep anywhere, and stifle a groan. We didn't even get to talk about our rather mortifying discussion on the road about whose friend Fox is.

Despite the weight of the soldiers that close in, my mind keeps returning to Marley. How I can't sleep without her and the beating of her heart against me as she slumbers, the breaths she draws gently soothing my mind into my own sleep. So, I surrender and think of Marley and of the questions I asked for so many years as I lay awake next to her.

Questions whose answers now lie outside the door.

Theo lets out a particularly loud rush of air, his lips smacking slightly, and I jerk out of bed, sighing just as loudly.

For fuck's sake.

But I don't really want to wake him.

I crack the door as quietly as I can and freeze. What am I going to do out there that I can't do in here with Theo? Trapped between two sleeping men I don't want to talk to – one because he needs sleep, the other because perhaps not knowing any answers is better.

'I'm awake,' Fox says quietly.

My breath catches. Of course he's bloody awake and sprung me here, stuck in the dark doorway.

'How many times?' I ask before I've moved, before the words even run across my mind and I can stop them.

'What?' he asks sleepily. Perhaps he wasn't awake until I came out.

I leave the shelter of the bedroom, where I didn't know the answer, and shut the door behind me. But I don't move closer.

'How many times did you sleep with her?' I ask into the darkness, relieved I can't make out the details of his face.

The image of Fox in that laneway, holding someone other than me against the wall, drives behind my eyes. The way his body moved with hers, the rhythm they found, haunted me for a long time afterwards. As did the impossible sadness in his eyes when he saw me watching. It was the last time I'd seen him.

My eyes adjust to the dark room enough to see Fox sit up and rub his face, his hair loose around his shoulders.

'That was the only time,' he says. His voice is soft and sad, like his face was then.

I close my eyes. I don't know if that's better or worse. I'd run so many scenarios through my mind to explain why he did it, why he disappeared forever afterwards. Part of me hoped he'd fallen so deeply in love he had no choice but to run away to fulfil his dreams.

Not that I wouldn't have been shattered by that, too, but the alternative was this. Knowing he gave up everything we had for a one-time thing. The history we shared, the little girl struggling to raise a family and the steadfast boy next door who made her feel like she could conquer the world.

And that he would help her do it.

All the firsts, the passionate arguments broken by physical exploration, the tears he wiped from my cheeks. The scrapes he cleaned on Theo's knees, the meals he cooked with my Papa. All of it – worth less than a one-time thing in a back alley.

I'd wanted to hate the girl for so long. Did hate her for a while. But then I knew the magnetic attraction to Fox. How much I adored being the focus of all his light, lit up from the inside simply by how he looked at me. How I would have been powerless against it as well. *Was* powerless against it. I couldn't begrudge another girl for wanting the same.

And emotions were running high that night. His last night before enlistment, before he started his career as a soldier in the Koamah Military. We were giving him the best send-off we could, and he was going to return to me after his two full seasons of initial training.

But, instead of us eking out the last hours of the night under the stars, I found him with his pants around his ankles.

Never to hear from him again. Until now.

Some things are better left unknown, I think as my heart sinks.

'The only time,' I say almost entirely to myself, my knees losing more of their strength than I'd like to admit. 'Must have been some fuck.'

CHAPTER TWELVE

I sit on the floor of the bedroom where Theo sleeps and listen to his snores. I want my little girl so badly my chest aches. She and Theo and Papa. They are mine. And I will forever be theirs. The pieces of my soul that will never disappear.

Dropping my head to my knees, I let the tears come. For a time, I'd let myself believe it was over. Done. I'd never see Fox again, and I didn't care – I'd let myself heal, carve out a life that was my own as much as it could be. Then I met Ash. Charming, funny, and sexy-as-hell Ash. But, hard as we tried, there just wasn't the right kind of love for us.

Ash cried when he told me, worried it would crush me; instead, I let go of a breath I'd been holding for years.

We agreed to keep the incredible friendship we'd developed and let each other move on. I never truly believed I would. If I wasn't able to have love with Ash after Fox, I'd never have it with anyone. Fox ruined me for anyone else. But I would let Ash have it.

And I was okay with that. Am okay with that for Ash. Having Marley filled me in ways I'd never even considered, I didn't need a different kind of love again.

Then Fox blew into the shop and shattered my false reality.

'Ruby,' Fox says through the door. 'Ruby, please, talk to me.' His voice is pleading, and I press a hand against my chest.

I rest my head back on the bed I lean against.

The door groans gently where I imagine Fox has leaned his own head.

Drawing a steeling breath, I move to stand. Not because I feel guilty for walking out, but because I show up for people. It's what I do.

Right now, I need to show up for myself. I need to finish this.

My body feels every fight I've won and lost as I unfold myself from the floor and face Fox in the doorway. I let him take my hand and lead me to the small couch, but I can't hold his back. He lights a lamp, placing it on the table where our food bowls still sit, and closes the bedroom door once more, the light flickering around us. The gentle sound of Theo snoring is shut away.

He joins me on the couch; his face is tight, dark brown eyes devouring the flickering light. The scar on his cheek shines gently where it catches the lamp before disappearing into his short beard. He faces me and takes my other hand in his as well.

'It was one time,' he says. 'And it never should have happened. I – I wish it hadn't. I wish I'd been strong enough—'

I can't help but scoff at the same time a sickness fills my veins.

'Was she really *that* attractive you couldn't say no?' I shake my head. 'Don't answer that – it doesn't matter.'

He desperately searches my eyes for something.

'I'm not sure what you want from this, Fox – I'm not sure what *I* thought I'd get from this.'

His fingers are light on mine, and I wonder what would happen if I took them properly, let them wander. But the poison of how it felt to be left turns the edges of my mouth down, and I can't imagine letting him touch me like that again.

'You slept with someone else, then you left,' I say, matter-of-fact. 'There's not a lot else remaining to be said. You could've chosen to stay and fight for us, for me. But you made your choice, and I wasn't it.'

I shrug against the heartache that still brings.

'I know that now,' he says. 'And every day I will regret taking that road. I should've taken a stand against doing it that way. I know you have ... a different life now—'

Taken a stand against what? How good at sex she was? I want to ask. Instead, I nod. 'Yeah, I do.'

'But I know I'm not nothing to you.'

My throat starts to close over beneath its bruises, but I force the words out. Force my hands to remain relaxed. 'What do you mean?'

He watches me carefully, as if I might be the one to suddenly run away. 'You told Theo I was nothing. I'm not nothing to you, I won't believe that.'

Slowly, painfully, I withdraw my hands from his and place them in my lap.

'I'm not sure why you care now, when you so clearly didn't then.'

He opens his mouth, but I continue.

'No, Fox,' I say gently. 'You're not nothing. You are a memory of my best friend, my first love. For me, you are a memory. But, apparently, you are still Theo's friend. One that is currently risking everything to help him, and helping him in a way I can't do on my own. So, no, you are not nothing to me. Only because you are something to him. And I will do anything for him – I would imagine that's something you might remember about me.'

'Okay,' he says, his voice nothing more than air.

He clears his throat, his Adam's apple bobbing with the action. I resist the urge to look at his mouth, and instead turn to the table and stack the dirty bowls.

'We should probably go,' I say, letting our immediate next step erase the possibility of any others. 'Can you take us somewhere we can watch the station? I want to see if Theo's theory, and the timing, are right. If it is, and the medallion giving him a secret means someone will be looking for us quickly, they should be arriving soon.'

The three of us lie in a ditch in the dark and watch the soldiers crossing the green square of the Traders' Station. Straight into the inn we'd just been in.

Their uniforms are olive-green.

Oskrinya.

Fox swears under his breath. 'I think this is unusual enough to say your theory is correct,' he whispers to Theo. 'I almost never see Oskrinya here. Can you tell us each time you're ... told a secret?' he asks Theo.

I can hear the frown in his voice at the awkward use of language, but I don't know if I could do any better. A piece of metal is telling Theo things he shouldn't know, and somehow alerting others to its – and by extension his – presence.

'I'll try,' Theo says just as quietly. 'So far, it's been a slow growing of awareness that comes with a chill, as opposed to a sudden knowing. But I'll try.'

Fox rolls on his back and points behind us, over his feet. I can just make out his shape in the dark.

'There's bushland in that direction, but we won't be able to light the way. We can cut across from there to where I will get us horses.'

We wait for long, long moments, the night dark around us and the ground getting increasingly cold until we're comfortable enough the soldiers are settling in for the evening.

Then, we make a break for it.

The ground is mostly flat, but there are enough tufts of grass and holes to make running in the dark too dangerous. None of us needs an injury to carry. I only breathe a little more freely when we're deep in the bushland and I'm confident I can't hear the slashing of Oskrinya machetes behind us.

'We can't let those men get that medallion – or you, Theo,' Fox says.

'I know,' Theo says seriously. 'Just ... don't make Ruby be the one who has to kill me.'

His statement, and how clearly he seems to have thought that proposition through already, steals all thought for a moment.

But I don't tell him I will kill myself before I let any harm come to him.

The better-than-expected relief Fox's balm gave my blisters is wearing off by the time the sun graces the sky. A nicker sounds, and my heart screams in delight. If I don't have to walk another step, I might just pass out from happiness.

'Please tell me those horses are for us, Fox. It might literally break my heart if they're not,' I whisper, risking the sound for confirmation of this fact.

He smiles at me, the corners of his eyes crinkling softly. It doesn't remove the shadow of sorrow that's still in his eyes. The one that happens sometimes when people reminisce for too long. Like when Papa thinks of our mother and tries to remind us of the goodness in her – something I have never witnessed.

'Your heart is safe. They're ours.'

Theo looks at me from the other side of Fox, eyebrows raised high, a smug 'told you' on his face, and I focus on the pain of my blisters, not the somersaulting sensation behind my ribs. No way is my heart safe from Fox, but it doesn't need to be. It will never be his again.

'If there's one that's not entirely terrifying, I might just kiss the owner,' I say.

'Even if they look like the backside of said horse?' Theo asks.

'I can't see any better options, can you?' I ask.

Fox slides his gaze to mine before looking ahead and continuing to lead us on.

'You might be convinced yet,' he says. A sly grin appears on his face, but he keeps his eyes averted.

The sounds of a farm grow as we make our way through the scrub. Beyond the tree line, I can just make out timber fences, buildings, and a large, dark animal circling in the yard. Sand kicking up in its wake.

Fox whistles a three-note tune and steps us out of the trees.

The circular yard is complemented by a smattering of buildings in different stages of upkeep and disrepair. The one that's clearly a house sits the furthest away, to the left. Four people appear, each from a different part of the farm.

Each holding a weapon.

'We good here?' I ask Fox quietly, suppressing the sparking need to get in front of Theo lest I spook them.

'Definitely,' he says without looking at me. 'I would never take you – either of you – somewhere you weren't safe.'

I bite back the retort that nothing about what we're doing says 'safe'.

I look to the foursome that approaches. The woman carries a blade that's seen more blood than I care to know. The blade shines like the sun, no blood to be seen, but it's obvious in how worn the handle is. Whether that's her lifestyle here, or something more sinister, I don't know. But I'm not prepared to take any chances.

The man who looks like he's come from the yard with the horse – a brownish one who's now tied to a post panting softly, waiting for the man to return – walks forward the closest. His shirt is undone almost to his navel, and sweat beads between the muscles on his chest. Blonde, curly hair frames his face and his smile, when it finally breaks, is blinding. But it's the kindness that shines from him that catches the breath in my throat.

'Well,' Theo says quietly. 'I could certainly be convinced.'

Me too.

Fox chuckles, and I tuck an errant curl of my own behind my ear. Fingers drifting to the piece of fabric around my neck to check it's in place.

'Convinced of what?' the man asks when he's a pace or two away.

Fox steps forward and takes his hand.

'Brode,' Fox says. 'Good to see you again.'

'And you,' he says, his smile remaining. 'I've heard things are getting bad in the city. I assume we'll be seeing more of you?'

'Hopefully,' Fox says. 'I'll do as many extractions as I can, but it may not be enough. We'll have to reassess our resources.'

Brode nods at Theo. 'I'm being rude, apologies.'

He extends a hand to Theo who grips back tightly as he shakes it and introduces himself. He moves to me next, and I fight a blush as his large hand envelopes mine. I hold his gaze and refuse to look at either Theo or Fox, given my earlier comments about kissing the horseman.

Although, it would certainly be no hardship to kiss this man.

'This your place?' I ask.

Brode shakes his head. 'Freya's. Been in her family for generations.'

Theo clears his throat, and Fox glances at him.

The other three wander back to where they came from, apparently convinced we pose no threat, and Brode leads us to the horse yard. The stables lie on the other side of the sand-covered yard, and I can just make out the rumps of two other horses. I swallow, my gut starting to skitter. I've never ridden before, but I'll be damned if I'm not going to try.

'I only have two today,' Brode says, and my heart sinks a little. We will be slower with one of us still walking. And I can't stomach the idea of walking any further than absolutely necessary. My blisters ache in anticipation.

'The other,' he says, looking into the stables, 'is lame.'

'We'll make it work,' Fox says.

Theo leans against the railing next to Brode, a tension running underneath his casual pose as he looks back at Fox and me.

'We should keep moving,' he says, hazel eyes sparkling in the sunlight.

He holds my gaze to make sure I understand – another secret.

'I'm sorry you can't stay,' Brode says, 'but it's probably for the best. We've had both Koamah and ... Oskrinya ... soldiers through in the last few days. There's movement afoot, that's for sure.' He shoots a meaningful look to Fox, but gives nothing more away.

He steps away from the rail and into the stables; Theo watches him go.

'Another one?' Fox asks quietly, keeping a watchful gaze around the whole farm. No doubt watching for the others to return. Or soldiers.

'Yeah,' Theo says. 'I'm pretty sure Freya's great-grandfather killed someone on behalf of the Kingdom and was gifted this farm in return. They don't know about it.'

I suppress a shudder. If Freya is the woman with the large knife, perhaps she takes after her great-grandfather more than they know.

Brode emerges from the stables with a chestnut-coloured horse trailing behind him.

'This one's for you,' he says, handing me the reins. I stare at the leather straps in my hands, my mouth dropping open. 'She's quiet,' he reassures, 'don't worry. And you'll be in good hands with Fox.'

He walks the other horse out of the yard and hands its reins to Theo. We look at each other. Theo's hair continues to get darker as he gets older, and it's now growing down over his ears. His hazel, green-brown eyes are wide as we take each other in. I imagine I look much the same. My colourings are different to his, my skin several shades lighter, along with my eyes, but the stunned look would be much the same.

Brode holds Theo's horse, Trumpet, and helps him on. The black horse doesn't seem to move a single muscle until he shakes his head a little and lets out a snort. Theo smiles in return. Brode grabs his heel and pushes it gently towards the ground, Theo's toes staying in the stirrup.

'This is go,' he says, pressing Theo's heel gently against the side of the horse. Reaching up to the reins, he places them in Theo's hands and indicates pulling back. 'This is stop.'

They lock eyes for a moment, long enough to catch my attention, before Brode smiles and the sun seems to light Theo up from the inside.

'Ready?' Fox says, breaking my attention.

I nod.

'Left foot in here,' he says, holding the chestnut's stirrup out to me. I hop a little to get my foot in and hold on to the top of the saddle for balance.

'Jump,' he says.

I spring myself off the ground, my momentum helped by Fox's hand on the back of my thigh. I land heavily, and the horse shifts.

I wince, gripping the saddle. 'Sorry, sweet girl.' Sweat makes the reins slip in my palms.

Fox's hand rests on the top of my thigh where it's traveled as I found my seat. I watch it for a moment, how the expanse of dark tan skin covers my pants. How the span of his fingers curves around the top of my leg, warmth seeping through beneath them.

'You'll be fine, Ruby,' he whispers. I close my eyes briefly and breathe out.

'You'll need to take the secondary path,' Brode says. 'The *Oskrinya* soldiers took the normal one.'

His blue eyes flash as he hands a pack of food to Fox, who ties it on the back of Theo's horse.

Fox looks up at each Theo and me. 'One day till we reach the Varelai, and you won't have to run anymore.'

One day until Theo is mine again, and not Fox's.

One day until I can start my journey home to Marley.

CHAPTER THIRTEEN

The walk from Brode's farm is far more pleasant than the one in. Almost entirely because I am no longer on my feet, and Fox has decided we've made it far enough to talk properly. There is nothing but bushland around us as far as the eye can see. And this worn, dirt track.

'Where exactly are we?' Theo asks.

'Almost at the junction of borders between Koamah, Solynara, and Oskrinya,' Fox replies.

Slowly, I look around. Bushland that only a moment ago seemed calm – peaceful, even – now feels like it could be hiding any number of Oskrinya, whose dark green uniforms would blend perfectly into this landscape.

Fox walks between Theo and me, the horses heads at his shoulders. He'd started out leading us, but has since let go of the reins as the horses just plod along the dirt track. His long, dark hair is tied back in a small knot at the back of his head; strands that have seen too much sun run like gold through the rest.

The sleeves on the black shirt he wears stop part way down his upper arms, exposing the brown muscles there. A deep brown, like he'd return from his regular visits out of Koamah when we were growing up. At home, his skin would pale a little as we went to school and worked in Papa's shop together. Then he'd go away at different intervals to visit family and return like he'd spent all day in the fields somewhere.

Each time he'd come back, he'd just slide back into life with us. He spent more time with us than in his actual house next door. When Theo arrived, Fox helped change his nappies during the night, even though he was only a little less of a child than me.

A hollow feeling rises as I recall what it felt like to watch those shoulders walk away each time. What they looked like hunched over someone else when I was supposed to be the only one cocooned in his space.

I watch his body move between the scrub around us, the trees getting larger and taller the further we go. I can't help but sigh. He's not slow, but my skin crawls with the need to go faster. And it's uncomfortable to watch him walk while we ride.

'Okay, your turn,' I say, preparing myself for how my blisters will protest again.

He glances back over his shoulder at me.

'Finally,' Theo says. 'I was wondering how long that would take you.'

'And yet you didn't feel like you should offer in my place?'

Theo raises one shoulder. 'Fox and I together will be too heavy for Trumpet.'

'I wasn't suggesting we ride together – I'll walk, it's fine.'

'Forget it, Ruby, your blisters will split again if you walk. I can go faster,' Fox says. He picks up the pace, the horses skipping slightly to change speed.

My cheeks heat.

'Stop,' I say. 'Just get on already.'

I wriggle my feet out of the stirrups and shuffle forward as far as I can go without impaling myself on the pommel I'd hauled myself up with. My legs feel strangely heavy as they hang from my hip joints off the side of the horse.

Fox takes the rein closest to me in one hand, pulling it further towards the back of the saddle than before so the leather lies across my thigh as he pops a foot in the stirrup where mine was a moment ago. My heart beats a little faster as his eyes find mine, and he waits. Like he's giving me a moment to change my mind. I blink and he's swung himself up and around behind me, his chest pressing into my back.

I suck in a breath.

'Posy,' he says in my ear. 'Her name is Posy.'

Little shivers sneak down my neck and into my shoulder as his breath meets my skin.

Fox's arms snake around my waist and I freeze, back arched away from him. He takes the reins, one in each hand and guides Posy onwards. His bare forearms ripple with the movement and I tear my gaze forward.

'How long?' I ask, dragging a breath through my nose.

'About an hour until we'll stop for lunch,' he says. I can feel the vibrations of his chest against my back. 'There's a place we'll stop that will give the Varelai time to know we're on their land – they have a small parcel here. Then we'll go further until we can meet with them properly, further away from other jurisdictions. But we need their permission to travel that far first.'

I breathe out.

'Not too far now, Ruby, and I'll take you back to your family.'

I look around Fox's shoulder to Theo, who looks more comfortable on a horse than I ever could have expected. He smiles, one of his true, all in, smiles that reminds me I did well with him. Despite the odds, and my age, I raised a good man.

His smile slips a bit.

'Fox,' he says, brows coming together slightly, 'you're still our family too, you know.'

I let my eyelids float closed for a moment, against the tide of emotion his statement brings, and let myself breathe into the knowledge I will be with Marley again soon.

Theo was on sandwich duty again before we left the Inn, and I inhale mine as Fox hands me a mug of steaming tea. I almost moan as I take my first scalding sip. The horses graze happily in the grass, their reins held loosely by the low branches of an old tree. The quiet burble of a creek hums in my ears.

'It's so beautiful here,' I murmur, stretching my legs along the soft grass in front of me.

'It's one of my favourite places,' Fox says. He looks across the meadow, towards the horizon over the hill. 'Oskrinya is just over that rise.'

I shudder.

'Marley would lose her mind to ride a horse.' Theo laughs as he imagines it, and I smile, watching him.

She would. Her little face would light up, a squeal on her lips. There would be no fear in her eyes as Fox led her around the lush green meadow. I can see her screaming 'faster, faster' as he ran around with her bouncing along behind. And then she'd fall so in love I'd have to find a way to take Posy home with us.

I drop my gaze from the vision before me. A horse is not something I can give her in Koamah, and she's not here to enjoy this one.

Fox bumps my shoulder with his knee where he sits on a fallen tree branch just behind me, and I glance up.

His finger is pressed to his lips.

Theo watches Fox with his sandwich held halfway to his mouth before his gaze slides to mine. I slip the knife from the ankle strap I still wear and press myself to standing. Fox and Theo follow, each of us turning slightly to take in the surrounds. The meadow stretches away before us, trees guard our back, but I don't see anything out of place.

A chill tickles my spine.

Theo takes a step closer to Fox and me, hand hovering protectively over the pocket the medallion lives in.

'Welcome to the Atrium.'

I spin back to the meadow, a scream threatening to leave my throat.

A tall woman with a flowing, grey fur cloak stands before us. Dark charcoal hair, shot through with white in tiny matted rows, is pulled back from a face that's covered in piercings, a thick band of white paint graces her throat.

'Laramie,' Fox says on his exhale. 'Thank you. We are honoured to be received here.'

She inclines her head slightly and several more people appear, flowing back from her in two angled lines. They all dress similarly, although Laramie is the only one with a painted throat.

Her eyes move to Theo, and a stone drops through my stomach.

'We heard you were coming to seek entry to our lands,' she says, watching him carefully. 'I understand a series of events have been set in motion and you have a request.'

Series of events is one way of putting what we've been through since my mother's visit.

'You're the Varelai?' Theo asks quietly.

Laramie examines him for a long moment before nodding, her dark hair shifting heavily behind her shoulders as she does. None of the others make a sound, their eyes riveted on Theo.

'You've come for us, yes?' Laramie asks.

It's Theo's turn to nod slowly as I look at the group of Varelai. There is no question these people are capable of incredible things. Even if their quiet, steely presence didn't speak volumes, the way the space around us – the Atrium, she'd called it – seems to thrum with something I've never felt before makes it clear. Goosebumps run along my skin at the sensation and the stillness of the air.

'You need us, no?' she asks.

Theo opens his mouth but no words are forthcoming.

'We do,' I say, clearing my throat. 'My brother – Theo'—I gesture towards him—'was ... unwillingly given something he shouldn't have been, and we understand you can remove the mark it's made.'

'I think ...' Theo says finally, not taking his eyes off Laramie, 'I think you're someone I was supposed to meet.'

The group of Varelai witches silently turn their stares to me and I realise I must have made a sound. My palms start to sweat under their scrutiny.

'You have the medallion,' Laramie says. 'Are you sure you wish to remove its claim?'

'Yes,' I reply without hesitation.

But Laramie pauses for a moment, still watching me, but somehow seeming to observe Theo and Fox with the same intensity at the same time.

'Even if it will tell you the second part of the prophecy?' she asks.

I frown. *Second* part of the prophecy? But that implies the first part has something to do with why we're here.

'No,' Fox says. 'We're not here because of the prophecy, only the medallion.'

'Perhaps they are not as separate as you might think.' Laramie's searing gaze flies to the tree-lined edge of the Atrium. 'It's both too early and too late for us to intervene now. None of you can be taken here – you must protect that medallion at all costs.' Her voice takes on a slight urgency and I glance over my shoulder.

Nothing.

'We will help you when the time comes – you have business with us that's as yet undone.' The others bow their heads. 'You must travel beyond the rise and through the fall. We will meet you there and do what we can with the mark to buy you more time.' She's quiet a moment before looking back into the bushland around us. 'Fight hard.'

The temperature drops, plunging us into an ice bath, and then they are gone.

Fight hard?

Theo looks wide-eyed at Fox and me. A slight tremor runs through my knees.

Fox's mouth kicks up at the sides. 'The Valerai have accepted us.' He smiles completely. 'This is excellent news.'

I blink at him. 'Were you worried they wouldn't?'

Trumpet skips, pulling back on his reins, and a crash sounds in the trees behind us. Faster than I can track, Fox has two knives out. Spinning them each in a hand as he focuses on the treeline.

He jerks his head at Theo to get behind him.

'Move,' he says.

I step side-by-side to Fox, who blanches.

'Get behind me, Ruby,' he says, teeth gritted but not looking at me.

I ignore him and watch the trees. Birds twitter as they abruptly flee the now disturbed forest.

'More Varelai?' I whisper.

Fox shakes his head once, and I look back into the trees. Large, dark shadows shift between the silver trunks, the undergrowth crunching. Something grunts. The dark shapes fan out as they move towards the meadow.

Fox puts an arm in front of me and presses us back a step. Another.

I glance back at Theo, his face pinched. The singing of a machete through the foliage finds us and he pales.

Another joins it, and I breathe through the rising nausea. Images of machetes hacking through the people on my street.

Papa dragging me away.

Screaming for Theo.

And so much blood.

Marley, I'm sorry.

'You're a long way from anywhere civilised.' The first Oskrinya soldier breaks the treeline on a handsome horse. Black boots finish his green uniform, a black beard shot with white cups his face.

'We're just travelling through,' Fox says.

'Armed?' the soldier asks.

Fox shrugs. 'Wouldn't you be?'

'Nothing but us out here, son – Oskrinya rule these parts. Surely you don't need to be scared of us.'

'You tell me,' Fox says, keeping his knives out.

The other mounted soldiers join him, six in total that I can see. Two haul a limp form behind them. The rope cutting into the wrists they bind is soaked in red.

Fox glances at the form and grips the knife in his right hand tighter. He nods at the shape.

'Was he unarmed when you took him?' he asks.

The main soldier laughs. 'Wouldn't have made a difference for him. Heard a rumour he's been assisting people in the Kingdom of Koamah. Been sneaking witches out and crossing our border in the process.'

He looks each of us over, shrewd eyes squinting slightly in the sunlight. Sweat breaks out on my palms as I think of Atticus and his secret tunnels.

The knowledge that Atticus can, and does, get people out on a regular basis. That Fox knew where those passages were.

'You three wouldn't happen to be among those he's assisted would you?' he asks.

The form shifts and groans, blonde curls falling into the grass.

Brode.

His kind smile flashes behind my eyes.

Oskrinya bastards.

'Never mind,' the soldier says, looking between us. 'I have a feeling you've got something I'd like anyway.'

Two others dismount and amble over.

Fox holds his knives out from his sides slightly.

And then he moves.

The two soldiers drop before they blink, red rivers staining the grass. Theo stifles a gasp. I can only stare. Those hands were once so gentle and loving and now they ... now they've—

Fox doesn't look at me as he turns back to the main soldier.

'We go nowhere with you,' he says.

Blood drips from his blades.

'You will,' the soldier says, his dead soldiers not even changing his tone. 'I know what you've got, and I'll be taking it. You can come alive, or stay here dead. Up to you.'

A crack splits the air, and the horses strain against their ties. As I drop to the ground, an impossibly tight bind of leather around my neck, I see Trumpet snap his reins and skitter free. A soldier moves after him, lunging for his free rein and bringing him to a fierce halt.

My lungs heave, trying to draw breath around the vice-like hold around my throat. Above me, a soldier grins as he grips the end of a long, black rope.

A whip.

My vision blurs and tears seep from the corners of my eyes, but I think Fox pulls up short when he sees me.

He holds his hands up, knives gone.

'We'll go,' he says. 'We'll go.'

Theo, I try to ask, but my voice doesn't come.

CHAPTER FOURTEEN

Everything hurts. My burst blisters stream, and my throat is sore. But it's my neck that really makes it hard to focus on anything but the pain. Worse than before, the broken skin where the whip cut stings in the afternoon sun. Drying blood itches my skin.

The soldiers herd us along, riding behind and leading Posy and Trumpet. Mostly they laugh, or ignore us altogether. Until the one with the whip decides to practice.

Fox convinced them to strap Brode to Trumpet and that, if they did, he wouldn't kill anymore of their men in his protest.

I walk between Fox and Theo and glance at each of them in turn. Theo walks with his head down, defeat in his shoulders. But there is a faint bulge in his pocket; he still has the medallion – for now. He and I are the only ones with hands bound. I think it's only our captors' arrogance that has left Fox's untied as he walks before the men on horseback.

Fox is determined, his head held high as he strides along the path, bearing the brunt of the crack and the sting of the whip. His shirt is shredded and blood marks his skin. I know in my bones he won't break like this, he'll die before he lets them see his defeat.

But it doesn't stop the fire that flies through my limbs at seeing him bleed.

Theo stumbles and drops to his knees, his bound hands unable to stop his fall.

I gasp, making my way to him just as the medallion rolls out of his pocket.

Fuck.

The soldier behind me barks a laugh.

'Didn't even have to get you back to camp so the boss could search you himself,' he says. It's the same one who did the talking in the meadow.

I freeze. Protecting Theo will always be my priority, but I can't help the flicker of worry for the continent if this man claims the medallion. What his rule would be like. What Roan's rule would be like if he handed the medallion to him instead, like he's obviously been ordered.

Feet hit the ground behind me as he dismounts.

The brass glints in the dirt. It's multiple, hexagonal faces calling to the sunlight.

Come, it says, like it's talking directly to me.

I kneel beside Theo and look him over, trying to block out the curse Fox is delivering to the armed men. Theo's eyes remain glued on the medallion.

Throwing myself towards it, I try to twist as I land – putting my hands where I might have a small hope of clutching at it. But I land badly and the Oskrinya laughs, kicking the medallion out of reach before scooping it up in an easy move, his face splitting into a grin. But there's no moment of pain, no light spilling of blood like when it claimed Theo.

He slips it into his own pocket.

The group comes to a stop, and I look up at them from the dirt where I lie, the sun shining down and warping my vision. I squint. Theo is still beside me, head bent. I can't see Fox but I know he can't be far behind me.

'No need to keep them now, I suppose,' the main Oskrinya says. 'Bleed them. But make it slow – they can pay for the boys they took from me.'

Theo makes a small sound, one I think only I can hear, and I scramble to stand. Fox presses in closer to my side, the soft snicker of a machete being drawn from a belt rings in my ears, my heart clogging my throat.

Galloping hooves thunder down the road before us; the new horses skid to a stop. Fox looks straight at the man in front, standing tall as if challenging him. Another group of Oskrinya soldiers. This land doesn't even belong to them.

There are eight in this new group and they pause, eyeing up those that herd us.

The one in front looks at Fox once more before Fox shoves me back to the ground. Dirt clouds my eyes and fills my nose, but I can see Theo in the same position, on the other side of Fox.

Screams and swords sound above us. Horses stamp, and the ground thuds with the fall of the dead.

On instinct, I crawl towards Theo. Towards Fox. We shuffle to the edge of the road and I stand, ready to run – however awkwardly with bound hands. Fox halts me and tucks the three of us behind a tree instead.

'Wait,' he says quietly – calmly – wincing with each move of his back.

'We have no idea what this is. We need to run,' I say.

A gurgling scream cuts the air.

Fox pulls me to him and presses me against his chest. I realise how badly I'm shaking when I feel myself shuddering into him.

'Trust me,' he whispers against my ear.

I reach blindly behind me for Theo and breathe again when I find his skin, my shoulders pulling painfully to keep hold of him, too.

The three of us huddle together amongst the trees and wait.

'We're done,' a voice says from the road.

Fox's sigh is heavy before he leads Theo and me from the into the open, my elbow in his hand. I pull back against him, but he looks back and squeezes me gently until I step forward.

'You have an excellent sense of timing,' Fox says.

I take in the soldiers in front of us now, so similar to the first group. Machetes. Olive-green uniforms.

Roan's soldiers.

Oskrinya.

The leader of this group shares a look with Fox who nods his appreciation.

My thoughts fall away. All I can see is Oskrinya.

But also ... dead Oskrinya.

'We'll escort you to the border,' the leader says, gentle authority radiating from him. I look wildly at Fox.

'You'll find shelter there for as long as you need,' the still mounted leader says to Theo and me. He looks at Brode, whose chest is rising in uneven heaves. 'We need to get someone to tend to him quickly.'

I widen my stance, readying myself. I feel badly for Brode who helped us, but I won't go down without a fight. Theo needs the Varelai.

Fox glances at me. 'We need to go with them, Ruby,' he says. 'I need to get help for Brode.'

I shake my head, looking between him and Theo. Looking at the marks on Fox's back.

'But Theo—'

'He needs help, Rubes,' Theo says. 'More than me right now.'

'So we're going with the *Oskrinya?*' The panic in my voice takes it up an octave.

One of the soldiers glares at me. 'For fuck's sake. We're not going to hurt you,' he spits.

The leader of this group looks at Fox, who remains silent. He looks at me again, imploring.

'We'll get someone to help Brode,' he says, 'and then I'll take you to the nearest Varelai. Please, Ruby. I owe it to Brode to get him help.'

The compression in my chest when I look at Brode, still unconscious on the back of the horse, threatens to overturn my ribs. Theo's face is marred with worry that matches my own. Brode is a bloody pulp because he helped us, I owe him the same.

But the Oskrinya ...

Who just *saved* us?

From Oskrinya.

Fox cuts the binds on our wrists, Theo rubbing where the rope has burned his skin. He strides to the dead Oskrinya who taunted us and rummages in his pockets. The dead man's body moving slightly with the force.

Without a word, Theo subtly takes the medallion and returns it to his pocket, not daring to look at this new group of Oskrinya, who watch intently. Then they strip the rest of the dead of all of their weapons, including the ones they'd taken from us.

We all mount, Fox behind me and leading Theo on a new horse as we're surrounded by this group. The soldier who's done the talking so far leads Brode on Trumpet.

This time, I lean into Fox and his steady presence as we follow, turning around often to check on Theo.

'I'm not sure I'm going to make it home to her,' I say quietly, closing my eyes as the pain threatens to overwhelm me. 'I was never meant to leave one of them behind.'

I can't leave her. I won't be like—no. I won't leave her.

Fox wraps an arm around me, and I don't protest as he pulls me tighter. Pretending, just for a moment, that all of this isn't on my shoulders alone.

The ride is relatively quiet, but I can't focus on our surroundings. Fox's arm is still tight around me, the other guiding the reins of Posy. The reins of the horse Theo rides are looped around the pommel of Posy's saddle. I trail my fingers over them as I hold on.

We were almost killed by Oskrinya soldiers – and then saved by them, too. Perhaps only to be killed by the second group, anyway.

My head aches trying to piece it together.

'How far from the Varelai are we travelling?' I ask Fox, keeping my voice soft. I can't focus on how unlikely it is I will get home to Marley, so I concentrate on what I am supposed to be doing out here. Saving Theo.

Fox's chest rises and falls in time with mine.

'From where Laramie suggested we go, far. But there are some Varelai scattered through these parts – one in particular. It will be faster for us to talk to her now than to try and cut back.'

My heart sinks a little further as my hopes of returning to Marley tomorrow burn alongside the raging dread of the growing target on Theo's back.

Just keep moving forward, is what Papa would tell me.

One step at a time, one fight at a time.

Chimney smoke rises past the small hill in front of us and I make myself look around. Green, rolling hills with lush, towering grass smattered with blue flowers sways just beyond the forest we're about to leave, the sun dancing on the petals.

I could almost live here. If life was so very different.

And this forest wasn't teeming with witches and Oskrinya soldiers. Things that, if they didn't kill us themselves, would easily have us banished from Koamah simply for interacting with them.

The lead Oskrinya turns in his saddle, his machete angling across the back of it. I lean a little further into Fox, away from the man who slaughters Koamans for a living. Koamans like Theo and me.

'How do you want to do this?' he asks.

I frown.

'We'll stop here.' It's Fox that answers and I stiffen. A growing sense of cold realisation settling in the pit of my stomach. 'The local healer can see to Brode and Ruby. The horses could do with some rest as well.'

The soldier chuckles. 'So, the easy bit first, then.' He looks at me and how Fox's arm squeezes my middle. 'Or perhaps this is the hard bit.'

Fox doesn't respond.

White buildings with brown tiled roofs come into view. Theo looks wary but tired when I glance over. His gaze finds mine, the weight of his guilt crushing. I give him a sad smile; it's all I can offer right now. But I will talk to him when we stop. However I'm feeling in this moment, I will rally my energy enough to soothe him.

The soldiers lead us onto a stone road, the horses clacking hooves announcing our arrival to the small town. A white, timber building with a peaked roof flanks us. Little faces press up against the window as we enter the town, desperate for a look. And then the children come streaming down the front steps, squealing and waving in delight at the Oskrinya.

Not screaming and crying at them like they did in Koamah.

A little girl with blonde hair waves at us and my mind empties. I close my eyes briefly and find myself gripping Fox's forearm.

The soldiers laugh and smile, joking with the children as we pass. They turn right, just past the school – a town this little can surely only have one – and escort us to the large stables at the end of the road. It's a complex not unlike where we met Brode, but in better condition and with more horses.

Two young men wander out, one wiping his hands on a cloth he then swings over his shoulder.

'Sir,' they say to the soldier in charge.

They each nod at Fox before taking our horses in turn, everyone dismounting and leaving it all to them. We look at each other awkwardly, but no one draws a weapon. Or mentions a cell, or torture, or sale, like I would have expected in Oskrinya. Like what the first group of soldiers definitely had planned for us – or worse.

My legs ache to be stretched and moved before collapsing. But I can't do that now. Now they need to be ready.

'I'll leave you to it,' the main one says. The others have left all the talking to him. 'I'll get you some basics sorted, but let me know if you need anything.'

Fox thanks him and waits until they all walk back down the street. He glances at one of the dwellings in the horse complex – a small log cabin, where the healer is now with Brode.

The air is cooler now as evening starts to claim the day. But that's not the cause of the chill that settles in my bones, hard enough for me to shake.

I grab Theo and pull him to me, my knife out.

'You – you know them,' I say. 'You're Oskrinya.' My mind swirls. 'You let them hurt us.'

Fox takes a step to us, and I point my blade at him. Hurting Fox might haunt me forever, if I can manage it, but I will go down fighting to protect Theo from him.

'Ruby,' he says. 'I can explain. I would *never* let them hurt you, but they wouldn't do it, anyway. It's not who we are.'

'I have *no idea* who you are,' I say. The nausea in my gut is all consuming.

He winces but keeps walking back to us.

'You know the important things, Ruby. You both do.'

I look into the dark brown pools of his eyes and shudder at what they hold. It's too much for me to absorb. He reaches us and stretches out a hand, gripping my wrist and taking the blade from me. My skin fires under the contact.

But I can't move away.

Fox places the blade in his belt and turns to Theo. 'I'm—'

Theo's fist connects with Fox's jaw, sending him stumbling sideways and spitting blood. We stand together as we wait for him to recover himself.

'An asshole,' Theo says, shaking his hand out. 'I trusted you, Fox. I was fucking *rooting* for you. Praying one day you'd put our family back together.' My heart cracks further than I thought it could go as he paces in front of Fox. 'Shit,' he says before dropping his head. 'What a fucking mess.'

'Please, come with me,' Fox says, his whole body pleading.

He holds a hand out, and I leave it hanging in the air as I walk past him and into the cottage. I will see to Brode, it's not his fault he's been dragged into this, and then I'll work out what the fuck to do next.

CHAPTER FIFTEEN

Brode lies on his back on a short bed that's not wide enough for him. His breathing has evened out somewhat, and there are several bandages wrapped around his arms. A pink stain rings the ones at his wrists. Purple and black bruises flow down his face and across the part of his chest that's still exposed.

Theo's gaze runs along him from head to toe before he looks at me.

'Do you think you should take a look?'

I shake my head.

'They've done a lot, and they're probably more skilled than me, anyway,' I say softly.

I look at Fox and point to Brode.

'Does he know what you are, or is he just collateral, like us?'

For a moment, I think he's going to object to what I've said – it's in the way his face falls slightly. 'He knows,' he says quietly.

'This goes back to when Oskrinya and Koamah were allies, doesn't it?' Theo asks.

Fox's eyes flick to him, burning in their intensity. 'Secret or guess?'

'Guess.'

Fox lowers himself into one of the many chairs around a large dining table off the area Brode sleeps, but where we can still see him. Theo takes a step but hesitates before he takes the last few and sits down, as far from Fox as he can get.

I look between them, taking in the hurt on each of their faces, the pain that hangs on Fox's body that's not just emotional. He's still wearing the whip marks from earlier. I lost Fox, but perhaps I don't have to watch Theo do the same.

You know the important things, he'd said. *Trust me.*

I sit between them, each of us separated by at least one space. Stones in a river, trying to come together against the force of what divides us.

'Talk,' I say. Against everything in me that says to run, there's a growing voice that says stay. One I want to silence. But not until I have answers.

Fox combs the loose strands of hair around his face back with his hand. He closes his eyes, and Theo and I wait in silence.

'I'm Oskrinya,' he says. 'But I am also Koaman.'

He opens his eyes and looks between us.

'Tensions between our regions were so high but we didn't really know why – we'd been such good allies for decades. Koamah started lying about Oskrinyan attacks on the city, and we were painted as the villains across the continent.

'Roan secured an agreement for marriage, one he believed would unite our people and restore the alliance. One we each desperately wanted to hold against Rehdree.'

'The badlands?' Theo asks.

'Not all the horror stories about them are false,' he says, looking at Theo. 'But the marriage didn't go ahead.'

'He was betrayed,' Theo says.

'Secret or guess?' It's my turn to ask.

Theo's face shutters. 'Secret. Roan was betrayed by his lover. He was so jealous when he found out Roan was intending to marry Queen Astra that he found an opportunity to take the power of that arrangement himself.

He sealed an alliance on his own and cut Oskrinya out of the picture. And left you to fend for yourself against the badlands – Rehdree.'

Fox blows out a breath. 'That part is correct, but the timing is wrong. The breakdown in the alliance between Koamah and Oskrinya happened in my parents' generation. Roan is not too much older than me. Oskrinya was trying multiple ways to gain information and turn things around well before Roan thought he'd solved it with the proposition of marriage. And, all along, we battled the Rehdree, who saw us as a stepping-stone to conquering Koamah and her sister nations.'

'So how were you – are you – involved?' I ask, bracing myself.

'I was a plant,' he says.

Ice rushes my veins. A plant. Someone trained to lie and cheat and pretend.

And disappear.

I scoff a laugh. 'I don't know what's more plausible, that you're a plant, or you left because you'd got the fuck of your life.'

He shifts forward in his chair and leans across the table, facing both of us, wincing with the movement.

'I may have been a plant, but my life in Koamah was the only thing real to me. I was sent there to live with strangers – other plants – at five years old. You two, and Ted, you were my family. You were ... everything. I came here once every few weeks for training, and to ensure I wasn't a total stranger in my birth country.'

I think of the times he would visit family. This is where he was, learning how to betray.

'But I always came home. You were home.' He looks between Theo and me, as if silently pleading for us to understand.

Theo's eyes shine.

'And now?' I ask. 'Is that why you kept seeing Theo?' And not me.

Fox nods. 'He may as well be my brother too, Ruby.'

'Oskrinya weren't the ones that attacked us in the forest – nor are they behind the assaults on Koamah,' Theo says. 'That's definitely a secret.' He doubles over and groans, his head in his hands. 'Oh, that's a particularly painful one. So many people have died for that secret.'

My chair falls over as I push back and rush to Theo. He sits up as I grip his shoulders.

'I'm okay,' he says, patting my hand and blinking as if clearing his vision. 'It's going.'

'And they'll be coming,' Fox says.

'Oskrinya?' I ask. 'We're already here.'

'No, those posing as Oskrinya – like those who had Brode.' He stands up and moves to the seat next to Theo. 'I'm sorry I couldn't tell you. I didn't want to risk your lives by getting you involved. But it doesn't change this.' He gestures between Theo and himself.

'I believe you,' Theo breathes out heavily and nods. 'I'm still pissed as hell, but I believe you.'

Which just leaves me.

I squeeze Theo's shoulder, pleased for him that this relationship will stay intact. His love for Fox was something I never questioned – their bond something that only made me love them both more. To know that love is stronger than the hurts between them is ... comforting. At the same time, I wish I'd known. Wish there'd—

'How come you didn't know?' I ask Theo. 'Why didn't the medallion tell you?'

I think on some of the secrets it's given him so far. The truth of Traders' Avenue, the soldier at the inn, the secret about Roan as we were talking about him. Each one seemingly triggered by our proximity to those places. And yet it was silent about Fox.

He shrugs, my hand moving with the action. 'I don't know. Maybe it's testing how I go with less ... painful ... personal secrets first?'

I check on Brode. He's slowly returning to a normal colour and stirring a little in his sleep. Waiting with him – for what, I don't know – feels like the right thing to do. I suppose I've looked after people so long, I don't really know what else I am supposed to do.

But, as I look at the marks on Brode's face, I realise I like doing the supporting. The helping. It's exhausting. But … it's me.

Theo comes up behind me. 'I'll watch him for a bit, you two should talk.' He pauses and gives me a meaningful look. 'He also needs medical attention, Rubes.'

I can't find the words to object, even though I narrow my eyes at him – of course he's playing the 'someone needs help' card. I'm not sure I really want to object either, but finding the energy to face it is draining just by thought alone. How many ways can he betray me? But he does need help, something Theo knows I won't walk away from.

I wander back to the horse yards and locate Posy. She nibbles gratefully at a hay bag that's been deposited in her stall. Briefly, she extends her nose over the gate and I stroke her face before she returns to the hay.

Not a single person interferes with me. Or asks what I'm doing.

The night sky is beginning to sparkle with stars when I leave her in peace, and I wonder if Ash has taken Marley into the yard to see them recently. Drawing a rallying breath to prepare myself to see to Fox's wounds, I walk back to the cottage.

Fox blocks my way, sitting on the stoop.

He looks up at me, illuminated by the fire and lamps inside where Theo still watches Brode. Fox's hair is messy where his hands have been running through it, an old tell of his tension – same as Theo's. But it's those loose strands blowing softly in the breeze that make me sit next to him instead of going inside.

'I'll tell you anything you want to know,' he says.

'I'm not sure I know what to ask anymore.' I'm just numb.

'I know what I want to tell you.' He looks down at his hands. 'But I don't think you're ready to hear it, and it's not fair of me to tell you, anyway.'

My throat feels thick as my heart leaps into it.

'I live with the guilt every day, you know,' he says. 'I've done pretty terrible things for a good cause, but it's always your face that haunts me. I'd never ask you to do that to someone else.'

'What do you mean?'

'You have Ash, Ruby. Whatever is still here, between us – and don't say nothing, even if it's only a memory as you say, it's there – I won't put you in that position.'

I have an out, I know. He thinks I'm with Ash. I could let him keep believing it, keep him at arm's length without even asking him to stay away.

But Theo would know it was a lie, and so would I. And ... despite everything I could, and possibly should, hold against him, I'm just not sure I can weather more lies between us.

My limbs tingle.

'Fox, I ...'

He watches me and my fingers itch to touch his face. To see if he's real. Does he feel the same? Does being Oskrinya change who he is?

'I'm not with Ash. I haven't been for a long time.' My stomach flutters with the admission. Not because I wish it were different, or I'm ashamed of what Ash and I shared, but for the first time since we explained it to Marley and our family, I'm nervous about how it will be received.

He stills.

'So, it's not loyalty that's keeping you away,' he whispers.

'Can you blame me?'

He smiles slightly. The aching smile of those who are seeing defeat and wondering why they ever thought they'd win.

'I probably would've killed me by now if I was Theo,' he says.

'Theo doesn't know it yet, but he is the best of both of us.'

He nods and looks back at his hands. His fingers loop together and drop between his knees. The black pants he's been wearing all day are still dirty where his legs have rubbed against the saddle.

'You need a wash,' I say. 'The cuts in your back need one, too.'

He looks up and holds my gaze, searing my insides from the other side of the gulf between us. My heart beats to close the distance, a drum pushing me on.

'I was under orders,' he says, searching my eyes for a reaction. 'The right ones. Taking any ... attachments into the next phase of my assignment was too dangerous. You all would have been taken down with me if I'd been found out, even if you still knew nothing.

'I was told to break any connections I'd formed, they weren't supposed to be genuine anyway, so I was told it should be easy. I knew you would see through me if I told you I didn't love you anymore, but I refused to put you – any of you – in danger because of who I was born to be. That was not a choice I would ever make. I shouldn't be making it now.

'So, I cut it off the only way I could think how.'

It's my turn to search his face, my eyes tracing the full, deep pink lips that peek out from his short, dark beard. His strong nose and blazing eyes. That scar that keeps drawing my gaze.

There's nothing but truth on his face. Does it matter where he's come from? Even if it did, have I been wrong about the Oskrinya my whole life?

We were saved from Oskrinya – or what I thought was Oskrinya – by other Oskrinya. Is what we've seen here real? No bars, no cells, no torture for those of us from Koamah.

But he came back for Theo, despite 'orders'. Theo, and not me.

'How can I tell what's real?' I ask.

'With me or the world?'

'Both.'

'The genuine Oskrinya have altered our uniforms. It's subtle, but we have a piece of jet sown into our collars with a small ring of brass. Look for that.'

'Who are the others, then?'

He shakes his head as he looks at me. 'We don't know.'

My skin prickles under the intensity of his stare, one half of his face in increasing shadow as the depth of night increases.

My chest hammers.

'They're good people, Ruby, the true Oskrinya.' He sighs. 'As for me – as long as I'm not hurting you, it's real.'

Fingers appear on his face. He inhales sharply, and I realise they're mine. I trace the beginning of the scar and trail it from near his nose, along the cheek bone under his eye to where it disappears into his beard.

His eyes close and he presses into my fingers slightly.

'How did you get this?' I ask.

'A false Oskrinya.'

'Were you in Koamah uniform or true Oskrinya?' I'm not sure why it matters.

'Oskrinya.'

Slowly, he reaches up and his hand cups mine, pressing it flat around his face. His beard tickles my palm.

'There's something else I need you to know,' he says.

I brace myself.

'I take my orders directly from Roan.'

I exhale.

'He's brutal,' I say. Then frown. 'Isn't he?'

His fingers stroke mine. 'Only as much as we all are, when we need to be.'

'But?' I ask, reading the hesitation in his shoulders.

'He's my brother.'

CHAPTER SIXTEEN

Theo focuses on washing Brode's forehead instead of looking at either of us as I tell him of the conversation – or parts of it – I just had with Fox on the outside steps.

'Roan?' he asks flatly. 'As in the actual terroriser of Koamah, Roan? The one I am supposed to protect the medallion from?'

'Well,' Fox says, 'I don't know where the last part came from exactly, but I can understand why you'd say that.'

'And you want us to go to him?' Theo asks, re-soaking the cloth in the bucket I'd given him.

He hasn't had a lot of practice outside of helping with Marley when needed, but I taught him a handful of things I had to learn for myself when he was growing up. The cloth is wetter than I would make it, but he's doing well, washing the dirt from Brode's face without causing too much pain.

'There's a Varelai there – and defences,' Fox says. 'The timing of the last secret puts us on the move during the night again. We'll get to Roan's faster than back to Laramie.'

Roan. The man we have lived in fear of for more years than I can count. The man the ... false Oskrinya attacked my city, my home, under the name of. The one whose army children fell before. Including me, until Papa—

And, yet ... the children in the street today waved at the Oskrinya soldiers far more warmly than any soldier is looked upon in Koamah. There, the children shrink away in fear. Because, even if the Koamah soldiers try to keep us safe from the false Oskrinya, they still arrest us at will. Banish third daughters. Execute the women who displease them. Call us witches.

We're never really safe from them, either.

'We'll need to move soon. We don't want whoever is coming to come here,' I say, still thinking of the school children from our ride in.

Brode moans slightly, and his eyes flutter open, catching on Theo.

'Are we going home?' he asks.

Theo glances at Fox.

'Yes,' Fox says, looking back to Brode. 'We're taking you home.'

Home.

I take over from Theo so he can get some rest before we have to move out as Fox disappears. Busying myself with checking on Brode at regular intervals and washing up the cloths and changing the water in the bucket. My heart flickers at every sound and I tell myself it's not because it's wondering when Fox will return.

I wander on restless feet between Theo and Brode, checking each, and ultimately decide to finish Brode's sponge bath. I don't know him, but there's a pull to his kind spirit I can't deny. The softness he pulls forth in Theo's eyes when their gazes find each other catches in my chest.

Brode lies on his back, one arm hanging off the side, his knuckles resting on the floor. I leave his face, Theo's done a good job of that, and make my way down his throat and across his shoulders.

I jump as the door creaks open.

Fox.

A rush of air leaves my lips.

Silently, he moves to me and crouches behind Brode's head, lifting his shoulders. We ease him out of the torn and dirty shirt he still wears. He's paler on the ends of his shoulders, a deep tan running down the space where he wears his shirt open. We work together to clean his torso and the dirtiest parts of his skin around the bandages he wears. I stop short from dipping the damp cloth under the edges of the bandages. I haven't seen what's under there, and I don't want to unknowingly contaminate anything.

Fox moves back to the door and returns a few moments later with a clean shirt. Side by side, we wrestle Brode into it; he looks surprisingly different with his chest covered in fitted, soft fabric.

'Your turn,' I say.

Fox's gaze flies to mine, and I push down the rising panic in my chest. Deep brown eyes watch me as he takes off his torn and bloodied shirt and drops it to the floor. I keep my eyes trained on his face.

Slowly, he turns and lowers himself to sit crossed-legged on the floor.

I blow out a breath. The crisscross of shallow cuts draws it from my lungs. Thankfully, the soldier that dealt them was more interested in the laugh from those he rode with than inflicting permanent damage. These cuts could have been much worse had he had a different intent.

Still, they are enough to make Fox flinch as I pick up the last clean, damp cloth and run it over his skin. I kneel behind him, holding his brown shoulder in one hand, and work away the blood and dirt with the cloth in the other. His muscles ripple underneath my touch as he tenses.

But I keep the cloth moving, trying not to memorise the breadth of his shoulders or the new pattern that now dances on his skin. Eventually, he sighs and drops his head towards his chest as he breathes into the rhythm.

I can't help the extra stroke or two I make over his back, letting myself give in, momentarily, to the small part of me that doesn't want to stop touching him, that finds it hard to drag my hands away.

But then it's past time for me to finish.

'You should rest,' Fox says over his shoulder. 'We'll wake Brode before we go.'

I peel myself from the floor and move to the dining table; it's as far as I can go as exhaustion starts to weigh heavily on me, snaking its way through my limbs.

Fox sits next to me, his scent filling my nose. Sweat and dirt and horses but, underneath, something indescribably Fox. I inhale, a calm descending with his smell and the warmth I feel from his body on the edges of mine.

I realise, with a strange sensation under my rib cage, I'm not sure I even know his name. The smell of him, the feel of his presence...but not his name.

'Who are you?' I ask thickly.

He stares at me for a long time. 'I'm still me – Fox.'

'Is that your actual name?'

There's just the tiniest pause. 'Fox Castellan.'

A little rush of air leaves me. 'It's just your last name that wasn't real? Are you really Fox?'

He nods slowly, and I could swear his gaze says 'your Fox'.

'Sleep, Ruby,' he murmurs.

'I won't be able to,' I say, resting my head on the arms I cross on the table. 'You might as well.'

'Marley or Theo?' he asks.

I smile softly. 'Both.' My eyes feel heavy suddenly and sting with tears. 'I miss her, and I can't lose him.'

Fox mirrors my pose, and we watch each other. More weight descends and I couldn't move now, even if I wanted to. I try to focus on Fox's eyes and understand what's there. To know all the things that happened in the years we've been apart, what he felt then, and now. But my vision wavers and grows increasingly dark.

Finally, my eyes close of their own accord. Safe, under a watchful chocolate gaze.

'I can send her a message if you like,' he says. 'Give her somewhere to write back to, now we're here.'

A gentle stream of tears leave my closed eyes, tickling the bridge of my nose as they travel towards the table. I smile and try to nod. Callouses scratch my skin as Fox wipes my tears with his thumb, and a rush of warmth expands in my center, threatening to break the rest free. But I breathe through them, and let the stroke of the fingers that brush the hair from my face lull me into a peaceful sleep.

A chair scrapes and I jump, clutching at my neck as it gripes.

I spin, my throat closing over.

He's gone.

'I'd love to say good morning,' Theo says behind me, his voice thick, 'but this hour should actually be a sin.'

I turn back to him, blinking. Forcing air into my lungs. Trying to get my heart to start again. For it to not feel like it did then. When he—

My mouth opens, but I can't talk. Theo takes the few steps to me and holds my shoulders, concern lancing through his features. Hazel-green eyes narrowing at me.

'Rubes,' he says, 'are you—oh.' He smiles a little, a smug one he tries to cover by pulling me against his chest and talking into my hair. 'He hasn't gone anywhere. Well – he has – he's getting organised. But he hasn't left us.'

I squeeze him back, stifling a small sob as relief washes through me in waves. The last time Fox blew apart my life, he wasn't there to witness the fallout. The news of him being Oskrinya seems so much more bearable without him disappearing before I can process it.

Theo holds me for a moment longer before tightening his embrace in a gentle warning that he's letting go. Stepping back, he runs his gaze over my face. I can only imagine what my hair looks like after several days' travel.

'I couldn't do this without you, you know,' he says.

I place a hand on his jaw. How much further I have to reach each time I do always catches me by surprise.

'I'd never not be here.'

The door slams, and Theo's eyes fly over my head, his face relaxing into a full smile. I turn to look at Fox; his gaze flicks between Theo and me, a slight, questioning crease appearing between his brows.

'Packs are on,' he says, still watchful.

He drops a cloak at the door and joins us, looking quickly at Brode who's sitting up and rubbing at his eyes.

'Listen, we don't have to go to Roan's if you'd prefer not – it's just so much closer.' Fox's face is serious as he addresses both of us. 'I know it can be hard to accept Oskrinya aren't the enemy, that I'm not the enemy—'

'We—' Theo tries to cut in.

'It's okay, Theo,' Fox says. 'You've spent your whole lives thinking Oskrinya were to fear, and now I'm asking you to walk right into the heart of the country – with an Oskrinya. If you'd prefer to go back to Laramie, we can. I'll make it work.'

I look at Theo, his brown hair edging on dark in the firelight.

The medallion has found its way into his hand, and he rolls it subconsciously around his palm. I haven't begun to think through how we work out who to give it to once we remove its claim on Theo. Or how I avoid taking it back to Atticus – if I even want to avoid giving it to him. But I can't do that until I know the mark is gone, that Theo's safe, that there are no more secrets being told, and certainly no more … unsavoury people following whatever the fucking beacon does. And the quickest way to do that is to face Roan, and all his Oskrinya have to offer, so we can get access to the Varelai witch.

'Koaman, too,' I say.

Fox frowns at me, and I want to erase the line between his brows. I want his face to be joyful when he looks at me. My chest tightens at the realisation I no longer want to madden him. Or be mad at him.

'You said you're Koaman, too.' I glance at Theo. 'Theo trusts you, we go to Roan's.'

I look away from his face then. There are some confessions I can't bring myself to make just yet.

Posy shifts slightly under the weight of Fox and me, and I lean down to stroke her neck, trying to seem like I have any idea what I'm doing up here. Fox stills behind me at the movement, and I slowly draw myself back up, thankful he can't see the blush on my face at the memories that stroke my temples.

I close my eyes briefly against that mad train of thought and focus on Brode. We've been given an additional horse for him, but he still seems unsteady in his seat. Images of him toppling to the ground crowd me; it's not something I want to see for real. It's very clear his body has already taken a significant beating, he doesn't need to add a fall to it.

Theo is looking even more at home on Trumpet than his last ride, but he is also focused on Brode. Shrewd eyes seeming to do a continual assessment of the risks of having him on horseback.

A horse whinnies behind us, and I feel Fox turn.

'Mind if we join you?'

I vaguely recognise the voice.

'I haven't ordered you to,' Fox says, his chest rumbling along my back.

'Thought you could do with some additional … assistance if you encounter any other *Oskrinya* on the way.'

The physical release of breath from Fox betrays how anxious he was about us making this journey on our own, despite it being on true Oskrinya land. But I suppose the call of the medallion knows no borders.

'We'd love to have you,' I say blearily, looking awkwardly over Fox's shoulder. I feel Fox's gaze more than see it.

'Xave,' he says after a moment. 'Meet Theo and Rubilena. You know Brode.'

Theo and Brode nod.

'Let's move,' Fox says.

CHAPTER SEVENTEEN

The town's outer edge appears almost before we've ridden through the centre of it. The odd window shows a flicker of a hearth fire or lamp, but most are dark as their occupants sleep. But the windows don't strike me as empty, just content. So very different to Kaya's neighbours. So different to Koamah city. And that realisation sparks a foreign emotion in me – like I shouldn't just be hiding in the shadows of that city but leaving it – an emotion that brings a sharp pain with it. I've left half my heart behind in that city.

My eyes adjust enough as we move into the fields and then back into the forest that surrounds the town that I can make out Posy's head by the sliver of the moon, but not a lot else. Except Fox's arm where it rests around my waist, the other loosely holding the reins. I think the trail we take is closely guarded by trees, but I can only guess at that based on the occasional snapping of a branch against my legs.

Posy's movement is rhythmic. She is sure, and steady, and has clearly walked this path many times. I jolt as my head drops to my chin. The taste of sleep I had at the table still has its grip on my body, and I'm desperate to surrender to it. Vaguely, I wonder what it would feel like to surrender control completely. But, even in my fatigued state, I know that's just musing. I would never give up control enough to stop guiding, helping, my family.

What a luxury it must be to have someone do the worrying for you.

My eyes move past gritty and into pain.

I try to blink, but it seems to take a long time.

Fox's pelvis shifts behind me, and he tugs at my middle, subtly shifting my angle. He removes his arm just long enough to press against my forehead, the back of my head finding his shoulder, and then it's around me again. Holding me to the horse, to him.

'Sleep, Ruby,' he whispers into my hair.

I don't need any more invitation.

My mind wanders between the rhythm of Posy, the feel of Fox behind me, holding me, the sounds of the forest, and thoughts of Marley and Koamah. I drift seamlessly between them, unsure what's real and what's dream, and too exhausted to care. Underneath it all is the steady breathing of the body behind mine. A smell of trees, and dirt, and something rich.

'—the girl, I take it?'

'That obvious?'

Snippets of conversation filter through the darkness, and a man laughs.

'She didn't run.'

'Yet.'

A sigh.

'Give her time, and credit. She won't leave until—'

I shift in my seat, my body aching to turn around, and curl into the heat it's found. The safety that feels so close, and yet so far.

'Shh,' someone I know whispers in my ear.

'—I'm sorted. You have time to win her back yet.'

Marley twirls her dress in the kitchen, her face lighting up.

She burrows down into the covers where we sleep late. Snuggling.

My snuggle-girl.

An ache opens wider in my chest.

'Ruby,' Fox whispers.

He sounds so close, like he used to be. Always. Before he was just … gone. A gaping hole left where he once was. In the kitchen, the shop, where he'd come through the space in the fence. In my bed. My heart. My mind.

'Ruby,' he says again, a little more insistently, and I blink into the darkness.

I grip his arm. 'Theo?' I gasp quietly.

'Just in front. But we have company.'

Slowly, I pull myself from his front and sit up straighter. My pulse quickens as I try to scan our surroundings, but the darkness is complete.

'Xave has sent a pair of scouts to circle round behind, but we can't afford to stop.'

He gathers the reins a little tighter in his left hand and his legs squeeze under me. Posy's pace gathers, leaving the plodding behind.

'Roan's isn't far from here. Once we break the tree line, we're going to have to make a run for it – I can't risk the horses in here.'

I exhale, nodding, trying to clear the restless sleep.

'Make sure he gets there,' I whisper.

He holds me tighter still, a large hand cupping my opposite hip.

The air feels different as we leave the trees, something I can only tell we've done by the greater expanse of grass illuminated by the soft moon.

Trumpet's rump disappears into the darkness before me, and I stifle a gasp.

'Brode has him,' Fox says.

'Brode? He can barely—' my voice cracks.

Theo has gone from my vision and another gap opens in my heart. One I can now only hope I will close in a few scary, but short, minutes.

'Hold on,' he says, and I grip the pommel a moment after Posy launches into a gallop. Her movements are smooth and wild, but it's far from liberating.

Not when I can hear the thundering of other hooves behind us.

Pain lances through my knuckles where I hold the leather pommel, Fox's hand on top of mine, our skin chafing where it meets with Posy's rhythm.

Hair whips around my face, and I close my eyes to ease the pounding of my heart, aware that any moment we could tumble and be at the mercy of whoever comes behind. If we survive the fall.

The dotted lights of torches appear in the black sky when I open them again, and I can just make out the towering walls beneath them.

Roan's.

Fox pushes Posy harder, her breaths heaving between my legs. She snorts and drops her head as she forges on, sure footed even in the dark.

I focus on the growing torches, the flames beckoning us closer. Flame fingers reaching for the sky to show us the way to where I hope Theo has now reached the promised shelter; he would be faster with only a single rider.

Fox releases the pommel and his hold on me, the faint sound of his machete slipping his belt blowing away on the wind.

Shouts from behind reach my ears, closing on us, almost close enough to reach out and drag their nails down my back.

The walls loom, black sheets in the dark with a mouth of fire. Soldiers hold the wide gate open for us, light spilling out.

And then we're beyond the wall, past the blur of the torches.

Fox jerks Posy around, and I almost lose my seat, lurching precariously to the side. Facing back out the gate, pulling myself upright again, I can see the six riders who charge at us. It's too dark out there to make out their uniforms, but they move like the group of false Oskrinya.

I'm scooped around the waist and half dragged to the ground.

Brode.

Fox and Xave fly back out the gate on horseback, six other soldiers hammering out after them, covering me in dust.

'Close the gate!'

'No!' I scream. Spinning into Brode, who still holds me. I shove away from his broad chest. 'Theo?'

'In the stables.'

I nod vacantly, looking back to the closed gate. It's solid, like looking at a door to a void. Beyond which my life – Theo's life – could be changing once more. Completely outside my control.

Shouts and screams from the other side are muffled, but still find their way through.

Frantically, I search for something. Anything.

Theo is in the stables. Theo is safe.

I run.

Back towards the gate, then veer to the side where a ladder scales the wall. I go up, hand over fist, as fast as I can go. The metal is cold in my grasp. It doesn't quite reach the top and I haul myself up, my hands pressing into the ledge the wall creates and holding me up so I can see down.

It's ... a long way.

In the glow of the torches immediately outside the gate is a writhing mess of horses and bodies. Three riderless horses mill around the outside, totally unperturbed by the clamour and death around them. Horses bred for battle.

Two soldiers grapple on the ground closest to my vantage point, I can't tell who they are. A third stalks them. My blood sings that he's not one of Fox's. Not Oskrinya.

Pulling myself up the whole way, I don't give myself time to reconsider as I drag my legs up and over so I sit on the wall.

'Rubes!' I hear from behind me as I fall to the ground, dropping into a low crouch to absorb the impact. My stomach takes a moment to catch up from the free fall – and the knowledge that Theo watched me go.

A horse next to me shies at my arrival and loses his rider; I guess they're not trained in things dropping from above. Hopefully it's not one of ours.

Ours.

I run in a half crouch towards the soldier I know is an imposter. His back is to me and I have a clear advantage. For now.

Bringing myself almost to full height, I kick the back of his knee out and he goes down. Just not all the way. He recovers himself a fraction and kneels in the dirt, turning his head to find me. I jump on his back, pinning his arms behind him before he can stand. He struggles against me, my muscles straining in response to his weight.

I drag him back, his legs pinching underneath him, and make to spin him to the ground. A horse rushes by, and he sags in my grip. Dropping him to the ground, the slash at his throat gapes open, the blood black and glistening in the orange glow of the torches.

Scrambling for a rock just beyond my reach, I shimmy in the dirt. Fingers clutching at the ground before the cold stone bites into my palm.

I run again for the pair wrestling in the dirt.

Look for the jet. Where is the jet?

There – on the collar of the man on the bottom.

I drive the rock into the back of the head of the man on top and he slumps over the man under him, the wound on the back of his head glistening in the half light. The true Oskrinya climbs out from under him, eyes wide at me.

I search the faces I can see.

Xave is the only one I recognise; his short beard shot with the early signs of grey draws my attention even in the darkness.

A horse spins and races back to me.

Posy.

Fox.

He holds out a hand. 'Get on!'

Someone fists my hair and drags me backwards. Fox's face pales, but it's anger that crashes over it instead of fear.

The blade at my throat stings along the cut that's still raw from the whip. And then it's gone. The soldier I saved stands over the false Oskrinya, short knife in hand.

Xave is at my side in an instant, turning my stunned face to him. I drag my eyes from Fox and take him in. The blood that runs down his face and into his shirt. The piece of jet at his collar.

A low moan is silenced somewhere beside me.

'It's done now, you're safe,' Xave says. He grips my upper arm, a sly smile appearing. 'You were great. Pretty sure you almost killed Fox, though.'

CHAPTER EIGHTEEN

The stables are warm and inviting. Horses shift on their feet as they devour their hay. Some drop their heads low as they're brushed down. Posy rests her nose on Fox's shoulder as he turns into her and strokes her chest. Watching me over her withers.

He and Theo both watch me.

One radiating anger, the other expressionless. I turn away from the one I can't read, not ready to face the truths he thinks he now knows. I don't want to know them yet myself.

Theo's hair sticks out on end on one side, the brown strands covered in dust, residual fear in his features.

'What – exactly – were you thinking?' he forces out through gritted teeth.

I open my mouth, but don't even get the chance to try and make an excuse.

'I just—I can't even—that was so *reckless*, Rubes!' He throws his arms in the air. 'What have you *always* said to me? Don't be fucking *reckless*, Theo!'

He imitates me in a way that makes me want to both laugh and scream at him. But I know not to fight him on this. What I did *was* reckless. It was also right and, in time, Theo will see that.

The fact that Fox – his friend – is still standing here means it will probably happen sooner rather than later.

Fox stares at me. I stare at Theo, my skin tingling under the weight of the eyes on me.

Brode walks gingerly into the stables as the other soldiers finish up their horses and make themselves scarce. Probably due to Xave waving them on.

'Come, Theo,' Brode says, his gentle voice is slightly hoarse. 'She's alright. And has had a massive night.' His kind blue eyes flick to me, exposing all my vulnerabilities. My chest scrambles to contain them. The tremor in my knees at my part in killing those people. 'Let her get some rest, and you can chat about it when it all simmers down.'

I look back to Theo; he needs this moment to berate me. So often have I been the one hammering responsibility into him, and I just literally jumped into the worst possible place for my safety.

He points at me. 'This isn't over, Rubes. You're a fighter now, and I did that, I get it. But you do not have to fight *here*. And certainly not people with actual weapons!'

Brode grips his shoulder and squeezes. Theo is taller than Brode, but Brode is so wide it's hard to notice. His blue eyes skip to Theo's face, asking him to listen. Finally, Theo breaks his gaze with me and nods at Brode.

'How're you feeling?' Brode asks when he turns back to me, his hand sliding from Theo. Fox is still motionless, leaning into Posy's sweaty, dark chest.

'I - I'm not sure right now,' I say softly. 'But I'll be fine. I'm always fine.'

I won't fall apart here, in this room of strangers trying to be my friend. In front of Theo, who I am strong for. Always. And certainly not in front of someone I used to know.

Brode looks pointedly at Fox, and back at me when he gets no response from the man holding the horse.

'We'll get you both settled, and you can clean up before we grab you something to eat,' he says.

I blink. 'What about you?' I ask.

He frowns.

'You must be sore still?' I ask even though it's obvious in the way he holds himself.

Brode glances down at his body, as if he can see through the tight fabric to the bruises and bandages I know lie there.

'I've had worse.' He smirks.

Theo blanches.

Brode calls for Xave, who returns with two other soldiers in tow. Their uniforms are clean enough for me to know they weren't involved in the confrontation outside the gates. They both have those tiny jet badges on their collars – ones that are almost impossible to see if you weren't looking for them.

'We'll accompany you to the manor,' Xave says. 'It's not often we have anyone from Koamah here with good intentions.'

That drags me from my stupor.

'What does that mean, exactly?' I ask.

He rubs a hand over the beard on his square jaw. He's older than Fox, but his short cropped hair gives an impression of youth that's at odds with the crinkles near his eyes and the whiter patches of hair at his temples.

'It's nothing significant, I can assure you, Rubilena,' he says. 'Especially once word spreads of your involvement tonight.'

Theo scowls at me. 'Great, the whole of Oskrinya will know how stupid you are.'

I look at him, and he flushes slightly. He'll only get one pass with a remark like that. Even if it might be true.

'But,' Xave continues, looking between us, 'many Koamans have been particularly unfriendly to us – understandably, given what they think we do. This is nothing more than showing you have our support and making sure you're undisturbed. I assume you'd like a wash sooner rather than later?' He smiles; his slightly crooked front teeth only add to his character.

'I'm in,' Theo says, begrudgingly taking the branch that's been offered – a change in direction from railing me. 'I'm quite taken with Trumpet, but I don't need to smell like him indefinitely.'

A secret smile sneaks onto Brode's face before he looks away.

Roan's place, Hartfield, is a large town behind a tall wall and is the capital of Oskrinya. But it's late, or early – it's too dark to tell which end of the night we're closest to just yet – making it hard to learn much more than that. The cool air bites my skin and promises a crisp day to come. There are soldiers moving around, not unlike in Koamah. But there are also plain-clothed people whose bodies move without the shackles of fear, even in the dark, with the Oskrinya soldiers.

Only two days ago I would never have volunteered to be here, terrified for what it would have meant.

Today, I killed for them. Or one of them.

I rub my eyes in an attempt to erase the confusing thoughts.

Theo and Fox walk on either side of me, Theo chattering away to Brode and Xave, Fox as silent as stone. Perhaps he's always like this after a fight. I only knew him before this career; I don't know how he processes death.

I don't know how *I* process this sort of death and my role in it. Killing my opponents was never something expected or encouraged by Atticus – even if there were times I thought I might have to do something drastic before I was the one killed on that mat. At the end of the day, in the club we fight for money and entertainment. What I did out there was ... not that. But it was also in defence of someone Theo holds dearer than almost anyone else.

And so I know I wouldn't have made a different choice. I needed to know where he was, what dangers he was facing, and to fight alongside him.

For Theo. Of course, for Theo.

But the sensation of how that soldier went limp in my arms sticks to me, as if I can't quite let go of him.

We're led into a large building, the details of which are hard to make out beyond more fire torches along the stone walls. The entrance is two huge timber doors with black, circular handles on each. Fox moves ahead and pushes one open, allowing us all through. His gaze brands me as I walk under it.

We're ushered into a large, rectangular receiving hall of some sort and up an expansive white, marble staircase that branches out to the sides. Its curved banisters are cool to the touch and sing with history.

The grit returns to my eyes, and the rest of the details slide past.

Even Theo's voice is losing its vibrancy as the opportunity for sleep draws closer.

'Any more?' I ask him quietly.

I desperately need more than half a day before we're on the move again. He needs to see the Varelai.

He shakes his head and yawns. 'Not yet.'

'We'll take the East Wing,' Fox says, walking away.

If I knew Fox, I would say he didn't want to see Theo's face as he takes in the place Fox is so familiar with. Or mine. But I don't know him, not anymore, despite what my body wanted to recall when I was pressed against him on Posy. That warmth, the solid muscle, it's not what it once was. He's not who he once was.

Nor am I.

He holds a torch he grabbed from a collection near the banister at the top of the stairs, the entrance now a dark abyss below I don't want to look at too long.

Theo and Brode begin to walk after Fox.

'We'll leave you here,' Xave says. He holds my gaze a moment, his own torch flickering light around us. 'Thank you, Rubilena. For tonight.'

I nod.

Xave glances over his shoulder, at the soldiers that amble back down the pale stairs, before finding my face again.

'He's shaken, not indifferent,' he says when he looks back at me.

Indifferent. That's what the uncomfortable pang is in my chest.

But I nod, Xave's right. Nothing about what Fox has been doing with Theo and me says 'indifferent', so I push away the thought that the pain in my chest is about him walking away. Instead, I think about the fact that an Oskrinya soldier – Xave – is standing in front of me … comforting me.

I smile at him, not sure what else to do. The adrenaline is fading from my system, the same as it does after I fight at Atticus's, and the sore and tired parts of my body and soul remember to make themselves known. Reminding me I'm not getting any younger.

The tiny ball of unexpended energy complains as I resign myself to storing it away for another day. Without Ash here to take the edge off the comedown of a fight, I feel strangely at a loose end. We promised we'd stop; he needs someone who can love him without worrying about me in that way. Perhaps this is the best way to achieve it – all at once, instead of a gradual decline.

The dark hallway seems to know all my stories as it looks back at me, and I hurry after the fading light of Theo and Brode.

Fox is waiting by an open door when we catch up. Warmth and light spilling out and across the carpeted hallway. I'm suddenly conscious of my dirty boots and the stains they're leaving.

'Trinialla been?' Brode asks.

'I sent word,' Fox replies. He looks at Theo and me. 'After you.'

I follow Theo into the room, its thick carpet and soft furnishings illuminated by the raging fire. Two large lounges frame the space in front of the fire, a sprawling rug stretching across the distance and making them one. It's a world away from the well-loved interior of my home in Koamah.

Three doors punctuate the wall opposite the fire to my left, their black handles beacons against the white timber panels.

'The bathroom—'

'I claim first wash.' Theo cuts Fox off.

Fox shakes his head with a laugh. 'I'd expect nothing less.'

Theo shrugs. 'Staying filthy can be her penance for stupidity.'

I lift my eyebrows at him, the jab still landing. 'See you later, Theo.'

He ducks away and into the room Fox indicated, its door almost behind the entry.

'Right then.' Brode looks awkwardly between Fox and me. 'Tell Theo I'll collect him in the morning. He wants to check on Trumpet.'

Fox watches Brode go, and I take him in. His dark shirt is darker in places, the stickiness of blood glistening in the light of the room. I swallow into the squeeze in my chest.

Unbidden, two of my fingers reach out to his torso. Tentatively.

I curse them. But they find the blood there all the same.

'Is this yours?' I ask, pressing my fingers into the wet fabric.

He opens his mouth to respond as Xave appears in the doorway. My hand drops back to my side as he glances at me and back to Fox, an unvoiced apology on his face as he takes us in.

'Roan wants to see you,' he says.

Fox looks back at me once before nodding at Xave and walking away. 'Give me your report while we walk,' he says.

I shut the door behind them and lean against it, listening to the faint murmur of their voices fade away.

When the hall is silent, I drag myself to the fireplace, warming the back of my body until Theo emerges. The pull to sit down has been a physical one, but I'm dirty, and bloody, and I know once I do I won't move again until morning. So I play a game with myself to pass the time – how long can I let the burn into my skin before I step forward for relief from the flames? The delicious heat that's both seductive and dangerous.

'Over to you, Rubes,' Theo says as he emerges with a towel around his waist, flicking water from his hair. His hazel eyes sparkle despite the tired weight in them. 'I think there are clothes in our rooms.'

CHAPTER NINETEEN

Two copper baths stand in the pale bathroom, the ridged white tiles that cover the walls winking at me.

It's easy to see which bath Theo has used. Not only because of the grime he's left behind, but the amount of water now on the floor around it. Hopping into the other tub, I sigh as the still-hot water climbs over my skin. I sink in and submerge my head, letting the pressure of the water push away all the thoughts that want to crowd me. The water tingles as it winds its way through my hair.

Instead, I focus on one thought at time and send it on. Fox appears in my mind more than once, but I can't articulate, even to myself, what that thought is. So, it leaves me with its trail of confusion.

I'm conflicted about the false Oskrinya. Now, having seen the two groups, I have no reason to doubt Fox's story and I'm not sorry there are less of them in the world after tonight. But I didn't expect to play such an active part in that. I shudder as the weight of the soldier seems to be in my arms again and I rub at my skin.

Yet here I am, always choosing brutality to save the people I care about.

And I do care about Fox, even if part of me still wishes I'd stopped a long time ago.

I break the surface, letting the air race back into my lungs.

Using my fingers, I scrub my scalp and brush out the knots in my hair, wincing. When I'm satisfied it's as clean as I will be able to get it, I reluctantly remove myself from the now luke-warm bath.

'Night,' I hear Theo tell someone, the door closing behind them.

I hope it was Brode coming back to talk about horses. Theo could use a friend like him, and an interest that's all his. Not Papa's shop or helping with Marley while I fight. Somehow, I will find a way to get him access to horses when we return to Koamah. As impossible as that seems in the middle of a city – with very little Kabolshi to spare.

I run my fingers over the fluffy fabric wrapped around me. Even the towels are soft here. New maybe. Unlike ours at home, that have seen too many washes. My skin sings where I pull the gentle fabric and wipe away the beads of water.

I stand naked before the gold framed mirror and assess my injuries.

There aren't too many. I certainly don't look like Brode with his cascading bruises. But the whip mark is vivid, raw in some places, over the yellowing marks the Koamah soldier left on my neck. A redness runs across my back, towards my spine where I must've taken a blow I didn't feel in the rush. Otherwise, I'm relatively unscathed. Nothing some rest and stretches for my sore muscles won't cure. Although they'd heal faster if I could make myself something.

I give my hair a last dry, the curls already springing back towards my head, and wrap the white towel around my body. It's large enough to almost drop to my knees.

Theo has crashed, and blown out most of the torches for me, so I creep out of the bathroom and across the now slightly darker sitting room to where the other bedroom beckons from the opposite corner. The hearth fire still rages and, for a moment, I hesitate in the middle of the room, tempted to stand in front of it again. Just for a moment.

Instead, I sigh – clothing calls. Then I might come back until my mind can settle enough for sleep. I take a step forward, yelping as I come face to chest with someone who stands from the patterned couch.

My heart hammers loud enough to drown out the crackling flames, and it takes me longer than I'd like to gather my breath, hand pressed to my chest.

'Ruby,' he whispers, doing nothing to calm the organ in my chest.

He takes another step towards me.

I freeze.

'Sorry,' he says. 'I didn't—'

His eyes graze my collarbones, my body responding as if he's touched me there.

We watch each other, gazes stubbornly held. Me daring Fox to look at my body again, and him resolutely not taking the bait. My chest rises and falls under my hand, the only thing that tells me time still passes.

'I should go,' he says at the same time I ask what he wants.

He draws a deep breath and sweeps his hair off his face.

'I wanted to know – I needed to know – why you went out there. Over the wall. Is it something I need to worry you would do again?'

I let the time spin away, staring at the man before me. The one who used to be a boy with so much to give, so much promise. Has he realised all of those things yet? The heat in his eyes tells me there is so much more for him to do. To give.

'I would do anything for Theo,' I say quietly.

He blinks and frowns. 'Theo?'

'I always wondered at his resilience when you ... left. He was devastated at first, and then ... within months he was himself again.' I close my eyes briefly. 'Now I know it's because you came back. For him, you came back. Whatever the risk was, whatever your orders were, he was worth it for you.'

My throat thickens with the truth of it. Equal parts gratitude on behalf of Theo and despair it wasn't for me.

He searches my face. 'I didn't think you'd want me to,' he whispers. 'You shouldn't have wanted me to come back.'

'I would do anything not to see any more devastation on his face, Fox,' I say, ignoring his statement. It's both too close and too far from the truth

– if I even know what the truth is anymore amongst all these secrets. 'Including helping you, and your Oskrinya, if I can.'

'His name is Landis,' he says. 'The kid you saved. It was his first time facing the false Oskrinya – who the Koamah believe us to be. And he was saved by a wild-haired woman from Koamah herself.' He smiles. 'He'll be a little wide-eyed for a bit yet.'

I smile gently back. 'He saved me, too.'

He closes his eyes for a moment. When they open again, the chocolate pools are dark pits of emotion.

'I'll be forever in his debt for that,' he says.

He steps forward until he's side by side with me, stopping as our elbows touch. My insides consider a riot as they tighten in preparation.

'Night, Ruby,' he whispers.

Roan's office is cold, despite the fire that burns in the corner. A large, grey fur rug lies across the centre, punctuated by brown leather armchairs on either side. Either he's had several rugs sewn together, or the animal large enough for the pelt doesn't exist in Koamah. Theo flanks me, chin held high. I notice he doesn't obviously hold the medallion in Roan's presence. It's a jolt to the system to realise Oskrinya's ruler doesn't look that much older than Fox.

Fox's brother.

The similarities are there if I look for them. The breadth of their shoulders, the way they hold their heads high. Roan's gaze isn't as dark as Fox's, and his hair is short, shaved close to his skin around the sides. His skin is a darker shade of brown, but the intensity that burns from each of them is similar, too.

We stand at the entrance while Roan finishes a conversation with a younger woman. Her eyes are sharp as she takes in what he asks. I watch her for signs of distress or mistreatment.

I find none.

She dips her head at me when she finally spins on her heel and marches out past us and down the hall.

Roan's eyes are on Fox when I look back at him.

'Welcome to Hartfield,' he says, slowly looking to Theo and me.

The charming name is just one more thing at odds with what I believed for so long.

He pushes himself out of his seat behind a large, polished timber desk and wanders over to us. He's slow and confident in his movements, a man completely at ease with himself and his surroundings. It's Theo's hand he grips first, and I stifle a shouted objection.

His hand is warm and encompassing when he takes mine. It's softer than Fox's, and has probably held less weapons. At least, his skin says he holds less weapons; he still looks like someone who knows how to handle himself if needed. Releasing my hand, Roan gives me a blinding smile before closing the door behind us and sealing us in.

I flinch at a hand on my lower back.

Fox.

He guides me into the room, Brode and Xave coming round from behind Theo.

'What we discuss now,' Roan says, 'is not to leave this room or extend beyond this group. Understand?'

He looks at us each in turn, waiting for a response. The uniform he wears is more pale than olive-green, a dress version of what his soldiers wear. But he has two jet pins on each corner of his collar.

'Please.' He gestures to the armchairs as he returns to his desk and leans against it. 'Sit.'

Theo glances at me, and I take the chair on the right. Brode, Xave, and Fox stand behind us. A human wall between Theo and me and the only exit.

'You have brought something of great value here, I think,' Roan says.

Neither Theo or I respond, and he nods.

'Bringing it here also brings a great deal of danger to my people.'

I suck in a breath. We weren't supposed to endanger anyone else, but he's right. No longer are we in the forest, on our own, or with Laramie and her witches. We're in the middle of a heavily populated capital.

It's the children I think of first. The horses second.

'We don't want to bring any danger here, Roan,' I say carefully.

He purses his lips in thought. 'I imagine that's the truth, Rubilena, but here we are.' I start a little at his use of my name. 'You are lucky one of my dearest friends is a highly skilled Varelai, who has agreed to remove the mark,' he says.

Theo's cheeks puff out as he exhales loudly. 'Thank you.'

Roan leans back a little and crosses his arms over his chest. 'Understand this, though.' I brace myself. 'You do not have the added safety of Varelai lands here. She will need to move fast, before any others come looking for you – and it will not be fun.'

Theo frowns but nods.

'Once the mark is removed,' Roan continues, 'no one – and I mean *no one* – touches that medallion. Understood?'

'Not even you?' I blurt out.

Roan's assessing stare lands on me and I straighten my spine. 'That's a fair question, I suppose, given the lies you are fed in Koamah,' he says, but the distaste is clear. 'But no, not even me. I have less than zero interest in being claimed by that medallion. And you will tell no one in Hartfield, outside this group, that it's here.'

He doesn't ask for a response.

'We should get started, Roan.'

I jump as a statuesque woman appears in my vision. Her deep-purple hair is swept off her face in tight braids that fall down her back and frame the sides of her painted throat. But that's where the similarities with Laramie end. This woman has no piercings in her face and, instead of white, a red-purple paint is feathered at the top and bottom of her throat. It's almost like fingers traced in the darkest hearts-blood reaching up and around her jaw, covering her pulse-points and dusting her collarbones. A vaguely familiar, multifaceted shape is painted in thin white lines on her forehead and points down the bridge of her nose to the white line that runs the length of her throat, over the rich purple.

Roan glances at her, affection in the movement, before looking forward again.

'There are two things I ask of you,' he says.

'Shoot,' Theo says, rubbing his hands on his thighs.

'Aestais will help you remove the mark, and protect both you and Rubilena from its effects. Neither of you will be able to be hunted because of its call, whatever happens to the medallion. In exchange, you will not return to Koamah until both she and I are comfortable you mean us no harm.'

'No harm?' Theo asks, his face scrunched. 'Of course we mean you no harm.'

'You have spent a lifetime hating us, Theo. You'll forgive me if I think it will take a little longer than a couple of days to change your mind,' Roan says simply.

I stare at Roan, searching for the words.

'I have to go back.' I try to stop my voice from cracking. 'We have family – a daughter. I have a daughter.'

His eyes flick behind me in surprise.

'It's not about the number of days,' Theo says quietly. 'It's Fox. And we won't betray him in any way.'

Roan looks behind me again, presumably at Fox, watching him for several moments. His gaze almost returns to me but he averts his attention to Aestais instead.

She nods.

'The second thing: I am in the middle of some ... delicate negotiations.' He looks at Fox again, almost apologetic. 'I need you to keep your history with Fox private. Here, he does not have a Koaman past – he is second in line to Oskrinya, the head of our Military, and *only* that.'

'How do you—' Theo starts.

'Not just you,' Roan says and he turns his attention to me. 'You too, Rubilena.'

My stomach bottoms out. The fragile grip I had on it at the prospect of not returning to Koamah giving way entirely. I look at Theo, who's a picture of confusion, and wipe any from my own face.

Someone shifts on their feet behind me. 'I thought you didn't want what they'd offered,' Fox says. His voice has a sympathetic edge to it and I suppress the urge to turn around and see what's written on his face.

'I'm almost there,' Roan says. 'But refusing, even gently, what they see as the greatest honour they could give does not make a people want to fight for you, Fox.'

Fox is silent in a way that tells me that's not an option.

Roan continues, focusing only on Fox. 'They can present whatever they like – saying no has other risks.'

Roan returns his gaze to me. 'Ruby?' he asks, clearly in reference to his question about keeping quiet.

'Of course,' I answer for both Theo and me, even as my heart sinks in protest. 'If that's what you need to help Theo, that's absolutely fine.'

CHAPTER TWENTY

The room Aestais leads us to is nothing like I would expect for a witch, and a Varelai at that. Not only is it light and airy, with large windows that look out over the gardens behind the manor, it's located in Roan's place.

A witch. So openly in the seat of power of Oskrinya.

Where, in Koamah, I could be banished for my balms – some of which I keenly miss and should have used on Fox's wounds – Aestais, one of the most powerful witches, wanders these halls with no fear. Those that greet her do so as friends. A visible and respected member of Hartfield.

Aestais's pale timber shelves whisper to me. Hundreds of brown glass bottles of varying sizes line the bottom two shelves. The middle is graced with neatly packed books and dried herbs. Drying flowers hang from rails over the remaining two shelves.

What I would give to see Marley's reaction to this space, too – to not have to stifle her abilities.

Aestais smiles gently at me as she selects a book from the middle shelf, using a long finger to angle it out. The pages are old, and the room dims a little when the pages fall open, dust spinning in the air.

I stand next to her. 'Is it hard to do?' I ask. 'Removing the claim?'

She cocks her head, graceful like a cat. Her blood-purple hair falling heavily from one shoulder to swing down her back.

'It's not so much difficult as it is unpracticed.' Her full lips are pale compared to her hair and throat.

'Unpracticed?'

She snaps the book shut and Theo jumps.

'Most who are claimed by the medallion are happily so. So refuting the claim is unnecessary.' She turns back to look at Theo, and he shivers. 'It is a brave thing to do, Theo, reject all knowledge.'

'Brave, or stupid?' he asks.

'We'll find out, I suppose. Your path is decided and this is it,' Aestais says. 'You don't need the medallion to fulfil your destiny.'

The sentiment of things being outside of our control reminds me of Laramie's question at the Atrium.

'Laramie said there is a second part of the prophecy,' I say, a little hesitantly.

As I wait for Aestais's response, I wonder if I really want to know. The echo of the cry from the girl in the market still rings in my ears in times of quiet and if that – and worse – is what happens in response to only one part of the prophecy ... I shudder to think what people might do in Koamah if they knew of a second.

'Yes,' she says, sliding the book back onto the shelf. 'It is not un-common to find an ... opposite for something. For every life, there is death. For every happiness, there has been sadness. For every promise kept, there is a risk another is broken. Only those prepared to make monumental sacrifices can truly know all its secrets. But even then, they would be bound to never share them.'

She crosses the room before I can really process what there being a sec-ond part of the prophecy means, and why I care, and pulls back a semi-sheer curtain that hangs from the ceiling to reveal a large bed. Theo doesn't need an invitation and climbs on. She directs him to lie down on his back with his arms and legs spread wide.

My heart lurches when she ties his ankles and wrists to the frame of the bed, but she shushes me, and a tiny voice in my mind insists I trust her.

Watch her, learn from her, trust her.

'Pass me the sage,' she says.

She lights the stick and stubs out the flames on the worn timber bench that runs under the window. Moving around the room, her robes shifting like liquid around her body, she fills it with smoke before cracking the window and watching it snake its way out.

'Now, we begin.'

She places two black stones in each of Theo's hands, and he circles them awkwardly in his palms, tumbling them against each other.

'The medallion?' she asks.

'Pocket,' he says.

She hands me an embroidered cloth, and I slowly wrap it in my fingers. I know what she is asking. I lean over and reach into Theo's pocket, careful not to expose any of my skin to the medallion. It's cold, even through the fabric, and pulls against me as if it prefers to stay with Theo.

My fingers slip in the fabric.

'It's just a piece of metal, Rubilena. Take it,' Aestais says quietly.

Come, it calls.

I glance up into her sky-blue eyes and grip the medallion in my fist. It slips out so easily I almost topple backwards from the effort I've overexerted.

She nods to her workbench and I place the medallion there along with the cloth. Moving to Theo, Aestais extends gold capped fingers and slices the front of Theo's shirt with the curved metal nail now crowning her index finger.

He hisses, and a thin strip of red blooms down his chest, chasing the sound.

I stare at her, my stomach turning at seeing someone I love bleeding. I want to trust her, I *need* to trust her – trust that she can stop Theo being hunted – but it doesn't stop the rioting in my stomach. She takes one of the stones from each of Theo's hands and places them along the cut, coating them in his blood and leaving them to rest on his wound.

Theo grips the remaining ones.

Aestais kneels on the bed over Theo, her knees pressing into his shoulders, and places her hands on either side of the cut.

Theo's face disappears into her robes.

Aestais looks once at me, and I nod, not sure if she is asking permission or not. She begins to chant. A haunting, rhythmic sound that reverberates through the room and down my limbs.

Until Theo starts to whimper.

And that whimper builds to a scream.

A scream I want to echo. Every fibre in my body has been built – designed – to stop my family hurting. Standing here watching Theo in the worst pain of his life feels like my biggest failure. Not because of the medallion. But because of *her*. The one person I couldn't protect him from. The one person, perhaps with Fox as the exception, that he built up to an impossible standard. One I can't compete with, but am *always* dealing with the ramifications of.

On and on, Aestais chants, and Theo screams, and I bite my tongue to keep from demanding she stop. From swearing I will kill our mother for leading us here. For turning me into that powerless little girl once more.

Mine.

The room around me blurs, and I drop to my knees at the bed, taking his hand in mine.

'I'm here, Theo,' I whisper into his screams. 'I'm here.'

His fingers twist under my palm until his hand grips my own, and he squeezes tight, crushing the bones.

Theo's voice eventually goes hoarse, and he slumps back into the bed.

Aestais leans back, her hands gently leaving Theo's chest, but the marks remain. She unties his binds, and I crawl onto the bed with him and cradle his head.

'He'll be okay,' she says softly.

'Is it done?' I ask, stroking his brown and gold hair off his face, my heart aching. Racing.

She shakes her head. 'It will take several more goes, but I have managed to push its claim back. Even if he learns another secret or two, we should have more time before others arrive on our doorstep.'

I exhale. Several more goes.

'You should get some air,' she says. 'I will be watching him until he wakes.'

Reluctantly, and after some time, I agree to leave. In large part to steady myself before I return. Before he can see the worry – the uncertainty – coursing through me. I am his, and Marley's, steadfast foundation. And that doesn't stop, even when I waver.

I find myself out in the hall, with no idea where to go or how to find a way out.

'How'd he go?'

I turn, stunned, to find Brode sitting in the hall at my feet.

'Walk me out?' I ask.

The gardens are a feast for my senses, and I struggle to soak them in after watching Theo in so much pain. Knowing there's more to come.

Brode leads me around the low hedges, past a water feature I pay no mind to other than the soothing sound of the water splashing into its base. Pink and white flowers dust some of the bushes, but they're almost accidental – sporadically dotted around the garden and throughout the lawns.

He waits until I'm ready to talk, his genuine concern for Theo and me filling the faint lines at the corners of his mouth and eyes. Then he listens as I tell him what happened.

After several minutes, he speaks again.

'I hope this isn't totally improper, Rubilena.' I want to frown, but I find I can't shift my face, the worry has already drawn it into that shape. 'Does he have a partner?'

I laugh. Not the question I was expecting.

Brode flushes deeply.

'Oh, Brode, I'm sorry – I – sorry.' I school my features back into some-thing neutral. 'No, he doesn't have a partner.'

He smiles to himself, one I don't think I'm meant to see.

He clears his throat.

'Has Fox told you how I came to be part of his unit?'

'Unit?' I ask, frowning, wondering why he would assume Fox has told us anything.

'Not his Koamah one, his secret one.' He takes my silent head shake as an invitation to continue, which I suppose it is.

'I was born in Rehdree – the badlands. At a time that was … particularly difficult. My sister and I were all that remained of our family. There are clan wars there often, you see, and ours hadn't done so well.' He laces his fingers behind his back as we wander. 'So, she escaped with me and took us to Koamah. How she managed it, I'll never know.'

His eyes are wide when I sneak a glance at him.

'She got us out of Rehdree, through Oskrinya, and into Koamah mostly unscathed. And we made a home there. A life we built from nothing. And then someone outed her as a daughter of Rehdree – I've never worked out who, or why. But she was taken by Koaman soldiers who charged her as a witch.'

It's his turn to look at me.

I close my eyes for a moment, remembering all the other women and girls I've seen torn away. 'I'm so sorry, Brode.'

'It wasn't Fox's team that took her – this was when he'd only recently joined the royal military, before they were fully set up, but he saw them. Saw me in the crowd. I'd promised her I wouldn't cry and give myself away. But I think being a statue in the crowd was my tell in the end, anyway. Luckily. Because Fox came for me later that night and smuggled me here.' He stretches his arms wide and smiles at his surroundings. 'When I was old enough, Fox let me join his unit helping others get out – it's almost always the women.'

'Where do they go?'

'We resettle them in the territory beyond Rehdree, mostly, teach them to fight. It's a pretty harrowing journey at times, but gives them a sense of power, of control that they haven't had before.'

'You teach them to fight?'

'Our people do, yes. Fox oversees it.'

I look around the garden and listen to the faint sounds of the town on the other side of the hedges. Its gentleness is almost unsettling. But, in a way, it feels like it echoes the gentleness of Fox's motives – the work he has been doing this whole time to try to give people a better life. Including those from the Kingdom of Koamah. A Kingdom that would execute him without blinking if they knew what he was doing under the cover of being a Koamah Military Officer.

'Did you find your sister?' I ask, looking back to Brode.

He shakes his head, pale hair falling across his face. 'Fox and I looked for a long time, but she was gone.'

'Do you believe the prophecy?' I ask, not knowing why it seems important.

His face shadows.

'*When three of she become one, the dark will rise with the sun.*

All that's dear will be reclaimed, all that's loved will be lost to flame.

A darkness none will defy, and all but blood will die.'

His voice is quiet as he recites it. 'I've always known it, of course, but I've never seen it so staunchly defended as in Koamah. I'm actually surprised this is the first time either you or Theo have mentioned it.'

I've often wondered myself why it isn't a greater part of our own lives and beliefs for the same reason. But the girls I have seen dragged away and exiled for even the possibility of being a third sister, or producing one, just ... never seemed dangerous. Instead of them reclaiming – or burning – everything I hold dear, their own lives were shattered.

And, on reflection, it's never been something Papa preached to us either.

Being a witch, on the other hand ...

'I don't know,' I say honestly. 'Perhaps because my grandfather wasn't going to have any more children – or that our mother didn't abandon any more children into my care after Theo. It just wasn't something I thought we needed to worry about. I had a lot to keep my mind busy with Theo, and then Marley. The only way I knew how to do that was focus on what was right in front of me, on what I could control. And I can't control if another woman has three daughters.'

'No,' he says quietly. 'But it's a hell of a control measure for the people in Koamah.'

'Yes ...' I murmur as I wonder whose control it would strengthen. I know Koamah can be brutal at times, but would our King and Queen, and those that came before them, really use a prophecy to control us? It seems extreme but, while I have doubted the existence of the prophecy for a long time, I can't deny the influence it now has over all of our lives. And, for the first time in a long while, I wonder if the prophecy – something that creates such devastation in some people's lives – is something I should pay a little more heed to.

Particularly if there is a supposed 'solution' in a secret second half.

Trinialla's grin elicits my own. Her straight, auburn hair is cut short around her jawline and swings as she throws her head back and laughs. I missed the remark Theo made that's caused such a raucous response, but the fact he's recovered enough from his time with Aestais to be joking is enough to make me smile.

Trini crouches in front of the hearth fire and pokes the logs with a gold poker, the flames celebrating at the surge of oxygen circulation. Hanging it back up and dusting her hands on her white apron, she looks back at us.

'You're not like I expected, you know, for people from Koamah,' she says.

I can't imagine her voice as anything other than friendly.

'How's that?' I ask.

She lifts a shoulder with a coy grin. 'I don't know. You don't breathe fire, for one.'

I laugh again. 'Nor do you.'

'You haven't seen me at night.' She winks, and Theo's laugh fills the room again. 'Particularly if you don't eat what I bring you.' She points a finger at each of us. 'You've got dinner in the hall tonight, but I'll bring supper up later.'

'What?' I ask.

'All of Roan's guests dine with him most nights in the hall. You arrived too late last night, obviously, so tonight it's "welcome to Oskrinya" time. I've brought clothes.'

She sashays her hips a little as she wanders across the room, dancing to some unheard music as she collects the basket she left near the main door and disappears into each of the bedrooms.

A knock sounds at the door. 'I'll get it!' she calls out.

I look at Theo, lounging on the couch, noting just how comfortable he seems here. But, given the differences in Roan's expansive manor compared to our cramped home, I suppose it's easy to see the comfort. For me, it just adds to my longing.

'Good evening, sir,' Trini says, a smile in her voice.

I turn around to find Fox standing in the doorway.

She picks up her basket and loops it over her arm. 'I'm off, can you get them to dinner?'

'Of course,' he says, eyes holding hers as if he can't look away. Or doesn't want to look at me.

She lifts a hand, and he smiles as she high-fives him on her way out.

'All yours,' she sings as she disappears down the hall.

'She is the happiest person I have ever met,' Theo marvels as Fox shuts the door and comes into the room.

'You and me both,' he says. Finally, his deep brown eyes look my way. 'I have something for you.'

I try to quell the hope that rises like a burning column in my throat.

He reaches around his body and pulls a small stack of envelopes from his back pocket.

I cover my mouth, eyes wide. 'Is that really ...?'

The joy on his face as he hands them over is almost enough to break my heart. The cream envelopes are simply addressed 'Mumma', I guess so there were no identifiable markers. Who gave them that advice, I don't know, but they must be part of Fox's network to get correspondence in and out of Koamah without using the royal postal service. And keeping all of us safe at the same time.

Gingerly, I reach out and take the letters. There are three.

'She's okay,' he says softly.

I close my eyes. How he could tell what terrified me about opening them, I don't know.

Theo sits up. 'Come on then.'

The letters are short and clearly written by a combination of Ash, Papa, and Marley. Even Kaya has left a little note. Marley's letter formation has improved since I saw her, which means Ash is practicing with her. I smile, thinking of how many times I've done exactly that in our humble little home.

I take the picture she's drawn of Theo and me having an adventure and hold it to my aching heart.

'Thank you,' I whisper. 'How long ago did you last hear?'

'Just today. There is a lag, but the message is no more than a day old.'

I exhale. One day should feel comforting, but it's so much longer than the few hours I have previously been apart from her. In those times, I still knew where she was, and what she was doing. Anything could have happened in the time since that news.

'Aestais thinks I only need a few more sessions, Rubes,' Theo says, resting his elbows on his knees, mimicking Fox's posture. His shoulders pull against his shirt the same way too. 'Then we go home.'

'If Roan will let us.' The heaviness in my soul is pressing. I can't not go home.

Fox stands and comes to take my elbows. 'Ruby, there is no way we will stop you going home to her.'

'But Roan—'

'Will very quickly see what I know. You are genuine, kind, and honest. You will never bring Oskrinya intentional harm.'

I stare at him, taking his words and tucking them away. Desperately wanting to believe they're true, that it's what he thinks of me, and more. But he drops his hands slowly and turns back to Theo.

'Time to get ready for dinner,' he says.

I don't ask what happens if we bring unintentional harm.

CHAPTER TWENTY-ONE

A familiar warmth swells in my chest as Theo comes into my bedroom. The dark navy suit Trinialla has given him is a perfect fit. His eyes sparkle, the blue flecks in his primarily green-hazel eyes enjoying their time in the spotlight.

He brushes the hair back from his forehead and immediately looks several years older.

'Do me up, will you?' I ask, turning to show him the buttons that run down the back of my black dress. The fabric is soft against my skin, and I hold my stomach in so Theo can pull the fabric together at the back.

'Well?' I ask when he's done. 'Not too bad for the first time I've worn a dress since ... ever?'

He makes a show of pulling a pensive face and looking me over.

'I'd say you look at least half as good as me.' His face cracks into a grin. 'Which is to say, smashing, of course.'

I laugh, but it dies out quickly and I look up at him, the surreal quality to this moment making me want to soak it in.

'You should do a twirl for her,' he says. 'She'd love it.'

My chest is giddy when I spin for Marley – the heart I've left behind. Theo smiles at me.

'Perfect,' he says. 'I'll tell her Mumma was beautiful when she spun in her dresses, but never as beautiful as Marley.' He drags me in for a rough hug, all frivolity dropping from his face too. 'I'll never forgive myself for bringing us here, Rubes, but you will go back to her. *We* will go back to her.'

'You'd do the same for her, right?' I ask, already knowing the answer.

He nods.

'That's all I need to know.'

Brode and Fox are in the sitting room when we leave the quiet of my room.

Neither of them says a word.

Brode is the first to stand, Fox dragging his form to full height a moment later.

Theo looks at me. 'Told you we looked good, we've rendered them speechless.' He laughs, but I don't miss the faint blush painting his cheeks as he strides over to Fox and Brode.

My own mouth goes dry, like it did when I saw Fox in his Koamah military uniform for the first time, and my skin prickles as his gaze drags to my feet and back up again.

Brode clears his throat.

'Shall we?' he asks gently.

The hall is somehow both large and intimate, with several long wooden tables positioned in rows. Numerous hearth fires are nestled into the walls and each table is dusted with a collection of candles and flowers in an assortment of tins and jars.

Trinialla squeaks from across the room and half runs to Theo and me, clapping her hands when she's in talking distance.

'I'd be a designer in another life, you two look impeccable!'

'You do have a good model, Trini.' Theo winks at her, and she bats him away.

She grabs my hand and leads us to a table towards the centre of the room, gently pushing me onto a bench seat facing towards what feels like the front of the room – the opposite end to the massive doors that lead outside and adjacent to the internal doors we came through. Theo and Brode sit together on the one side of me, already deep in conversation about Trumpet and the new training regime Brode would like to try.

Trini plops herself down on my other side, leaving Fox standing at the end of the table, looking a bit like a loose end. She looks at him and blinks before glancing back to me, a question in her eyes.

'Well, sit down, sir,' she says, pointing at the spot across from me.

A fiddler strolls into the midst of the crowd, behind where I now stare at Fox, and begins to play a welcoming, upbeat tune. The large timber doors to my right, those that lead back into the manor, creak open. People spill forth, dressed just as well – or better – as those of us at this table. Something in my stomach skitters at the onslaught of Oskrinya, but my gaze catches on their smiles. These are not people out for destruction, even if they do appear to notice Theo and I haven't been here before.

There also doesn't appear to be a weapon in sight.

'Roan, my old friend!' an older gentleman calls out, striding further into the growing mass of people milling around.

I glance at Theo, who's watching it all, a small smile gracing his face. People dressed in casual clothes and white aprons start to flow between the tables, placing plates before us and large platters of food down the middle of every table. I'm clearly not the only one whose mouth starts to water at the rich, warm smell that fills the room and, soon enough, every spot is filled. A deep-red wine is poured into my goblet and I lift it to my lips, thankful to have a distraction from the curious gazes that seek us out.

Trini taps my arm gently. 'Here we go,' she says, her smile stretching wider than I thought possible.

'Welcome, friends!' Roan's voice booms around the hall as he stands on a bench behind Fox. Fox twists in his seat to watch. 'I'm honoured to have you all here tonight, whether you are new friends or old. Please.' He gestures around the room, and Trini grins at me as she takes her own goblet in hand.

The hall raises their red-filled cups as one.

'To Oskrinya!' Roan shouts.

'To Oskrinya!' the hall cries back.

The food is better than anything I've ever eaten, the roasted cauliflower my favourite, and my stomach is full to bursting when I finally put down my knife and fork. The conversation has varied, but mostly Theo and Brode talk together on my left. Fox is drawn into different discussions from the strangers at our table, or those that seek him out, and I listen to Trini's never-ending chatter about who is who and why they're here.

Fox and I don't talk.

But his gaze burns me often enough that Trini stops mid-sentence and looks between us.

'Are you ...?' she asks, lifting a brow and looking pointedly between Fox and me. He pretends to focus on the conversation he's having now. From what I can make out, she is a family member of one of the soldiers who serves under him.

'What?' I ask Trini, my face heating.

She drops her voice to a whisper and leans towards me. 'You can't stop looking at our General.' She grins. 'You have a crush on him!'

Fox coughs, and the woman he's talking to lifts her brows slightly.

Trini squeals. 'Yes!'

Thankfully, those in the white aprons choose that moment to return to clear away the remnants of our dinner, and the fiddler returns with a full band in tow. The kind-looking woman moves back to her table, and I studiously keep my focus away from Fox.

Roan stands and helps push his table out of the way, creating a space in the middle of the room. He stamps his foot. Slowly at first, like a half-time heartbeat.

A deep note sounds from an instrument like the fiddle, but larger and standing on its end. The sound elicits a warming in my heart. And the fiddle and the other instruments, whose names I don't know, fly into a fast rhythm. Their musicians swaying and stomping with the beat.

The room erupts into shouts and applause.

Trini turns to me and grins.

'Sir!' she shouts over the music. 'Rubilena wants to dance!'

A gleam finds its way to his dark eyes when they look at me, questioning. Slowly, he leaves his seat, and I can only watch him walk towards me, my heart rate starting to kick up as he holds a hand out to me. I look back at Trini, my mouth agape, but she watches in anticipation.

Conscious of contradicting all the people around us and what they probably expect from his gesture, and that Fox and I are supposed to have no history, I slip my hand into Fox's. The memory of how it used to feel in mine presses against me. His is slightly larger now than it used to be, more calloused. And somehow it fits better.

I clear my throat as I push the thought away. Roan's gaze falls on me as I stand, and he slowly looks down our arms to our linked hands.

I swallow and nod at him, in acknowledgement of my promise, and a silent hope that he understands. Almost imperceptibly, he nods back.

Fox leads me to the dance floor and spins me, first away, and then back into him, catching me against his chest. He holds me there while the audience cheers, and just for a moment there is only the two of us in the space.

But it's Roan's space, and I take a step back as others begin to make their own way to the dance floor. The music pulsing through the room, I'm passed from person to person as other women seem to be, each person I dance with grinning from ear to ear.

Sweat beads on my forehead, and down my spine, but the music is relentless and so am I. The music, the movement, the happiness in this hall is intoxicating, far more so than the small amount of wine I have consumed. And I'm struck by what an incredible sense of freedom there seems to be here.

Eventually, I end up back with Fox, the familiar sense of his warm hand on my lower back making me shiver. The song ends, and we stare at each other a moment longer than anyone else. Then I break away and clap with the rest of the room, smiling at the Oskrinya around me. Wondering how it's possible two things I thought impossible not so long ago – that Oskrinya would be a safe haven, and that Fox would return – could come together so intrinsically.

What feels like hours and endless dances later, my feet are beyond sore and I drop back onto the bench seat.

'Good night?' Roan says, standing above me suddenly. I watch his handsome face as he sits next to me, facing the other way and leaning his back on the table, completely unsure how to take this ... softer version of Roan. But is he 'softer' because I've agreed to his condition of being here, or is he trying to catch me off guard after dancing with Fox?

'I don't think I've had a night like this in ... well, the last time may as well have been a different lifetime,' I venture.

'Aestais tells me Theo's first treatment went well.'

I nod. The music is loud, so I don't concern myself with making unnecessary comments. Fox dances with several other women as I watch. One in a pale purple dress makes a few more appearances than the others. I swallow against the feeling in my chest when his hands find her back like they did mine.

No history, Rubilena.

He catches me watching, and I look back to Roan to find he's turned slightly and looks between Fox and I carefully.

'Had I known you then,' he says, 'I might have given him a different order.'

A beat passes between us as I let that sink in. 'A lot of things would be different if you had,' I say, bringing my goblet to my lips and taking a sip. The red wine runs smoothly down my throat. 'But not all would be better.'

'She's not his, then?'

Surprise lifts my face to his. 'Marley? No, definitely not his.' I study him for a moment. He is decidedly handsome. Rugged, and yet infinitely polished somehow. I narrow my eyes at him. 'He knows she's not his, that's never been a secret.'

Not like so many other things.

He makes a sound in his throat, eyes never leaving my face. 'No ... but I think I'm starting to put a few things together.'

'I meant what I said, Roan,' I say, lowering my voice further. 'No one will know we have any history while Theo and I are here. I won't jeopardise Theo. Ever. And I will do everything I can to keep your people safe, too.'

He sighs. 'I think you mean that. I'm just sorry things have now moved too far to be taken back.'

An older woman hovers a polite distance away, clearly wishing to be next in line to talk with Roan. He takes my hand and squeezes it gently.

'Thank you for helping me, Rubilena.'

The comment strikes my chest in an odd way, and I have to remind myself that was Roan. *Roan.* Who I lived in fear of, along with my neighbours, for longer than I can remember. They're two realities I can't yet bring together.

He moves away to talk with the woman and I look down at my hand, thinking of all the ways life would have been so different if I'd known who Fox was back then. If he wasn't ordered to cut me out in the worst possible way.

Looking back to the dance floor, Brode and Theo leap and stomp happily. Trini is whirling between two young men ... and the woman in purple is back in Fox's arms.

My dreams of Oskrinya have never looked like this.

The music fades away behind me as we make our way back to where Theo and I are staying. Brode and Theo are enjoying the buzz of the red wine and chuckle with each other, shoulders bumping as they hurry off down the hallway. Beside me, Fox is hesitant about something, and I can feel his steps dragging. I think of the woman in that gorgeous lilac dress. It was Trini, in the end, who dragged her away under the guise of a dance, but perhaps that was unnecessary. Perhaps he'd prefer to be—

'I'll find the room okay if you want to head back in,' I say.

Voices filter to us from the hall as more people head in this direction. Fox grabs my elbow and drags me down the hallway, flinging open the first door on the right and shoving me in. Blackness envelopes me, broken only by the light seeping under the door, and my heart leaps.

'You only gave me one dance,' he whispers. Gradually, his face takes shape as my eyes adjust to the dark.

A cupboard, he's put me in a storage cupboard.

'I thought you were happily occupied,' I say softly. Not that it should matter.

The voices move past the door and only silence remains. My stomach skitters as I know there's no longer a reason for us to stay completely hidden – the whole hall likely saw us dancing. I wouldn't think walking down a hall together would be a problem. This cupboard, though, *this* could be a problem.

Fox presses against me. I don't move away.

My ears hum with the sound of our breaths in the dark, my body burning where his touches mine. His breath shallows, and yet he doesn't move.

I inhale sharply as his hand finds my face and tips it up towards his, an act as familiar as if it was yesterday we last did this. The pain in the memories stings my eyes.

He lowers his forehead to mine and I freeze, unable to decide if I can do this. No one would ever know what we did here. Roan included.

'I desperately want to kiss you, Ruby,' he whispers, the rush of air tickling my lips. 'I've wanted to kiss you again every day.'

He doesn't have to say since when. I close my eyes.

His thumb snags on my bottom lip. 'But I need to hear you say yes,' he says. 'If you don't say yes, it means no.'

I squeeze my eyes harder, heat pooling where it shouldn't. My body and my mind prepare to go to war. It would be so easy to say yes to him. But my heart wilts under the weight of the hurt and I press my lips together. Even if it was a yes, I won't jeopardise Theo – no matter the cost for me.

'I'm so sorry, Ruby,' he says when I don't respond. When I can't respond. 'I will spend the rest of my life sorry for what I did. For what I destroyed.'

Cool air races around me as he steps back. The distance is physically small, but it's an abyss I don't know if I will ever be able to cross. These last few days have asked so much of me to shift and change – how can I let go of everything I once believed? How many bridges will I be asked to cross?

CHAPTER TWENTY-TWO

'Up, up, up,' Trini sings from the door. 'Aestais waits for no one, and you need to eat first.'

She bursts into my room and lets out a small sound. 'Good grief, what happened to you?'

I look down at my sweaty shirt. 'I went for a run in the gardens. I'm normally more ... active, and I needed to get out for a bit.'

It's close to the truth.

My limbs have been restless since we got here, despite the endless walking it took to arrive. But both my need for movement and the haunting of Fox's hand on my face meant there was no sleep last night. Instead, I spent the nighttime hours oscillating between dreaming what could be, and fretting over Theo and what he faces again today.

'Then you need to wash. Quickly.' She pulls a face and leaves to rouse Theo.

I wipe myself down with the cold water in a pitcher in the bathroom and dress in clothes that don't feel much different to what I fight in – tight black pants and a sleeveless top. But the similarities end there. Where my Koamah fighting clothes are worn and well loved, these look like they've never seen a day of wear. The fabric is definitely far too delicate to fight in. Over it, I put on an elegant velvet jacket that cuts away to rounded points at the bottom and drops to mid-thigh at the back.

The boots that almost broke my feet go on last. I will tame them eventually.

Theo and I force back some breakfast to appease Trini, but he's even less interested in eating than me. The last bite falls from his mouth, and he presses a palm against his head, a low moan escaping his lips as well.

'Theo—'

He holds up a hand to silence me and, after a moment, he sits back up.

'I'm fine,' he breathes.

'Secrets or wine?'

He looks at me and blinks.

'The Varelai will follow me into battle if I ask them to,' he says. 'That's what I'm supposed to learn here, how to lead – not the secrets of the medallion.'

I can only stare at him. I have no idea what that means. His mouth drops, eyes widening in understanding.

'And ... Fox is creating an army. He just doesn't know it yet.'

He looks like he will say something else but then shakes his head, silently sorting it through.

Fox appears at that moment, looking a little awkwardly, but not apologetically, at me. Then his attention is drawn to Theo and his clammy face and he frowns.

'Brode!' he calls out, summoning him from somewhere in the hallway.

Fox launches into orders as soon as he appears, his brows drawn low over his eyes. I watch as his hands gently punctuate his words.

'I want a perimeter check, now,' he says. 'Start with Hartfield and then send scouts to each corner of the borders. They circle back to Hartfield until they find nothing but each other. Get me a report from each outpost, and find Xave.'

Brode nods, sparing Theo and me a single glance before disappearing once more.

'You're due with Aestais, yes?' Fox asks.

Theo nods.

'Trini will take you. Ruby, I want you with me – I need to show you something.'

I glance at Theo, readying to object. Trini looks between us, a slight tremor in her hands.

'Is it serious?' she whispers, finally focusing on Fox.

'It could be, but we don't know anything yet. Brode and Xave will find out,' he says gently. 'Keep it to yourself please, Trini. I don't want to frighten anyone unless I have something they need to know.'

'Of course, sir.' She draws a breath and pulls her head up high. 'Let's get you going then, Theo,' she says, striding out the door.

Fox watches me as my gaze trails Theo, biting my tongue to stop from calling him back.

'Aestais said we'd have time,' I say when I look back at him.

'I still need more than half a day to protect these people, Ruby. I also need to know who might come. The false Oskrinya or Koamah are the most obvious, but it's also possible Rehdree will turn on us again, too. Knowing who is coming helps me work out how to defeat them.'

'Turn on you?' I ask, meaning the badlands and hoping he follows.

He gestures to the door, and I fall into step with him, along the hallway and down the large stone staircase.

'We have been harassed endlessly, and bloodily, by Rehdree for a long time, but Roan is finally making some ground in winning them over as an ally. If they also get a summons by the medallion, they may give it up and begin to slaughter us again. The secrets of our world are no small thing in somebody's arsenal.'

An acidic taste coats my tongue along with the memory of soldiers cutting down people I knew, people I …

My heart aches at the thought of that happening here, in this gentle place Roan and Fox have created.

'I thought they didn't make alliances, even amongst themselves.'

'They still haven't proven that they do.'

Fox strides around the main square of Hartfield once we leave Roan's manor, pointing out the sentry towers at different parts of the wall, the weaponry room and stables. I look back to the manor, not having seen it from the front since we arrived in the dark. Its black and grey mottled stone contrasts with the white framed windows. A black tiled roof sits on top. Despite its size – it's clearly the centre piece of Hartfield, the square and the rest of the town rippling out from around it – it's surprisingly homely.

The main road leads straight from Roan's front door to the city gates. I don't know if that's accidental, but it feels like a statement that if anyone comes through those gates, they go through Roan first. Something that feels like a world away from the moat-surrounded castle in the middle of Koamah City. The first thing any attackers find there are the people.

The barracks are in the back corner of the town, close to where the wall is most compromised due to expansion. Fox tells me Roan is building more estates within the walls of Hartfield to accommodate the increasing number of Oskrinya who seek the safety of his home base.

I've always believed no one in their right mind is supposed to flee *to* Roan.

Yet Theo and I did. And, so far, there hasn't been a lot that's felt ... wrong about being here.

Finally, Fox shows me a space in the barracks complex that he calls his office. It's a tiny building with three rooms and a bathroom that looks strikingly like an old, repurposed house. The hearth fire is out and the chill in the air seeps through the rough timber walls.

General reads a brass plate on the door to his office.

'Are you as senior in Koamah as you are here?' I ask, running a finger along the top of the plate, dust coating my skin.

'Not quite. Although an unexplained absence for this long is likely to see me demoted ... as a best-case scenario.'

I spin back to him, my heart lurching.

'That's a problem for another day, Ruby.'

Ruby.

After last night, the nickname on his tongue sends a shiver down my spine.

He follows me into the room and unrolls a map on his busy desk, shoving different things aside.

'Here'—he points with a thick finger, his nails trimmed short—'is the northern border of Oskrinya. There are townships scattered throughout, between there and around Hartfield, but most of our population runs along the bottom channel here.' He runs his hand across the paper, south-east of the northern border before reaching for another map and laying it on top.

'This is Hartfield. Much of this should make sense now that I've shown you the highlights. If we need to evacuate—'

'Evacuate?' I lay a hand on his arm. 'Why are you showing me this?'

He looks at my hand and covers it with his own. The tiny action sends a ripple of awareness throughout my body.

'Someone will come. It might not be today, but Theo has learned more secrets and the medallion has sent its message. So they *will* come. Even Roan and I can feel it – like a stronger sense we should be here. If we're lucky, it will be a small number I can deal with easily. It could also be an army or more than one group.

'When that happens, I will need to lead our forces and protect Hartfield. It will be hard for me to do that and get you and Theo out as well.'

'So we're on our own?' The selfishness smarts even as I say the words.

'Never on your own. I've assigned Brode to be with you at all times—'

'But not you?'

He takes my hand from his arm and links his fingers in mine. I close my eyes and inhale the subtle scent of timber and sweat that surrounds me.

'I will find you,' he says when I open my eyes again, his face serious. 'I will always find you.'

There's an implication in his words of something I haven't been able to wrap my mind around yet – what happens after we're done in Oskrinya?

He tugs at my hand gently and leads me around the other side of his desk.

'I have something for you.'

He slides the top drawer open, revealing an assortment of papers, on top of which rests a black velvet bag. Slipping it out, he opens the pouch and slowly slides the contents on the desk.

A mess of black points stares back at me.

I look up at him as his gaze shifts from the desk to me. I haven't been this close to him in the daylight, where I can see his face, in a long time. The temptation to tuck myself in against his side and feel his warmth along the length of my body is visceral.

He clears his throat and gently drops my hand, picking up the sharp objects on the desk.

'I had these made for you.'

His voice is soft as he takes my right hand and slides the black stone on. My fingers glide into four rings with a slightly arched bridge over the top. I stare at the four sharp points that grace the bridge.

'Do you know what they are?' he asks.

I nod, still staring at the black stone that's cool on my skin and between my fingers.

'They're banned at Atticus's.'

'For good reason,' he says, closing my fist so the points sit fractionally below my knuckles. 'But if you choose to do something totally out of your mind again, like go over the wall'—he narrows his eyes at me, not quite forgiving of that yet—'then you will use everything you have.'

The thunderous pounding of hooves outside has us both looking in that direction before quickly moving back to the front door. I scoop the knuckle rings back into the bag and take them with me as we go.

Outside, Brode dismounts a grey horse who looks half asleep, despite the speed at which they came into the barracks.

'No false Oskrinya bastards,' Brode says, wiping his brow with his sleeve and leaving a smear of dirt behind. 'The perimeter is clear of them. But the leaders of Rehdree are on their way.'

My ribs squeeze and I watch Fox carefully for a response, for his body to launch into action. But he relaxes, his shoulders dropping minutely from his ears.

'They're expected – sort of,' he says to me. 'It's the alliance Roan has been negotiating. He offered to host them here for discussions, but they refused to commit to a time – part of their strategy of making sure he couldn't have a plan against them in place.'

He looks back to Brode. 'Can you get a message to Trini? She'll need to rally the staff and get ready to receive them.'

The whole of Hartfield is abuzz before I even get back to Roan's manor to find Theo. Horses and carts scurry along both the stone and dirt roads, in and out of the gate, and disseminate to their different locations. The most popular seeming to be the manor, barracks, estate, and where I think the central market is.

People stream up and down the stairs in the centre of the expansive entrance to Roan's with all manner of goods and tasks. I make my way back to Aestais's room, the thickly carpeted hallways thinning somewhat of people the closer I get. A pale, softly patterned wallpaper runs the length of the top of the walls, white timber panels mark the bottom. I glance behind me to check for dirty footprints; I do not wish to tell Trini if there are any.

'Come in,' Aestais calls when I knock on her door.

Theo is sitting up and rubbing his face, legs hanging over the edge of the bed. His face is tired but clear, even the hair hanging across his forehead seems like a more muted brown. My fingers itch to brush it back like I did when he was child.

'He's doing very well,' she says, and he laughs softly.

'She's making me out to be braver than I am.'

Aestais shakes her head at me softly, and I know much from that look. It's been hard, more painful than he should have to bear. Not for the first time, I curse our mother. For doing this to Theo, for endangering so many innocent people, and tearing me away from my daughter. If there was any possibility I could forgive her for abandoning Theo and me, it no longer exists.

My palms smart at the thought of how I've left Marley the same way. But at least my intent is wholly different. There is part of me that burns to know why she had the medallion, why she left it. But understanding her motivations has never come easily to me. If at all. And Papa has never shared his reasons for still believing in her.

'Your turn, Rubilena.'

I look questioningly at Aestais.

'I can't protect you from the claiming of the medallion, but I can stop its beacon if it does claim you – protect you from being hunted. Given how close you are to Theo, I assumed you would only trust each other with it until you work out where it goes from here.'

I stare at her for a moment, realising she and Roan truly never intended to take it. Truth be told, I haven't really cared what happened to it after this, as long as Theo and I could go home free. Without the terror of the world's armies chasing us, including the one from our home. But then Atticus's face looms in my mind – the threat of what the rest of my life will be if I don't bring it back to him.

A life so different to here.

And I wonder if, really, I have already been claimed by the medallion and no spell will stop my personal beacon to Atticus – the call back to Koamah and my debts.

'It is a burden,' Aestais says, as if she can see the thoughts swirling my mind. 'One you could escape if you wish. But I fear not all who would hold the medallion and its secrets would be as disinterested in its power as you and Theo. As two people with no desire to hold it for yourselves, I feel you would be well placed to work out where it goes. Or stays.'

'Think on it,' she says when I try to object. 'After all, should power over anyone be granted because of a possession?'

Or a debt? I think.

She points to a chair someone's brought in since I was here last and I sit, my spine straight against its hard back. A soft hand strokes the top of my head, her fingers trailing through my messy ponytail. Nostalgia for the motherly touches I never received washes over me and I close my eyes.

'Keep them closed.' Her voice is in front of me now. 'This will hurt, but not like Theo.'

The bed creaks a little, reminding me he's here in support.

'Hold this down,' she says, tugging on the neck of my top. I drag it down and out to expose my collarbones. She pushes along the ridges of bone and below, pressing into the thin muscle that covers my chest.

A slight metallic sound reaches my ears.

Then the pain starts.

Fractionally at first, an inconvenience. Eight distinct pricks of metal in my skin, running horizontally across my chest. The stings begin to burn as Aestais leans into my skin, breaking the surface. Even with my eyes closed, I can imagine her gold capped nails shining with my blood, the words she whispers spinning around me.

The eight entry points blur into two runs of pain, each travelling away from the centre of my chest. The pain licking under my arms and around my chest.

My whole torso starts to burn, flames licking my skin, and I think I cry out.

I count the beats in my inhales and exhales, but they are punctuated by my own hoarse cries. A blackness edges at my vision, and then the weight pushing against me gives completely, and I drop my head to my knees, pressing the heels of my palms into my eyes.

A hand cups my head once more and helps me sit up.

Aestais presses me back into the chair and I let my head fall back on the hard supports. I listen to her open a jar and brace myself for the assault of pain once more. The balm she paints on my skin, over what I can only imagine are significant tears, is cool and tingling.

But not painful.

'This will both seal the protection spell and your skin. You will have no scars,' she says.

Scars, I think. They are the least of my worries. If only there was a Varelai balm for ensuring the safety and happiness of everyone I love.

Maybe even including me. But as difficult and also refreshingly different this time away from Koamah is, I know what my life has in store after this point. And our debt won't clear itself.

CHAPTER TWENTY-THREE

Theo looks like he's been on the losing end of a fight with Marco. Just with a distinct lack of bruises. He sips slowly from a vial of bright yellow liquid Aestais gave him as we left, along with instructions to rest. In my own hand is a jar of the balm she put on my chest. A small part of me flutters with excitement to try and replicate her balm when we get home. Glancing down, the eight angry puncture wounds in my chest look certain to remain, but the pain has dulled to an inconvenience once more. Something I won't notice in the morning – if I could forget how much pain it means Theo has been enduring in his sessions.

I sit next to him in front of the fire, pocketing my balm and holding my hands out, warming my palms in the radiant heat. The bottom half of the walls in this room are white, like many in the parts of the manor I have seen, with a pale blue wallpaper on top. Dark frames with different paintings and embroidered images dot the area haphazardly. Like someone with the excitement – and patience – of a five-year-old was in charge of decorating. The warmth it brings to the room is undeniable, though, as is the constriction in my chest that never goes away. Missing Marley is something I just can't get around, despite the numerous distractions here.

'I don't feel any different,' Theo says eventually. 'I thought I'd feel powerful, knowing all the secrets of the Kingdom – but I still just feel like me.'

'I think that's a good thing.'

'Maybe,' he says, turning back to the fire. 'Don't you think it's a bit of an anti-climax though? I mean, I'm still going to have to gather our wood when we go back.'

I study the flames, hiding a small smile. 'I think it's a testament to your good nature, actually. That the power of knowledge hasn't rushed to your head and turned you into a fool.'

'I could find out more if we wanted to,' he says, hazel eyes finding me as he turns in his seat.

'How so?'

'They're all there for the taking.' He shrugs. 'I don't really know how to explain it, but I haven't been actively seeking them out. That's why they've been spaced out, I think, as the medallion tries to find a home. But ... it's like a library I can access at will. It just feels like I might not come out again if I go too far in.'

Cold fingers run down my spine. I search Theo's face.

'Your last session with Aestais is tomorrow. Please, do not go looking before then.'

I bite back the panic that wants to rise at the temptation that must be causing in Theo's mind. A pull towards an abyss of knowledge.

He laughs, but I can't join him.

'What's so funny?' I ask.

'I'm not going to go looking, Rubes. The things I want to know aren't held in this medallion.'

I frown.

'Like what?'

'Well ... I think the things I want to know are what Laramie can share with me. I have this ... knowing, almost, that I will spend more time with her at some point, and that feels more important than what's in the medallion. And'—a light takes flight in his gaze—'like why Brode blushes when I look at him a certain way.' A sly grin creeps across his face. One I now can't help but mirror. The sparkle in his eye tips me over into a soft laugh.

'Is that really a secret?' I ask.

'He thinks it is.' He winks.

We both chuckle then lapse back into silence. I'm not sure what to make of his comment about Laramie, but for now I'm just relieved he doesn't plan on searching within the medallion. Even if it means he has some hopes of spending more time with witches – I will cross that bridge if and when we get to it.

Trini arrives a moment later, bursting through the door without knocking, both of us twisting around in surprise. Her auburn hair is as perfect as ever, but her eyes fly wildly around the room. The toll the pressure of being prepared for Roan's visitors on her is clear even from where we sit.

The seven clan leaders, or their representatives, and different members of their clans arrived not long after we'd finished with Aestais. It was impossible not to hear the different conversations up and down the manor as Theo and I returned to our rooms for him to rest.

Other than knowing it as the 'badlands', there is not a lot Theo or I know about Rehdree. In Koamah, our focus is always on Oskrinya. The other two regions, Solynara and its neighbour, Talvore, are allies of Koamah – part of the Kingdom. Rehdree, with Oskrinya in between us, has always seemed too far away to be a credible threat or ally.

Only because of what we faced, or thought we faced, from Oskrinya.

But it's clear that most of the people in Hartfield are highly anticipating this visit and what it means, hopeful for a better future with an undercurrent of fear. The history of pillaging by Rehdree in Oskrinya has left a wound, one I don't even know the half of. But if they feel anything like we do in Koamah about the Oskrinya – or false Oskrinya – I know it will be hard to move beyond. Even being here, seeing every day the simple joy in Hartfield, only seems real if I ignore the fact we're in Oskrinya.

But clearly, however hard he is working behind the scenes, Roan is an excellent diplomat. What I do know about Rehdree is the seven clans have previously proven impossible to unite for any cause. Which makes me even more unsettled about who is actually parading as Roan's soldiers – because I can't imagine the clans acting cohesively enough to pull it off for so long.

A tiny flutter of excitement stirs in my limbs. Roan's dinners have proven to be quite enjoyable, if not a little challenging not to give away how well I know Fox. But that's an easy price to pay for Aestais's help. And seeing the clan leaders of Rehdree for myself is something I will never get to do again.

'Your dress,' Trini says, as she pulls out a heavy looking black bag that shouldn't have been able to fit in her basket. I follow her into my bedroom where she places it gently on the bed, the thick blue covers crinkling slightly.

'Your suit's already in your room, Theo!' she calls out as she undoes the buttons on the front of the bag. A deep, shimmering red fabric slides between her fingers, and she sighs.

'You will look gorgeous in this,' she says. Her gaze flicks to mine and holds my eyes a moment longer than I expect.

I frown quizzically at her.

One shoulder lifts a fraction. 'Sometimes it's good to make a statement.'

I laugh. I don't need to make any statements, but I never have the opportunity – or the Kabolshi – to wear beautiful dresses. I feel like nothing more than a brawling single mother in Koamah. I won't be passing up a chance to explore a different version of myself tonight.

Trini hurries back out, the spell of the dress snapping and her focus returning to what she needs to do, leaving me to dress and fix my hair in private.

The dress is like liquid against my skin as I step into it and wriggle the fabric up my body and over my hips. Finding the arm holes and additional fabric clearly designed to hold my breasts in place, I realise there is something wrong.

Trini has given me a dress with no back.

'Statement' is one way of putting what she's asking me to wear. Totally inappropriate is another.

But she's gone, and I refuse to see the clan leaders in my dirty clothes from the day. Not when I know how dashing Theo will look next to me.

The sleeves are full length, as is the skirt, the soft material clinging to me like a second skin. I look over my shoulder to try and see but, judging by feel in the places I can't see, the back only starts where my spine curves into my ass. Thankfully, the front is high and skims across my collarbones, hiding the marks from Aestais's nails.

Theo whistles when I join him in the sitting room.

'Did Xave say you almost killed Fox when you went over the wall?' he asks. 'You're certainly going to succeed in that particular mission tonight.'

I roll my eyes. 'Funny.'

But a tiny part of me shimmies at what his reaction might be. I look to the door expectantly, waiting for him and Brode to arrive, a nervousness I haven't felt in a long time skittering along my senses.

'They're meeting us there,' Theo says, and we make our way alone.

The noise from the hall is loud before we've even entered. Music and voices flow through the manor, paired with the occasional scraping of furniture or slamming of a heavy goblet. Theo offers his arm as we reach the doors and I take it, giving him a gentle squeeze. Time with Theo like this is so precious, and I press the image of the man he is into my heart.

He pushes open the large timber door and we find most of the tables already occupied. A different kind of nervousness makes itself known as I look out on the sea of unknown faces. The faces of people I once thought would kill Theo and me on sight, but have never shown an ounce of violence towards us. Not once.

'You are set to give someone a heart attack.'

Xave's voice is a welcome sound and I smile up at him. He's someone who smiles with his whole body when he wants, and it generates a genuine warmth in my chest. He leans into me and places a gentle kiss on my cheek; I return the favour.

'Come,' he says.

He leads us through the tables, weaving around those already seated. Halfway across the hall, I realise there is a different table at the front I haven't seen before. A long stretch of timber that is clearly the focal point of the night, seats on one side only. A number of men and women sit side by side, only leaving a gap in the middle of the table. They say little and watch much, each set of eyes roving the hall and glancing at the doors often. Varying designs of fur vests grace their chests and many have tattoos on their faces. One of the women's tattoos disappears down her neck and into her vest.

Trini squeals when she spots me from the table we sat at before. Clearly, she's been saving it for us and gestures wildly for us to sit down.

'You look beautiful,' I say when I reach her, taking in the midnight gown that plays off her fire-coloured hair. She blushes and swats at me, her gaze flicking briefly to Xave in his grey suit.

He clears his throat and I look between them. He must be almost old enough to be her father, but I'm sure there is a murmur of something different between them. Xave looks at the doors before giving my hand a little squeeze and sitting across from us, next to where Fox will join us.

Brode and Theo have already disappeared into their own conversation beside me, and I don't expect Theo to draw breath.

Xave thumps the table; the cutlery and I jump.

Brode joins him, and quickly the thumping is echoed around the room from all the tables, even those occupied by the Rehdrians. The doors open again, and Fox and Roan stride in.

I suck in a breath.

The white shirt Fox wears is open at the neck, exposing the top of his chest. A black jacket stretches across his shoulders, skimming the fitted black pants he wears underneath. Military medals are pinned to the side of his jacket.

Next to him, Roan is also in black, his shorter hair contrasting against Fox's length and beard. The polished ruler and the soldier.

Both impeccably handsome.

The Oskrinya cheer as the two walk to the table, Fox and Roan each smiling in return. Fox's face is slightly more reserved than Roan's, who grins warmly at everyone in his hall. Roan makes a beeline for the head table, and Fox falls in behind, his chocolate gaze searching the room.

My cheeks heat as he does a double take when he sees me, and his smile widens. I notice the matching red piece of fabric in his jacket pocket and look accusingly at Trini.

She scrunches her nose and Xave stifles a chuckle.

I wait for Fox to join us, but he gives me a slightly apologetic look and walks after Roan, joining him between the clan leaders at the front table.

Servers immediately swarm the hall and place platter after platter on the tables, filling goblets as they go.

The hall buzzes with the conversation and music as we eat, and a warmth grows in my chest and fingers from the wine. I let the words flow around me, a shimmering current of connection in the room that tugs at the corners of my mouth.

'You can go talk to him, you know,' Trini says. 'The longing looks between the two of you are almost enough to make me combust just sitting next to you.'

I almost spit my wine just as Fox catches my eye, a laughing question in his.

One of the clan leaders chooses that moment to stand, clearing his throat and saving me from having to answer Trini. It takes a moment or two, but gradually the hall quietens and all the faces turn to the man standing. His dirt-coloured hair is long and tied back in numerous braids, pieces of leather tying the ends together. The fur he wears is white and almost glowing against his dark pants.

'That's Andvett Starrisson,' Trini whispers. 'He's the ... leader ... of the seven clans. Unofficial, I think, but they all seem to follow him – rumour has it he's the most brutal of them all.'

I nod slowly, taking him in.

'From what I've heard,' Trini continues, her focus still on the front table, 'trying to negotiate with them has really tested Roan. He's used to people that play a similar game – the Rehdree, though, they just make whatever rules they want.'

I let my gaze travel the group of warriors lining the table, among them Roan almost seems out of place.

'What a feast!' Andvett says, his deep voice booming around the room as he brandishes his goblet and gestures to the rest of us watching. 'And what an occasion.'

The room waits, the anticipation of what the occasion actually is thick in the air. Even Roan looks purposefully composed in his waiting, as if even he isn't sure what this speech will entail – something I can't imagine is true, despite what Trini claims.

'For many years,' Andvett continues, 'the clans of Rehdree have protected ourselves against any threat – including the threat of Oskrinya.'

The Oskrinya in the room shift nervously in their seats. Fox and Roan go still.

Andvett raises his silver goblet.

'The Rehdree have proven ourselves a fearsome foe,' he continues and Roan nods softly. 'But we will prove ourselves an even better ally.'

Stunned silence greets him.

Roan stands and embraces him, Andvett thumping Roan solidly on the back.

Fox stands and shakes his hand and, finally, the room erupts.

Roan finds my gaze across the hall and watches me for a moment. I hold it, and a fleeting sense of regret crosses his features. I flash him my most encouraging smile. He's forged an alliance for Oskrinya that no one else has managed. Whatever my complicated views on his people, he's done this well. And they, too, deserve to be protected from whoever is parading as them.

Andvett raises his drink again and waits for silence once more.

'To solidify our growing friendship, we offer the opportunity for a marriage between our people, one I am sure will prove exceedingly fruitful.' He lowers the silverware and looks around the room.

A smattering of whispers runs the perimeter.

I glance at Roan, whose face gives nothing away. For some reason, I hadn't considered him to be the marrying kind. But then, I vaguely recall Theo mentioning a secret of a lost love, so perhaps he knows he won't find it again. A feeling I understand.

I sip my wine.

'We have brought with us some of our finest women and warriors, who are most pleased to be part of this historic union.'

Andvett gestures subtly with his free hand, and women from various tables stand, each more beautiful than the last.

He turns to Roan.

'Fox Castellan of Oskrinya, let me present to you—'

My mind goes blank. Trini sucks in a breath next me and Theo reaches for my hand under the table, swearing as he does.

I look forward, at Roan, whose eyes don't leave mine. Suddenly, his request that Fox and I hide our history all makes sense.

I lift my chin and squeeze Theo's hand. This will mean Fox definitely doesn't come home. There won't be the 'after' that seemed implicit in our recent conversation. Theo will leave him here. I will leave him here.

But then, this *is* his home.

The women form a line and walk towards the front table, bowing, nodding, or curtsying before Fox, who pointedly looks each of them in the eye as they do so. One draws a dagger from her vest and places it on the table before him. Her silver blonde hair snakes over her shoulder as she dips her head, not in submission, but one equal meeting another.

Theo's hand trembles in the fist we make on my knee.

I hold on as long as I can, forcing my body to be still despite the free fall that's ripped me from the unsteady balance I thought I'd found, refusing to be the jilted lover fleeing the room.

I'm not even his lover. I have no right to feel jilted.

As soon as the women have finished, the servers return, filling the goblets once more, and the room explodes into noise. Cheering, clapping, and music fill the air, completely at odds with the rampaging that's currently taking charge of all my senses.

I gently let go of Theo's hand, only to realise it's mine that shakes.

He glances up at me, his own heartbreak written all over his face. But I've been here for Theo all this time, away from Marley, letting my heart believe stupid things, and I find I can't comfort him just now.

'I think you need some air,' Xave whispers, appearing beside me and extending his hand. Numbly, I place my fingers in his and leave the bench seat as gracefully as I can.

I imagine rich, chocolate eyes watching me slip from the hall.

Wishful thinking.

CHAPTER TWENTY-FOUR

All I can focus on is the pressure of Xave holding my hand as he guides me from the bustling, celebrating hall and out into the night. It feels like I can only draw breath once the dark has enveloped me and the number of people watching me fall apart is significantly reduced.

The air is crisp on my skin, a sensation I needed to feel, needed to remind me I'm real. This is not some hideous dream of a love I am never destined to have. It is my reality.

A gentle rain has fallen while we were dining, while I desperately held on to the remaining pieces of my composure, and the garden path is damp as we make our way out into the welcoming shadows.

'You okay?' Xave asks seriously and I can't help but laugh. 'Should I take that as a no?' he asks, a bit of mirth sneaking in.

'It shouldn't be important,' I grind out, the cracking in my chest seeming to be reflected in the clenching of my jaw. 'It shouldn't ... in the scheme of things ... it's not—' but I can't actually make myself say it's not important, can't say those words out loud.

'Some would say there is nothing more important than love,' he says, matching my pace around the garden's water feature.

I grapple with that concept. With Marley, and Theo, and Papa, I would agree. Because that love fuels every decision I have ever made. And every decision I make is in their best interests. But this ... doesn't feel like that. Not right now. How can what is stampeding in my chest be more important than the alliances they are currently toasting to in that hall?

'He didn't think he'd see you again, Rubilena,' Xave says, the tone in his voice bringing my steps to a halt.

'What—'

'He thought he'd never have another chance with you – that it didn't matter what happened to him, providing it was in service to Oskrinya.'

Xave closes the small space between us and takes my elbows in his hands.

'Ever since you stumbled back into his path, he's been trying to get this marriage option off the table – for both him and Roan.'

I look up at him, hoping he can't see the tears in my eyes, but I'm too full of things I can't name to really care.

'Why didn't he tell me?'

'Would you have been ready for him to say he was calling off the possibility of a marriage because you'd come back into his life?' He smiles sadly, knowingly, at me. 'Even still, I'd say the look on his face tonight meant he did not see this coming.'

I close my eyes, thinking of the moment in the cupboard when he asked me to say yes – to kiss him – knowing full well what that would say about my feelings for him.

Xave draws me into a tight embrace and the absence of Papa stings worse than ever before.

'I know what it is to love someone you can't have, Rubilena and ... I'm sorry.'

I clutch at him for a long moment before I finally push back and wipe my eyes.

'Would you like me to walk you back to your room?' he asks and I shake my head.

'I'll stay out here a little longer, I think.'

As Xave turns and walks away, I wonder how long I would have to stay out here to heal what is tearing inside me.

The torches staked through Roan's gardens catch the drops in the bushes, lighting them up in a thousand crystals. This picturesque, gentle landscape is not one in which I belong. Koamah, with all its faults, is my home, and I desperately ache to go back. At least there I was in charge of my own pain, my own battles. Even the ones Atticus scheduled for me were ultimately my choice.

It was not my choice to be here with Fox once more. Fissures I'd patched so long ago have opened themselves again for a man I do not wish to care for.

But, then, that's a lie too.

I want.

I've always wanted. It's just that I can't have.

My feet pace around the gardens behind the manor. I can hear the last of the dinner guests begin to leave, past the large water feature of women and children frozen in time. It's both innocent and grotesque. I force myself to keep moving, partly to help the warmth move throughout my body, partly so I don't sink to the ground under the weight of the exhaustion that's descending.

I think of the blonde woman with the dagger.

He should choose her.

My blood bubbles with pure, unadulterated jealousy, and I want to scream at myself. For caring that someone else could be as deserving of him as me – more deserving of him. I don't bring peace for his people with me. For caring that they will have a clean start, with nothing but hope and peace to start their relationship. That they don't have a past spoiling the air between them with hurt. The rotting scent of jaded memories fills my nose as I pass bushes dotted with white flowers.

The gravel crunches quietly behind me, and I turn to face whoever lurks in the shadows.

And there he is. In all his suited splendor.

'Xave said I'd find you here,' he says.

It's not a question, and so I leave his statement hanging, not really sure what I'm supposed to do with it, anyway.

He closes the space between us with long strides and I straighten my spine further.

'I'm sorry for what happened in there.'

'It's fine,' I say, glancing at the sparkling bushes. 'Xave ... explained. You don't owe me anything anymore, Fox. Bringing Theo here is ... a lot. Enough.'

'I'm not sure that's true.' His voice is low, its vibration humming in my chest.

'We made no promises,' I say, finally bringing myself to look him in the face, unable to voice the 'this time' – we made lots of promises last time, all of which were broken. 'You're free to do whatever you please. Whatever you're supposed to do – need to do as ...' I trail off, gesturing vaguely to the medals on his chest and the manor behind.

He catches my hand in the air and clasps it between his two warm ones. The roughness of his skin in contrast to the image of refinement before me makes my heart stutter.

'Tell me you don't feel what I feel,' he whispers, his voice filling my mind. 'Tell me you feel nothing, that you don't want me.' My breath hitches as my throat threatens to close over. 'Tell me you don't want me to fight for you.'

He inhales softly. 'Tell me I'm wrong about us,' he says, 'and I'll stop looking for a way out of this with Rehdree – I'll walk away from you. I know I don't deserve your forgiveness, but I'm desperate for it, anyway. What I did to you eats me alive every day, but I don't want to hide from it. I want a chance to make our future so bright it burns away that pain.'

Traitorous tears sting my eyes and I struggle to hold them at bay.

'You broke me.'

My voice catches on the quiet truth it utters. Ignoring that we can't have the future he talks of, not when his future wife waits inside. When the people he leads to peace wait inside.

He deflates and pulls me against his chest, the red fabric in his pocket caressing my cheek as the cold metal of the medals on his jacket cut into my skin. The contradiction a mocking reflection of what's between us.

'I broke me, too,' he says into my hair. 'Ruby, I—'

'I *want* to forgive you.' I surprise myself with that statement, perhaps more than I surprise him. 'But ... I don't know how. You were there, you were everything, and then you were just ... nothing. *We* were nothing.'

His exhale is quick and he presses me closer for a moment, his palms on the bare skin of my back, before pulling back to look at me. The thick, dark brows that frame his face draw low over his agonised eyes. Taking my face in his hands, he runs his thumbs along my cheekbones.

'Not nothing, Ruby, never nothing.'

I close my eyes briefly and focus on the warmth of his breath on my face.

'What about all of that?' I ask, pointing to the manor behind him.

'I don't want any of that. I just want you.'

I just want you.

Words that have burned in my heart and mind for years, words that burned so hot when he left they branded my skin. Words he never said, but I needed to hear like I needed air to breathe. Words that never came. Words that were held back, kept secret from me.

Until now.

Now it's too late.

Hot tears spill from behind my lashes and down my cheeks, pooling in his hands. The pain and regret crackles in his eyes and I believe it broke him too. The desperation to move on, to forget, claws at my insides. But it's a weight I have carried for so long, it's become part of who I am. I don't know who I am without this wound.

Its twin is being dragged in parallel, another addition to the Fox shaped scars I carry.

His eyes close as I run a finger down his nose and along his jaw, the growth of his short beard almost soft under my fingers as I explore the planes of his face. It's not one I can let go of. The depth of his being I see in his dark eyes is not something I want to share with anyone else.

'Can I kiss you?' The tentative shake in his voice makes it so quiet I almost miss the question. My chest constricts in response even as the rest of me rejoices.

I can only nod, my words having disappeared.

His lips are soft and inquiring as they meet mine, my face still cradled in his hands. Parting my own, I give him his answer and take the kiss I've dreamed of since he left, wrapping my arms around his neck. Sensation rushes my limbs and through my centre, chased there by the urgent hammering behind my ribs. Fingers move into my hair, his other hand running down my back and pulling me against him again. My tongue finds his and my own secrets break free and take the strength from my knees – this is where I belong. Despite the time and the hurt, this is home.

Fox grips me tighter to save me from falling, kissing me harder. His hand slips to the curve in my spine, large fingers dipping under the very edge of my dress. He groans into my mouth and I take that, too.

'I'm yours, Ruby,' he murmurs, his lips moving on mine. 'I always have been.'

It's supposed to put my heart back together, to stitch up the holes.

Instead, it splinters.

Eventually, the cold air on my exposed back shakes my body and Fox sneaks us back into the manor. We take a staff hallway and access stairs before running down the hallway to Theo and my rooms, hand in hand.

He walks me to the fire and stands me in front of it, never letting go of my hand. The heat of the flames licks up my spine and I shiver happily as the cold is slowly driven out. Fox stands, legs wide, in front of me and I lean into his chest. Large hands trail up and down my back, assisting the spread of warmth in my blood. The pressure of his fingers increases gently, and I close my eyes. My focus narrows to the feel of his callouses dipping to the lowest point of the dress and running under the edge of the fabric once more.

'This dress will be the death of me,' he says roughly.

The corner of my mouth lifts into his jacket.

Taking his hand again, I move us to the couch. My heart is not ready for my dress to come off just yet, but also not willing to lose this moment altogether. His knuckles are scarred and my thumb seeks out all the ridges of scar tissue.

'How did you do this?' I ask.

He winces, the orange glow of the fire dancing over his face. His eyes slide sideways to me before looking down at our hands. After a moment he clears his throat. 'I ... may have found out someone ... important ... was having another man's baby.'

'Oh.'

'Let's just say I wasn't particularly gracious about it.'

'She and Theo are the realest things in my life.' I say, perhaps a nudge more sharply than I intended. 'And Papa, of course. I couldn't do any of it without him.'

I miss Papa as much as I miss Marley, but it's a tension I don't have to hold on to as hard. Papa is one person I know I don't have to consider every decision for. The wonderful man he is has never relied on me making good choices, or helping him make good choices. He just ... is. Loving him, having him love me, feels like the only guarantee in my life.

'She's a lot like how I remember you, you know,' he says, a smile in his voice. 'They're lucky to have you.' He turns and faces me fully, a glint in his eye. 'If I didn't want to do wicked things to you, I'd almost wish you'd raised me, too.'

Images of said wicked things flash in my mind and I try to laugh to distract myself from the heat that paints my cheeks. Fox's face is serious when I look back at him, its intensity wiping the smile from my face. There's only one thing that look says.

My heart beats so hard I'm worried he can hear it.

'We should go slow,' I force myself to say. Why, though, I'm not sure. 'No one can know. Roan—'

'I know,' he says, his body leaning into mine anyway.

I can't help but look at his mouth. It feels so familiar and yet different, the pull to him sucking the breath from my lungs. The beard is new, but he's also taller and more solid than before, his jaw a little squarer. Letting my gaze drift from his face, across his chest, and down his body, I wonder what else will give this contradiction of familiar yet brand new.

My body moves without instruction, driven on heat and memories, and I capture his mouth in mine, dragging my teeth on his bottom lip. Every part of me tingles as I'm pressed back into the couch, Fox's jacket straining around the frame he makes over me.

Soft lips trail my neck, sending tiny bumps running down my spine.

My dress pulls tighter on my chest as Fox pulls a shoulder down, exposing more skin. His teeth—

'Fuck,' he breaths as a loud knock breaks through the slamming sound of my pulse. 'Trini?' he asks, forehead resting on my shoulder.

'She doesn't knock.'

I push him off gently and head for the door, lifting the corner of my dress back where it belongs, looking back once to check he's put back together. A glower looks back at me and I smile.

I grip the handle and draw a steadying breath myself.

Only to come face to face with Roan.

My throat thickens at the barely concealed thunder on his face.

Fox and Roan stare at each other as Roan walks into the room and shuts the door behind him.

In four strides, Fox crosses the room.

Roan watches him come.

Waiting.

Fox swings, his fist connecting with Roan's jaw so hard I think I hear it crack. He staggers against the wall, throwing out a hand to break his fall.

Fox waits.

So do I.

Roan straightens, taking the bright blue fabric square from his jacket pocket and pressing it to his mouth – too much of a gentleman to spit the blood that's pooled in his mouth.

'You're an asshole,' Fox spits.

'And you're a short-sighted soldier,' Roan snaps back.

Fox clamps his mouth shut.

Roan sighs. 'You're right, I'm an asshole. But one who's trying to do the right thing for Oskrinya.'

'Have I not been a pawn enough for one lifetime?' Fox asks, his fists clenching at his sides. 'I did everything, *everything*, you asked of me regardless of what it cost,' he spits. 'Did you know that was coming tonight?'

'I knew,' Roan says quietly. The anger in his face dims, an apology taking its place so like it does on Theo's. I frown slightly, wondering where he is.

The force of the steam goes out of Fox immediately at the unexpected admission. But the tension in his jaw and shoulders gives away the simmering boil below the surface.

'Why didn't they want you?' Fox grits out, articulating the question that had been circling in the back of my own mind. 'Why did it have to be me?'

'You know why – they are a warrior people. What use is a soft-handed leader to them when placed next to our foremost general? These negotiations have been going on for a long time, Fox,' Roan says. 'Before I knew – shit, before *you* knew there was a possibility you would reconcile with Rubilena.'

I glance at Fox, my heart cracking at what could have been. But I squash back any tears that think they'd like to come.

'We need them, Fox,' Roan continues. 'We barely have the numbers to hold those false Oskrinya bastards at bay without them, we will never defeat them on our own.' He looks at me. 'Especially not now that medallion is here – sending its message of a new, weaker, seat of power. We are one country, Fox, and a small one at that. One country against the Kingdoms of Koamah – the armies and resources of *three* countries. And Rehdree sitting above us with their legions ... there are very few options here.'

'I know.' Fox deflates in defeat. I reach out and wrap my hand over his bicep. Reflexively, he twists his arm around me and pulls me into his side.

Roan's gaze flicks between us, taking in my widened eyes, that I can't quite relax into Fox. But can he see it's because Fox feels like the safe place I am consistently denied because we both have other responsibilities that have to come first?

In return, I look at Roan. This figure who has been a shadow in my life for so long, without ever knowing who he really was. Never knowing who, or what, he was really fighting for. His face is hard on the surface, not unlike Atticus's, but underneath it seems like genuine regret runs there. Like he would make a different decision if he was free from his responsibilities. In that we're not so different, I suppose.

But where I am responsible for a handful of people I'd give anything for, Roan has a whole country looking to him. And Fox has a role to play in that, too – one that started well before I was a factor.

'It's okay,' I say to both of them after several moments. My voice is quiet but steady, vastly different to how I feel on the inside. Vastly different to what I can show them. 'Joining with Rehdree could not only free your people from the tyranny of the false Oskrinya, and the oppression of

Koamah, but could also free Koamah as well if the false Oskrinya are dealt with.'

'What are you saying?' Fox slides away from me a little, studying my face.

'I won't make this difficult, Roan,' I say, looking at him and not Fox. I don't want to see the hurt on his face. The same, I imagine, that would have been on mine all that time ago.

Fox walks away from me, towards the fire, but doesn't sit down. Roan watches him before looking back to me and nodding slowly.

'I'll ensure you're not disturbed tonight,' he says softly, turning back to the door and pocketing the bloody blue square. 'And get Theo to Aestais first thing tomorrow,' he says over his shoulder. 'I can feel that fucking medallion's beacon in my sleep.'

CHAPTER TWENTY-FIVE

Fox stares at me as I approach where he stands at the fire.

'I can't risk Theo, and you won't either,' I say to his unvoiced opinions.

'That's almost done. Tomorrow—'

'Will you feel differently about Oskrinya, or Koamah, tomorrow? Will they stop being your homes? People you need to protect?'

He doesn't answer, and for several moments we just watch each other. The words too heavy to form.

'You feel the same,' he says quietly. 'About Oskrinya and Koamah.'

My brows lift. 'I ...' I frown. 'Yes, maybe I do.'

'You feel at home here?'

He watches me watching him as I weigh up my thoughts, my words. Watches the warring between my body and mind. And my heart in the middle that screams at me for letting him go, for not fighting the way I wanted him to fight all those years ago. It begs me to ask him to fight now, too, to find another way.

I'm not naive enough to believe that marriage alone makes love, but the acts that must be done in marriage can certainly make a family. And I know with every fibre of my being that Fox would never abandon his children.

And that is a reality that will only be a matter of time.

I rest my head on his chest, between my hands, as I gather myself – pushing thoughts of Fox's future children from my mind.

I can have tonight. That's more than I thought I'd ever have again.

I let a soft smile show. There's no risk here now. I know what this is – a chance to relive my past, to intimately know this not-really-a-stranger in front of me. To feel the expanse of his skin and know there is no tomorrow. No tomorrow for him to walk away and never return.

'There might be a fantasy of sorts I have about what home looks like,' I say, not only thinking of Marley and Theo with the horses I'd arrange for them.

'Oh?' His hands start to trail my arms, the fabric of my dress not thick enough to stop the warmth of his skin seeping through.

I spread my palms on his chest; they don't cover as much as they used to. Slipping them under his jacket and up towards his shoulders, I drop it back and he shrugs it off, throwing it on the couch.

His hands lift to the back of my head and cradle it. He's still while I grapple with where we are and how we got here. I long to hear him talk to me, tell me there is a way out of this, but what can I possibly expect him to say? I won't risk Roan's alliance any more than he will. And I will never put this before getting that fucking medallion's claim off Theo. Where it goes after that I no longer care. I want to go home and nurse my shattered dreams in peace, even if it means I owe the rest of my years to Atticus. At least I'd have a reason to hit something on a regular basis.

But I want this, too. Even if this one night, when it ends, will destroy me. Walking away from it, from him, in this moment is not something I can bring myself to do.

'I want tonight,' I say into his chest.

He sags beneath me.

'I want so much more than that,' he says.

His lashes glisten in the firelight when I finally look up at him.

I kiss his face, his eyes, and the new scar. Lifting his hand to my mouth, I kiss the scar that runs along his knuckles there as well. Deep brown eyes watch me. Standing on my toes, I pull his head to mine, and place a gentle kiss on the end of his mouth, right where I can feel both the bristles of his beard and the fullness of the mouth that peeks out.

'Kiss me,' I demand.

He looks at me for a long moment and I almost think he's going to say no – until hot lips caress my mouth, his tongue sweeping across mine. Gently he takes my bottom lip in his teeth and a current courses through my body. I press into him, his need already clear, and close my eyes as I tip my head to the side. He doesn't have to be asked twice, lowering his head and kissing a line between my shoulder and my ear.

I begin to tremble, a subtle shaking that starts in my knees and my fingertips.

Slowly, I find each of the buttons on his shirt and relieve them of the pressure of containing his chest. His hands skim the outside of my dress, cupping my ass and pressing me tighter still. A single hand moves back up to my head and loosely grips my hair. Pinning me against him with a hand on my behind, and one on my head, he bites my neck – hard. I let out a whimper as the current he creates burns through my core, threatening to light me up from the inside out.

Releasing me slightly, he drags his fingers up my spine and slips the dress from my shoulders, letting it pool around my waist. He sucks in a breath and my nipples go hard under the attention, his eyes blowing wide. I watch him for a moment, my body throbbing. He's the same but different to me. He's grown broader, taller, stronger. I wonder which bits of me are the same but different to him. This body that grew and nurtured a baby, and then grew hard to protect the child I didn't grow. It's a smattering of hard and soft now, full of things that will never return to what they once were.

My hands find the bottom of his shirt and tug it from his pants. I take one of his arms out at a time before dipping my fingers underneath the waist of his pants, slipping beyond the belt.

The murmur of the fire crackles, punctuated by Fox's ragged breathing.

Butterflies take flight behind my ribs as my fingers brush the top of him, straining against the fabric between us. His eyes devour me when I look up once more. Pools of molten chocolate.

We stand for a moment, staring at each other. So close to diving off this ledge, knowing we will only crash at the bottom. Slowly, so slowly I almost miss the beginning, Fox drops his head and brushes the faintest of kisses on my lips, and I'm powerless to stop the freefall. I crush my mouth to his, frantic now to have him, feel him.

I free the belt from its fastenings and undo his pants, all the while never letting his mouth leave mine. His hands rove over every inch of my bare skin. His pants drop to the floor and I let him kick off his boots as I shimmy all the way out of my dress and lead him by the hand into my bedroom.

We come together in a flurry of limbs and skin and teeth, my body screaming to claim all of him. To let him claim me. But it's a process that was completed so long ago. Even as I fought against it tooth and nail, broken as I was by his absence, I knew I would never love anyone like I did him.

So I take him now and let the new feel of him add to the memories of how he used to feel. Where his then slightly smaller, softer hands once roamed, larger, calloused ones do now. Where his once soft face ran, his bearded one does now. But his eyes are the same. The same all-knowing, bottomless pits that draw me out, that glitter with an emotion neither of us will be able to name in this time we have. The name for what we thought we had now doesn't seem enough.

But even saying that will be too much for what we can handle now. Far more than I am ready to consider. It was there once, but the gulf between now and then is wide.

Now, all I can give him is this. All I can take is this.

Tears run down my cheeks as he slides into me, filling me and overflowing the space in my chest that has always belonged to him. I rock where I sit astride him, my tears falling into the dark hair at his chest. He reaches up to cup my cheek as we move together, an unbearable ecstasy building in my core. I want to delay it. I want to stay here, on the precipice of giving it all away without suffering the fall out. But he drives harder from underneath me. It's clear he knows I'm close, and he will stop at nothing to make me go over. Those dark eyes watch me go to pieces as my body slips into oblivion and clenches him into his own release.

Eventually, I slip off him and nestle myself into his side, head on his chest. His fingers trail in the ends of the mess my curls create, the gentle tugging sending tingles across my scalp. The same as I circle mine in the dusting of hair over his heart.

We don't talk, and I finally drift off into sleep. The familiar wishes that things were different with Fox slinking in the shadows.

The sky is just starting to lighten outside, dawn not quite here but racing ahead for the day to start when I slowly open my eyes. Warmth envelopes me from behind, a large brown hand wrapped in mine between my breasts. I close my eyes, hating that morning is here and I have to leave him. At the same time, a stone that's sat in my stomach since my mother appeared in our shop is starting to dissolve.

Today, Aestais will complete her removal of the mark from Theo. Today, we can be free of the hunters of this land and others.

Gently, I ease myself out of Fox's embrace – the last time I will ever feel it. His face is magnificent, even in sleep. I dress quietly while I watch him, smiling softly – bitterly – at the fantasy of waking up to him like this every day. Collecting my boots in my hand, I pad over to the bed where I stretch over his still healing back and place a soft kiss on his cheek.

Then I leave the room, gently closing the door behind me.

Theo is already in front of the fire when I come out, looking at the clothes Fox and I left there. His face is sad when he sees me. He points vaguely at the suit and dress crumpled together – a memory of a different life.

'I don't think this means what I hope it does, does it?' he asks.

'If you mean does it change that he's marrying someone from Rehdree – no.'

He pulls at his unruly hair, pain flickering over his face as he looks at me in the pre-dawn light. I follow the regret creeping across his face, over his straight nose and pulling the skin near his eyes, tugging at me for what I haven't been able to give him. But he just nods slowly and stands.

'Let's go,' he says.

I let go of the breath I'd held, bracing myself for his apologies, unsure if I'm strong enough to hear them. Not when I have failed him, too. I didn't protect him from our mother, and I haven't been able to put our 'family' back, as he calls it. The three of us always a team, even when I thought one was absent for so long.

We walk the halls in silence, the slumbering manor calm around us. There's an anxious skitter to Theo's steps, and I don't blame him. We're finally at the end of this nightmare and we can go home.

If I can prove to Roan that we will give away no secrets of Oskrinya. If what he saw between Fox and I last night doesn't delay us. But I was truthful in my stance that I won't make it difficult. Fox is a … complex dream. A beautiful one, but complicated. Theo and Marley – they are my life. And I will give them everything I have.

CHAPTER TWENTY-SIX

Aestais is tying her purple hair back from her face when we enter her pale room. She's got the fire well stocked this morning, and my skin laps up the delicious warmth spreading through the space.

She smiles generously at us.

'An exciting day for you both, I think? The claim will be gone when you leave this room,' she says.

Her blue eyes rake over each of us and she cocks her head to the side, the deep scarlet paint on her throat rippling as she does. She makes a sound behind that paint, her eyes narrowing. 'Perhaps you've each become a little more attached to Oskrinya than you expected?'

'Perhaps,' Theo says flatly. 'Or one of us fell back in love, only to have it snatched away again.'

'Theo,' I admonish, but what can I really say? There doesn't seem much point hiding anything from Aestais. We won't be here much longer anyway.

'Please don't say anything,' I ask her. 'It's nothing, really.'

'I thought you didn't like secrets?' she says.

I frown slightly. I don't, but I don't recall telling her that before.

'Theo's exaggerating, and I promised Roan I wouldn't make his alliance with Rehdree difficult.'

She watches us for a long time. Long enough for Theo to start to fidget under her gaze.

'There are many paths to the same destination,' she says.

She gestures for Theo to take the bed as per normal.

'The Oskrinya have been hunted for so long, it's hard to remember a time they truly knew peace before Roan,' she says, grabbing the sage she always burns at the start of a session. 'They've gone from being violently targeted by Rehdree, who coveted our lands, to vilified by prophecy Koamah for the attacks on those people. Being wrongly – and so very publicly – accused of those crimes is a terrible thing for a people to bear.'

The sage smoke drifts around the room before finding its way out the window she has cracked.

'It caused a lot of in-fighting, too,' she continues as she gathers her gold nail tips. 'Even the Oskrinya believed the stories at first, raging at Roan as to why he'd attack Koamah without their knowledge – needlessly sacrificing the sons of Oskrinya. But it's not something we can stop until we know who is behind it.' She glances at me as Theo removes his shirt, but not for his privacy. 'We feel for the people of Koamah, you realise, even if it's disappointing they don't see the truth. But we know you are controlled by an incomplete understanding, a terrifying twisting of the prophecy, and genuine fear of the false Oskrinya.'

I widen my eyes at her. I don't know why I expected her to think differently, to not truly believe in the prophecy, even though we've talked about it before. Perhaps because she would be banished and likely executed in Koamah for being what she is, I didn't expect her to believe in the same things as a regime that would persecute her.

The nails tinkle, a sound at odds with the pain they create.

'I don't know if it's fear of the prophecy itself so much,' I say eventually, 'as fear of the military's actions to avoid it.'

'And do you know why they take such actions?' she asks as Theo shifts himself into position. 'Why they would go to such lengths to enforce an incomplete understanding of the prophecy instead of trying to learn its true meaning?'

I open my mouth to answer, but I realise I don't have a good one. I've been so focused on the *how* of my life – completely unable to answer the *why* of my mother and her actions with Theo and me – I eventually gave up asking for reasons. I never even asked Theo *why* he wanted to go into competition with Atticus. If I think about that now, I would say it was because he wanted to share some of the burden of our life. But back then, I just saw it as another obstacle to get through.

As Theo sits up on his elbows to listen, I almost feel like I'm looking at a slightly different version of him. Was that why he tried to set up that ridiculous business – to help? Not because he was a reckless kid who didn't know any better?

'I do not believe the purpose of the prophecy is to have people cowering in fear,' she continues, the last of her nails slipping into place, 'but knowing the second part of it is likely the only way to change that.'

'If only you were our Queen instead,' I mutter. 'So, what do you think the second part of the prophecy is? And why is Koamah so frightened of the first part when Oskrinya doesn't seem to be?'

She looks between us for a long moment, as if preparing herself for a hard conversation, and I can't imagine how we look to her – a brother and sister so far in over their heads it's laughable? Or just two people with good hearts, trying to do the right thing?

'Did you know Koamah leaders, and the rest of the Kingdom, used to have Varelai as advisers?' she asks.

'Witch advisers?' Theo asks. 'Wow – ours must have really pissed off the King.' The small smile in the shape of his mouth is immediately replaced by a look of intense curiosity. One that makes my heart beat a little faster.

'Don't go looking for the second part,' I say to him. 'Not now.'

'Yes,' Aestais says slowly, ignoring my comment, 'I believe your last one did.'

'And what could be so offensive to cause them to want to wipe out witches altogether?' I ask, not sure I really want to know.

What I do know is that what I – and Marley – can do with different ingredients, like those lining the shelves next to me, is enough for us to be included as 'witches'. And that is enough for me to stay as far away as possible. Except for right now, of course, when I have to help Theo. And that includes keeping him from getting too attached to the knowledge at his fingertips. But we are a long way from Koamah right now.

'What else but stand in the way of a powerful man and what he wants?' she replies.

'Which was what?' Theo asks, medallion now spinning in his hand.

Aestais draws a long breath, one that's not released in a sigh, more of a … rallying inhale.

'She advised your Queen not to ally, by marriage, to Solynara – not to marry King Boaz. The Queen had already agreed, with the support of her advisers, to a marriage with Oskrinya and her Varelai felt that was the better arrangement for the good of the people of Koamah. There was something in Boaz she didn't trust. But Boaz's influence was stronger than hers in the end, and the Solynaran marriage went ahead. She was banished, and later all witches hunted. Boaz uses the twisted interpretation of the prophecy to support the outlawing of magic and to hold on to his seat of power in Koamah. I believe the first part of the prophecy actually tells what will happen if we don't know, or understand, or somehow bring about the second part. But without being able to know what that is – and most people not knowing it even exists – the King is able to do what he likes while the Queen is absorbed in her superstitions.'

'And Oskrinya was and is left in the cold,' I say, shuddering at the weight of responsibility that Theo could bear. One I have just asked him to step away from, condemning Koamah to never change in the process.

'With enemies on both sides. At that point in time, at least,' she says, her gaze turning a fraction softer. 'It seems part of our predicament is to be rectified.'

By Fox marrying into Rehdree.

I clear my throat.

'If you think the second part is so important, why are you not asking me to find out what it is?' Theo asks, medallion spinning faster.

'Well,' Aestais says, brows lifting a little, 'some *would* say that's the greatest secret of all. Knowing both how to bring about the prophecy – or stop it – essentially gives the bearer of the medallion power over the whole world. Individual countries and alliances mean nothing under the weight of a prophecy for the whole world. If Boaz knew the whole prophecy, would he be even more powerful? Probably – he knows what the prophecy says about ending the world, imagine what he could do if he knew how to save it, too. But what if saving the world isn't his goal? What if his other values outweigh the continued existence of our world as we know it?

'But I also believe the prophecy is more complicated than simply knowing. These things are usually a train of events that start well before we even think to consider the consequences of our choices. And for you, dear Theo, to be so untempted by the secrets of the medallion ... I would suggest that's quite clear evidence you are destined for something else entirely.'

I can't help my gaze sliding to Theo, who stares at Aestais. Boaz's values. All I know of them is that it doesn't include a broad spectrum of women's rights – or any real value for human life. My stomach turns over itself as I look at Theo. What I would give to read that look, to know if we are on the same page or not. To know what guidance I need to give him to steer him away from finding those secrets – ones that could have him going up against Boaz and all he stands for. Away from the mystery, the power, and back towards safety. The known. Away from whatever destiny Aestais thinks might be in store for him.

Back to me.

'Do you know what any of it means?' he asks her and I swallow, imploring her with my eyes to not tempt him too far down the path of keeping the medallion.

She doesn't look at me, but I can't help but feel like Aestais understands the curiosity, the ... desire ... that might be piqued in a young man who suddenly has not only a crown, but the world potentially at his fingertips.

Or in the palm of his hand.

'I know,' she says carefully, 'that it can be interpreted in different ways. I know that medallion was created by a most powerful Varelai, and I trust that the many generations that have come before me have always had good intent for this world. So, I trust that the key to the prophecy was hidden away for good reason – in the wrong hands it could be lethal to many more than Boaz banishes or executes.'

The words Aestais speaks are heavy, laden with truth. Theo and I look at each other – giving the medallion to Atticus suddenly feels like a very bad idea. I'm not sure that much power should be held by any one individual. And I certainly don't think Theo and I are qualified to decide who is. After all, everyone has their secrets.

'I also know,' she says, moving back towards Theo, who doesn't lie back down, 'that the pursuit of all knowledge can mean losing oneself. That, sometimes, knowing all the secrets can be more than any one person can hold. In the case of the medallion, only one who binds themselves to be a guardian can know *all* it does, and they can never share that knowledge.'

A gentle breeze seems to pick up in the room slightly and my skin prickles.

'Making that medallion was the final act of the first Varelai,' she says. 'And more than one has made great sacrifices to keep it safe. Shall we?' She gives Theo a meaningful look, gesturing towards the bed.

My pulse is loud in my ears as I turn to Theo once more, the intensity on his face one I very rarely see.

Slowly, he lowers himself back down on the bed and I watch Aestais's shoulders relax a fraction. A feeling that is mirrored in my gut.

She kneels above Theo's head on the bed as she's done before. He grips the bed frame and I notice he's not been tethered this time. As if he's practiced in this pain now.

'Rubes,' he says tentatively. 'Do you mind waiting outside.'

I smart. My skin actually stings like he's struck me.

'Oh, sure. I … yes.'

Aestais turns sympathetic eyes on me, indecision there. 'The burden of secrets can be heavy, he wishes to spare you knowing more than you need.'

Theo sucks in a breath as the nails prick his skin.

'Tell me though, Rubilena,' she says, 'would you want to know the secrets if they were about you?'

I think of Fox's duplicity in our childhood, Theo's actions that led me to Atticus, the look on his face just now when he could have decided to keep the medallion. Would I have loved Fox then if I knew? Would I have wanted to know what Theo was doing before it all blew up in our faces? Do I want to know now just how tempted he was?

'It would depend what it was,' I say, gathering the little scraps of my pride and leaving Theo to face this final test on his own.

But he's carried a huge burden all this time, too; he deserves to see it through in his own way.

He's beaten it, after all.

CHAPTER TWENTY-SEVEN

Fox is standing in the hallway when I focus my eyes, arms crossed over his chest. The space is filled with him, close enough for me to reach out and touch. I keep my hands by my sides, fingers stinging with the fresh memories of how he felt beneath them.

'You left,' he says quietly. The hypocrisy of his statement flickering in his face.

'I wasn't sure what else to say.' My voice is laden with guilt, he's not the only hypocrite in this.

'These came for you.' He passes me another thin pile of letters and my heart leaps.

This time, Theo and I have letters from both Ash and Papa; the latter I tuck away to read with Theo later. Ash's update is good but bare, like there's something he's not saying – or something he didn't want read by someone else. But then we've never written to each other before, so perhaps it's just his writing style.

Marley's drawn me another picture – of soldiers in the street. One of them is in an Oskrinya uniform. The blood drains from my face and I feel every drop leave. Wordlessly, I hand the picture to Fox.

'Do you have anyone in the city right now?' I ask, trying to keep my voice steady. Keep my mind from racing forward to Marley being in a city with—

Is it another attack? One in which they killed Koamans without thought, or care – or just the blood.

So much blood.

'What—shit,' he says, eyes sparking as he deciphers the drawing.

The hallway thuds quietly as Brode approaches, watching the two of us. Fox drags his gaze from me and I feel colder without it. Exposed. Like the reality of that drawing is about to come crashing down on me.

'Still no word from our outposts,' Brode says by way of greeting. 'But I've had word from Koamah City.'

The tension that ripples through Fox is palpable. He looks at the door that hides Theo.

'Has there been more secrets?' he asks me.

'No.' At least, I don't think so. Theo's face just now, his clear request that I not be in there …

I don't have to ask Fox if we should be concerned about Marley's drawing, or the lack of communication from his patrols – it's written all over him.

'Aestais's work should have made it harder to pinpoint who has it and exactly where it is, but we can't rule out that others are already on their way here,' Fox says.

'Could it have brought the Rehdree early?' Brode asks.

My breathing is loud in my ears. Theo is here, Marley is there. With false Oskrinya. Nausea threatens to overtake me, my face going numb.

'I don't know,' Fox says. 'But we should make Roan aware, just in case. And send a second wave of scouts to the outposts.'

I gasp as Theo's scream pierces the air and close my eyes. Leaning against the door, I find I can't look at Brode or Fox. Can't see them wondering why I'm not in there for this monumental event. My hand lifts to the door as I turn back to face it so I don't have to look at their questioning faces.

Instead of reaching for the handle, I rest my palm on the timber. Focus on the sound of his scream.

He'll be okay, he's okay. I chant to myself.

And then we're going home to protect Marley and the rest of our family from those soldiers – today. I can't bring myself to think about how long the journey home is. How many people might be dying in the meantime.

It can't be them. It can't be them. Ash and Papa – they'll keep her safe. They'll keep her safe.

'He's just trying to prove his independence.' I jump as Fox's voice whispers in my ear. I didn't hear him cross the hallway.

I nod, unable to form words. Listening to my baby brother, *mine*, cry out a sound that sends chills down my spine is worse than Aestais's nails lodging in my own chest. I want to be in there, I want to feel that wound, have that pain. Anything to stop his screaming. And I need to be with Marley, the abyss that yawns in the depths of my gut at not having her with me threatens to devour me whole.

Please, don't let her be screaming too.

The sound goes so long I sag to the floor, on my knees before Aestais's room.

Fox stands beside me, his fingers trailing soothingly in my hair. I lean against his leg, my head on his thigh as I wait. All I can do is wait with him for Theo to be done. Then I can help him again. Then I hold Marley again.

They'll be okay.

My bones feel like they're shaking, the floor below me literally trembling with my impotence. My inability to help either of—

'What is that?' Brode asks.

I'm only vaguely aware of him, Marley's picture overlaying Theo on the bed in my mind. False Oskrinya soldiers, machetes drawn. Screaming. Aestais. The medallion.

Fox's hand leaves my hair and his thigh tenses under my cheek.

I stand, the shaking floor making me stumble into Fox. He holds me there, and I don't move away. Brode's gaze moves up and down the hallway, but no one appears.

A blinding light ignites beneath the door to Aestais's and we're thrown backwards, a slithering spark surging through my chest and out the other side. The breath is forced from my lungs as I slam into the wall, head cracking on the timber moulding halfway down. My vision goes blurry momentarily, but no blood comes away on my fingers when I tentatively touch my scalp.

If nothing else, my fighting with Atticus has taught me to get up quickly, despite the blows I receive. My feet are steady as I leap into a crouch. Brode blinks groggily as he steps away from the wall, a small crack where his head connected with it.

Fox is in front of me – I didn't even see him recover – pulling me from the crouch.

'You good?' he asks.

'What the fuck was that?' Brode asks, rubbing the back of his head.

Silently, we all look to Aestais's door as it opens and a wild Varelai witch steps out, terror flying into the hallway with her. She grips the door frame, holding herself upright. Theo's blood stains the ends of her nails. I shove past her, knocking her into the frame with a grunt, my eyes scanning every inch of the room.

'Theo!' I scream, a constriction winding through me, the walls pressing in. 'Theo!'

'Here,' he says hoarsely.

I spin to find him leaning against the bookshelves, sliding his shirt back on. Racing to him, I grip his head in my hands.

'Oh fuck,' I breathe. 'Are you okay?'

He looks over my shoulder, at the others who I can hear have joined us. I listen to the door close before I collect myself enough to let go of Theo's face. His gaze bores into mine as I release him, silently convincing me he's okay.

'Was that you?' Fox asks, no sign of the brewing panic I feel in his voice. His control almost calms me. Almost.

'Me or the medallion, but yeah,' Theo says. The rawness of his throat still evident in his speech. 'I think it was a ... distress signal.' He drags his hands over his face.

Aestais pales further, the paint starker against her skin.

'I ... I didn't know it could do that,' she says, starting to move restlessly around the room. She plucks books from her shelf, flicks through them and discards them. Her eyes not really seeing. 'It's not meant to be able to do that.'

The door flies open and Roan skids to a halt, slamming it again behind him.

'Tell me what the fuck that was. Now.'

No one speaks for a moment. It's Fox who takes the lead when it's clear neither Theo or Aestais can say anything. Aestais rings her hands around the long ends of her hair.

'The medallion sent out a'—he frowns—'a distress signal.'

Roan's sudden composure makes me doubt he's understood.

'I think,' Theo says quietly, 'it panicked about losing its claim on me. It wants a home. And so it's put out the call.'

Roan shuts his eyes as Fox and Brode look at each other. A single moment passes before they launch into plans. To send stealth scouts to the outposts instead of their regular ones; pull remaining food sources inside the walls of Hartfield; advise the surrounding towns and assist evacuations to Hartfield; hide the medallion; prepare—

'Wait,' I interrupt the methodical, ordered voices. 'We need to go home.'

The three of them stare at me. Brode glancing to Theo, who's still leaning on the bookshelves behind me.

'No,' Roan says abruptly.

I go deathly still. How dare he try to keep me from my daughter. There's a fizzing in my blood that hums in my ears. I step forward, fingers curling together. It's been a little while since I hit something, the desire to change that quickly focuses my gaze.

Fox steps between us.

'We need to go home,' I repeat, slowly, looking solely at Roan. 'The claim is gone, you can have the medallion for all I care. We're leaving.'

'I have already told you,' Roan says levelly, 'I do not want the medallion. I offered Aestais's help in good faith that you wouldn't rush home and betray Oskrinya. You will not leave until I am satisfied that is the case.'

I take another step forward, Fox now close enough for me to feel the heat coming off him. But he doesn't stop me, yet.

'And I am telling *you*, my daughter is in the City of Koamah without me. With false Oskrinya soldiers on our streets. I will *not* be stopped from getting to her.'

Roan looks between us, the news of false Oskrinya in Koamah is obviously news to him, too.

Theo swears.

A slow throb starts in my jaw.

Roan watches me, too calmly.

'Ruby,' Fox says gently, a hand lifting to me, stroking the back of my arm. 'You can't leave on your own.'

A hole opens up inside me. 'What?'

I glare at him.

'I know I promised to take you back to Koamah but—'

I step back, out of his circle of warmth, a vice pressing in around my skull.

'Think carefully before you finish that sentence,' Theo says from over my shoulder. The violence in his voice is new to me. But he loves Marley as much as I do, so it's no surprise he would also do anything to get back to her.

Fox drops his hand. 'We need to be smart about this.' The gentle tone is slowly replaced with that of a calculating soldier. 'There are two possible threats here – that one or more armies are currently descending on Oskrinya right now, and false Oskrinya in Koamah – we believe.'

I start to insist it's not a belief, it's a fact. Marley hasn't been close enough to those bastards to know their uniforms before. There is no possible way she has made up the olive-green-uniformed, machete-wielding assholes in that drawing.

Fox half lifts two fingers to halt me. I stare at him, my chest rising and falling heavily.

'The first, I need to verify – urgently. If there are armies on their way, Oskrinya needs to be ready for them. The second means you and Theo going to Koamah could be suicide.'

'A risk that's not for you to decide,' I spit. Something flickers across his face. I grapple for calm. 'She's my *daughter*, Fox. The only way I will abandon her is in death.'

'I know, Ruby,' he sighs. 'I'm not suggesting you do. I'm suggesting we get her *out* instead of you going *in.*'

Theo's exhale behind me mirrors my own.

Marley out of Koamah.

I can do that.

'How?' I ask, not looking at Roan's impassive face.

I know my own is still hard when I look at Fox and wariness flashes behind his eyes. But there is a blinding pain in my chest that won't go until I have her safely in my reach once more.

He turns and looks at Brode. 'Get a message in, I want three of our contacts camped in their house as soon as possible. Okay?' The last bit is directed at me and I nod. 'Find Xave, tell him I'll meet him at my office – we have work to do here.'

That dark gaze returns to me and I ignore everyone else, an anxiousness stirring the deepest parts of me, desperately wanting to believe he can do this, he can help me get Marley. Protect her – protect Papa, and Ash, and Kaya. My heart is spread in too many different places and I don't know how to keep it together.

'We will have armed soldiers in your house before the day is out,' he says.

My heart plummets at the thought of that, too; this is not something she should have to experience. Ash will be beside himself. Despite our work, we have tried everything to keep violence from Marley's frame of reference.

'As soon as I know what reaction the medallion has incited, I can get her out.' He steps towards me again and lowers his voice. 'This is not because she's less important.' Unbidden tears prickle my eyes. I glare through them. 'It's the fastest way I can keep both her and Oskrinya safe. Okay? I *will* get her Ruby.'

Just not now, is what he's saying.

He pulls me closer and I want to be able to melt into him, to have the hole in me closed because of his presence. But my body is stiff and, as much as I yearn for him, the only person who will take the pain away is my daughter.

Marley and Theo make me whole and one of them isn't here.

I can change that.

Fox's contacts will be in there today, keeping them safe. I don't know exactly how long it will take me to get back. But, if I leave now, I will get there not too long after. Fox said get her out. He can't do that right now, and as much as it pains me – selfishly pains me – I understand his responsibility is to those in Oskrinya under threat.

But I can.

I can save Marley, while he protects Oskrinya.

CHAPTER TWENTY-EIGHT

The red dress eyes me from the corner of the bed. Gently placed there by someone – Trini or Fox, I don't know. Sweat beads on my forehead as clothes I've never laid eyes on fall to the floor or are shoved aside, spewing from the drawers as I rummage through them. I need the bag I came with, the pack Atticus gave me, and I can't for the life of me remember where it is. It was such an inconsequential detail when I arrived.

Fuck.

Theo's room.

I rifle through his things, but there's nothing familiar here, either. Except a drawing from Marley that halts the breath in my throat.

I'm coming, baby girl, I'm coming.

'What are you doing?' Theo asks.

My hands jerk, dropping his clothes. At least I have a reason he will find more palatable today than when I was forced to check his room at home.

'I was trying to pack.' I look around the room quickly, there's no bags here either.

'To do what?' he asks, but the look on his face says he probably already knows.

'I need to get her now, Theo. You're safe here with Fox and Brode, and I know they have things they need to do but I can't, I just can't, leave her there until Oskrinya is clear of threat. Can you get me a horse?'

I look back to him when he doesn't respond.

'A horse, Theo – can you move?'

He's spent so much time with Brode and those horses, he knows far more about them than I do. The hand he's massaging the back of his neck with drops back to his side.

'Horses,' he says. 'I'm coming, and don't even think about arguing.'

A beat passes and then he strides to the bed, dropping to his knees.

The two empty packs slide out.

'Thanks,' I mutter.

I throw pants, shirts, and a woolen jumper on the bed for him to pack. Moving to the cupboard, he catches the cloak I throw at him in one hand.

'We'll need weapons,' he says. 'Brode showed me them too – I'll grab some on the way. Food?'

'And water.' I close my eyes to think for a moment. 'They're stock piling, let's see what we can find on the way out.'

'Wait,' he says, stilling for a moment. 'What if they don't let us out the gate?'

'Then we go over the wall.'

'With no horses?'

Shit.

'We'll make them let us out,' I say, thinking of the knuckles Fox gave me. 'I can't stay here and wait, Theo – I just – I can't *sit* here.'

I move for the sitting room, taking the other pack with me to fill.

It took us three days to get here from Koamah, but Fox took us the long way, aiming first for the Varelai. If we go directly south, we should be able to cross the border into Koamah in one and a half. Less if we travel through the night. And I don't intend to stop.

A squeal snaps me to attention as I almost collide with a body.

'You gave me a heart attack!' Trini exclaims, pressing her hand to her chest.

I smile to cover the hammering in mine, but it feels like a grimace. 'Maybe you're just jumpy today.'

'So should you be,' she says tersely. 'We're about to be under attack.'

Heat burns across my cheeks and down my neck. I have one job as Marley's mother – protect her at all costs.

'How long?' The words are thick in my mouth and I almost choke.

She looks down at the bag in my hand, the fist it's clenched in.

'Not long enough for you to get clear, Rubilena.' Her voice softens but it brings me no comfort. 'I know you feel you need to go ... I'm so sorry, I can't even—'

'Please. Don't.'

I don't want to be rude, not to Trini, but I can barely focus on the words coming from her mouth. I have no capacity to hear apologies for something so far out of her control. There are lines around her eyes when I properly look at her face. Parts of her auburn hair sticking out, one strand stuck to the side of her sweaty face.

'Who told you how close they are?'

'Xave,' she says quietly, searching my eyes.

It makes sense he would make sure she knows everything; I haven't forgotten how they looked at each other last night.

How long ago that now seems.

'Who are they?' I ask.

'The false Oskrinya,' she says softly. 'They've surrounded our southern border. You'd have to go through them to get home – if you could get through Fox's units first.'

Theo places a hand on my shoulder and squeezes. 'I'll find Brode, see if there's anything he can do. Another way.'

My head moves up and down slowly of its own accord, but I know there's nothing. Even if there was, I highly doubt Brode would go against Fox's wishes. Orders.

I have two impossible choices – leave Marley where she is, knowing how terrified she will be, or take Theo straight into an oncoming army.

With nothing else I can do, I pace. Visions of Marley filling my head, the phantom feel of her arms around my neck, her little body pressed against mine. The wild blonde hair that tickles my nose, the tantrum she threw because I poured her milk wrong. I press the sides of my head with my hands as I pace, my body threatening to come apart.

How shockingly I have failed her.

Trini claps her hands and I jump. 'Come, we have work to do.'

She's a rigid taskmaster but, eventually, I welcome the distraction. I hadn't given Trini's role much thought before, but it's now clear she runs Roan's manor. Or the staff in it, anyway.

The hall is rearranged with a combination of long and small round tables in one half and empty space in the other. Piles and piles of bedrolls and blankets are stacked against the walls on the empty end. Wood is stocked in the fires and smaller collections of toys and books for children are deposited in a corner.

I trail Trini as she rushes from room to room in the manor, checking on all the preparations – everyone seemingly understanding their role. Satisfied with the inside of the manor, she takes me outside. Even here the air is coated in anticipation. It rolls around inside the walls, unable to break over and free, the weight of it on the shoulders of everyone I pass.

Structures have been placed at staggered places along the walls, two sets of steps leading up to each. Horses are saddled and loosely tethered outside the stables. I expect them to be shifty, radiating the fear in the air, but they stand still. The same as the horses in the fight I jumped into.

Followed Fox into.

It's a physical effort to push away the image of the man Fox killed for me. The one I held down to have his throat slashed. Is that what's happening in Koamah City right now? Men, women, and children being slaughtered?

I scan the spaces we pass in Hartfield, the market square, town hall, the stables. But there's no sign of Theo or Fox. Or Xave or Brode. I glance at Trini to find her doing the same – eyes jumping over the town. Then she straightens and focuses her eyes in the direction of the back wall and I know where she's headed.

Fox's office is filled with broad, muscled, and now uniformed, men. The olive-green still sends an immediate chill along my limbs, until I remember to look for the jet on the collars. Even then it takes a moment for the feeling to return to my lips.

They're different, Rubilena. Not the people currently in Koamah.

Their conversation halts entirely as we enter the room, the papers they look over curling up at the edges on Fox's desk. I slip a hand into my pocket and finger the cool jet knuckles he gave me.

Xave's chest relaxes a little when he looks at Trini. She holds his gaze for a beat and looks away, her eyes finding mine as a desperate place to land. She lifts her chin slightly, but remains silent, her focus shifting between Fox, Xave, and me.

I open my mouth to ask what's happening, but Fox talks before I can. Whatever secrets he might keep from the general population to avoid panic, it's clear he won't keep them from me. Something that would have been useful years ago, but that life now seems so unimportant compared to what we face now.

His dark eyes soak me in, hesitant but resolved.

'Less than an hour,' he says.

The heaviness in his words finds me slowly, but it finds me all the same. The people who filled the hall at Roan's dinners dance around me. The laughter that sounded echoes in my ears. Now that laughter will be replaced by screams. By the dying sounds of the people of Oskrinya, people I once thought should die. Until I knew who they really are, and what they haven't done. Until I knew them as the people of Hartfield.

And they will die because I brought Theo here.

Like I watched the people of Koamah die.

Spots appear in my vision and I blink to clear them.

'I've been looking for you.'

Theo's voice brings the focus back into the room, and I turn to him. His mouth drops into an 'O' as he realises he has a greater audience than expected. 'Sorry,' he says, glancing at me. 'I was hoping to talk to Brode.'

'It's okay, Theo,' I say, Fox's gaze hot on my face. 'There's work to do. The Oskrinya—' Xave bristles, although not at me directly. At how easy it is for people to forget it's not them. 'The false Oskrinya,' I correct, 'are almost here. There's no time.'

'No,' he says, his eyes shining. 'There has to be time.'

Fox looks between us, his shoulders sagging a little.

'Only time to prepare,' Fox says.

He walks to me, uncaring of the opinions of the others in the room. His hand winds up my neck and behind my head, pulling it to his chest. The fabric is stiff under my forehead, but the warmth of his body seeps through.

'Ruby,' he breathes, leaning down to talk against my ear, 'I will get her. I promise.'

I let three tears fall, their tracks clear on his shirt.

Clearing my throat, I lift my head. Meeting his gaze head-on is almost a mistake, and I grit my teeth to contain the sob that wants to escape. The desperate scream for Marley that builds in my chest.

'What do you need us to do?' I ask.

'Be safe,' he answers, without missing a beat. 'Trini will take you back to Roan's. There's—'

'No. Out here, what do you need? I can fight, you know this. Theo can help Trini with the kids—'

'Not a chance.' It's Theo's turn to interrupt.

I turn away from Fox and look back at Theo. He's wearing fighting leathers. My stomach falls to the floor, a familiar weariness settling into my bones. We've done a similar dance many times before.

'Theo,' I say gently, 'you can't be out here.'

I walk to him, leaving the others to discuss the rest of their arrangements around Fox's desk behind me.

Hazel eyes burn through the slits he's narrowed his eyes to.

'I can, and I will, Rubes. This is on us. On *me*.'

He's trying to hold back the anger in his voice, much like he did when he was a child and didn't want me to know something. He's never really believed how readily I can read him, anyway. But, I think, remembering his face when Aestais talked of the prophecy, maybe I don't know everything he's thinking.

I shake my head. 'No, Theo. I won't allow you to be out here, or over the wall, when they arrive.'

'You don't get to make that call.'

He's so much taller than me now, almost as big as Fox. My eyes run over his body, his stance is weak right now though. He doesn't expect me to do anything physical to stop him.

He's wrong.

'I'm afraid I do, and it's no.'

Someone coughs slightly behind me – I ignore them. Theo balls his hands into fists at his side. He shifts on his feet, correcting his stance slightly, but this push and pull between what he wants and what I know is best for him is an emotional fight I have had with him a thousand times, and I won't back down now. Someone needs to protect him, keep him safe.

And that falls to me. Always has, always will.

He's mine.

He widens his stance and crosses his arms over his chest. If I didn't know him, my heart rate would be slightly elevated as I prepared to take him down. Starting with a kick to the knee that's currently holding most of his weight.

'You fight, I fight, Rubilena. I'll accept nothing else.'

'I—' the back of my neck tingles where the others watch and I lower my voice. 'No, Theo. I'm not sure what's so hard to understand about that.'

Trini moves to my side and the voices behind me go quiet.

'You don't get to tell me no, Rubes, not in this.'

His voice is quiet, serious. The voice of a man and not a child. But he's still a child to me.

I raise my palms at him, placating. I'd prefer not to do this with an audience, but he's not giving me a lot of choice. Part of me wants to let him get a win here, in this room of strong and capable men he's diligently trying not to look at. But the thought of Theo going anywhere near those soldiers who decimated families in Koamah, left the dying in the street, who bound us and dragged us behind their horses, who now march on Hartfield to kill and maim in pursuit of the medallion, is one that hollows me out.

Replacing all that I know with an all-consuming blackness.

He will not fight them.

'Theo,' I try again, willing calm into my words. 'Listen—'

'For fuck's sake!' His hands fly up as he gives into the wave of frustration. 'You can't tell me what I can and can't do – you're not even my fucking sister!'

The world stills. Trini grips my elbow.

'Really, Theo,' I say quietly, raising my brows – pleading with my eyes for him to see reason. 'You've moved on from telling me I'm not your mother, now I'm not your sister, either? How childish do you want to be?'

I regret those last words as soon as they're out, the quick clench of his jaw shows the sore spot I've hit. And it's a low one.

But it's his lack of response that punches a hole where my heart is supposed to be, the truth written on his face. Aestais's words come back to me. *Would you want to know, Rubilena, if the secrets were about you?'* The ties that bind me to him pull taut – painfully cutting into me as the blood drains from his determined face – desperate to patch it over, pull him back close where he belongs.

'But you're mine,' I whisper, tears stinging at the sudden vacancy of another child's place in my soul.

I blink furiously as he curses under his breath, his hands on his head as he watches me trying not to go to pieces.

He takes a step towards me and I can't help but step back, accidentally pressing into someone's chest behind me. Inhaling, I recognise Fox's earthy scent, but it doesn't ground me this time.

'No ... no, that can't be right.' My words are so quiet I don't think he's heard me.

Then he shakes his head, tears on his own face.

'The medallion,' he says, his voice splintering. 'It told me.'

Fox's hands curl around my upper arms and hold me to him. My own hands flutter between my face and my chest, unsure what to do with themselves.

'I have a family,' Theo continues, 'but it's not you.'

I start to fold in the middle like I've been kicked in the stomach – the feeling is the same – Fox's hands the only thing keeping me from falling to the floor.

I watch Theo's grown face as his gaze travels over my head, the sounds in the room disappearing – sucked into a river of protests only I can hear.

Fox's hands squeeze me once before they slacken with realisation.

Over my head, leaving me under the current of their own, unique connection, drowning alone, Theo holds Fox's gaze, and I know who he means.

Who he really belongs to.

Who his family is.

CHAPTER TWENTY-NINE

'Tell me it's not right,' I demand.

Aestais turns to me when I enter her room without knocking, the door flying wide and hitting the wall behind. She watches it bounce back towards me, but makes no reprimand. Her once tidy room is strewn with open books and papers. The medallion, though, still sits in the white fabric she wrapped it in the first time we came here. A circle of calm around it, a space in which nothing can touch it.

Her sky-coloured eyes hold mine steadily, but there's a magnitude of other thoughts spiraling behind them.

'I don't hear the secrets that are shared,' she says. 'But his reaction would tell me it's true, yes.'

'I just – what am I supposed to do with this knowledge?'

As I scan her features, the knitted brows, the painting on her neck and face, I realise how desperately I need her to have this answer. Papa would tell me it makes no difference – that Theo is still Theo, regardless of his blood ties. We never knew who his father was, anyway. Mine, either.

But Papa's not here and, as I stare at the normally so collected Aestais and her disheveled room, it seems to reflect the turbulence of my insides. And I need the answers to my own chaos to be here, too.

I close the door as if it can hold the oncoming army at bay while I collect my pieces. As if they will patiently wait until I can recover from this and bring Theo back.

Aestais clasps her hands, the white of her knuckles showing the strain of the patience she gives me instead.

'I've done everything, *everything,* for him and my daughter.'

The ghost of every hit I've received in Atticus's club finds my body. The training, the blood. The soldier Marco killed so we could get away. The time I've spent away from Marley. Her face when I'd come home bruised, the disappointment on it.

'I *left* my daughter for him and he's not – he's not even mine?'

Cool hands take my own and lead me to a timber chair where Aestais pushes on my shoulders to make me sit.

Eons pass before she talks. I wait like a ghost, stuck in the moments of my life I've devoted to raising a stranger. My mother's face comes to mind and I wave it away, the energy to be angry with her will come later. For now, she doesn't register as much more than a flicker. The enormity of the direction she sent my life for a lie is just too big to understand.

Aestais kneels before me, taking my hands once more.

Up close, I can see the silver flecks in her pale eyes. The tiny creases at their corners.

'I won't ask you if it really changes anything,' she says in a papery lilt. 'You know the answer to that.'

She squeezes my hands in hers and I dimly note the scent of sage still in the room. And something like sweet orange.

'But ...' she says, and my gaze locks back on hers. 'I think he was brought into your life for a reason.'

I sigh. It's so like what Papa would say. My heart cracks a little further at telling him the truth. Perhaps I won't. There is only so much heartbreak a father should suffer because of their child. How unfortunate it is that child is my mother. I don't need to make Papa hurt more because of her lies.

'Don't dismiss me for a sentimentalist, Rubilena.'

I purse my lips. What else do I do with that statement?

'I need you to know something.' She glances at the door as if she can see where the army approaches the wall. 'You know Koamah's thoughts on the medallion are wrong ... incomplete. The prophecy as well. But did you know the Varelai that advised Koamah was once here, too?'

My eyes close of their own volition. That fucking prophecy always comes up at times I simply do not wish to discuss it. The weight of the crucified women and children, watching their lives blown apart, is something I can't forget. But I am powerless to take action without risking my own daughter.

And yet, you left her there anyway.

'To date, the theories on the medallion and the prophecy have been separate.' Aestais talks as if she can see the distaste on my face. 'We believed the medallion was created *because* of the prophecy – to bury its secrets. Other secrets were added to it over time and then it became all-powerful in its own right – know all the secrets of the world, and you can control those they affect.'

If Theo isn't related to me, why did my mother have him? Why did she leave him with us?

I try to push the questions aside – and the voice in the back of mind that wonders if the medallion could tell me – and focus on Aestais. On trying to follow what she's saying. What else she has found in the papers currently strewn around her room.

'And so, the medallion is unbelievably valuable,' she continues, 'it could literally contain the answer to the prophecy and how to save the world. This remains true.'

She pauses, thinking.

'But?' I ask.

'But ... what if the medallion and the prophecy are connected in a greater way than the knowing of secrets? What if the medallion is actively trying to fulfil the prophecy? What if it needed to get into the right hands for it to do that?'

My eyebrows shoot to the sky.

'As in ... it's sentient?'

She drops my hands and hurries to her table, picking up an old notebook. Scanning whatever she's got in there, she walks while she talks.

'Not necessarily sentient, but getting desperate as the magic of the prophecy begins to take effect.'

Are both Marley's and Theo's homes about to be destroyed?

I shake my head as I stand. 'I'm sorry, Aestais, I need to go. They're coming for that hunk of life-destroying metal and, whatever Theo is, he is not someone who's going to die on my watch. I can help—'

'Think about it,' she says, dropping the book to the floor and gripping my arm. 'Why wasn't it already claimed before Theo touched it? Why hadn't the Queen or King claimed it for themselves? Because it didn't *want* to be claimed by them.'

'Aes—'

'The signal – distress beacon, whatever you want to call it – has never been as strong in all of history.' She says this like I am supposed to understand.

'So ...' I venture, 'it let Theo claim it, and didn't appreciate him having the claim removed?'

'I think ... it let Theo take it because he was *closer* to where it wanted to end up.'

I search her face, but she looks like she's still putting this together as she talks aloud.

'And so by bringing him, and it, here ...' I say, not entirely convinced of anything other than my need to get out of this room, 'I brought it closer to where it wants to be?'

'Yes! And when I forced it from Theo, it panicked, desperate to be claimed by its rightful owner. Because its rightful owner, along with the medallion, will be able to fulfil the prophecy.'

My mouth falls open slightly.

Aestais stands tall. The light catches on the shape painted on her forehead.

'It's you,' I say. 'Aestais, if it's you – you need to take it. Stop the call to the armies!' I grip her shoulders and shake her slightly. 'You can stop the attack, Aestais. Take the fucking medallion!'

She shakes her head.

'It's not me, I tried, in a moment of desperation. The role of the Varelai remains true – we are guardians, advisers – not the rulers or destroyers.'

The breath leaves my lungs. It might be too late to stop the army that's about to crest the hill and storm these walls, but we can stop others.

'Then why is it painted on your skin?' My tone is more accusing than I'd intended.

'Because I am to help guide it and its owner come together. Help the secret of the prophecy be known. Shepherd them into stopping the dark gods.'

I take a moment, but it's not long enough to understand.

'Roan?' I ask, dropping my hands from her robes.

'I don't think so,' she says. 'He's shown almost no interest in it.'

I laugh then. Of course.

'Fox,' I say.

She nods slowly. 'It seems most likely.'

Of course it's fucking Fox.

I move to grab the medallion, less worried about touching the metal now I think it has a view on who it wants. The door flies open behind me and I spin, fists at my chin in less than a heartbeat.

Trini's not so perfect hair swings around her chin with the force she's entered the room, the door handle gripped in her hand.

'It's starting.'

Gone is the music and liveliness of Roan's hall. Replaced by a softly pulsing crowd, one ready to combust with the fear that seeps into every crevice. Weapons of all kinds punctuate the crowd. Many have short swords and blades tucked into their belts. A few have what look to be the pitchforks from the stables, and I can see at least two axes and a shovel.

Outside, Hartfield is far from quiet. People shout orders, tools bang, and the running of footfalls on the streets echo even in here.

Roan stands on the long table that featured the night my future with Fox was cemented. But perhaps Fox really did that a long time ago. Or I did, by not going after him.

Andvett Starrisson of Rehdree and Fox stand on either side of him. Fox's uniform has gone, replaced by fitted, black leathers that give my body a flicker of memory, despite the circumstances. I scan the room, but there's no sign of Theo.

The contents of my stomach start to churn.

Fox catches my eye and I hold my breath. Subtly he glances down, near to where he stands, and I understand.

Theo is there, with him.

'I will be quick, and frank,' Roan says, addressing the crowd. 'A large number of soldiers, parading as Oskrinya, march on us.'

The crowd is mostly silent, they know this already. It's what comes after that matters.

'We are ready to meet them head-on.' Roan gestures to Andvett. 'Rehdree is here in support and, today, we fight our first battle together. For an army that marches on one of us, now marches on the other.'

A deafening banging drums the floor and, over the heads of the crowd, I can just make out the top of bladed spears the Rehdree clans slam on the floor.

Silently, a blonde, fur and leather clad woman steps up on the table beside Fox. The multiple blades she wears along her strapping catch the light and she holds a long, pointed spear in her hand. Fox nods at her as she plants her feet and looks out at the crowd, chin lifted against the incoming threat.

The woman with the dagger.

He chose the one I would have.

Roan keeps talking and Fox meets the eyes of the people before him, showing them his courage and determination, imbuing them with the confidence in his ability to lead their forces to victory. To save their homes and their families.

Eventually, his gaze finds mine again and I want to kick myself for waiting to see how long it would take him to look me in the eye. I hold it because anything else feels too significant. I can't bring myself to nod, I said all I could say last night, but I still can't give this approval. But nor can I look away and send him into the enemy thinking I hate him – I am very far from hating him. And I certainly can't smile.

I just have to get through this. Get Theo through this – this battle – and then I'm going to Marley.

Time itself waits for us to decide our next steps as the room around me slips away. The blonde Rehdrian looks at Fox, nodding when he meets her gaze. They all leap off the table and the people around me burst into sound. I push through them, Trini hot on my heels, as I force my way to the side door they go out of. I know without doubt Brode has gone in that direction. And so has Theo.

Out to join the fighting.

Fox is shouting orders when I find them outside, it wasn't hard. There is a small army inside the walls of Hartfield – all clad in black leather – not an Oskrinya uniform in sight. If it's just practical to save confusion around who they kill, or because their patriotism has been clouded, I can't say. Although, seeing the sheer numbers of them taking up weapons probably tells me all I need to know about how they feel about Oskrinya.

They listen intently to Fox, not a single one questioning his commands, the tension in the air completely at odds with the gentle sunshine.

On the other side of the square are the Rehdree, most still in their white and grey furs.

Aestais strides out from somewhere, also in form-fitting black. A sword the length of my torso is strapped to her back. When she steps up, side by side with Fox, the soldiers of Oskrinya cheer, the sound vibrating through my bones.

Fox grins at her and she slams her sword into the sky, Fox's army following suit.

'Rubes.'

Theo is at my elbow and I yelp. Less in fear than relief, but his face is still resolute enough for my chest to crack a little further.

'I'll stay with Brode,' he says.

I look to the huge man beside him, his shirt done up all the way to his throat, covering the almost-healed wounds that are there, but I know they will still give him more grief than he needs today. There's a seriousness in his gaze that marginally lessens the worry in mine.

'Let's get changed,' Trini says urgently.

I let her take my hand and start pulling me away.

'Be safe, please,' I whisper to the man who used to be my brother.

Most of the teams Fox assigns are inside the walls, just to the sides of the gate, and dotted around the walls. I'm no strategist, but my guess is he doesn't want the oncoming forces to get a good feel for his numbers.

He sends four teams of about twenty each outside the gate to defend it. Led by Xave.

At first, the silent waiting is excruciating.

Not a soul in Hartfield makes a sound. I can't even hear any children, frightened or oblivious.

The wind blows a handful of leaves across the road where I stand, behind Fox's teams at the gates.

A roar sounds from outside and every person I can see tenses, their bodies twitching and ready to pounce.

The Rehdree who flank Fox's soldiers lean casually on their spears.

Theo trembles slightly next to me, and I hope Trini has locked herself away inside.

'I'm going to assume you're out here because you know how to use one of these?' Fox says as he winds his way towards us, holding out a long blade to me.

I look at it a moment.

The last time I held one, in an experimental fight, my opponent had a long healing process. Atticus added a large sum to my – Theo's – debts. 'You can't deprive me of fighters and not expect to pay,' he'd said. He's avoided fights with weapons since, but he still made me train with them. He liked the way swords built muscle, he said.

I nod at Fox.

Screams and shouts from the other side of the wall scurry through the square, winding their way around all of us who wait. Fox hands me the sword with one last, long look before he strides off. Another piece of my heart breaks off and follows him. How much of it is allowed to be owned by others? Others that don't belong to me.

Too soon, the brutal screams and chants of war are replaced by silence, and the timber gates groan under the strain of something slamming into them.

They splinter and crack, and an olive-green tide washes through the entrance, the sun shining on the excess of blood on their uniforms.

Uniforms with no jet pieces.

'Run!' I scream at Theo as the world around us explodes.

He drops into a partnered stance with Brode, slightly back-to-back so they watch each other. Reality crashes into me.

He is not the helpless child I've looked at every day.

He's been training.

And the machete he holds looks at home in his hands.

CHAPTER THIRTY

'Focus, Rubes!' Theo yells, and I snap back to the olive-green stream.

A tall man, a red beard on his chin, smiles at me as he shoves a true Oskrinya soldier aside. The soldier recovers quickly and slides a blade between his ribs. The red man's face slips into surprise as he falls to the ground.

The Oskrinya soldier spins away, slicing another of the enemy across the middle. Pink and white and red spill from his uniform. I look away and narrow my gaze to the olive-green uniform now striding towards Theo and Brode. They fight at least one soldier each, their machetes hacking wherever they land.

The metallic sound joins that of the metallic smell that clogs my nose.

They've only moved a handful of steps to the side. I leap over the fallen Oskrinya beside me, I didn't see him die, and slide my blade across the back of the heels of the man encroaching on Theo. He drops to the ground with a yell and Brode drives a blade into his chest, subtly spinning Theo behind him.

He looks at me and things become crisper then.

Theo is with Brode.

Right now, it's better than being with me. I can barely keep track of who is dying and who is a threat.

My skull rattles as an elbow finds my temple. A whirl of fur and blonde spins beside me, an enemy soldier falling at her feet. She holds out a hand to pull me straight, and I don't hesitate to take it. Her face is half covered in blood, but there's something familiar about her – about all the Rehdree that have filled Roan's halls. But there's something more about her, like she was in the line of women who were introduced—

'Inglet,' she says by way of introduction. Her voice is slightly accented and even more breathless. 'You going to get in the game here, or are you asking to be slaughtered?'

Olive-green uniforms swarm with black leathers and blood colours everything.

Theo and Brode remain a unit, even as they move further away from me. I spin.

'He's fine,' she says, not having to ask who I look for. I don't have room to be secretive about it. 'Ready?'

It's late for her to be asking the question, given the blood and the death that surrounds us, but it's what I need. Wordlessly, I follow her as she springs into action. Her spear taking down those too far to reach with my sword, my fists catching anyone that gets beyond the two stages of our defences.

Fox makes a shout and abruptly she peels off to go to him.

'You like to fight, little girl,' says a soldier, spitting at my feet and nodding at the jet spikes on my hands.

I arc my sword towards him, his lifting in response. The impact when they join fires down my arms. My skin pinches under the knuckles where they grip the underside of my fingers.

'I don't like to fight,' I say, teeth gritted as I stalk him, blow after blow.

His eyes go a fraction wider as he realises he's underestimated me. But it's only a moment's reprieve, and then he pushes back, a glancing slice landing across my ribs before his sword presses dangerously close to my face. Held back only by the pressure I force into mine. He holds it there, the silver blade taking most of my vision.

I drop my left hand and drive it up into his chest.

His muddy green eyes go completely wide then, his sword arm giving. His blade tumbles to the stone road slowly. I watch it go before I look back to him, his chest blooming with the blood of a thousand bodies. The holes are small in his uniform where the spikes on my knuckles have pierced. But they've run through something vital in his chest, and blood pushes through in great chugging throbs.

'I fight because I have to,' I say, turning away before I watch him fall to the ground as well.

Inglet is holding her own against three soldiers when I find her.

There's no sign of Theo or Brode.

Or Fox.

Trini flashes in my mind when I realise I haven't seen Xave come back in from outside the walls, either.

We fight on, my sword taking who it can, my knuckles pulverising the rest. My left hand isn't my strongest, but it's the one I use now the most. My right's grip on the sword is too strong to let go, it's a safety net of distance. And the blood that now coats my left would only compromise its grip on the handle.

And so it goes. Slashing with my right and smashing with my left.

'Andi!' The terror in Inglet's face is at odds with the calculated calm she's been smothered in until now. She's across the square from me; I watch as she lashes out at the soldier gaining on her, cutting him down.

Then she runs towards me.

I land another upper cut into the stomach of the man before me and kick him away. Over my shoulder, I see what's captured her whole attention.

Andvett is pressed against the inside of the wall of Hartfield, seven – maybe eight – uniformed soldiers circling him. He spins a double ended axe over his head in one hand, the white fur of his vest clumped with blood.

Inglet hasn't reached me yet and I glance between them – the distance between Andvett and me is much less.

From where I am, it's clear his gaze is not on those in front of him, but her. The blonde force of nature carving down her opponents in an attempt to get to him. I think of Theo, of Fox. Of Marley.

I run.

The bodies that fall around me are soundless as I focus on Andvett and the men that press in. Vaguely, I hear them taunting the leader of the badlands. A head flies, victim to Andvett's axe, and they quiet. But they don't back away.

Seven remain and still I run, leaping over the dead.

'Andi!' Inglet screams again, this time in rage.

The sounds of the battle are louder now as I give myself to the moment and act. The soldiers surrounding the Rehdree leader don't hear my laboured breathing, I imagine they thought they'd cleared this part of the square. I slash at the back of the first's thighs and he goes down. Spinning to the next, I slam my spikes into his spine. He doesn't make a sound as he drops, legs crumpled beneath him.

Andvett's axe swings again and a dark head of hair rolls by my feet.

Pulp covers my hands as I drive my sword and the spikes into everything olive-green. My skin tightens as Inglet watches me, running and fighting her way over.

I don't know who he is to her, and I don't care. The fear that ripples from her is all too familiar, and I will save him if it means one less person can have their life ripped out from beneath them. If one less person can be powerless to stop the void that opens up when those most precious are taken or gone.

There are two left, and Andvett and I take one each.

Andvett's is hoisted in the air with the force of his axe up and into his chest cavity.

Mine watches me as his throat gapes open.

He's younger than Theo.

I stare at Andvett, his breathing heavy, dark-blonde beard smattered with almost as much blood as his vest. Inglet grinds to a halt when she reaches us and Andvett's fiery stare finds her instead. They stand there for what feels like an eternity, the sounds dying away behind me.

Awareness pulls at me and I turn to find Fox on the other side of the square, bloodied machete in hand. There is a mountain of dead between us, and yet nothing at all. But I can't tell if he's horrified at the brutality behind the deaths I've delivered, or happy his gift for me was the right one.

He points, my question not even asked yet but there, a little further along, are Theo and Brode. Brode with his hand on Theo's shoulder and talking softly to him.

A groan to my left drags my attention away from the slowing square – the battle field clearly ours. Oskrinya's. And I pick my way through the bodies littered in the gateway. Pulling himself to standing with a grunt is Xave.

Shining rivers forge their way down his front, his leathers too dark to see the colour of the liquid that runs until it drips over his boots and onto the stones.

A pool of red at his feet.

My sword clatters to the ground as I leap to him, the relief at seeing him quickly draining from my body, and drive a shoulder under his arm.

'Got you,' I mutter as I drag him along.

Fox is with me in an instant, crouching under Xave's other side.

'Stay with me,' Fox says quietly as Xave's head drops onto his chest.

'Healers?' I ask.

'Hall.'

We carry Xave to the external doors of the hall, the people of Hartfield a sombre mixture of cheers and tears as the reality of the battle sinks in around us. Rows of bodies line the floor with multiple people moving between them, offering what healing they can. Aestais oversees them, her sword tucked safely back into its strap on her back.

I didn't see her in the square as we battled, but her smeared paint and the smudge of red on her cheeks tells me she definitely stayed out there. Trini spots us from across the hall and freezes.

'There's too many here,' I say. 'Let's get him to Aestais's.'

We back out of the room and move around the front of Roan's manor. It's a longer but easier way with less people. Trini meets us at the front door, the apples of her cheeks flushed. She lets out a whimper when she sees the blood on Xave's front, his form still lifeless. But she picks up his legs and three of us carry him up the white stone stairs and down the hall.

Blood trails on the carpet in our wake, dripping down the stairs.

Trini gently drops his legs when we enter Aestais's room, a small groan slipping from him with the shift in his weight. Quickly, she shifts vials and papers from the table to the work bench under the window, clearing a space for him.

She whips the sheet from the bed and throws it over the table before scooping up his legs once more and we hoist him onto the table. In moments, the pale yellow sheet is marked with dirt and blood, sticking to the timber underneath.

There will be no way to stop the stains.

Fox undoes the leather straps and vest over Xave's chest as I grab a knife from his belt. Lifting the neck of his shirt, I run the blade down – shearing it in two and exposing his chest.

'Pants,' I say.

Trini takes a respectful step back and Fox and I strip him to his under clothes. I inspect both of his legs first, running my fingers along the corded muscles dusted with hair, but there are no major injuries there.

Xave takes a shuddering breath.

'I'm okay,' he groans, trying to sit up.

Fox presses his shoulder back down and pins him to the table.

There's a myriad of bruises already beginning to show over his torso, along with several bleeding cuts. But the wound that concerns me most is a narrow, but deep, hole in his side. Trini hands me a warm damp cloth, hands shaking, and I press it against the hole. Unable to look at her and the desperation I might find there.

Tipping him on his side, I pour jugfuls of water I demand from Trini over and in the entrance of the wound. Xave braces himself against Fox's chest where he's propped up and I try not to slip in the dark-pink puddle at my feet. As satisfied as I can be that it's clean, I jerk my chin at Fox, gesturing at him to lay Xave back down.

Fox takes another cloth from Trini, who's stepped back again, and washes the blood from Xave's clammy face and torso.

Three blood-soaked cloths later, the bleeding has slowed enough for the hammering in my chest to ease as well. Trini retrieves a blanket from the bed, and I cover the lower half of his body to keep him warm.

His eyes blink open, unfocused until he finds Fox.

'I need a drink.'

Fox laughs and Trini bites back a sob. Fox looks between them and back at me, realisation dawning in his features.

I rummage gently in the vials on Aestais's bookshelf, looking for something to help keep the entrance clean, and Trini hands me a needle and thread.

I swallow. I've only done this once before – and I didn't enjoy it.

I thread the needle and breathe through my nose. Fox returns from somewhere with a bottle and a glass of dark-yellow liquid for Xave. I snatch the bottle from him, the burn flowing deep into my belly before tipping it over Xave's wound. I hand it back to Fox as Xave curses, and focus on the narrow opening in his side.

I palpate around it gently and he hisses. But no more blood gushes out. It's the best sign I'm going to get that there's no more significant internal bleeding. The skin dents under the needle before giving way and sliding across the slim piece of steel. Oil coats my insides as I pull the thread through and over, continuing until he's sealed shut. I tie it off and snip the ends with the gold handled scissors Trini silently hands me before I let out a breath.

I peek at Xave, who's watching me, teeth marks in his lower lip, and Fox bracing his shoulders.

'I should probably have let you drink first,' I say, my voice shaky.

'I wasn't the one holding the needle,' he says roughly. 'Will it add to my appeal, do you think?'

A red bloom appears across Trini's cheekbones and I nod at Fox. He's okay enough for us to leave, I think.

'Wipe this on it,' I tell Trini, handing her a vial of ointment from the shelf. 'The bleeding might not stop completely just yet, but we're looking for small seeping only, not dripping. And it must stay clean and dry.'

She stares at the small, brown bottle.

'Trini,' I prompt gently. 'I need to find Theo.' And Aestais – I need her to look at Xave, to check what I've done.

'Of course.' She jumps forward and takes the bottle. Back to business.

'I'll be back,' I say as I walk out.

In the hallway, the light of the day is dimming around us. The sun tired now from all she's witnessed.

I lean against the wall, just for a moment. The scenes from the battle hurtle towards me and I drop my head between my knees. A moment, I just need a moment.

And to not be sick on the carpet.

The hands on my knees still wear the jet spikes. The spikes that drove into countless ribs and flesh. And hearts. I feigned ignorance on the field, focused on staying alive, but the black points on my left hand wear the deaths of so many.

A presence fills the hallway and the door to Aestais's clicks shut behind him. He smells of sweat and blood and steel.

I close my eyes.

He kneels in front of me, gripping my jaw and lifting it level with his.

There's a narrow channel of blood on his face, mostly dried now. It creates a scarlet lightning strike along his forehead and down his cheek, crusting in his dark beard. It's the brown lakes of his eyes that hold the most pain, the fracturing of seeing Xave on the table, I think. And the countless others. He hurriedly scans my body.

'Are you hurt?' he whispers.

I shake my head, ignoring the twinge on my side as I do. His exhale blows the hair back from where it's fallen around my cheeks.

'Your head?' I ask.

He shakes it sharply. 'Fine.'

My shoulders sag, hands slipping on my knees. Sliding to the floor, I lean against the wall.

Fox holds my gaze, and my face, as I go.

The mass of words in my throat is too thick to talk past. To assure him, and me, that I'm okay. To protest that was my first time killing with my own hand, even if I looked very practised at it. That my heart is tearing in two as I look at him, the fear that stalked me across that square taking root, never to let go, even though he's not mine.

That the same heart that wants to beat for him has been shattered at the loss of Theo.

'How long have you been training him?' I ask, instead of the outpouring of emotion I can't find the words for.

He smiles gently. 'Since he tried to hit me after I came back to the shop the first time and he landed on his ass instead.'

I want to laugh but it won't come. I need to see him. Whatever he is to me now, whatever anger still simmers in his veins at me, I need to lay eyes on him again and remind myself he breathes.

Fox pulls me to my feet, our bodies coming together in the hallway.

We hold there, unable and unwilling to let each other go.

After the death and dying and spilled insides today, the hurts of before seem ... not quite trivial, but so much more inconsequential than they did yesterday. And if we have one more private – secret – moment, before he's actually married, what harm can that do in comparison?

Fox lowers his head to mine and rests his forehead there, our breath mingling.

I close my eyes and lift my face slightly.

Someone clears their throat, and Fox turns to them.

Inglet stands in the hallway, eyes narrowed as she looks between us, hands slack at her sides. Fox looks back to me, too many sorries dancing on his features, and steps back.

And I let the reasons why she was familiar in the fight seep in. She's the woman with the dagger.

'We're needed in the hall,' she says, her gaze landing on mine before she spins and walks away.

CHAPTER THIRTY-ONE

The commotion in the hall is loud enough to push against my skin. The victory of Hartfield buoys everyone in sight, even those who are gravely injured. I enter with Fox and Inglet, and a cheer races around the perimeter. I step back and Inglet raises Fox's arm – the crowd loses their minds for their heroes. The two who are uniting their countries against all forces and just led their first crushing defeat together.

The burning in my skin and along the shallow slice in my side is close to pain. I seek out Theo, spotting him across the hall, not far from where our usual table has been but is now pushed aside to make way for those that stand, clamouring for a view of the heroes of Hartfield. He looks almost as unsettled as I feel, even with Brode pressed against his side.

When our eyes collide across the room, a sense of home sparks in me, stronger than I've felt before. But perhaps that's because I want something I used to have.

But Theo looks equally relieved to see me.

Inglet drops Fox's arm and he stops dead. She looks questioningly at him, and he leans down to whisper in her ear. I rub at my own arm where the skin has started to crawl and glance away.

I look over at Theo once more. He smiles up at Brode, the gap in my chest still sore at the edges. Another wound I will have to grow around. The noise in the hall is overwhelming – too much sound, and not enough space. I am suddenly acutely aware of not belonging here, where I have no choice but to watch those I love not need me. My fingers are still tingling slightly, a pretty standard sign the fight hasn't quite left me – even if this one was very different – and my feet are restless.

I'm halfway back to Aestais's room to check on Xave and Trini when fingers grip my elbow, spinning me around. The air whooshes out of their chest as my fist finds the soft part of their belly. Luckily for them, my jet knuckles are back in my pocket.

'Ouch,' Fox mutters, sweeping his almost shoulder length hair back out of his face.

'Oh – shit.' I grip his arms. 'Fox, I – I didn't mean to.' I drop my hold and look away. 'Sorry, I'm … still a bit … pent up. What are you doing scaring me out of my wits, anyway?'

He takes my hand in his, threading our fingers and I look at them. The blood that still stains them both.

'I have a promise to fulfil.'

He crushes his mouth to mine, the low burning fire that's my constant companion in his presence instantly sparks to life. I don't have time to kiss him back before he pulls away, leaving me staring after him, at the space he occupied just a moment ago, wondering what in the world just happened.

With nothing else to do, I continue to Aestais's to see Xave and Trini.

Gently, I crack the door and peer into the darkness. Trini has lit two torches that crackle softly in the corners of the room, dousing them in warm orange light. Xave lies where I left him on the table, surrounded by the filthy yellow sheet, Trini's head resting on the timber beside his chest. His rib cage rises and falls heavily, but it's steady and his head bows towards hers, as if he knows she's there, even in sleep.

Silently, I finish washing Xave down in the dim light, removing the blood smears Fox left behind, and gently raising one arm at a time to remove the grime. He sighs softly, and I move to his face and hair last, wiping away the traces of the day.

Trini whimpers in her sleep, her fingers twitching where she lays a hand under her head.

Xave inhales deeply, and cracks an eye.

'It's Rubilena,' I whisper and he nods, letting his eyelid drift closed again.

I wash the cloth and ring it out, tossing it into a pile I've gathered near the door where it lands with a soft smack. Trini shifts in her sleep and my heart goes out to her. I feel like I have lost so much in the last few days, but none of the people I love are lying on this table. I push away the urgent voice that tells me I don't know anywhere near enough about the ones I love in Koamah City. I take Trini's shoulder softly and shake her awake.

'Let's get you washed up,' I whisper.

She frowns, sleep dusting her features, and shakes her head.

'You'll be better for him when you're feeling better yourself. You need to eat, too.'

Her stomach grumbles in response, and I lead her away by the hand, her face still turned over her shoulder at Xave.

'Do you have a bath in your room?' She nods. 'Can you take me there?'

Wordlessly, she moves back down the hall, towards the sweeping staircase and across the other side the manor. She regularly looks back to where we've come from, and I can't blame her. The distance is pulling tight for me, too.

Her room is smaller than mine, with no sitting room, but someone has tended to its torches and fire and its homeliness wraps me in a warm embrace as soon as I shut the door. A small bathroom is off the main room, its door just past a small table and chairs. But it's big enough for a bath and some kind soul has already filled it with water and lit the coals underneath.

A bucket of water sits by the wall and I roll up my sleeves, exposing my pale skin that's flecked with blood and marks that my shirt couldn't stop, and I scrub. I fumble through an assortment of things on a small timber stool and grab a bristled brush. Scraping it over my skin and under my nails, I get clean. Or cleaner.

As satisfied as I'll get, I dry my hands on a dark towel in Trini's bathroom. Thankfully, she won't notice any stains until tomorrow.

She stands mutely and watches me, her eyes still heavy with fatigue, but the worry that creases her skin is the heavier burden.

'I'll wait in your room,' I say.

But when she doesn't move, I walk to her and loosen the waist tie of her dress. Tugging it off her shoulders, momentarily thankful for its wide neck, I wriggle it down her arms and to her waist. When I've got both her limp arms free, I drop it from her waist and lead her to the bath. It's definitely more awkward than undressing Marley for the bath; little limbs are much easier to manage.

Trini blinks at her legs before she lifts one, and then the other, over the edge of the tub as I hold her under the arms and she slides in, curling her head to her knees. Gently, I pull her shoulders backwards so she leans against the bath and is better submerged in the water.

'I thought—' she takes a breath that wracks her body, the tears she's held on to threatening escape despite her.

'He'll be okay.'

'I want to go back, do you think he would mind if I went back? I feel like ...'

I think of Xave's head tilted towards her in sleep, of how he looked at her in the hall before it was full of the wounded, how he keeps her informed of everything and anything that happens in Hartfield that might matter to her. And I imagine she feels so much like I do, being away from my family – a distance my body physically calls out to be closed.

'No, I don't think he'll mind,' I say, a smile in my voice. 'But you need to recover a little, first. You can't look after him if you haven't first looked after yourself.'

I ignore my blood-stained clothes and gritty eyes as I watch the back of her head. Filling a pitcher with the warm bath water, I instruct her to lie deeper. Until just her head and her knees poke out of the water.

She closes her eyes as I run the water over her hair, shielding her eyes like I do for Marley. The water cascades over my hand, running down the sides of her face and through her hair. A sigh escapes her when I dig my fingers into her scalp and massage it, running the water over it once more.

I let her get out once she's clean. I'd prefer she'd stay longer to restore her energy, but I know it's solely focused on the room in the other wing. It would be a disservice to keep her from being with him.

She towels herself off as I leave her in the bathroom, appearing a moment later wrapped in the soft fabric to search for something clean to wear.

'He's old,' she says quietly, avoiding my gaze.

I frown at her. 'Why does that matter?'

'I don't—people think I'm his daughter.'

My question still stands, but I don't voice it again. Of all the things I have had to hide, age has never been one of them.

'He thinks he would be keeping me from some great love affair of the young.' The sadness in her tone tells of the conversations she's had about this. At least in her mind.

'Has he said that to you?'

'Not in so many words, but he's a romantic, you know?'

'Romantic is nice, Trini.' Memories of Ash and me in the early days flood my senses, when my heart fluttered with the possibilities, even though it beat for someone else. 'And he's not that old. If I had to guess, I'd say he's scared.'

She glances at me, the pale blue shift she now wears moving slightly around her bare feet. 'You don't think he's too old?'

My heart pangs with her desperate need for approval. Or perhaps its reassurance.

'You're, what?' I ask, running my eyes over her. 'Mid-twenties?' She nods. 'And he's about forty?'

She closes her eyes.

'Trini, it's *older*, not too old. If he is kind, and loving, and respectful – honestly, who cares how old he is?'

Her tears come then, but she smiles through them, the eyes that match the colour of her dress sparkling. She wrings her hands.

'Do you think I can convince him it doesn't matter?'

'Only one way to find out,' I say, a sinking feeling taking over the pain in my side. And I realise how badly I'd like my own opportunity to love – to give and receive in equal measure, instead of having it all decided for me by some external force.

My room is quiet when I return, echoing the emptiness that's building behind my eyes. The bath has been filled here, too, and I peel the clothes from my body. The dried blood stings a little in places where it's stuck my clothes to skin.

The water is lukewarm when it gathers up and over my body, and I scrub myself until I match the colour of the stained water. The cut on my right side stings worst of all as the water washes over it, but I'm lucky it's not worse.

Pulling myself from the now cold water, I drag the gentle fabric of my sleeping clothes over my relieved limbs and stumble to my bedroom. I avert my eyes from the dark door of Theo's room, wondering if I should give him space, but my feet lead me there anyway.

Cracking the door, I hope the firelight from the sitting room will illuminate his room enough. Just so I can know he's here. Safe. Someone else's, but safe.

His bed is lumpy in the rough shape of a body.

Beside him is another.

The second leaps from the bed and holds a knife out at me.

Instead of the fear that should raise its head at the sight of the broad, bare-chested man with death in his eyes, I sigh, a warm rush of gratitude flooding my limbs.

'Sorry, Brode. Just checking he's ... okay.'

He quietly puts the knife on the small table by the bed and walks over. If he's embarrassed he's only in loose, soft sleeping shorts, it's too dark to tell. A hand tucks his mop of blonde curls from his face when he gets to me in the doorway.

'Ah,' he looks back at the bed. Okay, perhaps there's something bigger than being half-naked that's worrying him. 'Rubilena, I – we—'

I place a hand on his warm shoulder.

'I'm going to skip the talk about how I'll kill you if you hurt him.' He raises his brows. 'I hope that goes without saying. How is he coping?' I ask, looking back at the rumpled shape.

Brode draws a breath. 'Better about the battle than finding out about you.' He glances behind him and drops his voice to a whisper. 'It's been a pretty big hit to his foundations, I think.'

I nod. *Mine too.*

CHAPTER THIRTY-TWO

My body is a weight I can't move, sunk into the soft bed surrounded by Fox's earthy, heady scent. A place where, on the bridge between awake and asleep, I can pretend he's here. That Marley curls into me, and Fox brings me a warm drink to start the day. A place where Theo and Brode tend to the horses, and Papa opens a new shop. Ash and Kaya—

'Up, up.' Trini strides into the room.

I unwillingly cross the bridge into consciousness and any visions slip away, too far to recall their detail, and I groan into the pillow. Muffling the sound around my face, my hot breath catching in the fabric.

A tiny flicker of hope starts in my chest as I recall my dream of Fox and Marley. The promise he talked about.

The blue shift she still wears is the only sign Trini's been up half the night. The light in her cheeks is enough to tell me Xave is recovering well enough.

'Roan and Aestais want to see you.' She lifts a brow at me when I open my mouth to speak. 'No, I can't tell you why, but at least it will give you something else to focus on today.'

The more I think about it, the more sure I am that's where Fox has gone – to Marley. And the time between now and seeing her stretches impossibly before me. I haven't seen or heard from Fox since the moment he kissed me in the hallway. But getting her out can be the only promise to me he's trying to fulfil. And I am both immensely grateful, and terrified. What if he doesn't come back? What if he doesn't even make it there? Or it's too late? What if I never see either of them again?

'You did well yesterday, I understand,' Roan says, leaning back against his dark timber desk, one ankle crossed over the other, hands holding the edge of the desk. Aestais is back in her robes; the image of her in the black leathers and long sword now seems like a distorted dream.

'A lot of people did well yesterday,' I say carefully, unsure exactly what this conversation is about. 'And a lot ... didn't.' I haven't forgotten Roan is keeping me here. Even though I know we never would have made it past the false Oskrinya in time, it's hard to keep the bitterness out of my tone.

'I'm thanking the ones I don't command.'

My lips purse, unsure how I should feel about that, about the blood on my hands that shows I both took and saved lives.

'Your history is Koaman, correct?' he asks.

I can't help but frown. 'Yes ...' I say, thinking of Molly and her family, of my childhood, Theo's. Until Fox smuggled us out, all of my history has been Koaman.

'And what history do you have with Astra and Boaz?'

My mind goes blank.

'The King and Queen of Koamah?' I ask, the names finding their places in my mind.

Roan just watches me.

'None. I'm a citizen of Koamah – one that tries very hard not to come to their attention.'

'And, yet,' he says slowly, 'their medallion ended up in your store.'

I glance to Aestais, suddenly afraid I've said too much to Roan. What if he sells me out in Koamah?

'I've told Roan of our discussion about the medallion,' Aestais says.

I'm still not sure what to say, my mind spinning through the possibilities. The risks.

'That we agree it might be trying to find its way to Fox,' she offers.

I refuse to look at Roan to see what he might do with that information. He's used Fox significantly, for at least two purposes I know of: a plant in Koamah, and a trading tool with Rehdree. There is no telling what he will do with this.

'Queen Astra and King Boaz are on their way here, Rubilena,' Roan says, a curtain of stone crashing down on his face, his expression unreadable. 'We need to know how much of that has to do with you, or the medallion.'

I sink into one of the brown leather chairs that faces the desk and look up at him and Aestais.

'I don't know them,' I say, shaking my head. 'But—'

No, he wouldn't do that. And even if he would, he doesn't know I'm here. Would he really turn us in without waiting to see if he could get the medallion first? Perhaps that depends what else he was offered in exchange.

'Yes?' Roan asks evenly.

'My ... employer ... has connections. He knows why we ran, he connected us with Fox. But I can't imagine he would give us away.'

'Atticus,' Aestais says. 'I've heard of him and I think you're right, he would not send them.'

'He doesn't even know we're here – he thought we were going to Laramie.'

Aestais nods as if this would have been a sensible strategy.

'Then it's the medallion's beacon only,' Roan says. 'I'm not sure if that's better or worse. But the King and Queen will be here by nightfall.'

Once more, the manor is in full swing. Trini races from room to room, shepherding people and things in every direction. The wounded are re-housed in the barracks and I spend most of my time with Aestais assisting with small healing tasks.

My mind regularly drifts to Xave and how he's doing, but I haven't had a chance to see him yet. Aestais checked his wound – and my stitching – which lifted one of the weights pressing on my sternum. She also insisted on a balm and dressing for the slice on my side, scolding me gently for not taking the time to make my own.

The market square is being cleared of bodies when I find myself outside, but the sight of blood being scrubbed from the stone makes me turn away, an uncomfortable acidity in my stomach.

A horse whinnies and I wander in that direction, a man in a leather apron nodding at me as I pass. There's a dark horse in the stables that watches me lazily as I walk to him.

'Hi Trumpet,' I murmur, stroking his nose.

'He's here.' I jump back from the horse, who is apparently not Trumpet, to find Theo. Leaning against the stables, he looks older in this light. His shoulders broad, and the thickening forearms crossed over his chest are bare.

Trumpet, blacker than the horse I mistook for him, nibbles at his shirt gently and Theo pushes him off.

'Where's Brode?' I ask, trying to make myself look at him.

'Ah ... filling in for Fox, I believe.'

My eyebrows draw down.

'They have some of the survivors. The false Oskrinya,' he says. 'They're determined to work out where they're coming from.'

'Where?'

A flicker sparks in his eyes.

'Barracks. I'll go with you.'

I've spent so much of my life fearful and hiding from who I thought were Oskrinya. There's a tingling in my fingers and a whispering in my heart I need to follow – I want to see who they really are.

Theo and I are silent as we walk to the barracks, our arms swinging side by side but never touching. The chasm between us is one that's never existed before. An awkward space that I don't know how to cross. The apologies I'm so used to seeing in his eyes pale into insignificance compared to the guilt that now resides there. Liberties once taken with a family member, a sister, mother, are not ones he would take with a stranger.

I glance at him, his purposeful stride so like Fox's, the resemblance one of many I'd put down to his turning into a man. The thought of him as anyone other than my brother doesn't fit. It's a jagged piece of glass catching and tearing at the silk of our bond and our memories. Trying to shred what I know of us.

But what if I simply turn the glass away? What if we just decide that the secret won't define us?

Grabbing his arm, I spin to him in a stop.

'The medallion,' I say, desperately searching the hazel flecks that look back at me for guidance, 'the things it told you – we get to decide what it changes, right? *If* it changes.'

He searches my face, a tiny slice of the young boy he once was peeking back at me. I walk my fingers down his forearm as I pull it to me and squeeze his hand. His skin is dry. Not yet as calloused as Fox's, but his work with the horses and the hold on the machete is just starting to show.

'I don't care what label we put on it, Theo.' The words are quiet, the subdued bustling of Hartfield ebbing around us. 'Even if we don't call it anything'—I press my free hand to my chest—'it can't change what's in here. In here you're my brother – more than my brother. You're part of me, you always have been, and no antique piece of metal will tell me otherwise.'

His eyes glitter as he looks down at me. He's grown even since we've been here.

He nods and squeezes my hand back once before he drops it again.

'Okay,' he says, turning back towards the barracks and walking on.

I follow a step behind, but not before I notice the subtle shift of weight in his shoulders and the shadow of a returning confidence in his step.

The barracks are quiet when we get there, all the Oskrinya soldiers deployed to other parts of Hartfield to clean up and reassure the survivors it's over. Sweat and dirt are the smells that assault us, walking through the rows of rectangular buildings, their walls dark grey with black roofs and doors. Practical colours. Yet they're sombre, even in their robustness.

Empty windows watch as we pass and my mind is dragged back to the night we left Koamah. To the dark windows that watched then as well. They were more closely packed together, some with the flickering light of a fire or torch. But despite that being my home, somehow even the memory of them is more sinister than the ones looking at me now.

A groan sounds from my left and Theo immediately jerks his head in that direction, shoulders squaring.

The wet smack of a fist on skin meets my ears, the sound as familiar as my own breath. One I almost miss.

We approach the partially open door of the building closest to us, the last in the row of barracks, and Theo pauses, drawing a lungful of air before he walks ahead again without looking at me. The door creaks gently as he pushes it open all the way and we're greeted by darkness, the only light spilling in from the yard behind us.

I blink as my eyes adjust and focus on a man, seated with his head hanging low on his chest. Brode spins to us as we enter; his bright blue eyes, now dull in the low light of the room, catch on Theo.

He drops his fist as if he's been burned, never taking his eyes from Theo's face.

Theo holds his gaze and I clear my throat.

Brode slowly moves to look at me. 'You shouldn't be here.'

'Have you found anything out?' I ask.

He sighs loudly, looking between us and then the floor. It's bare dirt in here, splattered with fresh spots of blood.

'No. They're all the same. I just get silence. Every now and then this one mumbles a prayer.'

'What kind of prayer?' Theo asks.

Brode rubs his face, the blood on his knuckles catching the small beams of sunlight as he shakes his head fractionally. 'Not one I know. But it's not going to help him now, anyway.' He glances back to Theo, looking away before Theo can meet his gaze. 'He can't leave here,' he whispers.

Theo jerks his head to him, but says nothing.

The man, his dirty hair hanging down over his face, obscuring it from view, mutters under his breath. He's semi-conscious, ragged breaths filling the empty room. I crouch down beside him, the stench of his own filth bringing tears to my eyes.

'Who are you?' I ask quietly.

The mumbled prayer is his only answer, the words in another language.

I don't understand it, but I turn the sounds over. There's a corner of my mind that calls to them. Reaching for that space, I stretch out in my mind, willing myself to find what's caught on them.

But just as I close around the feeling, it disappears like mist.

I stand, pushing my hands off my knees.

Bile rises in my throat at the memory of the destruction these people have caused – dressed in the fake Oskrinya uniforms. The death and destruction in Koamah, the fear. And the pain in Hartfield, a place so sensitive to their damage, and what parading as Oskrinya has meant for them.

Brode's face pleads with me as I walk past him and back to Theo.

'We'll wait outside,' I say, gently gripping Theo's shirt and tugging him along behind.

Leaning against the wall of the building and listening to the gargling that slowly stops inside, I know why it's the last one in the row.

Brode looks between me and the ground when he comes out, physically unable to look at Theo. He doesn't see the short stride Theo makes before pulling Brode's head against his shoulder. They shift into a hard hug and Brode looks at me over Theo's shoulder, his eyes closing against the emotion in them.

A warmth spreads along my chest and wraps around my shoulders as I watch them, strong arms binding the other to them.

They stand like that for several long moments and I take a step away, but Brode opens his eyes and reaches a hand out to me. Theo pulls back from Brode and they welcome me into their circle of comfort. Their large bodies enveloping mine as we squeeze each other.

I disentangle myself to wipe away the tear that's found its way down my cheek and into the neck of my shirt. Theo grips my hand in his.

'Doesn't change it for me, either,' he says.

CHAPTER THIRTY-THREE

I get myself dressed in another of Trini's stunning finds for dinner – a blue dress that does nothing but remind me how far from home I am. But then, I was wearing fighting leathers just yesterday, so perhaps it's not so far away at all.

Brode and Theo are waiting for me when I emerge in the sitting room, Brode letting out a soft whistle. I grin at him and he takes Theo's hand as he stands up.

'Looking good, Rubes,' Theo says as we make our way down the white staircase of Roan's manor.

If it was designed to be impressive, it more than achieved its goals. The cool of the polished stone banister under my palm steels my spine before I let my hand drop at the bottom and move to the doors of the hall that opens off the large foyer. The sound that filters through isn't as loud as the night before the battle. Now that the frantic pace of preparing for an unexpected royal visit, so soon after a bloody win, has abated, the people of Hartfield seem ... subdued.

After all, this is the King and Queen who told the whole of Koamah, and our world, that Roan's Oskrinya were the enemy. And the wounds of battle are still very fresh. The nagging in my mind at the reason for their visit is almost loud enough to drown out all other sounds. I glance up at Theo to find him already looking at me.

'I know,' he says. 'But they don't know for sure it's here. And they don't know we had it. The claim on me has gone, Rubes.'

I nod slowly. *Hide in plain sight*, Roan had said.

The flickering, uncertain undercurrent from every person on the other side of those doors rises to greet us as we walk through. We take our usual table just before a man in an off-white Koamah uniform strides into the hall. His chest is densely decorated with military medals and they catch the light of the multiple fires as he walks the length of the hall. Roan, seated at the head table with Aestais, Andvett, and Inglet, rises.

The others do not.

The King and Queen don't rule here, try as they might, and it seems they will be treated as such. The Koaman soldier, how high ranking I don't know, talks quickly with Roan. Roan lifts his hands and motions for silence from all of us in the hall. The soldier nods towards the door he came in and ten others file into the room, taking positions directly behind the long table.

Roan watches them come but doesn't turn around and see where they stand, totally unfazed by the threat they could pose at his back – at least outwardly.

Andvett shifts in his seat and places a short knife on the table in full view of the room.

The space pauses, balancing on a precipice of something, but not knowing what.

Two tall figures enter the hall, looking only straight ahead, completely ignoring the full hall. They're both dressed in slim pants and full length, tailored jackets. His is white, hers a deep blue so dark it's almost black.

I flick my gaze back to Roan as they walk down the path between tables, but he remains expressionless. I suppose making them greet him in a hall full of his people is a message in itself.

Queen Astra has pale skin and jet black hair that glitters in the torch-light. Light that catches on the silver crown on her head, its branches travelling around and down the back of her head and up into points.

King Boaz is the colour of honey. Everything from his crown to his skin, including his eyes. Having heard him speak in Koamah, I know he has a honeyed tongue as well – when he's not calling for someone's execution.

At the table, Roan nods to each of them but doesn't bow. He directs them to seats on the other side of him, the King directly on his left, Andvett on his right. There's no warmth in their greeting.

Servers immediately fill the silence, the clatter and clang of platters finding the hard timber tables and glasses being filled takes over the room. But it doesn't erase the knot in my gut that tells me neither the King or the Queen should be here. If Theo was still held in the magic of the medallion, would we be better informed about their visit? Know the secrets and lies that bring them here?

Eventually, after many looks at Roan and the royal couple who now grace us with their presence, we start to eat.

The meal is painfully slow, made better only by the smell of the food – food I can't bring myself to actually eat around the Marley shaped vice my stomach is gripped in – and Trini's non-stop commentary on what she thinks is happening. Xave sits on my other side, not across from us like previously, so he faces the front of the hall. Only two tables lie between us and the one at the front – I assume so he can keep his own eye on Roan and the King and Queen. And Andvett. Not that his wound will be even close to healed enough to take any action if needed.

As the last of the small plates of sweets are cleared away, King Boaz stands silently.

It takes long moments, but the rest of the room eventually quietens, shifting uncomfortably under his scrutiny. He waits as the last smattering of talking ceases. Queen Astra just looks out at the crowd before her, assessing every one of us. A chill runs along my skin – that look is exactly like I remember from the square the day that poor girl was taken away, while Marley listened to her scream. All to prevent the fulfilment of the *three of she*. Suddenly, the weight of the violence committed in the name of the prophecy threatens to crush me as I brace to hear the death knell of Boaz's voice once more.

'People of Oskrinya.' The King's voice is smooth and commanding, leaving no room for question. Vastly different from Roan's open and inviting tone. It does nothing but call back more memories of the last time I was at the market in Koamah ... like the peony cough syrup I never got to make. 'We understand you have faced a fierce opponent in recent days. An opponent, it seems, we have also faced. One we mistakenly believed to be you.'

The room stills, and Xave tenses beside me.

Trini grips the dinner knife that remains on the table in front her.

'A fact I have told you time and time again,' Roan says from his seated position. Not looking at the King.

The only sign King Boaz is annoyed is the slow rise and fall of his chest as he steadies his breathing.

'That may be so,' he says. 'But it is rare for an enemy to take responsibility for their atrocities. Your denials were particularly hard to fathom, given they wear your uniforms.'

Roan's dark eyes flash, but he stays silent.

'Our visit here,' the King continues, 'is a gesture of our goodwill for our relationship moving forward, and I sincerely hope we can be ... useful to each other in the future.'

His gold eyes slide to Roan, who looks out of the crowd before standing slowly, gathering himself to his full height.

I glance to Queen Astra to find her searing stare on me. Heat rushes through my body when she refuses to look away. She searches my eyes, her gaze never leaving my face, her own remaining totally impassive.

'The people of Oskrinya,' Roan says, and I gladly take the opportunity to look away even as my cheeks blaze, 'my *friends*, will be of use to people who are of genuine heart. Your Majesty.' The words are spat from his mouth.

Xave pulls himself to standing beside me, his hands coming together in a clap that cuts through the air.

Trini joins him.

And soon the whole room is applauding Roan and his steadfast commitment to his people.

Including me and Theo.

And still the Queen watches.

Eventually, people start to leave and I glance at Trini. She's absorbed in something Xave has whispered in her ear, a secret smile dancing on her face.

'I'm going to head off,' I say to Theo, who's watching Brode talk to someone I don't recognise. 'You'll be okay here?'

'I'm going to wait for Brode.'

I smile, but I'm not sure it reaches my eyes. Theo looks sideways at me.

'He'll bring her home, Rubes. Here. I know he'll get her.'

I gently press a knuckle to my lips, the veneer I've kept in place since we left her behind dangerously close to cracking. I nod and squeeze his shoulder when I know the tears won't come. Theo just watches me, giving me time to pull it together, his own worry in his eyes.

Deciding I will look for Aestais before I go to bed, I head for her room. Part of me wonders if this worry that's sitting deep in my bones could be channeled into something more productive, like helping her restock the different healing aids. Although, I probably shouldn't do anything to draw attention to my connection to that knowledge right now. Now that I think about it, I didn't see her at dinner – which isn't surprising given Koamah's views on witches.

I pause in the hallway in indecision. The blood trail Xave left has vanished and I vaguely note I don't know how that happened. I hope it wasn't Trini who cleaned it.

'—the fuck are you playing at?'

I freeze.

Roan's voice sends a shiver down my spine, the edge of violence in it very far from the calculated calm he normally presents.

CHAPTER THIRTY-FOUR

I press myself to the wall. Roan is behind me somewhere, perhaps just tucked into a room on this hallway. Somewhere I must have just passed on this long, straight hall.

'You have known, every – single – time those attacks were not me. Not Oskrinya. And yet you've crucified us anyway! Do you know how many of my people have suffered at your hands? How many have been slaughtered by your fucking vigilante groups? Or run to me for refuge after being in Koamah for multiple generations and then *outed* as Oskrinya? What that has meant for them?'

It's King Boaz's voice that responds, almost mocking in the face of Roan's anger. 'We can easily put an end to this, Roan.'

Ice gathers in the middle of my gut.

'I know you've never moved on. I know what you want,' King Boaz continues. 'There's only one thing I need, and I'm all yours.'

I all but freeze over.

'All … mine?' Roan asks slowly, the pain in his voice finding a crack in my heart. I've been intimate with that feeling for a long time.

'In exchange for what I came for – the medallion and those that brought it to you – I'm yours.'

Black edges at my vision.

Theo.

But to get to him, I need to go back past Roan. Roan, who is about to turn us into the King.

'I don't have what you want, Bo.'

I don't breathe.

'It's here, Roan. Astra *knows* it's here. It was a gift, Roan, one she's particularly—'

'You're wrong,' Roan says, ignoring the last statement. 'I have moved on. There was nothing real in what you and I shared. You wanted Oskrinya, not me. Then, you realised you could have Koamah instead.'

It takes me a moment to remember the King is not from Koamah, he married the Queen as part of an alliance. Much like Fox and Inglet. He's from the neighbour on Koamah's other side – Solynara. Same as Marco. The alliance Koamah's last Varelai advised against.

Fabric rustles. 'You sure about that, Roan? You sure you don't want me? Do you remember when I would—'

Someone takes a step, the floor creaking slightly.

'I'm sure.'

My feet move before I tell them to and I make my way back down the hall, glancing into the open doors on my left and right as I do. It's in the third I find Roan. I take a steadying breath as I peek in, not quite sure what I'm about to do. I should be staying as far away from King Boaz as I can.

His back is to me, almost completely blocking the doorway – and Roan's exit. It's that subtle position that raises the hackles on my neck. I know Roan can defend himself, but why should he have to? Why should Boaz think he can intimidate – or worse – all those around him?

'There you are! I've been looking *everywhere* for you,' I say lightly, extending my vowels with a slight Oskrinya accent. I squeeze myself past the King, his white jacket rustling with the movement, and plant myself next to Roan.

Roan's eyes flick to me the same time King Boaz sneers, but he quickly schools his features back into indifference. I slide my fingers into Roan's and press against his side, standing on my toes to press a kiss to the corner of his mouth. A beat passes when the room is quiet, and I fucking hope I've made a good choice here. He leans into me a fraction later, accepting my kiss and squeezing my hand in return.

Roan's face cracks into a warm smile.

'Your Majesty,' I address Boaz, meeting the King's gaze straight on.

Hide in plain sight.

Fuck.

His golden eyes run the length of me, and a thousand insects run over the surface of my limbs. I grip Roan's hand a little tighter to repress my shudder. He returns the pressure, a reassuring gesture, taking a moment to let his own gaze run over my face before lazily looking back to the King.

'I'm afraid I haven't had the pleasure,' King Boaz says, extending his hand as if for me to kiss the back of it.

I let it hang.

'No, I don't believe you have.' I smile as wide as I possibly can.

He lets his hand drop, along with the carefully curated mask of civility he wears. 'The offer stands, Roan. If you don't accept, I will take what I came for anyway.'

My lips stick to my teeth where I hold them in a forced, saccharine smile, until he turns and walks away.

Slowly, Roan lets go of my hand and pokes his head out of the door, clearly making sure the King is actually leaving. I don't breathe a word until he comes back into the room and closes the door behind him, blanketing the room in a protective gloom. It's too dark to make out his expression. Not that I have any idea how to explain what that just was. But the way he played along, the way he held my hand – it's hard to feel like that was a mistake just now.

He strides to the window and wrenches open the drapes, allowing the moonlight in and leaning part way out the now open window. His jagged breathing is audible from where I stand across the room. He crouches low suddenly and smacks his head on the window sill. Purposefully.

'Fuck,' he curses under his breath, his barely contained rage bubbling to the surface.

I'll take it.

I'll take it.

The King's words echo through my mind. The medallion – he's going to take it. I curse myself as I realise I might have saved Roan from a horrible encounter, one I think he was grateful to be out of. But ... *I'll take it.* Doesn't that mean that Roan either hands over Theo and me – and at this point, I can't see any way to escape, if that's the road he chooses – or ... King Boaz will take it by force?

'Did I ... just commit you to war?' I stare at Roan, hardly hearing the words that come from my own mouth. So hard I've tried to protect the people around me and now I—

'I think I may have done that for us.' His voice is low, like a rumbling of thunder in the distance as he stands and turns.

Roan's dark hair absorbs the light, unlike Fox's, which shines. It's swept off his face tonight, showing his high cheekbones and full brows.

'Why didn't you give us up? Is that ... for real?' A small part of me doesn't know why I'd risk asking it. But there was something in the way he responded to my potentially very ill-advised insertion into his conversation with the King that says ... maybe we are – or could be – friends? Something that means I want to hear him say it out loud.

He sighs and leans the back of his hips against the window frame.

'Don't get the wrong idea,' he says. 'It wasn't entirely for you.'

I wait.

'Let's just say, I know what it is to find out someone you loved isn't who you thought.'

'Boaz?' I know I'm right, but it still seems extraordinary so I ask anyway.

He nods before hanging his head briefly. 'I would have burnt the world to the ground for that man.'

'What happened?'

'He met the Queen.'

'She seems very cold compared to you,' I say, still grappling with the thought of Roan and the King. Or the King with anyone, really.

'I realised too late that's not what mattered. Bo was – is – only interested in himself, how high he can climb. For a long time, I thought he'd come back to me, to fulfil the dreams we had for Oskrinya. They were good, noble dreams for my people. And then I started hearing whispers of Oskrinya attacking Koamah. I knew immediately it wasn't my forces, of course. But it wasn't until then I properly realised how little he knew me … and I him, I suppose. Now, I know what didn't serve him was unimportant. Still is, it seems.'

I kick off my shoes and sink into the carpet near the door, rubbing my feet.

'I'm sorry that happened to you.'

He watches me from the window for a moment before joining me on the carpet, sitting crossed legged next to me and leaning against the wall.

'I'm sorry for you and Fox, too.' He glances at me. 'The upside for you is that you do truly know him. I don't think he's ever been able to hide himself from you – I'm not sure he ever tried.'

I lean my own head against the wall, the pins Trini placed in my hair pinching into my scalp. I expect to dissolve into tears. Instead, I find the weight of his words heavier than tears right now. Since Fox left, I have wondered who he really was. Wondered how I so completely misjudged him.

'He was better at that than you think.'

'Perhaps, when forced,' he says looking back towards the window. 'But, even then – and I know it sounds unbelievable – he tried to make it cut and dry for you. To give you everything you needed to hate him and move on. He never wanted you to have uncertainty about where you stood.' He sighs. 'It was an underhanded way to do it, but I told him to – ordered him to. It seemed like the most straightforward option at the time. I wish I'd seen then what I see now.'

'Is it really too late?' I whisper.

He's silent for so long I think he's not going to answer.

I close my eyes.

'Do you want a way out of it?' he asks.

'I don't know.'

'After everything he's given for Oskrinya, I can't now give him false hope, Rubilena. If you don't know, leave it be. Let him at least do this great thing for his country.'

'I'll fight with you, you know. Against Koamah,' I say. 'Providing my family is safe, I'll join you. They have ruled that country with a skewed, iron fist for too long.'

'Unfortunately, we will need many more than you, more than we have, but I appreciate the commitment nevertheless.'

I tilt my head against the wall, looking at the dark ceiling. 'Theo ... he said he might be able to help. In a way.'

A single drop of light – hope – soars in my chest, even as a yawning pit opens in my gut. Here I am, willingly offering Theo up to be part of this world. To step out of his innocence so completely he will never be able to return. But perhaps that's already happened. Now, all I can do is guide him through what comes next. The thought sickens me even as I'm bolstered by the knowledge of the man he's growing into.

'I'll talk with him,' I say. Roan looks like he wants to argue, wants to take control himself. But the exhaustion of the day, or his interaction with Boaz, is laid over him like a cloak. 'Did you know he's your brother? Or your half-brother, at least?' I frown as I ask.

'Brother. The youngest of three of us, obviously. I knew—' he blows out a rush of air. 'I knew we had another, I was here when he was born. Our then Varelai adviser took him away – with the blessing of my parents. He was never spoken of again. Fox was already gone by then, sent away by my father. By the time I took over, so much time had passed I assumed any remaining brother would be long dead, or lost. It never occurred to me to tell Fox about him.'

'Somehow, he ended up with my mother. It was exactly the same pattern she'd shown with me. I had no reason to doubt he was mine.'

'The exact motivations of my parents aren't clear to me, either – it was a different place here when my father ruled. Perhaps he helped make it so easy for the people of Koamah to believe we were terrorising them. The false Oskrinya look so very like us, after all, why question what you're told when those two things line up?'

'I'm sorry I was one of them.'

That fact sits heavily on my shoulders and they slide a little further down the wall.

'We've all jumped to conclusions at one point or another, and even I know this one wasn't a big leap.'

I look at Roan, a spark of recognition firing in the recesses of my mind.

Leap.

Fly.

Leap and you shall fly.

They were the words the soldier Brode killed in the barracks was saying – the ones Marco translated for me.

Marco …

I jerk off the wall and smack a hand into Roan's arm as the realisation takes hold. His eyes go wide as he looks at me.

'I think I know who—but it doesn't make any sense. I—' My stomach turns over as I think it through, still holding Roan's arm. 'The soldier Brode had, he – he said something I've heard before but couldn't place.'

Roan searches my face and I stand, unable to sit still. Slowly he joins me.

'I think they're from Solynara.'

Roan pales in the moonlight. 'No, he wouldn't do that,' he says.

He stands and paces to the window and back.

'No, Rubilena, you must be wrong. He – he betrayed me for a crown. But that – that's very different to actively – *knowingly* – using his *own* Solynaran armies to attack his *own* people … and claim it was me.'

I say nothing. What more can I possibly add? It could be a coincidence that soldier was repeating Marco's words – words so old most of Solynara don't know them. But, somehow, the crawling feeling the King left me with, along with his treatment of women – witch or otherwise – makes it feel like a short step to this sort of manipulation. Not to mention what I've just witnessed him do to Roan.

I'll take it, he'd said. Without even the slightest pause or reflection of whether it was the right thing to do. How many people might be lost in the process.

Roan is like a kettle boiling on the stove as he paces the room, the scorching water about to start spewing out. He picks up a chair on his path back to the window and slams it against the wall with a roar.

I wince.

'I hope I'm wrong,' I whisper.

'But if you're not ...' He squeezes his temples in one hand, the chair completely forgotten. 'Fuck – I need to see him. Stop him. I need him to fucking *explain*.'

Roan charges from the room and I chase him down the hall, the carpet soft on my bare feet. We fly down the stairs, me not really understanding the need for such speed. Surely the King and Queen will be retiring in their rooms?

The hall is quiet when we arrive, the last of the servers clearing the space.

Roan doesn't even stop before he races for the stables. The stone road slows me without shoes and I lose sight of him as he disappears inside. Just as I reach the stable door, limping slightly, Roan appears again, almost toppling me over as he storms back out. He stops abruptly and takes my arm gently, leading me back towards the manor.

'They've gone,' he grinds out. 'Fucking asshole has gone, laughing at what he's done to us, most likely.'

I let him lead me along, his hand warm on my arm.

'This might be good, Roan. He doesn't know we know, and now you have time to think. To be sure.'

'I'm going to do more than think. I'm going to fucking destroy him.'

CHAPTER THIRTY-FIVE

Blood soaks my fitful dreams until I wake at the breaking of dawn. The time since I left Marley feels like an age, but it's the time since Koamah filled with foreign soldiers that's been the most painful. My insides turn on themselves at the thought of the risk to Marley and Papa. Ash and Kaya.

I ball my fists in the bed covers and clench my teeth against a growl. The rage at the injustices of this world and the choice I made of one child over another. The knowledge I did the best with what I knew at the time is of little help. It does nothing to quell the uprising of self-loathing in my soul.

I left her. It's as simple as that.

Just like my mother would have.

Did.

Forcing my fists apart, I get up. I wish I was someone who could sleep through my worries, but I need action. I need to hit something. Clearly, there is only so long I can go without smashing someone's face – something Atticus would have words with me about were I in his club.

Dressing in clean pants and a shirt, strapping on my leather vest, I move to the sitting room to look for tea. Until I realise I'm awake before Trini normally brings it and I have no idea how to get it myself. The sudden urge to be at home, making Papa tea in the mornings and mixing my balms, burns my throat.

Marley is coming here, but then what?

I stare at the empty sitting room, the fire down to red coals. I take several breaths before I crouch down, taking wood from the pile and placing two medium logs on the coals. Watching for the flames to start licking up the sides.

I'd head to the stables to find Brode and ask him to train with me, but I'm pretty confident I heard him come back here with Theo last night and I haven't heard them since. I don't want to wake them early, only to have to tell them the battle in Hartfield was nothing. Not compared to the full scale war Koamah will bring down on us. It seems clear, at least to me, that the King will stop at nothing to get what he wants. And, right now, he wants that medallion.

Because of Theo and me. Well, what my mother did to Theo by giving him that medallion.

A door creaks slightly, my heart leaping into my throat. But it's just Theo.

Standing, I take a breath. They could be days away – she could be days away. I can't think about her not arriving at all.

'Morning,' he says. 'I thought you might have been Trini. I'm starving.'

'I don't even know where to get us anything.'

'Have you really not seen the kitchen? I'll take you.'

'Theo?' I ask abruptly, unable to contain my spinning thoughts of the conversation I had with Roan last night.

He hums an acknowledgment of my question.

'You said the Varelai would follow you if you asked,' I say, 'that you felt like you were going to spend more time with Laramie at some point.' It's a thought I hadn't let take full shape in my mind until last night. When I could see the quiet devastation on Roan's face at what is to come and how vastly outnumbered Oskrinya is.

Theo eyes me carefully, almost suspiciously – like I might be able to shut down the thought for him. At the same time, I can see it there. The beginnings of light for what his own future might hold.

'What makes you think that?' I ask.

He clears his throat. 'When we met her in the meadow,' he says quietly, 'I just had this ... feeling – different to when I got a secret – that she was someone I was supposed to meet. Like ... there was a connection to her that was – is – more important for me to explore than knowing everything that's in the medallion. Like ... she's an opportunity.'

I let the silence between us fall as I turn this thought around in my mind, try to breathe around the literal distance it could put between us. And at a time I want him closer than ever. But, if he's right ...

'Would you be okay for me to let Roan know?' I ask.

'Sure—'

The main door swings open. Thank goodness for Trini and her tea.

'Mumma!'

I spin to the door, my mouth dropping.

And there she is.

My heart cracks and bleeds and stitches itself back together.

Marley, with her wild blonde curls and gold skin, runs towards me with her arms outstretched. Already I can see how much bigger she is, that her arms poke out a fraction too far from her sleeves.

I drop to my knees and hold my own arms wide.

She slams herself into me and I throw a hand to the floor behind myself to stay upright. Then I wind both arms around her where she tucks into my body. Inhaling her, I can still make out the sweetness of her skin under the dirt and the horses. I bury my head into her neck and let the tears come.

She clutches at me like she's never going to let me go and an impossible lightness takes flight behind my ribs, where at the same time there is a sinking that I ever left her. That I put her through this.

'Mumma, Mumma,' she whispers. Her little voice breaking around the emotions she doesn't yet understand.

My body wracks with tears and I hold her close. Only to pull away so I can take her face in my hands and look at her wide eyes and dark lashes, to feel the softness of her cheeks beneath my palms, stroke her soft and knotty hair.

'Oh, my snuggle-girl. I missed you so, so much,' I say quietly, still searching her face.

She wraps her arms around my neck again and squeals, bouncing on my lap.

'Hi, you,' Theo says. 'Can I get one of those, too?'

Marley squeals again and peels herself away from me, the emptiness rushing back in as she races for Theo, who scoops her up, swinging her around in the air before holding her tightly against him.

I press the heel of my hands into my eyes to stem the flow, taking gulps of breath and brushing away the tears with my fingers. Slowly my eyes focus on the rest of the room.

Ash stands over me, grinning, a hand held out, and I gratefully accept it. He pulls me into his chest and I cover my face with his breadth until I can compose myself.

Gripping my face much like I did Marley's, he looks at me. 'Fuck, it's good to see you, Rubes.'

Kaya hovers at his shoulder, looking between us, and I reach out and take her hand, pulling her into us. Ash smiles wider and squeezes hard.

Kaya blushes and I quirk an eyebrow at her.

I know that look.

I disentangle myself and glance back to Marley, who's being introduced to a crouching Brode. A faint dusting of pink graces her cheeks as she grips Theo's leg while peeking at Brode.

Fox waits at the door. I can't quite see him properly with all the bodies I'm suddenly surrounded by, but I think he's still wearing the same clothes he left in.

'Where did you hide Papa?' I ask.

Marley looks back to me, ignoring Brode, and tears fill her eyes.

The rest of the room goes quiet.

'Fox?' Theo asks, but the question in his tone is a different one. A harder one.

He looks to Theo, to the back of Ash's head. Then to me and I can see it there, what he can't bring himself to say. Ash takes my hand and gestures to Theo to join us. Fox doesn't move.

'Ted – um – we had an *inspection*. We hid in the space behind the shop storage room. But he insisted it would be unusual for the shopkeeper to not be present.'

Unusual.

I stare at Ash, unable to voice one of my greatest fears in case it comes true, desperate for him to say something – anything – other than what I know is coming. The one thing I never really considered. The one constant in my life I never doubted, never had to fight for. He was just always … there. For me.

He looks at Marley – how much does she know?

'He's not with us anymore, Rubes, I'm sorry.'

A pain in my stomach tries to double me over. Ash's soft, sanitised words for Marley's benefit tell me what I need to know. However my grandfather was murdered, it wasn't quick, and it wasn't easy.

And it sure as fuck wasn't right.

I bite the inside of my lip, hot, angry tears stinging my eyes. I stare at the ceiling and will them away. Turing my face from Marley's.

'When?' I ask.

'The day before Fox arrived,' Ash whispers.

I rub my face.

'One day? *One* fucking day?'

He nods.

The floor sways underneath me, a hot emptiness swirls around my limbs. I look between Ash and Kaya.

'I'm so sorry,' she says. Her voice is gentle and she stays pressed against Ash. I blink at them.

I can only stare at her.

They all watch me for a moment but I don't notice Ash move to Marley until I see him introduce himself to Brode.

Strong arms turn me on the spot and Theo collects me into a hug, his own tears spilling down my neck. I hold onto him for long moments as my world shifts, tilting precariously into an unknown void.

Theo pulls me closer and I find Fox halfway out the door. He pauses, one hand resting on the door frame, and looks back. His eyes sweep the room with a sad smile.

Then he walks away.

I release myself from Theo and cup his cheek gently before leaving him for Brode to gather up. Marley is smiling at something Kaya has said and I glance at Ash. He nods, understanding what I need to do.

Running to the door, I spin round the corner and into the hall. I can just see his shoulders disappearing.

'Fox!' I shout.

He stops and turns slowly, too far away for me to make out his expression.

I run, arms pumping by my sides, feet thumping dully on the soft flooring until I'm within reach and then I leap.

He catches me as I throw myself at him, legs circling his waist and arms clasping his neck, and takes a step back to absorb my weight. The muscles in his core flex between my thighs as he supports me, crushing me to him. Matching my desperation.

'Thank you,' I mumble into his neck.

He smells of sweat and horse and dried blood, and I don't care as my lips graze his skin.

'Thank you,' I say again, whispering as the tears that never quite stopped fall down my cheeks.

With a mind of their own, my hands run up the back of his neck and into his long hair as I sit back a fraction and look at him. The dark brown strands are tied back but they've come loose in his travels and I easily thread my fingers against his scalp.

His eyes close and I rest my forehead on his.

'I'd do anything, Ruby.'

Ruby.

A shiver runs down my spine.

Someone clears their throat and I glance over his shoulder to find Roan, his head cocked as he watches us. I slide down Fox's front and hear the softest groan of protest as I take his hand and turn him to face Roan.

There's nothing more important than love, Papa would tell me. I breathe through the pain in my chest that wants to be released.

'I want it,' I say. 'The out.'

I sense Fox turn his head to me, but I stay watching Roan. It's his turn to close his eyes.

'What out?' Fox says, looking between us.

Roan looks down the white staircase I'd been too focused on Fox to notice. Too absorbed by not letting him walk away thinking he wasn't part of us, part of my family, I didn't notice we're standing at the top of the manor entrance.

With a crowd of people looking back up at us.

Inglet and Andvett at the back, closest to the front doors.

'The Rehdrians are sending an envoy back to their lands to gather their forces. I was ... just seeing them off,' he says.

The void in my soul yawns wider, it knows what lies beneath Roan's words.

It's too late.

'What "out"?' Fox asks again, more insistently.

I look at him, the dark marks under his chocolate eyes giving away his exhaustion.

'Nothing,' I whisper. 'Nothing important.'

It's the most important thing there is.

Slowly, I let go of his hand and turn back to Roan.

'There have been some disturbing developments since you left,' Roan says carefully to Fox, saving me from whatever comes next.

Or at least delaying it. Saving the scraps of my dignity in front of the people of Hartfield. I glance down, a mistake, I know, to see Inglet still looking back up at me and the tears that still course down my cheeks. Her face is entirely unreadable before she walks out the huge front doors, followed by Andvett.

'Koamah has effectively declared war, unless we hand over the medallion,' Roan continues quietly. 'But we can't talk here. You need to wash, and then we meet.'

'Fuck. We talk now,' Fox says.

'You smell like the ass end of whatever beast you rode here on, Fox. Wash.'

'I'm going to see to Marley and then I'll get Theo and join you,' I say, my voice hollow.

Roan nods once before striding away and back down the stairs, smiling at the people who wait for him.

'Tell me he didn't do anything awful,' Fox says when Roan's out of ear shot.

I look back at Roan moving through the crowd and I don't know how to tell him I did the awful thing. Without meaning to, but the consequences are the same – we go to war. 'He protected us, at great cost to Oskrinya.'

CHAPTER THIRTY-SIX

I force myself to walk away from Fox and not look back; I've given
Oskrinya and the Rehdrian's enough to talk about for one day.
Having them see the remaining pieces of my heart – those that don't
already belong to Marley and Theo, or have been obliterated by losing
Papa – being turned to dust is not something I can manage.

Marley's tucked up in front of the fire when I get back to the room,
her eyes falling closed. Trini emerges from the bathroom, having drawn
and heated the water, and smiles at me.

'Today is a good day, Rubilena. I'm so very pleased to meet your little
one.'

'Thank you, it is. And she will love you.'

Trini smiles wider.

'Roan needs me,' she says, 'so I'll leave you and send someone else up
with breakfast.'

I watch her head out the door before kneeling before Marley. I scoop her up and savour the feel of her in my arms again, my mouth pulling up at the sides.

'Let's get you washed, my snuggle, and then you can sleep.'

She barely murmurs during her bath and I scrub her clean, as if I could wash away the time since my mother's last visit. As if I could return some of her innocence, take her back to before she'd suffered a major loss. To when Papa would read to her every night and teach her silly songs during the day.

Her head lolls on my shoulder even as she stands before me while I dry her off. I carry her into my room and lay her on the bed, awkwardly dressing her in my sleep clothes before I tuck her in.

I lie with her a moment and listen to her breathing, soothing the wounds I carry as only she can. But being with her in the quiet allows the thoughts to come. Too many, too quickly, and all I can see is Papa. All I can hear is Papa.

And all I can feel is the darkness left in his wake.

A hole that's filling with the acidic taste of guilt.

I wasn't there.

And he died alone, on the cold floor of the shop. The place we supported everyone else we could, but no one came to support him in his hour of greatest need.

My sobs start to shake the mattress and I clamp my hand over my mouth as Marley winds herself tighter around me.

'I'm so sorry, Papa,' I whisper. 'I'm so sorry.'

What feels like hours later, my eyes are drier but gritty when Ash pokes his head in. 'Can I talk to you?'

I gently back off the bed to leave Marley to her much needed rest and join Ash in the sitting room, wiping gently at my swollen eyes.

Kaya stands before the fireplace, her own eyes shadowed and ready to close. I can only imagine how exhausting their trip was. I don't even know if it was straightforward or difficult. Something I will need to discuss with Ash at some point soon, so I know what I might need to help Marley through. As if being left in Koamah without me and losing Papa isn't enough.

'Theo's gone to get ready at Brode's,' he says quietly. 'He seems happy there?'

'Very, I think. I wanted to tell him to take it slow, but we know how well that would go down,' I say. Kaya grimaces. 'And Brode is a thousand times better than Atticus, who was making eyes at him when we left.'

'You're joking?' she asks.

'The downside of being good looking, I guess,' Ash says. 'Listen, Rubes—'

'I have so much to tell you,' I interrupt. 'But I honestly don't know where to start. It's so ... big.' I sniff.

I wonder what Papa would have said about the situation I have brought down on Oskrinya. Would he tell me it was worth it to keep the people I love safe? Safer? Would he be as forgiving of my actions as he was of my mother? For the first time, I wonder if I was too hard on Papa for supporting her all this time; if, in my attempts to be the one that made him proud, I have taken a similar path to her in some way. Perhaps now I will never understand.

Ash nods slowly. 'Let me start, then. I can tell you what we already know as well.' Glancing at Kaya, he continues. 'Fox filled us in on the removal of the mark, and what that caused here. We also know the Oskrinya in Koamah are not really Oskrinya – that took a little more convincing to get us to come here. But we both knew we could trust him.'

He walks to me and, taking my hand, leads me to the couch setting that faces Kaya and the fire. Sitting next to me, he turns to face me, perched on the edge.

'Marley's okay,' he says. Another piece of the weight in my chest lifts, only to be replaced by what she's lost. 'She's taking the loss of Ted hard, which is to be expected, but she's been okay. She will *be* okay, Rubes. We've got her.'

I squeeze his hand, hard.

'I missed her so much,' I choke out. 'I didn't think I'd remember how to breathe when I found out the false Oskrinya were there.' He goes blurry through my watery eyes. 'Thank you, Ash, for keeping her safe. I – you – thank you.'

He returns the pressure on my hand.

'She's my daughter, Rubes. I'd die for her.'

I swallow my tears. 'I know.' And I do know. I've never once doubted Ash's love or commitment to our girl.

'We can't go back to Koamah,' he says. I look sharply at him. 'I know Oskrinya isn't—look, I don't know what our options are right now, but we can't go back there. It's too unstable.'

I look to Kaya. 'Is that how you feel, too?'

Kaya clears her throat. 'There was a ... shift while you were away, Rubes.'

'In Koamah?'

'Well, yes,' she says. 'But perhaps not only what you're thinking.'

Ash stands and walks to her, and I remember the look she gave me earlier. I pull my head back a little as I watch them, blinking through my still blurry vision.

He threads his fingers in hers. 'I finally saw what's been in front of me for a long time, Rubes.' His voice is quiet, tentative.

Her face is furrowed and she drops his hand, kneeling in front of me instead.

'I – I don't really know what to say Rubes, but I—'

'Nothing, Kaya, you say nothing. This is ... good. I—okay, weird, I think.' My brain whirls around this new development. 'But good ... and I don't even have to have you shipped to Oskrinya – you got here all on your own.'

She smirks coyly as she knocks my shoulder gently. 'Funny,' she says. 'But I'll take the fact you're not currently dragging me out of the room as your approval.'

I laugh softly. 'It would be a little hypocritical of me to have you in Marley's life as our friend, and not Ash's ... *girlfriend*.'

A soft pink stain graces the tops of her cheeks.

'But how do you feel about Koamah? Your house?' I ask.

She sighs sadly. 'I feel the same – I'm done with Koamah, and it's no place for Marley.'

'No,' I agree quietly. I don't have an alternative plan yet, but with no more Papa, or the store he loved so much, I feel at once burdened with an incomprehensible grief, yet freed of the ball and chain of Koamah.

Until a sickening thought slices my mind like glass.

'Atticus?' I ask.

'I'm working on it,' Ash says. 'He's not going to let you go easily. But we'll talk about it later – now it's time for your update.'

I lean back and rub my forehead, Kaya taking Ash's place beside me. I talk them through the most important elements, and the hardest. That Aestais protected both Theo and me from the medallion, but removing its claim on Theo came at great cost. About the King and my suspicions about Solynara. And the war that threatens. That Theo doesn't belong to me.

It's not eloquent, and not even in order. But somehow I get through the key bits, even though I don't have the time or the energy to discuss them at length.

'I need to get Theo and join Roan,' I say.

'That still seems very surreal – that you're friends with the terroriser of Koamah,' Kaya says, eyes wide.

'Tell me about it.'

'Speaking of friends,' Ash says as I stand. 'He's a good guy, Rubes. This is what we wanted right? People that made us each happy?'

I smile at him. Unable to tell him that's just one more thing I've lost.

I peek in at Marley before I leave, and can't resist tip-toeing across the room to kiss the soft apple of her cheek. She lets out a huff of air through her mouth, and I want to stay here forever. With my little snuggle-girl safe and firmly within my reach.

Ash and Kaya are barely standing when I leave my bedroom after making sure the coverings on the windows are drawn.

'You two need to wash up and get some rest,' I say. 'But you'll stay here, right?'

'I can barely move after our trip here,' Kaya says. 'I'm not going anywhere. I'm literally going to sleep on this floor, in front of this fire.'

'I'll make sure you get fed once you've had a rest,' I say affectionately. 'I don't really know why Roan has suddenly chosen to let me in on these discussions, but I can't pass it up. Theo will have a role I need to work out and—'

'He'll get your support,' Ash says. 'We know. Go.'

He musters what looks like the last of his energy and gives me a soft smile before I head off in search of Theo. Instead of finding him in Brode's room – not that I really know where that is – I find them both at the base of the stairs, ready to go to Roan.

My eyes land on Fox first. His very presence takes up so much room in my chest I can barely breathe. And then I remember how proud of him Papa was and fresh pain slices through me, my lungs expanding in the bleeding gash left behind. How can I even think about what I've lost in Fox when Papa has just gone? And yet still feel whole with Marley and Theo back with me? When I look back now, I realise the visit from my mother cleaved my world in half, and I now feel like two people, with two sets of emotions around what I have, and what I have lost. There's just too many to fit in this single body.

Roan is standing over a map, talking to Fox and Xave, the latter sitting in a chair close to the table. Roan's almost black eyes flick up to us as we enter, waiting only until the door is closed before talking again.

Fox's eyes don't leave me.

'Best guess,' Roan says, 'we have two days before the Koaman forces are here.' He looks at me, a hint of sympathy there, but he ploughs on. 'Probably along with Solynara – the bastards posing as us.'

Neither Fox or Xave look shocked by this, Roan having already told them it seems, but their faces darken.

'I beg your pardon?' Brode's voice is slightly higher pitched than normal.

'Rubilena can fill you in on the "how" later, but it seems she has been able to help us identify them,' Roan says. 'I sent messages to our scouts on those borders, and the timing of the comings and goings from there appear to match many of the attacks in Koamah. We haven't had time to work it through more thoroughly, and they were wearing their own uniforms then, but'—he looks at me—'I trust our intel here.'

'They will leave some forces behind,' Fox says. 'But with effectively two armies at their disposal, we will be vastly outnumbered.'

Roan stands from his position bent over the map. 'Rubilena had a theory about that, I think.'

I swallow.

Fox looks between us, unconcealed surprise on his face that Roan is inviting my thoughts. I look back to Theo, giving him an opportunity to back out before I commit him to this new path in front of everyone here – so many of them the same people who witnessed our worst moment as brother and sister.

He nods gently.

'Theo and I have been talking'—Theo holds my gaze as I talk—'and we think the Varelai would come to our aid if he asked.'

Every set of eyes settles themselves on Theo, but he doesn't falter.

'To be clear, it wasn't the medallion that told me this,' he says, 'more … an unspoken understanding with Laramie. All I have to do is call, and Laramie will bring an army of witches.'

The silence in the room is almost deafening. Apart from my own heartbeat.

'The Varelai answer to no one,' Roan says, narrowing his eyes, disappointment starting to flicker there. I wonder if it's more at himself than at me – for not asking me more about this before now.

Aestais clears her throat. 'That's not entirely true,' she says, gaze fixed on Theo.

'And they won't answer to me either,' Theo says. 'But I can call on them. For the liberation of people, they will come.'

'For Laramie's future apprentice,' Aestais says, 'they will come.'

Brode shakes his head and mumbles something I don't catch. But, judging by the look on his face, I think he just fell a little bit more in love with Theo.

'They are … fearsome,' Xave says, breaking the sense of awe in the room. 'Having them with us could mean … well, we could have a chance, Roan.'

'The medallion did tell me something though,' Theo says. He looks at me as if for permission this time and I nod, my heart warming at doing this with him. He moves his focus to Fox. 'It said you were creating an army as well, but you didn't know it.'

Fox's face is a mask of confusion.

So is Roan's, spiked with something darker.

'Fox?' he asks levelly.

'The women,' I say with sudden realisation. 'It's the women you get out of Koamah, Fox. Brode told me they're trained to fight once they're resettled in the banished lands.'

A small fire of hope starts to smoulder in my chest, and it ignites in Fox's features.

'They've been coming along incredibly,' he says, his eyes wide. 'But they're all at different places in their training – and they've never fought together. I would not call them an army.'

I walk to the table between us.

'But would you say they're fighters?' I ask him.

'In their bones.'

Roan looks sharply at Brode. 'Send the messages. I need to know how many will come – those that are willing need to leave now. See if Andvett can help get them an escort through Rehdree.'

The sentence isn't even completely out of his mouth before Brode runs from the room; Aestais and Theo go as well, I presume to contact the Varelai. Roan returns his focus to the map on the table, reassessing what the numbers might be.

We spend hours talking through the different strategies. Xave, Fox, and Roan leading the conversations, and Brode contributing when appropriate. Theo and I mostly listen when he and Aestais return, still stunned we're allowed to be here. That Roan trusts us enough not to try to get information back to Koamah.

Not that it ever crossed my mind to send information to the King and Queen, but I will be talking with Fox about how we evacuate more people from Koamah. The war will be on the doorstep of Oskrinya, but they will not be safe in Koamah.

Eventually, Roan calls it a day just as I'm starting to pace with the need to get back to Marley. Theo heads away with Brode and I avert my gaze from Fox as I leave, bidding them all a good night.

Wondering what fresh wounds we need to prepare for.

CHAPTER THIRTY-SEVEN

It's almost evening as I make my way back down the hall to my room. Trini said she'd organise food in our rooms tonight, and my stomach grumbles in appreciation. All the torches have been lit, the light they throw is hypnotic across the wainscoted walls and soft carpet that creates a channel through the hallway. The long hall stretches before me, the edges of polished timber reflecting the torches as I walk past the top of the now empty stone staircase.

Passing the cavernous entry, a server walks towards me and smiles.

'Dinner's ready when you are,' he says. 'I've left enough for Fox as well.'

'Oh, I won't see him, I left—'

'Thanks, Dante,' Fox says, just as his footsteps register behind me.

I try to cover the flinch in my spine at his sudden proximity – and the comfort it brings.

'Thank you,' I say. Dante smiles and continues walking past me.

Us.

'Hey,' I say quietly, turning to him. 'Um – so, dinner?'

The torchlight catches his white teeth as he smiles. We walk side by side down the hallway that suddenly feels a thousand times longer, the back of his hand occasionally brushing mine.

The silence between us feels alive, throbbing and running over my skin. I rub my arms over my shirt and tug my vest down as I walk, the pliable constraint of the leather bolstering me, holding my insides together. I wore a vest like this for almost all my fights in Atticus's clubs, and yet I never realised how much it feels like armour.

We arrive at my room and I reach out to the door handle, but Fox grips my wrist halfway, his skin burning into mine. He holds it gently and tugs it towards him, pulling me with it.

I don't resist.

The front of my body stops just before I come into contact with him. That final piece of space is molten and I don't know if I should touch it. I want to. But Roan's message – *it's too late* – thrums in my mind. How can it be too late, when Fox's eyes burn with the same sensation that runs through my veins? With what was temporarily a secret, and is now out for the whole of Oskrinya – and Rehdree – to see?

'I'm sorry about Ted, Ruby,' he says softly.

I look into his eyes, so thankful he didn't ask me if I was okay. But the pain in his face makes the dark hole in my chest deeper. Papa was like a father to Fox, too.

'I'm sorry, too,' I whisper.

A single tear leaks from the corner of his eye and I catch it with my thumb. We stare at each other for long moments, the language of grief too large and cumbersome to voice. Too painful.

'Tell me, Ruby.'

'What?'

'About the out you want.'

The stone that reappears in my gut is larger. And sharp. We've talked about numbers for the whole day. With all the options – Varelai, Fox's forces, and the Rehdrians – we might just be able to win against Koamah. But we need Rehdree. They are the only other experienced fighters Oskrinya has access to.

'It was nothing, Fox, there is no out. Don't worry about it.'

Whatever is between us, I won't ask him to risk the safety of his people for me. He takes a step towards me and I close my eyes, letting the molten heat wash over me even as I step back. He moves with me until I'm pressed against the wall.

'What was it, Ruby?'

His constant use of my name like that, like a promise, runs along my spine and he knows it. He places a hand on the wall next to my head and leans in.

'Ruby,' he whispers. 'Please.'

I can feel his breath on the side of my neck and I want to close the gap between us. The pull is so strong someone may as well have tethered the centre of my chest to his. I want him to kiss me. I want him to come inside, to have dinner with my family – *his* family. I want to curl in front of the fire with him.

But it's the want of him holding me while I let my tears for Papa fall that cripples me the most.

'Do you know what it did to me, to have you scream my name?' he whispers.

I just stare at him, liquid warmth pooling at the low, breathy words.

'It was like my heart was being called home.'

He shifts the hand on the wall to cup the back of my head and I lean into it. The other still holds my wrist, his thumb making small circles on my skin, the tiny touch a relentless wearing away of my defenses.

Even before I speak, I know I am condemning us. But I didn't tell Papa how thankful I was for him before I left, and now I'll never get the chance. The thought of Fox going into a war without finally, truly, knowing is no longer an option.

'I wanted an out of your marriage to Inglet. I ... asked Roan to help me.'

He exhales loudly, blowing the hair from my face. His gazes dances over my face for a moment, as if absorbing my words.

'That means you want me,' he says. 'That's what you're saying.'

It's not quite a question, but he's looking for my confirmation anyway.

I search his face; his eyes are as black as Roan's in this light, and they look back just as intently as mine.

'I want you,' I whisper.

The Fox shaped scar in my heart doesn't open, it doesn't bleed. What-ever happens here doesn't change the hurt from then. But knowing what I do now, about circumstances and choices, that ... alters it. But, more than that, what I know about Fox as he is now – that he's older, wiser, more scarred – and yet he's still the same person who fills me with heat, and fire, and love. A physical passion that stems from the dreams he inspires in my burning heart. For Marley. For Koamah. For me. An unwavering certainty that this world can be better.

And better includes him.

Lowering his head further to mine, the bristles of his bread tickle my lips.

'Say it again,' he says against my mouth.

'I want you, Fox. I had everything in my life that should have made me whole before you appeared in the shop. Happy. And I was ... but I never moved on from you. I never stopped loving you. And now—' My voice breaks, and almost nothing but air passes my lips. 'Papa has gone and life is so ... *fragile*. And with so many ready to break us to pieces, I don't want to spend more of my life doubting who should be in it. Even if I can't keep you.'

His forehead rests on mine, the heat from his touch caressing my temples. The fingers in my hair send tingles down my chest.

The bearded mouth achingly close to mine stretches into a smile.

'You love me?'

But I can't respond. I've spent so long trying to hide from, ignore, or change my feelings about Fox and now, at the worst possible time, I have spoken words right from the deepest part of me, my bruised and torn insides that haven't yet comprehended what it really means to not have Papa.

I have no more words.

Fox places the softest kiss on my lips, just enough for me to feel the warm skin of his own lips on mine.

I close my eyes.

He nibbles gently at my bottom lip, bringing the hand that was holding my wrist to my hip. Strong fingers lift the hem of my shirt, under my vest, my armour, and caress the delicate skin that once held Marley.

I part my mouth for him and his kisses change in an instant. He presses harder against me, his tongue against mine. His grip on my hip tightens a fraction and I pull myself into him. It's a kiss of memories and possibilities. An all-consuming heat, ignited by the tingling down my spine, sparks to life. I wind my own hands around his neck and pull him closer, against my now hardening nipples, wishing there was nothing between us.

He kisses down my neck, dragging his teeth where my shoulder starts, and I shudder. Drawing back to look at me, his eyes still dark with hunger, I hold his gaze. He presses another kiss to my lips, a gentle, lingering one that speaks to promises.

'So, dinner?' he asks.

Roan's garden is magnificent. Seeing it through Marley's eyes is better even than the first time I was here. And so very different to when I was here with Fox, kissing him for the first time again. My mind takes me back to last night as I watch Marley run and squeal in delight at the different flowers and statues. It had taken some time for the flush in my skin to abate, and Kaya kept glancing sideways at me as we ate in front of the fire.

'A picnic!' Marley had happily declared.

I wanted to let my happiness flood my senses. Marley was grinning from ear to ear, dancing and singing every song she'd ever heard, plus some of her own. But even as the flush in my skin and tremble of my core remained at the proximity of Fox, his fingers within touching range next to mine, a heavy layer coated the room.

Every time Marley sang a line from one Papa's songs, my throat swelled. I caught Ash looking sadly at Kaya and wiping a stray tear, despite the gentle smile on his face.

Now, as I watch Marley talking with a statue of a small child with birds on their hands, the pain redoubles. Papa would have howled with laughter at the stories Marley will make up about this place, and then joined her in the statue chats. The image makes my heart a little warmer.

'Mumma!' Marley shouts as she runs back to me, the little dress she wears trailing out behind her.

She'd spent the first part of the morning making the skirt twirl around her in the sitting room. She reaches her arms out to be picked up now, and I hoist her on to my hip. Strictly speaking, she's verging on too big for this, but I will pick her up for as long as I possibly can.

Her little face is serious when she looks at me.

'Is this our new home?'

A question I should have expected, and one that coils tightly in my stomach. But I promised her she could ask me anything and I would always tell her the truth. An appropriate version, of course, but the truth all the same. As long as there were no secrets in our family, we could get through anything.

I shake my head at that. How naively I once thought we could be free of secrets.

'I'm not sure where our new home will be yet, snuggle.'

'So, we're never going back?'

'There are some things we need to do here first, and then we'll work that out,' I say.

'After we win the fight?'

I tuck her hair behind her ear, my mind scrambling for a moment. This is a secret I wish I could keep from her.

'How do you know about that?' I ask. I said I'd tell her the truth if she asked, but I don't volunteer things she is too young to understand.

'I heard you,' she says quietly.

'Yes ... there is a fight we must win, and then we will work out where we will go. Will you think of what sort of home you'd like, and tell me?'

'I already know.'

'Oh?' I ask.

She stretches back, the muscles in my arms pulling with her, and bops me on the nose.

'I found it. Theo showed me where the houses—'

'Rubilena.' Aestais's voice cuts across the garden, and I turn to find her robed figure standing not far from the back entrance to Roan's.

'She has purple hair,' Marley whispers and I grin.

I put her down and hold her hand as we walk back to Aestais. She offers an enchanting smile to Marley, who stares at the paint on her throat. Aestais keeps the smile on her face as she looks back to me.

'You remember our theory?' she asks. Marley dashes off to the garden beds that run the walls of the house.

'Not too far,' I call out. She doesn't acknowledge me. Typical.

'About the medallion wanting to be with Fox?' I ask.

'I think it will stop calling when it's with who it wants to claim.'

'So, he has to take it.'

She's silent for a moment and a single butterfly takes flight in my stomach.

'Aestais?'

'I just ... yes, he will. Boaz knows it's here, so this war will come regardless. But after, the medallion will continue to call until it's claimed by who it wants. We saw with Theo it will still call once claimed with every secret it divulges to the wrong bearer.'

There's something underneath her words that stirs in my chest.

'But,' she continues, 'I didn't expect its ... emergency cry when I removed its stake on Theo. I also don't know what to expect when it's with its intended – if it will allow itself to be removed again. If we had time to research, or talk with Laramie, maybe we'd know more. But ... I think we're just about out of time.'

Just like that, a thousand butterflies join the first and rush through me, leaving coldness in their wake.

'I don't understand,' I say.

'It's about the prophecy, I know that. But is it trying to make it come true? Or reveal how to stop it? Its secret must be known, Rubilena. This war will be nothing compared to the others that will follow, and the only possible weapon we have is the second part of the prophecy – even if we could hold back the forces that will come, we will stand no chance against the dark gods should they rise.'

I glance to Marley, who's neared the corner of the large house and looks back to me. Testing her next steps. I beckon her to return so she stays in sight.

I press my hand to my stomach to quell the unrest there.

'But the prophecy talks to "three of she"? That's what will bring the darkness, not a single man.'

'Yes, but there are many ways to interpret that,' she says. 'I need to consult with the other Varelai to understand the link, but it is possible it's because Fox is the middle brother.'

I breathe hard through my nose, focusing on the cold rush under the bridge. A little too cold and raw to be comfortable, but it keeps me in the present and not spiralling into the what ifs.

'So, his mother could have been the "she"?' I ask. 'She's the reason the brothers were split up?'

Keeping my voice calm is tricky. For so long, I have focused on the actions taken in the name of the prophecy – and steadfastly rejected them, even questioning if there was a prophecy at all. Yet, now, I seem to have a front row seat to the person who is destined to take the medallion and either bring about the prophecy and raise the 'dark ones', or stop it entirely. And he is definitely not a daughter of Koamah.

But I understand what Aestais is saying – the medallion is still an unknown quantity in this world. Regardless of the outcome of Boaz's attack, it will still be pursuing whatever its goal is in regard to the prophecy. My stomach swirls uncomfortably again as I realise there might only be one way to find out.

'I don't mean to burden you with this,' she says gently. 'You're the closest I have to a Varelai colleague right now. And ... I guess I think of you as the medallion's guardian. You brought it here, you should get a say in what we do with it. Theo will look to you, as well.'

'We need to talk to Fox.' I swallow down the bile that's rising.

Because I already know what he will want to do, what he would die trying to prevent.

CHAPTER THIRTY-EIGHT

'I should take it now,' Fox says after Aestais fills him in on her theory.

I shiver in Roan's office, my body disregarding the heat thrown out by the hearth fire. But not with fear. It's the knowledge of a premonition coming true. Somehow, I know Fox is linked to both the medallion and the prophecy. And I knew he wouldn't hesitate for the good of his people.

'You've missed an important part,' Roan says, trying to sound patient. 'The claiming itself isn't the issue. It's what happens after. Will it destroy you? Bring about the destruction of the world?'

'People will keep dying if I don't.'

'They might keep dying if you do,' Roan counters.

'You're both right,' Aestais says, her face more composed than earlier but still tight with tension. 'Which is why it's important we know what the medallion can tell us about the prophecy – either way, people are in danger and will likely be lost. The question is, can we contain that to Oskrinya or will the whole continent be impacted?'

Fox looks at me. He's been trying to not look solely at me since we came into Roan's office, but our eyes keep finding each other anyway. Too many unspoken, unfulfilled, promises lie between us.

'Ruby?' he says quietly, moving his restless feet towards me.

There are only the four of us in this room, and I no longer bother to hide my feelings about him with only Roan and Aestais as our audience. Now I'm not hiding it from myself, I struggle to understand why it would be anyone else's business. Until I think about how badly we need the Rehdrians to fight with us against Koamah. Fracturing the alliance Roan has spent years building would not be a good start.

He twines his fingers in mine and my eyelids droop as I soak up his warmth.

'I struggle with the existence of the prophecy, I always have,' I say. 'But the more we learn about the medallion, the more I think I might be wrong. But if I am, I just can't understand how a *medallion* could be evil, why it would actively seek to fulfil something that would destroy us.

'That aside, we don't know what it will do when it makes another claim – particularly one who might be its target, whatever that means. But I think it's clear the medallion is a danger to far too many people. So, if you claiming it now means we have a shot at reducing that risk, I think we need to take it.'

I look between Fox and Roan. The thought of a war raging around Hartfield, with Marley right in its middle, is a towering black sheet I can't see past. Not without becoming tangled to the point of wanting to vomit.

'We are already going to see so much death and destruction when the King marches on Hartfield,' Roan interjects. 'I can't risk adding to the already significant threat to the people of Oskrinya.'

Fox steps closer to me, the parts of my body that don't care about war igniting in response to his proximity, and all my vulnerabilities rise to the surface.

'Roan's right about that and I'm not sure we have the time to chance an unknown quantity,' he says, looking at Aestais and then Roan and me. 'But ... right now, we've got a pretty good handle on who is against us and who might stand with us. The longer that medallion stays in play, the longer we have for our allies to turn against us. *If* we get the support we're counting on, we have one battle in us. One. If the medallion wants me, and I take it, it stops the call.'

Why does his logic have to sound so much like mine?

'I can't watch it hurt you,' I breathe, unable to keep the fear to myself.

He tips my chin up with his free hand.

'We don't know anything would happen.'

'We don't know that it won't. Look at what it's brought about when Theo had it – if you are its intended, what will it do then?'

His fingers run along my jaw and tickle the hairline at the base of my skull. He leans down and whispers against my ear.

'I'm never leaving you again, Ruby. Never,' he says as my thoughts turn to water and run away.

Never.

Even though I know it's impossible, my heart latches on that word like it will never let go. Never. Never. Except for Inglet. Rehdree. Oskrinya.

Roan clears his throat but looks genuinely apologetic when I lift my head from where it's landed on Fox's shoulder. But his expression is not only for me and, as he holds my gaze, I can see the vulnerability there – the sentiment he won't share in this room. That he's terrified he can't win this fight without Fox. Not against Boaz, a man he used to love. One who has far more resources than Oskrinya could ever dream. That there is too much risk in what could happen to Fox when he takes the medallion for Roan to risk before battle.

'You can't – and won't – take it now,' Roan says, his demeanour shifting to hardened leader in the blink of an eye. 'I can't have you incapacitated be-fore Koamah's army gets here. The soldiers need to see you. It won't change Bo's course now, anyway.' His gaze turns slightly harder. Commanding. 'As soon as it's done, then you take it.'

It's every bit the order it sounds like, and Aestais closes her eyes against it briefly, but says nothing more. She has told me herself she is an adviser only, it is up to the leaders to make their calls as they will.

Fox nods and squeezes my hand, a tiny flicker of what looks like relief in his gaze. Perhaps because Roan has made it an order, taking the choice from him.

Roan walks towards us and places a hand on Fox's shoulder.

'Thank you,' he says, shoulders dropping a little.

I can't move. Even long after Roan and Aestais leave, my feet are stuck to the floor. Fox pulls at my hand, and sits me in one of the brown leather chairs, kneeling before me.

'Talk to me,' he says.

I stare at him, the darkness Papa left in me yawning wide, ready to devour more. Fox grips my face in his hands. I can't help but think the dark ones the prophecy talks of couldn't feel this awful, but perhaps that's naive. Everything – every time – can always be worse.

'No, Ruby, don't you disappear on me. Not now.'

'I – I don't want to,' I say quietly, looking him straight in the eye. 'Disappearing is the last thing I want either of us to do. Not now. But the medallion ... what if we survive the battle, only to have the medallion – or the Rehdree – take you from me anyway?'

He takes my hips in his hands and scoots me forward on the chair, pushing my legs apart until he kneels between them. I loop my hands around the back of his head, fingertips in his hair.

'I know you're scared you're going to be hurt again,' he says. 'I don't blame you for that. But I am never leaving you again, Ruby, medallion or not, Rehdree or not. We will figure it out.'

I suck in a breath, desperately wanting to cling to the dream he offers.

His hands rove my body, constantly, the warmth they leave in their wake loosening my limbs. I lean into him.

'In the meantime, we can take advantage of every moment we have,' he murmurs.

My body tingles in response to his breath on my skin and I will my heart and mind to catch up. I don't know how to stop political alliances, or if I should even try. Or about prophecies and distress calls and sentient fucking medallions.

But I know this.

This man and how it feels as his hands go over my knees, fingers trailing the sensitive spots on the inside of them.

I can only assume the answer to why the medallion is so important – insistent – is in the medallion itself.

But is finding out worth denying what I have in front of me right now?

Fox edges closer, his hard torso pressing gently against mine where he still kneels.

Perhaps we won't even make it through the onslaught of Koamah and the prophecy, and the medallion will be someone else's problem? Just for a moment, I wish that was the case. That I could let go of all the things that weigh on me, the things I need to manage and just … be in this moment.

Fox starts kneading my thighs gently. The chocolate pools of his eyes travel from my knees, towards my throbbing centre, and slowly, intently, up my front.

My thighs clench in response.

I press into him.

Can I just let it go? Just for right now? Wouldn't that be a relief in itself? Even if I have to pick up all my responsibilities, losses, and debts as soon as I leave this room?

'Okay,' I whisper. 'We'll figure it out, but I want all the moments in between.'

He smiles as his fingers move up my legs and he traces the seam of my trousers with a knuckle. Two.

I suck in a breath and he gently pushes me back into the chair, bending with me and placing a soft, promising, kiss on my mouth.

Promises I want him to keep. Always.

But I only have now.

'Please, Fox, don't break my heart again,' I whisper. I know it sounds plaintive, so much weaker than I have sounded in a long time. But there is also part of me that is so *relieved* to be able to voice it, despite what I know is coming for us.

Hooking his fingers into the waist of my pants, he yanks them off in a smooth move, his knuckles returning with only my underwear between us. I groan and a wicked grin graces his face. He leans directly between my legs and looks up at me.

'This is the only way I will destroy you, Ruby.'

His hot breath does nothing to stem the fire building in my core, but it's the tickle of his beard on my thighs that makes me clench my legs around his cheeks.

I watch as long as I can as he tugs my underwear aside with a finger and kisses me. Deeply, wholly. Teasing me with the length of his tongue. But then his insistent rhythm forces my eyes closed and I throw my head back on the chair.

He scrapes his teeth ever so gently along the bundle of nerves at the very top, just as he slides two fingers deep inside me. And I'm gone, lost to a place of no words or thought. A place filled only with the rise and fall of incomprehensible pleasure.

And the image of Fox's face between my legs.

When I can recover myself enough to sit up, Fox helping to wriggle my pants back into place, I trace the side of his neck with my finger.

'You got good at that,' I say.

A flicker of tension dances across his shoulders, but I have no intention of giving him a hard time about what other experiences he may have had in the time between. And it would be rude of me now I'm the beneficiary of such experiences, anyway.

I kiss his mouth, my taste on his lips.

'I expect you to do that again, you realise,' I say.

His smile stretches our kiss.

'There are many, many things I will be doing to you, Ruby.'

My name on his lips never ceases to run hot, gentle fingers over my skin. 'Then you better make sure you live through this, and that medallion. I won't accept anything less.'

He kisses my mouth softly, another promise. And then my forehead, which sends a thrill of a different kind through me. One that feels so much like being loved.

I want to see Marley, and tiredness is starting to seep into my bones. The emotional exhaustion of recent days is making itself known. Standing, I pull him up with me and hold him close as we stand against each other. I have no idea how to make him mine, properly mine, and the complications of what comes after the war with Koamah swim in my head.

Marley needs a home, but it's gone.

We need income, but Papa and the shop are gone.

And I still owe Atticus.

The thought of how I even get a roof over our heads is overwhelming, let alone how I keep everyone I love together. When I want Marley as far from threat as possible, but I can't keep Fox from his duties here. When I want her to have unobstructed access to Ash, but he has a new life to start with Kaya. When Theo belongs with me, but he is more than ready to leave me behind and start whatever his new journey with Laramie might be, perhaps with Brode now at his side instead.

I rest my head against Fox's chest and hope the answers will come to me through his presence alone. So much feels like it's in the right place when I'm with him. But when I look up at his watchful face, I'm no closer to knowing any of them.

'I want to see Marley,' I say.

He nods and takes my hand. 'I'll walk you.'

He opens the door of Roan's office to find Theo with his fist raised, ready to knock. His eyes go wide when he sees us, peeking over my shoulder to check we were, in fact, alone.

Then he glances at our joined hands and his face just about splits in half. 'Does *this* mean what I think it means?' he asks.

Fox's grin matches Theo's and I elbow him.

'It means we're ... trying,' I say. I think we are? Or is it hopeless? 'There are a lot of—'

'Yes!' Theo fist pumps the air and I can't help the smile that graces my own face. The exuberance of the young.

'We're *trying* Theo,' I say. 'It's not a guarantee of anything.'

Fox looks at me sharply.

'It's a guarantee,' he says. 'I won't accept anything less.'

I raise my brows at him, but he only leans in and presses his soft and sinful mouth against mine.

'Oh. Ugh.' Theo cringes dramatically. 'I just realised I'm watching my brother and sister make out.'

Marley's hair tickles my nose and the body heat from the leg she has thrown across my middle is almost overwhelming. I throw off the covers and gently shift her back to her side, my awkward grunts soft enough not to wake her. Taking her small hand in mine, I close my eyes again and let sleep take me once more.

A gentle stroking of my cheek pierces my dreams and I lean into its hypnotic rhythm. Inhaling the scent of sandalwood and spice, I smile in my sleep. Soft lips press against mine and I take the kiss gratefully.

Blearily, I open my eyes to Fox crouching beside my bed.

'Hi,' he whispers.

'What are you doing here?'

There's a moment of silence when I wonder if he's going to crawl in with me, scoop me into his arms. I hope he does.

'They're coming.'

If the sudden nausea didn't drag me from my half-sleep, the thundering of my heart would. I look frantically to Marley.

No.

'She has time to sleep,' Fox says. 'But our other forces are also almost here, and I thought you'd like to be up to speed before they arrive.'

Of course.

But Marley ...

Once again, my chest pulls in different directions.

Gently, I get out of bed and gather my clothes as quietly as I can. The thick, fitted black pants are clean and warm. The shirt is soft and thin, cool on my skin. My leather vest dangles in my hand when Fox crosses the room to me.

He wraps a hand around my waist and I can feel the warmth of him seeping through the fabric of my shirt.

'I'm sorry it's come to this, Ruby.' The words are whispered, as if they're going straight to my heart.

'None of this is on you.' I look back to Marley, who's sprawled out again on the bed. 'If anyone is to blame here, it's my mother. And King Boaz.'

'Not if all of this has been so the medallion can find me.'

I close my eyes and inhale. 'Perhaps there are some things bigger than us.'

'Like love?'

I tremble a fraction under his gaze. Even the dark of the room can't mask the intensity there, and everything starts to warm from the inside out.

'You sound like Papa.'

He smiles sadly. 'He was an incredible man, Ruby. And closer to me than my own father, so I take that as the highest compliment.'

'He would have been so very proud to know that.'

Fox kisses my cheeks where tears have started to fall. I take them gratefully for a moment, before I clear my throat and stand a bit taller.

I roll Marley towards the edge of the bed where I can scoop her into my arms and carry her across the sitting room towards Theo's room – now occupied by Ash and Kaya. Fox trails me and helps ease the bedroom door open, but stays outside.

Moving towards the right hand side, I'm jolted by the knowledge I still know what side of the bed Ash sleeps on.

'What's wrong?' he asks, his voice rough with sleep.

'I need to go with Fox, it won't be long now. I'll come before it's time, but I need you to take Marley.'

He nods against his pillow and lifts the covers so I can slide her in with him. She groans in her sleep and turns into Ash, curling herself against him. At least, I think to myself, despite the winding road it's taken, I have given her more people that love her than I could possibly have imagined for myself.

CHAPTER THIRTY-NINE

The air around us as we walk through the manor, despite the hour of the night, buzzes with the inevitable. The tension of wanting the time to never come, and wishing for the waiting to be over.

'Is the room ready?' I ask Fox.

'Trini's seen to it.'

Roan has given us use of the large, walk-in safe in his office – installed there by their father for his own safety, and not a place Roan ever intends to hide in. But he offered it to me for Marley, and I couldn't bring myself to say no. Even though I know there are more children in Hartfield than Marley that deserve the same protection, I couldn't turn down the additional safety for her.

Sending her or not sending her would rack me with guilt either way – and I'll take the guilt that keeps her living. It's a risk. A huge risk. If the Koaman forces breach the manor, Roan's office is likely to be the first place they will look for the medallion. So it won't be there. Just Ash, Kaya, and Marley. Hiding.

Pressure builds at the base of my head.

But Atticus has made Ash and Kaya experts in hand to hand combat now, just like me. And I know there is nothing that would stop Ash from killing anyone that tried to harm our daughter.

Fox leads me out of the manor, past the stables, and back towards the gates he fought outside of when we first arrived. There's no sign of Theo, and I hope he is inside somewhere, making the most of the rest he can get now. In the corner of the wall, where it starts to curve back around Hartfield, one of the large structures from the last battle is left in place. As I think on it, they all are.

He takes me to it and we climb the timber staircase on the right, me just ahead of Fox. My fingers tremble as I remember the last time I did something similar – scaling the wall to drop down the other side. To where Fox was.

The top is a large platform with a single rail for safety, but it sits below the height of the wall. Crouching down, I press against the cold stone and peer over the top. Beside me, Fox does the same.

The darkness of Oskrinya around us swallows my vision. As my eyes adjust, small pricks of light come into view in a dotted line that runs right across the front of Hartfield and disappears out of sight around each side.

'Fires,' I breathe.

'That's where they want us to see them coming from.'

Fox sinks down and sits on the platform, leaning against the wall, but I can't drag my eyes away from the fires and who might sit around them. Do I know them? How many are from my neighbourhood? Did they ever visit our shop? Did their parents know Papa? Are they excited, terrified?

'We'll have archers up here,' he says. 'The priority is keeping them outside the walls as long as we can, but they will be breached.'

Slowly, I turn to sit beside Fox, bringing my knees to my chest and placing my head on the arms I rest there. Sighing slightly, I look out over Hartfield and the hurried preparations for another fight.

'I just can't fathom this is all because of Theo and me – because Roan refused to hand us over along with the medallion.'

Fox exhales heavily.

'It's not just about that, Ruby. It's about a power hungry man who's happy to destroy as many people and cultures as he needs to get what he wants. It's about making sure the power of the prophecy does not fall back into the hands of someone like that.'

There's a bitterness in his voice that contains more than the battle we're about to face. More even than the injustices against Oskrinya by Koamah's lies.

'You know what he did to Roan.'

He grits his teeth. 'I don't think Roan knows I do, but yes. Theo confirmed it with the secret he blurted when I first told you who I am.'

I let the time wash between us, in this tiny bubble that will burst in too few moments.

'You said that's where they want us to know they are?' I ask.

He nods, the back of his head scratching against the stone.

'He has two armies. I'm expecting he will come from the front – out there – and behind. The far wall is being extended for the new estates on the other side of Hartfield. He'll know that's a weakness. My guess is Solynara will come from there. As far as I can tell, Talvore are staying quiet as long as they can and Boaz will have enough force with Koamah and Solynara not to need them just yet.'

'I wonder what uniforms they'll be in,' I say absently. 'But you're ready for that?'

'As we can be. Most of Oskrinya and Rehdree will be inside the walls, split between here and the other side of Hartfield. The Koaman women who have agreed to fight, along with the Varelai, will stay outside the walls – assuming the rest of them get here in time. They will come from behind where we need them and help us crush Koamah and Solynara between them and us. Boaz doesn't know about them so, in that respect, they are one of our greatest weapons.'

'You're good at this.'

'I'd like to not have to be.'

I turn my head against the wall to look at him. For all the time before, Fox's dream was to join the Koamah army – for reasons I now know I didn't truly understand then. But finding him with a similar role in Oskrinya ... I never considered he'd want to do anything different.

'If this wasn't our reality, what would you do?'

It's his turn to look at me. The night sky is holding out her last stance against dawn, and the dying moonlight catching in his eyes.

'Serious question?' he asks.

'Of course.'

He turns his head away and looks up at the last of the stars.

'I want to ... lead a fairly quiet life. Maybe make something – I like furniture. Raise a family. Have a shop, even. I loved that one of yours.' He sighs heavily. 'For so long, all of that seemed out of reach. And now ...'

I can't look away.

'Now – if we can get through this next bit – I'd really like to go for it.' He looks at me again. 'If I can find someone to do it with.'

His gaze flicks over my face and the uncertainty there opens a crack in my heart.

'You will,' I say, leaning across to kiss him, unable to voice his other commitment. We're both very well aware of it. 'You will.'

'Can I show you something?'

I follow Fox back up the staircase and into the manor, urgency starting to creep into his stride. The night is fading quickly. Instead of turning right at the top, towards the guest wing Theo and I were taken to, we turn left, the same direction Trini's room is in. The colour scheme is the same on this side of the staircase as the guest wing, but the rooms are a bit smaller, more like Trini's.

At the very end of the long hall, Fox hesitates before the door. He glances back at me before opening it and leading me through.

I know immediately this is his space, and the charge in the air changes. The smell of him envelopes me and I suck it in like I might never have it again. The bed is rumpled from when he last lay in here and I struggle to keep the blush from my cheeks, despite the intimacy of our time in Roan's office.

He moves to the worn chest of drawers that stands against one of the walls and digs out a small, metal box from the middle right drawer. Moving back to me, he holds the box in his hands.

'Open it,' he says quietly.

Leaving the box supported in his outstretched hand, I lift up its lid, the metal hinges screeching slightly in protest. My heart skips as I take in my name in his handwriting. It's been a long time since I've seen it, but I recognise it all the same.

'What is this?' I whisper.

Just as I lift my fingers to feel the first letter, he snatches the box away, the lid closing with a snap. A cheeky grin tinged with embarrassment stretches across his face.

'I wrote to you. Even when … I thought I'd never see you again. I knew I didn't deserve it, but I wished for it anyway, and I thought writing to you might help it come true.'

'I want to read them.'

His smile grows temporarily. 'You'll have to wait until after.' A solemness takes over his features. 'I just wanted you to know they were here – just in case.'

I stare at him, the pit in my stomach opening wide, but I can't find any words. He places the box back in the drawer and returns to me once more, reaching out for my hip and pulling me flush against him.

'I have no intention of dying, Ruby. I suddenly feel like I have everything to live for.'

I pull his face to mine and crush my lips into his. He matches my need, the sudden desperation, and his hands rove and grip and claim, and I surrender. I give everything to him in our feverish meeting of teeth and limbs.

I yank the shirt from where it's tucked into his pants and run my hands up his torso, his nipples puckering under my touch. Pushing him back on the bed, I lose myself in the feel of his skin on mine and the smell of him in this bed. Gently, he changes the pace and spins me on my back, rocking back on his knees to remove my pants. He settles himself between my legs, bracing his elbows by my head. Soft kisses rain down on me before he fills me and I bite his lip, hoping none of this is the last time.

'You do have everything to live for,' I murmur, rocking my hips. 'I'll give you everything.'

Aestais bows low to Laramie when she enters Roan's office. Laramie nods shallowly at her before her eyes are rooted on Theo. He doesn't flinch.

'It's nice to see you again, Laramie,' he says.

'You did well to survive the medallion – and its removal,' she says in response. Her gaze flicks to mine momentarily. 'It is good you are both here. I had a feeling each of you would have larger roles to play when we met in that clearing.'

I look to Aestais, as if she might be able to interpret what that means, but she remains watching Laramie.

Laramie reaches into the folds of her soft grey cloak and hands Theo an amulet of some kind. He eyes it, trying to keep the suspicion off his face, and her eyes light with amusement.

'Yes, I suppose it makes sense for you to be wary.'

'The last medallion I had did get us into a spot of bother,' he says, holding her gaze.

'I would suggest that's subjective,' she says. 'Prophecies never have been a perfect science. This one, though, will help keep you out of trouble – it will allow you to get messages to me quickly so I know where to position the rest of my Varelai.'

He wraps the long chain in his fingers without further hesitation. 'Thank you.'

The room falls silent for a moment, Laramie's presence seeming to fill every space.

'You have a secondary plan to keep the medallion from the King, I take it?' she asks.

'Yes,' Aestais responds. 'I have theorised that the medallion placed its claim on Theo to get here – closer to the middle brother, Fox. These three being the "three of she".'

Laramie is quiet as she listens, but I can't help but feel like her attention is on me.

'But I cannot guess at the intent of the medallion,' Aestais says.

'Can you not?' Laramie asks. 'You have spent much time away from us, Aestais. Perhaps too much,' she says gently. 'The medallion was created to protect the prophecy – to stop someone willfully bringing it about. The "dark ones" it talks of are old, formidable creatures – three siblings, in fact – that my ancestors banished from this world a long time ago. Should they be allowed to return, it will only be with vengeance in their hearts and minds ... if those things still exist for them.'

Three people? Surely we could deal with three people, instead of this war Boaz is marching on us.

'Do not think you can beat them,' Laramie says, and I slide my gaze to Aestais again, wondering if it's a coincidence my thoughts have just been answered. But perhaps it was the way all the men in the room shifted their stances, as if preparing for battle right now. 'The dark ones are akin to gods. If they are let loose on this world again, they will rule it without question.'

'But,' I say, the prophecy still grappling for purchase in my mind. 'These three'—I gesture to Roan, Fox and Theo—'are ... good. Why would a world-as-we-know-it-ending event be brought about by three good people?'

'Because gods can be vindictive, Rubilena,' she says. 'And what better way to punish people than targeting the good among them?'

I shake my head, processing her words.

'I just need to understand this,' Theo says. 'The secret of the prophecy is that Roan, Fox, and I are the "three of she", and therefore us being together can bring about the return of the dark ones.'

Laramie nods gently as he talks, her long charcoal hair shifting slightly with the movement.

'I'm going to guess it's too simple for us to just separate again?'

'Yes,' she confirms. 'The separation was useful until you – the youngest – came of age. But the unfolding of the prophecy has long since started and war is now gathering here, is it not? Violence begets violence, and the dark ones merely wait their turn.'

'So ...' Theo continues, 'to stop the prophecy, we have to win the war and destroy the medallion so its secrets can no longer be found?'

'The bridge between you will need to destroy it – or its power, yes,' she says. 'Should that fail to occur, the secrets of the medallion – the blood that's shed for them – will all mean nothing in the face of the dark gods' return.'

The bridge between the brothers. The middle brother. Fox.

CHAPTER FORTY

'I don't want you to go, Mumma.'

Marley's eyes are shining with tears, and my throat is tight as I watch her. But I know I can't cry now, can't show her the tremble in my fingers. Or tell her my stomach is heaving. Because I'm her Mumma, and that's what I do. She needs to believe there is only hope for today. I refuse to think about how much of a lie that might be. Because, right now, hope – and Roan's enormous safe – are all I can give her.

'I know, my snuggle, I do. And I promise I will be as far away from the fighting as I can.' She looks up at me with her large, blue-green eyes. 'But I need to be able to see what's happening so I can keep you and Theo safe, okay?' A small nod is the best I get. 'Daddy and Kaya are going to be right here with you.'

'And I will have soldiers at the door.' I jump at Fox's voice behind me. He walks in and crouches in front of Marley, next to me. 'Do you remember how fierce they are?'

She nods silently.

'Well, your Daddy is fiercer, and he'll be right here with you,' he says, and I think I fall a little more in love with him.

Marley throws herself at me and I hold her tight, thankful she can't see how quickly I feel like I am falling apart. Ash takes her from me and pulls me into a firm, one-armed hug. I kiss Kaya on the cheek.

'Give it to them good, Rubes,' she whispers into my ear. 'I've got things here.'

I squeeze her hand gratefully.

'Shouldn't you be with your troops?' I ask Fox as we leave the room, forcing myself to smile brightly at Marley before I disappear out the door.

'Yes,' he says. 'But I should also be with you.'

We're silent the rest of the walk through the manor and towards the gates. The scene as we leave Roan's large front doors is vastly different to when we came out here during the night. Dawn is now just about to break, the grey light mirroring the muted feeling that runs around the inside of these town walls. Walls that have already seen too much death and destruction for a once happy people and place.

The hundreds of Oskrinya soldiers Roan has called forth both from Hartfield and regional Oskrinya are gathered in the square between the manor and the gates, flanking the stables. Roan has been honest with them about the King's deception with the false Oskrinya and, despite the battle weary gazes, a fire of retribution burns beneath them.

'Walls first,' Fox says to me, 'this space second. They're our first two priorities. After that, anything we can do to stop the destruction of Hartfield will be done.'

I nod, as if this is something I can really comprehend.

'If the square looks like it will fall, though,' he says quietly, 'I will need to claim the medallion and do what I can to destroy it without bringing about the prophecy – before Hartfield and Oskrinya are no more.'

I swallow, wishing there was something else I could do. Another solution I could find. But I gave Marley hope, and now I need to give it to myself too. Perhaps Fox taking the medallion will be fine.

As before, large numbers of people shelter in the hall on the left side of Roan's manor; multiple units of soldiers are stationed in there as well, in case of a breach. But I know that hall can't house the entire population, and there are people still in their homes, in inns, and sheltering in the barracks who also need our protection.

The city of Hartfield has swelled in numbers in the last few days as Oskrinya sent words of warning to the outlying towns. Many of those chose to stay where they are, which is a relief on Hartfield's resources, but it's hard to say where is safer. They will certainly be safer there in the short term but, if Hartfield falls today, Koamah will plunder every remaining village until Oskrinya is completely under the control of Queen Astra and King Boaz. If they also reclaim the medallion and, under the guise of knowing all the secrets of the prophecy, call more than Solynara to aid in entirely conquering Oskrinya, there will be nothing more we can do.

And that's assuming our theory on the 'three of she' is correct and Boaz or Astra can't be claimed by the medallion and truly access unlimited power.

If they can also do that ...

But no, our only hope is that they would have done that already if they were able – before my mother somehow stole the medallion.

The leather-clad Oskrinya before us are wearing black once again, and are neatly held in their formations.

I now know from experience it won't stay this way for long.

In the middle of the different units are those of Roan's inner circle, the leaders of the Rehdree clans, and Aestais. Including Theo and Brode, standing shoulder to shoulder. Being part of Fox's people-smuggling ring, Brode doesn't officially belong to any of the units in front of the gate, despite being a key member of Fox's team. But he's clearly a highly valued individual. Looking at them now, two halves of a whole, I know he and Theo will partner again in today's battle.

And I feel a little relieved. The worry that has a permanent home in my thoughts where Theo is concerned doesn't abate, but I can see – objectively – how capable he and Brode are together.

Roan says something I can't make out as we approach and Brode runs off in the opposite direction.

The chain of Laramie's amulet catches the first rays of sun as Theo turns to find us, a grim smile on his face. Aestais is dressed again in her fighting clothes, massive sword on her back and purple hair tied back up out of her face.

To die by that sword, with her painted face bearing down, would be terrifying.

'This is where we leave you,' Roan says to me. 'If it looks like it's going south, get into that room with Marley. Fox, you go for the medallion.'

He looks at Fox and Theo, who each give me a fast embrace before they turn as one and walk away with Roan. Fox will stay close to his fighters, I know, and I will stay closer to Marley and the medallion. As I watch them disappear, Roan lands a heavy hand on Theo's shoulder and tugs him a fraction closer for a moment, the brotherly moment warming something behind my ribs.

The town of Hartfield draws a collective breath. A breath in which it feels like the world starts to shift. This strange, quiet calm before what we all know will be a horrible storm.

The dawn is beautiful, the sky a melding of pastel colours.

Peaceful colours.

And yet, we are about to paint the day red.

There's a beat. Just one. Where I hope we are wrong, Boaz is here for another reason—

'Incoming!'

I duck unconsciously as a large volley of arrows whizz through the air, over the wall, and down. Roan's army crouches and throws up their shields. I don't know how I expected a battle with Koamah would start, but having the waiting dawn broken by a single, quiet, volley of arrows isn't it.

It almost feels like an anti-climax.

But as the moments tick by, slowly at first, and then with gathering speed, the arrows increase – as do the moans of the soldiers they hit on this side of the wall.

Our forces let them send another round and then Fox's voice bellows around the inner wall.

'Return fire!'

I can't see where he is, but the command in his voice sends shivers down my limbs and, again, I understand why Roan wanted to be sure he would be here for this.

The soldiers on the top of the platforms on either side of the gate launch into action. They work in pairs. One behind each archer lights the oil-dipped arrows, and then those flaming arrows fly over the wall.

Screams rise to meet us as the burning tips find their marks.

A shuddering starts right where expected – the gates that have been fixed since the last time we fought out here. The body of Oskrinya soldiers there shifts as they ready themselves for a breach.

A small number of leather clad Oskrinya catch my eye as they make a run for it. My heart lurches until I realise what they're doing – relaying messages. To Fox and his leaders, I assume, but I can't see their destination.

Thunder cracks the sky and I glance up.

It's blue.

I spin, looking for the source of the sound.

Inglet races to me and it dawns on me I haven't moved from the space between the soldiers and the manor. I snap to attention, dragging my thoughts from Marley in the house behind me, and Theo in the fray somewhere.

'With me,' she says, gripping my arm.

The fine chain mail shirt Fox gave me pinches my skin where she grips me. Everywhere else it slides almost like a second skin under my shirt. Before us, a tide of Solynaran soldiers spews through the square from the direction of the barracks, and I understand what the thunder was.

The back wall has come down.

Our weakest spot.

I glimpse Theo tucking behind Brode and gripping the amulet, calling for support. I keep running, Inglet dragging me across the front square of the manor, the gate on our left. We run to where Rehdree and Oskrinya create the human wall that stands between the manor – the medallion – and the clashing army.

I don't know why I expected there to be a reprieve between the two events – first the breaching of the wall and then the gate – but as I watch the recently repaired gate shake, I know I would have done the same thing. Why wait to bring it down?

The gate gives way.

A roar ripples through Hartfield and the Oskrinya soldiers move at will. The sounds of the slashing and stabbing washes over me. I grind to a halt behind the line of soldiers, taking my place as I slip the cool jet knuckles back on my hands. I bounce from foot to foot, trying to see over the Oskrinya soldiers in front of me.

Then it's my turn to grip Inglet.

'We need to go through!' I scream over the noise.

She smiles and takes my hand as I shove through the lines of soldiers. I need the line in front of Roan's manor to hold and, to do that, I need to be taking down as many Koaman and Solynaran soldiers as I can before they reach it.

The first soldier I encounter is dressed in a false Oskrinya uniform, and a boiling in my veins takes over.

He drops, mouth agape, before he even sees my punch coming. The once foreign sensation of blood dripping down my hands and the jet spikes returns. With it, so does my thirst for vengeance.

Inglet and I work together to carve through the soldiers that come this way. Her face is partly covered in blood when I glance at her, but she shows no signs of fatigue. My own arms are starting to burn. My fights in Atticus's clubs never lasted this long. But the thought of Marley in that house behind me spurs me on.

Under no circumstances will one of these bastards get into that manor.

With every punch and crunching of bones, or irreparable puncturing of skin and organs, I imagine I am one step closer to keeping her safe.

Theo safe.

And keeping Fox from taking that medallion. Or, at the very least, being there when he does.

The Oskrinya soldier next to me screams as a Koaman sword drives through his gut. I can't even watch him fall before I have to turn back to the soldier in front of me. Leaving him dead on the ground and the Oskrinya soldier in line behind him to take care of the one from Koamah.

I don't get close enough to the next soldier to avoid his blade and I catch a burning gash in my left arm. Gritting my teeth, I slam my elbow into his face and drive a knee into his gut. Bringing the hand of my weakened left arm underneath his chin, I look away as the spikes pierce the soft part under his jaw.

Just as all I can see is blood and death, the numbers start to thin. Still, I can't see anyone I recognise but Inglet and the death-grip fear has on my heart tightens. We break through this oncoming line of soldiers and my stomach turns. The ground before us is littered with the dead and dying. So many I can barely see the ground.

But it's not the dead that worry me the most.

Theo, Brode, and Fox are surrounded by a growing circle of Solynaran soldiers.

A high-pitched cry pierces the air. It's Aestais, her purple hair flying out behind her, racing towards them. Several other Varelai join her and they cut down the circle as I watch. A tiny amount of breath whooshes out of my lungs as their huge swords slice through the air, not even slowing as they move through the soldiers before them.

'Rubilena!' Inglet screams and I whirl to find her.

She's stalking backwards towards the manor, several Koaman soldiers pressing her back. One ducks around her, towards the doors.

'Stop him!' I shout at anyone who can hear me.

A young, black-haired Oskrinya soldier sees me pointing and takes off at a run, tackling the Koaman soldier before he reaches the door.

Come to me.

I spin back to Theo but he's engrossed in covering Brode.

Come to me.

A sinking dread runs down my legs as King Boaz strolls through the busted gates, eyes fixed firmly on the doors of the manor.

The medallion is calling.

Fox, Andvett, and a number of other soldiers I don't know are trying to stem the flow of false Oskrinya coming from the back of Hartfield.

Smoke rises from that direction as Hartfield starts to burn.

And the square is falling.

Just beyond Fox, Roan is deeper in the fray. A marble statue come to life, cutting down his opponents without so much as a flicker on his face.

I watch in slow motion as Boaz spots him from across the square and slows his gait.

An Oskrinya soldier hesitates before him and Boaz slashes his throat.

Come to me.

Three more soldiers descend on Fox, but I'm too far away to help. And he's too far from the manor, from the—

A grey-bearded soldier in an off-white, red-splattered uniform advances on me. I bounce on my toes, calves burning with the continued effort. But instead of ducking into his space, I run away.

Towards the manor.

Bodies litter my path and I leap over them, stumbling when I trip on someone's limb. I don't stop to see who they are, if they are alive or dead.

Come to me.

I run around the side of the manor. Not to the front doors I know are barred from the inside, but to the small rubbish outlet near the kitchen. I scramble through, racing through the empty kitchen and up the white stairs. The blood on my jet knuckles drops and splatters as I go.

Come to me.

Footsteps pound up the stairs behind me.

Come to me.

Aestais's room is just ahead and I can't comprehend how different it feels in this quiet, empty building to the scarlet-stained mayhem outside.

Someone slams into me from behind, driving me towards the floor. I spin into them, landing hard on my back with a Solynaran soldier sitting astride my hips. He smashes a fist into my face and my head spins. Clenching my core hard, I drive myself upwards, wrapping arms around his middle and dragging him back with me. Throwing my hips and free arm, I jerk us around until I am on top.

And then I beat his face until only a red pulp remains.

Come come come come come.

I check the hallway, leaving the dead soldier where he lies, and dive into Aestais's room. Yanking open the door at the bottom of the bookshelf,

I scramble inside for the hidden compartment. Fox needs to claim this medallion. Needs to stop it calling for Boaz to hear.

The white fabric slides through my fingers as I feel for it in the small hole at the back of the cupboard. I slide it out and the fabric falls open, the gold and brass metal lying in my hand.

I am yours and you are mine I am yours and you are mine I am yours and you are mine …

My head spins, the room swaying around me.

When three of she become one, I am yours and you are mine, the dark ones will rise with the sun, I am yours and you are mine, come come come …

I slip the fabric off entirely and grip the medallion.

Searing pain lances through my palm and up my arm, slicing into my head.

The room stills.

Then sighs.

My hand shimmers.

When three of she become one, the dark will rise with the sun.

All that's dear will be reclaimed, all that's loved will be lost to flame.

A darkness none will defy, and all but blood will die.

Foundations bound by the light of dawn, a bridge across a chasm forms,

Only then will darkness abate, the flames consuming those who wait.

I stare at the medallion in my hand, its multitude of faces gleaming back at me like blinking eyes.

Staring at my tiny reflection, I realise … the medallion just shared the second part of the prophecy with me.

When three of she become one, the dark ones will rise with the sun.

When three of she …

The bridge, Laramie said.

When three of she—

The brothers are the three.

A bridge across a chasm …

Aestais is right about Fox, he is the bridge. The middle brother.

I have to find Fox.

Pushing myself to my feet, heart hammering in my chest, I scramble upright and out of Aestais's room, back down the hallway, following the spots of blood back the way I came. I glance again at the medallion in my hand as I step over the man whose faceless body lies in a pool of blood, hastily shoving it down my shirt, into the tight binding around my chest and out of sight.

I slip in the blood on the last step of the pale staircase and twist my ankle, heat flaring in my joint. The medallion sits between my breasts like it was always supposed to be there, tucked inside my shirt.

Scanning the yard, I find Theo and Brode fighting the never ending pulse of Solynarans from the far side of Hartfield. They come from every street and alley, swarming towards the manor.

But I catch a glimpse of a long sword behind them.

The Varelai. They came for Theo – just as he said they would – and something in my blood sings.

Boaz has gained on Roan where he fights before the splintered gate, stalking him, blade out.

Slowly, I move across the space between the manor and the fighting. No more soldiers come through the front gate, and Oskrinya focuses its remaining efforts on those coming from the back of Hartfield. My limbs tingle with the need to locate Fox before Boaz wins here and there are none of us left to stop him.

But, right now, all I can focus on is Roan.

Disbelief crashes over Roan's face as Boaz takes the first strike. Roan's machete comes up and blocks the blow, but he doesn't retaliate. Instead, he steps back. Boaz does the same again, and again, and Roan just blocks and steps, blocks and steps. Back towards the Solynarans, who will take him down from behind.

And then I'm running again. To Roan, out of Boaz's line of sight, my ankle screaming in protest.

I stay crouched low, running along the bodies and behind the few soldiers still fighting on this side of the square. My left arm is heavy, the knuckles weighing it down. My own blood now mingles with that of the soldiers I have taken down, dripping to the ground.

Boaz lashes out at Roan, his hits coming harder and faster. He knicks Roan's face just as he jerks away before he loses an eye.

I let the world empty away and focus only on Roan's face.

I know what he can't do.

What he won't do.

But I won't let him fall to King Boaz.

I don't let my loved ones fall.

I creep behind, not having to be too mindful of noise – Boaz would never hear me over the rest of the fighting – but I don't want to be caught in his peripheral vision.

Roan doesn't make direct eye contact with me, but his face tightens in understanding.

I wait.

I will do what I need, but I give him a moment to give me permission.

I'm close enough to reach out and grab Boaz's long jacket.

Just for a moment, Roan inclines his head.

I spring up from my crouched position and drive my knuckles under the King's armpit. My spikes puncture his skin and slide back out just as readily.

Roan's machete drops to his side as Boaz falls to his knees, the flat side of the bloody end smacking softly against his calf.

A gurgling noise comes from the King's throat, but I watch Roan's face.

He spares Boaz one last look and turns away. The world stills as he holds my gaze, his eyes totally black. But he lets me see the pain there, the cracks in his soul that so few know exist.

'Thank you,' he mouths silently before snapping out of our trance and snatching the crown from Boaz's head. He races for the now abandoned platform Fox and I sat on as we watched the fires.

'The King is dead!' he screams when he reaches the top. 'Lower your weapons! The King is dead!'

The crown of Koamah waves in his outstretched hand.

CHAPTER FORTY-ONE

Hartfield bubbles with confusion, uncertain silence winding its way through the town. Weapons are lowered around the square, bloody and tired faces looking between Roan and their companions. The leather-clad Oskrinya begin to cheer.

The medallion warms against my skin.

When three of she become one, the dark ones will rise …

I frown, but no one else seems to be focusing on the medallion and where it might be.

Was that it? A tiny voice in the back of my mind asks. All I had to do was touch it and be told the second part? If so, I should have taken it from Theo a long fucking time ago.

'Boaz has fallen,' Roan shouts across the square. 'The day, and the crown, belong to Oskrinya. Oskrinya!' He slams the crown to the sky once more as Theo and Fox join him, and the deafening sound of the liberation of a desperate people echoes around us.

When three of she become one …

Mutely, I try to take in the scene around me. A feeling of unease starts to crawl up my spine.

A bridge across a chasm forms...

The prophecy. I know the second half of the prophecy.

The Oskrinya, Varelai, and Rehdree begin to round up the remaining Solynaran and Koaman forces.

I need to find Aestais. Or Laramie. They need to know.

The sun stretches into the sky over Roan's head and positions herself in the middle of the blue expanse, as though she will judge the bloodbath below her. As if an indication of what she finds, the edges of the world begin to grow dark.

The sun herself shadowing.

Soldiers around me fall silent. Oskrinya, Koaman, and Solynaran alike, looking at each in wonder. And terror. Their weapons momentarily forgotten.

The sky starts to bleed black and I back away, towards the manor.

Towards Marley.

'Boaz was right,' someone near me whispers, 'the prophecy is coming true. This is the end.'

The whispers build until it's all I can hear echoing off the walls of Hartfield.

Don't run, the medallion sings to me. *Don't run.*

'Aestais!' I scream, spinning in the growing dark. 'Fox!'

The fear in the soldiers dissolves into anger and they remember their weapons. The darkness creeps around their limbs and snakes around their necks. They choke on the life that's strangled from them.

'March on Oskrinya!' Cuts through the air. 'The prophecy cannot be fulfilled!'

Fight it.

The medallion is in my head, the opposing pressure of dark and light crashing behind my eyes.

'Ruby!'

Fox staggers towards me in the growing dark, his machete dull with blood. At his call, the soldiers of Koamah and Solynara turn almost as one.

To look at me.

This wasn't supposed to happen. I'm not supposed to have caused—

Soldiers start to close in on me.

I plant my feet, despite the churning in my stomach and my dimming vision. The manor is no longer somewhere I can go.

Fox spins, hacking into the necks of those that rise up behind him. Tearing at my armour and shirt, I try to grasp the medallion.

I force myself to step forward, the pain in my head dropping me to a knee.

Don't run. Find the answers. The medallion seems to pulse against me.

'Oskrinya!' Roan roars. 'To me!'

Andvett's voice joins his from somewhere and the Varelai call, their eerie war cry like nails down my back.

Roan joins Fox with his back to me, and Oskrinya and her allies fight to form a wall around me. A wall Aestais punches a hole through as she charges at me.

She drags my hand from my head and pries my eyes open.

'Talk,' she demands.

'Claimed.' My words are choked as I gesture to my chest where the medallion hides. 'I know ... the second ... the prophecy ...'

Her sky-blue eyes blow wide, reminding me of the colour the expanse above me was just a moment ago. How quickly darkness takes the place of light. She glances up to the sky that's now more black than blue, the sun desperately trying to hold her own.

'The medallion—' She grips my head as it wavers on my shoulders. I wince at her touch and the daggers it calls forward in my skull. 'It will tell you how to fight the prophecy. You brought us here. You know the second part now, find the secret of how to use it.'

I close my eyes and the darkness spins around me. Theo talked of a library of secrets. I look for the door.

In here.

In here.

I follow the vaguely familiar voice and scramble through what it shows me. A carousel of images, thoughts, and dreams. The spinning increases and I gag. Aestais's cool hands on the back of my neck are the only indication this isn't a dream of my own.

But the secrets here do nothing but weigh me down.

I drag my eyes open against their wish to be known and find Fox's back in the bodies, blood, and mess before me.

The darkness recedes enough for him to be bathed in sunlight, glancing back at me even as his machete finds its mark.

'Find the secret,' Aestais says in my ear. 'Follow the guide.'

I look at Fox and I let the memories of our recent time wash over me. Our second first kiss in the garden. The promises he made. The ones I made in return. Theo bursts into view and sprints to my side, taking my hand in his.

I can do this, I think, gripping his fingers.

For Theo, and for Marley, I will find the secret.

I am here, the voice says.

The darkness crashes back in, a scream from my right coming with it.

'They don't touch her!' Fox shouts, and I flinch at the thud of a body landing behind me.

Aestais grips my wrists and presses her thumbs into the pulse-points at the base of my hands so hard my fingers start to go numb. And then I can see her in my head as well. Part of the library, like she was always supposed to be there.

'Listen,' she says, the urgency in her voice growing. 'I am with you, Rubilena, but you must listen to the guide.'

I kneel in the dirt and the blood, barely able to see my own hands, and I curl myself into a ball.

I'm here, the voice says again. *You just have to open yourself to me.*

The breath in my lungs turns to flame as I place the voice.

It's me, Rubilena, it's me. Look at me.

Her voice is in the depths of the catalogue the medallion showed me, and I unravel myself, my breathing laboured. The sweat that runs down my face feels warm. Steeling myself, I turn in this strange image – one of shelves and shelves of what looks like ... shimmering paper. I both don't want to see her, yet am desperate to know the secrets my mother holds.

The ones that died with Papa.

'Rubilena,' she says, taking form between the dark timber shelves. They're like an overlay on the shadowy fight scene underneath. Somehow, I know I can't focus on the battle, or this image will evaporate into nothing.

'Don't say my name,' I say flatly. 'Are you the guide?'

I can't tell if I'm talking out loud. I focus on my knees which I can feel pressed into my chest. Aestais's hands on my neck. She pushes the pads of her fingers into my skin.

'I am,' she says. 'I knew Boaz was intent on claiming the land – on finding a way to exploit the medallion. Bad things happen when men believe they can control gods, Rubilena. When he banished me for advising Astra against him, I found another way to protect the secrets of the medallion. I am both guide, and guardian.'

'So you chose the medallion over us – over me.'

Her face doesn't change, even though I look for regret there. A sorry, maybe.

'By the time I knew I was pregnant with you, my path had already been decided. As had yours—'

'Bullshit,' I spit. 'I made my own path.'

Now, she does seem to take a slightly longer inhale. The pale grey robe she wears rising slightly over her chest.

'Yes, and no. You were in my belly when the magic to bind me to the medallion was done – binding you, too, in a way.'

The battle seems to rage harder for a moment, or perhaps that's my attention on my mother slipping as I struggle to understand what she's saying. But she was trying to protect the world against Boaz, and a prophecy I have only recently started to believe in. My resolve against her starts to slip a little, too. I could never understand why Theo was so keen to forgive her, hope for another brief visit from her. Now, I suddenly feel like all I want to do is spend this time understanding her secrets. Her decisions.

Another soldier falls near me. I can't tell which side she's from.

'Why couldn't you stay, then?' I ask quietly. 'If we were both bound, why did you leave me?'

'Because no one could know you were the daughter of the disgraced Varelai adviser. And ... I wanted you to have as much control over your life as you could. Until now. Being Guardian means I can't share the secrets –

having me in your life would have been more complicated and ... confusing, than not.'

Varelai?

'I'm ...'

'You've noticed the things you can do with ingredients, I know. As I know that shop of my father's was full of things he didn't make on his own. You are a Varelai descendant, Rubilena – maybe one day you will explore that for yourself.'

'And Theo?' I ask, the pain of discovering he's not mine as fresh as it was the moment I found out.

'I knew you would need people – good people – that is something I could control for you.'

My vision starts to fill with tears, her words are dangerously close to something I have felt for both Theo and Marley – keeping Ash in her life, keeping Theo away from Atticus.

'I was the adviser here, before I went to Koamah.'

Aestais's predecessor, I realise.

'Roan's – Theo's – mother knew a powerful house where a woman had three incredible sons would draw the attention of those wanting to test the prophecy. So, she sought advice from Laramie, and made the hardest choice.'

There's a tearing sensation in my chest as I think of Theo's mother.

'She gave up her last son,' my mother continues, 'before anyone outside the family knew he existed. Then I took him to you. You were so young,' she says, 'but I knew you would keep him safe until, together, you needed to do this. He gave you purpose, and you have given him a life that has prepared him for his own destiny.'

Purpose. Fuck. If I wasn't already kneeling, I don't know if I could stand.

Purpose, yes. But so much more.

My heart starts to race a little harder. How much time do we have? Not enough for me to really understand, I know that much.

But 'people' she'd said, not 'person'.

'Who else?' I ask, even though it's starting to already take shape in my mind, the outline of the one keeping the Koaman and Solynaran army away from me right now.

'I wanted you to have friends, Rubilena – people you could count on, always. The Castellans, along with being integral to the prophecy, to both our destinies, are those people.'

A tear slips my defenses and I close my eyes. Not so much at the magnitude of what she's done – or what it means for the control, or not, I have had over my life. But because they are decisions I would have made if I was separated from Theo and Marley, too.

I understand impossible decisions, impossible choices between those you love.

Someone groans and I desperately look away from the image of my mother and the shelves. How much time am I wasting asking about my own secrets?

'The prophecy, how do I stop the dark ones rising?'

She smiles sadly.

'You're the bridge, Ruby.'

The bridge.

'Between the brothers?' I ask.

She nods. 'You are the key that drew the pockets of our world together – the Koamah Kingdom, Rehdree, the banished lands, and Oskrinya.'

I frown. 'But that's not right, we fight Koamah.'

'Boaz has gone, yes? The people will move against Astra without Boaz to bolster her. Then who will rise in their absence? Who rules the underground of Koamah? Who owns half that city, and now all of it with no King?'

'Atticus,' I breathe, not sure I really understand. But I suppose he does own me.

I swallow. 'The prophecy?'

'You're the bridge – you *command* the bridge – and you need to burn it so they cannot pass.'

'Burn ... myself?'

'Sacrifices must be made for those we love, Ruby.'

Suddenly, the fighting is no longer blurred by shelves but a bridge – one that starts at my feet and leads into the thickest blackness. Three shadows seem to sway there, edging towards me.

'They cannot pass,' she says gently.

Dimly, I'm aware of her reaching out to me, a small bottle in her hand. One that glows green and gold. One that takes me back to time in my home in Koamah with Papa.

Firestarter.

I chance a look over my shoulder, where it seems the battle has shifted, but I feel completely disoriented. I can't see Fox, or Theo, or anyone else I recognise, and I let my gaze travel to the manor. To where Marley hides, waiting for her life to return to normal.

I can't give her normal. Not now. But I can give her a life.

One I know Ash, and Theo, and Kaya will defend with everything they have. Fox too. And maybe that's as much as I can control.

I want to be brave in this moment, but the bottle of firestarter shakes in my fingers. But, through the thickness that's lodging in my throat, I know this is the right thing to do. Making sacrifices for Theo and Marley is something I have grown up doing. It makes sense this is the last thing I will be able to do for them.

To burn the bridge – the one before me, and myself. To stop the dark ones, who seem to be taking more and more solid form as they move towards us, so close to crossing this final threshold.

If I had more time, I would question why it had to be this way. But I spent a lifetime questioning the prophecy and the actions taken in its name. When, all along, the prophecy was correct – and it was people that skewed it. I can stop that from ever happening again.

Because, after this, there will be no prophecy.

Swallowing, I step onto the bridge before turning and pouring the firestarter between me and Oskrinya. More in the image than out of it now, the battle has almost completely faded away from me.

The flames are a dark green as they start to lick the edges of the bridge and I shudder from the cold of the three shadows encroaching behind me.

My mother stands beside me as I turn back, and I'm somehow not surprised to find her there. Gently, she takes my hand. I look down at it, a hand I've never held before. They're the same shape, and the tears escape my lashes as I understand I will never know if grown Marley's are the same as well.

I love you, snuggle-girl.

'I'm proud of you,' my mother says as the heat from the flames starts to burn my cheeks. Words she's never said to me before. 'But it's time for you to go.'

'Wha—'

'A sacrifice, Ruby. You need to let me go.'

'Please, Rubilena,' Aestais says from faraway, 'we're running out of time.'

Through the flames, I can just make out Fox – on his knees, but fighting.

The questions I want to ask my mother swirl in my mind, the papers on the shelves I could read. But I care far less about them than the woman standing beside me now, in these last moments, like she never has in life. Or, at least I thought she hadn't.

A sob starts deep in my chest. Full of all the things I never got to say to her. Never got to hear from her.

'It's okay, Rubilena,' she says. 'It's okay.'

And I decide to trust her.

Trust the woman who gave me away, who left Theo, who left Papa. Because she's right, she's also the woman that gave me so much of what I love. And I won't let the darkness take them, not if I can make this choice for them.

Slowly, she removes her hand from mine and points back to the battle. To where Fox is on his back, a soldier bearing down on him, their swords at a standoff between them.

My breath is hot with the flames as it tears into my chest with my sobs.

I can't lose him again.

But I need her – I have always needed her.

My mother puts her hand on my lower back and gently nudges me forward, just as a shadow of fingers starts to reach out for the back of her robe.

'Go,' she whispers, and I leap.

Flying through the flames, I slam my outstretched hands into the soldier bearing down on Fox. I shove him aside, where Theo drives a blade through his chest.

I turn – just in time to see the last of the bridge engulfed in flames.

And no sign of my mother.

I blink into the light and my body gives way until I lie on the sullied stone of Roan's manor, next to Fox. He turns his head to me, his dirty, partially swollen face drawing a painful pull behind my ribs, and joins our bloodied hands between us.

CHAPTER FORTY-TWO

'I would suggest now is a very bad time to be sleeping,' a woman's voice that is definitely not Aestais's – or my mother's – says, and I drag open my eyes to find Inglet looking down at me.

She reaches out a dirtied, bloodied hand, Roan and Andvett on the other side of her helping Fox to his feet, and I take it, letting her pull me to standing.

'Why have you allied with us?' she asks Roan sharply.

'Inglet,' Andvett says, 'this is not the time for that question.'

'I would say it is the perfect time,' she says, her gaze not leaving Roan's.

Fox shifts on his feet slightly, but I am not convinced he is in good enough shape to do anything more than that.

'Because we can secure better futures for both our people if we combine our might,' Roan says, not missing a beat.

'And where does marriage fit into the picture for you?' she asks.

Andvett growls, low in his throat, and I can't tell who the sound is intended for as his fierce gaze stays on Inglet. Just like hers did on him that day in the square.

'Inglet,' Fox starts, a faint note of resignation in his tone.

'Cease.' She holds a finger to him, never moving her focus from Roan.

'Marriage,' she repeats.

Roan looks between Fox and me, and back to Inglet.

'I understand a marriage between our people would be appealing to some,' Roan says, his voice steady. 'But I think our bonds now run deeper than a convenient marriage.' He gestures around us at the aftermath of the battle. 'This speaks volumes to me.'

I hold my breath.

Fox stills beside me.

'Good answer,' she says through gritted teeth.

But the tension in her shoulders starts to drain away. She turns to Fox and me and smiles, the beauty of her face almost painful.

'I would say this is a good day,' she says cocking her head, silver hair falling away behind her shoulder. 'You get to keep each other, without losing the support of Rehdree.'

Her intense gaze slides to Andvett behind me and I finally release my breath. She stalks towards him and I turn to watch.

'And you'—she pokes a finger in his chest—'will marry me as soon as this god fucked day is done. Understand?'

Andvett wraps his hand round the finger in his chest, a slow, wicked grin creeping into his face.

'The pleasure will be all mine,' he says.

He leans in to kiss her but Inglet stretches away. 'You will give me as much pleasure as I demand, husband-to-be.'

And then she kisses him.

The familiar scent of lavender and cloves twitches my nose as Marley rubs my balm into my ankle. The circular massaging movements of her fingers is so gentle, caring, that fresh tears spring to my eyes. When did she get so good at this?

You're a Varelai descendant.

The air whooshes out of my lungs. If I am, she is too.

I didn't break my ankle on the stairs, thankfully, and the swelling has reduced almost entirely over the days since Boaz brought two armies down on us – and I destroyed the way for the dark gods. Marley has been my constant, thoughtful, healer; although Aestais insisted on being the one to stitch up the gash in my left arm.

Watching Aestais help her, with never ending patience, is an opportunity I never imagined we'd have.

I glance out the window, where the sun shines. Each time it dips below the horizon I find myself reaching for Fox, needing to lay my fingers on him. Feel the warmth of his skin and not the clammy, cold hand that held mine as we lay in the square.

'All done,' Marley announces, a smile on her face that grips my heart.

'Thank you, my snuggle. You're the best healer I know.'

Her face is serious when she looks up at me. 'No more getting hurt, Mumma, okay?'

'I promise.'

Part of me wonders if I really can promise that. The shadows of the dark ones were consumed in the flames, my mother with them. But there is still Atticus – and a debt that seems so surreal, almost trivial, compared to where we are now. But the medallion, while still here with me, has lost its shine.

And no matter how long I spend staring at it, just in case, it doesn't call.

I push myself off the couch in the sitting room, barely wincing at the remaining pain. Fox left in the early hours of the morning and, despite the sunshine, I can't stem the aching need to see and touch both him and Theo. Just to feel the relief they are still here, with me.

'Ready?' Trini asks as she pops her head in the door.

We're still occupying the suite in Roan's manor, and it's surprising how much it's started to feel like home now everyone I love is here.

Almost everyone.

Papa would have loved Oskrinya, I think. I can imagine him with a little shop in the square, stocked by a parcel of land just outside the walls.

I shudder. I'm not sure outside the walls is somewhere that will feel safe for a while yet. But then, the square will always hold memories too. Worse ones.

'Yes!' Marley squeals, breaking into my thoughts, and runs to catch Trini's hand.

'What for?' I ask.

'You'll see,' she sing songs as she walks out the door.

Fox and Theo are in the hallway when I get there, Fox's face broken into a grin. One eye is still slightly swollen, but Marley has been seeing to that as well, and it's already much improved.

'Hi,' he says before pressing his mouth against mine. 'How is my lady of light?'

I elbow him in the ribs. He's found a way to get that in every day since the bridge burned, bringing the sun back with it. Without the steady presence of Aestais, and her cool fingers on my neck, I don't know if I would have had the courage to delve so deep into the medallion – past even the shelves that Theo spoke of, the library of secrets.

But it was my mother who was there for me in the end, in a way she'd never been in life – a contradiction my mind and heart are still processing. Something Papa obviously knew. My rejections of his attempts to get me to trust his faith in her now sit a little uncomfortably. Though I know he asked something almost impossible – to trust something I couldn't see when I was so focused on what was right in front of me.

I've barely seen Roan, who has been busy negotiating the terms of Queen Astra's surrender, including compensation for his people – and his retention of the crown. The outcome of this battle is now going to reshape the allegiances of the continent as we know them.

But Theo has been like a mother hen, barely leaving my side, and my heart couldn't be gladder for it.

'Where are we going?' I ask as we follow Marley and Trini along the hall and down the central staircase.

'Marley has a surprise for you – she swore me to secrecy,' Fox says, winking at Marley, who grins up at him.

Theo smiles, but I don't miss the flash of uncertainty in his eyes when I glance at him. Obviously I'm not alone in my wariness of other people's secrets.

We walk through the square that still bears the wounds of the battle, the blood not yet completely washed away – perhaps those stains will always remain. Most of the prisoners were sent home under Oskrinya guard after swearing fealty to Roan. Having seen the light streaming from the medallion at my chest, and the defeat of the darkness, it didn't take much more for them to want to join Oskrinya for real.

But there will be a true Oskrinya presence in Koamah for a long time yet. Just in case.

I close my eyes and tip my head up to the sky, relishing the sun on my face. Something I'd never given much thought to be thankful for before now.

Strolling through Hartfield, the smell of smoke still in the air, it's almost like a different town. There are many buildings that now lie empty – their previous occupants having moved on from the reminder of those they lost here. It won't be long until they are claimed by the inevitable movement of people after such a huge power shift. But it's still the quaint, walled town it was when I first arrived. The stone houses with their thatched roofs and picket fences like something from a storybook. One my heart calls to, like a dream just out of reach.

Marley skips ahead, down one of the little roads.

Fox's hand is warm in mine and he gives it a little squeeze as we walk.

'It's okay if ... this isn't—' he starts.

'Mumma, look!'

Xave and Brode are waiting for us just in front of a house. Its roof has mostly gone, but its stone walls still stand. Marley runs to me when I reach them all, Theo and I glancing at each other – clearly the only ones left out of the surprise.

'Sit, sit,' Marley instructs, pulling on each of our hands.

We sit in the grass, Marley standing over us, the others around us smiling. Only Fox shows any tension in his jaw.

'I figured it out,' she says.

Theo's eyes narrow. 'Figured what out?'

Marley looks at me. 'Mumma said she wasn't sure where our home was going to be … after. So I asked Roan and Fox to help me find us one.' She claps her hands and jumps up and down.

I turn to Theo, whose just as slack-jawed as me. A sly grin creeps across his face and he tugs Marley into his lap, tickling her sides.

'Do you like it?' she asks.

He glances up at Brode, whose cheeks are pink.

'I love it,' he says. 'Although I expect you to fix that roof.'

'Mumma?'

'It's amazing, Marley, you've done a wonderful job.'

But my heart sinks. There is no way I can afford this house – even without a roof. Fox reaches out a hand and I take it as I stand, Marley having run off to Ash and Kaya.

'It's yours if you want it,' Roan says. I jump and turn to face him. 'They both are.' He gestures to the house across the road that's in slightly worse shape. 'We can help you fix them. There were others but'—he looks at Marley—'she liked these for some reason.'

I smile. Even my daughter knows there is beauty in broken things. Something I think she inherited more from Papa than me. But, watching her and Theo, particularly after seeing my mother, I feel like I understand him on a level I didn't even think to wonder about before. Because I know I would have done everything both he and she did, and more, to keep these people safe – no matter what else those secrets cost me.

'Thank you,' I say. 'I love them. I—'

Roan pulls me in for a hug. 'You're the one who brought us three brothers together, and defeated the darkness,' he whispers. 'I can't very well have you homeless, can I?' I hold him tighter. 'And debt-free is a good way to start life in Oskrinya, I think.'

I jerk back to look at his face.

'What?'

'It's done. No more Atticus's fight club for you – any of you.' Roan looks over his shoulder, his cheek length hair tucked behind his ear. 'He's going to be busy enough making an honest man of himself, running that city on my behalf. He did, though, think there might be someone else who'd choose to be here.'

I peer behind him to find Marco lumbering along the road, the tattoos on his dark arms shining in the sunlight. Three little Marcos trail behind him and my heart sings.

He holds his arms out shyly and I race into them, my feet lifting as he grips me and holds me high against his house-sized chest.

'Leap and you shall fly,' he whispers against my cheek in Solynaran.

I can't help but smile at him through my tears.

'Leap and you shall fly,' I repeat.

I turn to Fox, his quiet gaze having never left me. The others chatter around us, Kaya and Trini already discussing what furniture will go where. Ash and Marley claiming Marco and his family, Marley peeking out from behind Ash's legs.

'Did you really know about this?' I ask.

He nods, a crease between his eyes.

'But you don't—'

I take the two short steps to him, putting myself nearly flush with his chest, close enough I can feel the tremor under his skin. I listen to Roan walk away and join the others and I let their conversation fade away.

'Is this what you want?' I ask, placing my fingertips on his lips.

'I just want you, Ruby. In any way I can have you.'

'I promised you everything.'

He gives a soft, disbelieving laugh. 'I thought that was just pre-war jitters.'

I take his hand and place it on my stomach, where a little secret of my own has taken root. One Laramie confirmed for me before she left, telling Theo she will see him soon – when he's ready to start his apprenticeship with her. His eyes narrow, the questions flickering over his face.

I nod, unable to hold back the smile on my face.

'Mumma! Hurry up – I'm giving a tour.'

Fox takes my face in his, pressing his forehead to mine as he exhales.

'Fuck,' he breathes. 'I thought this much happiness was impossible.'

I take his hand and lead him into the house, where Marley is loudly pointing out all manner of spaces and the things she has planned for them.

The medallion is tucked safely away in Aestais's room once more, but I still feel its warmth envelop my chest. A reminder that some secrets are simply not worth the cost of keeping. True power is in knowing those that keep you tethered to the ground, and those you need to let go before you can truly be set free.

And in understanding the difference.

'Not when you belong to the light,' I whisper back.

Acknowledgements

Writing a debut book is scary. But, perhaps scarier than that, is writing a brand new story, in a brand new world, with brand new characters, and hoping readers love it just as much as, or more than, the debut series.

If you have read this far, I am truly, *truly,* grateful and I hope you have enjoyed the ride. I loved writing Ruby, Theo and Fox and there are elements of their story that will stay with me for a long time.

To family, literally none of this would be possible without your support. By this point, I think that's clear!

A huge thank you also to my critique partner, Erin Ogilvie - you're the best and I adore you and can't wait to have your stories on my shelf.

To my beta readers – Erin Thomson, Katherine Turner and Bron Swasbrick – thank you so much for all your glorious insights and help to make When Secrets Beckon sing. Your time and energy is truly valued.

To my editor Danikka Taylor of Authors Own Publishing (https:// authorsownpublishing.com), you are a seriously valuable partner in this writing process and this book, my writing, and my author career would not be the same without you, my friend.

WANT MORE?

AMBER WOLF (DRIARN DUOLOGY, BOOK 1)

FRIEND. GUARD. ORPHAN.
Lish Taylor thinks she knows who she is.
But when her tactical team begins to investigate a series of abductions, the haunting questions she's carried since her mother's murder come flooding back. With the case growing increasingly suspicious, Lish leaves her climate-ravaged city to seek answers, even after she's ordered to stand down—only to be abducted herself.
Captured by the brutal General Siosal, Lish is determined to free not only herself, but also the General's other victims. With the enigmatic cell-guard, Lochlain, as her unexpected ally, Lish's escape catapults her into the hidden world of the Calahi, where magic pulses through the land. But, even with its incredible differences, Lish can't ignore that this world is also suffering.
The threads of her investigation soon draw Lish into a war for a dying kingdom. To survive – and reclaim her future – she must bring those she loves together and prove that healing a broken world begins with standing in your truth.

Amber Wolf is an adult, dystopian fantasy with forced proximity, found family, fated mates, climate themes and hidden worlds. If you love family secrets, slow burn open door romance and epic magic, this is for you.

BLUE POINTED STAR (DRIARN DUOLOGY, BOOK 2)

A new queen must save the Realm.

But those who would deny her the crown are strong.

Lish Taylor knows that she is the rightful Queen of Airlie. But, before she can officially claim the throne, she is accused of murdering the previous queen – her mother. Forced to retreat to a neighbouring court, the shadow of regicide at her heels, Lish's only chance to regain her throne, and prevent the collapse of both the Human and Calahi lands, is to reassemble the shattered pieces of the Blue Pointed Star.

Underground assassin, Aeyva Kaylneau, is one step closer to fulfilling her lifelong dream of becoming a Sentinel to the Queen. But Aeyva's past allegiances threaten to jeopardise everything she has worked for, and the secrets she keeps have the potential to not only push away the woman she loves, but bring the entire Court of Airlie to its knees.

As the Human and Calahi realms crumble around them, Lish and Aeyva must unite a network of allies across rival courts and the boundaries of magic, to expose a sinister conspiracy that imperils the very fabric of their worlds. As Queen and her Sentinel, they must show that the future belongs to those who fight for more than power.

Blue Pointed Star is the final book in the Driarn duology (sequel to Amber Wolf). Lovers of fated mates, slow burn open door romance, sapphic romance, found family and becoming who you were always meant to be will adore this thrilling conclusion.

WHEN SECRETS BECKON

Every secret has its price...

Rubilena Lanmiere can barely remember how it felt to live life for herself. Or what it feels like to live a life in the open. Raising her daughter in a world where it's dangerous to be noticed, her days are spent selling forbidden remedies in her grandfather's shop — and paying her brother Theo's debts in an underground fight den.

When their absent mother returns to gift Theo a mysterious medallion, Rubilena and Theo find themselves fleeing their home in Koamah, hunted by the entire Kingdom and its enemies. With the secrets of the medallion painting a deadly target on her brother's back, Rubilena is forced to seek help from a man who once broke her heart, and her trust.

In search of the mystical witches who can free Theo from the medallion's claim, the group find themselves wrapped inextricably in the tendrils of a prophecy. But as the fight for the ultimate knowledge intensifies, the weight of secrets already between them threatens to tear Rubilena and her allies apart.

And they can't be sure if the medallion is seeking to fulfil a deadly prophecy, or save them from the encroaching darkness...

*When Secrets Beckon is a standalone adult, dystopian fantasy with an epic second chance romance, siblings, clashes with royalty, prophecy, witches and a single mum FMC. If you love your fantasy with forced proximity, touch HIM and d*e, and open door romance, this one is for you.*

TRAITORS' CREED (TRAITORS DUOLOGY, BOOK 1)

Truth makes traitors out of even the most dutiful.
Zanteera Island has a secret: it has two prisons. Vana, the one the world knows and fears, and an unnamed compound lined with comforts. Serving her National Duty at Vana's secret counterpart, Luka Brideoake doesn't question the unorthodox disciplinary system, or the VIP status of the criminals. But when the Warden offers her a prestigious new assignment in Parliament, she starts to see the prison and its inmates in an uncomfortable new light.
Then, her childhood best friend and his brother show up sentenced to Vana, and   Luka is forced to go against every rule she's upheld to seek a dangerous new ally. All the while, the Warden's cryptic advice suggests a political web far bigger than Luka could have imagined.
As inmates start to die and the authorities move in, her path intersects with a man as enigmatic as he is powerful. But how much of the life Luka thought she wanted is she prepared to trade...for the truth?

Traitors' Creed is an adult urban fantasy with an epic slow burn romance. If you like your love interests cold to everyone but the FMC, with wings as sharp as blades (literally) and a touch of forced proximity and forbidden romance, this should be your next read. With political intrigue, high stakes and a found family that will sacrifice everything to save each other, you will love Traitors' Creed.

Traitors' Promise (Traitors duology, Book 2)

Even the greatest escapes don't guarantee freedom.
With the gilded facade of Zanteera Island's prison smouldering in her wake, Luka Brideoake prepares to make her status as a traitor official. But nothing could have readied her for a summons to a second National Duty. This time, in the heart of Nuntainia's poisonous corruption: Parliament House.
Tasked by Quillian with finding the evidence needed to expose the political tyranny, and armed with an invitation printed with government ink, Luka has no option but to report for duty. Alone.
But as the net of her government's lies closes in, Luka risks returning to the island and the prison she didn't burn—Vana. This time, behind bars. With neither time nor magic on her side, Luka will discover just how much she can endure to reveal a truth that will unseat the highest powers.
Traitors' Promise is the final book in the Traitors duology. Full of an epic romance, open door spice, friends to die for, political intrigue, rebellion and high stakes, this is an adult urban fantasy not to miss.

FIND YOUR NEXT READ

All of Lauren's books can be found here, www.laurenparkerrhodes.com/buy, or at all good bookshops and online platforms.

To stay up to date with all new releases (and inside stories...) subscribe here or at www.laurenparkerrhodes.com

Loved this book by Lauren Parker Rhodes?

I'd love you to leave a review wherever you purchased from or on Goodreads! Just a sentence or two, or even just a star rating, will go a long way to supporting this duology and it would mean the world to me.

After all, without readers, stories go unread and unheard.

Escaping to fantasy worlds is a specialty of Lauren's, either creating her own or reading other people's – providing there's a strong romance, Lauren is all in. Living in semi-rural Australia with her husband and two little wildlings, Lauren tries to teach her children of the wonders of nature. About the impact of all our tiny decisions and that, sometimes, it only takes one person to make a difference. When she's not living vicariously through her characters, or kid-wrangling, Lauren can be found at her second home, the coast; feeding her coffee and chocolate addiction; or trying to fit in a yoga class...even though Archie the labrador would much prefer a walk.

Instagram: @laurenparkerrhodes
www.laurenparkerrhodes.com